SEE YOU MAYBE

KATE BREITFELLER

All characters and events in this publication, other than those in the clear public domain, are fictitious and any resemblance to real persons, living or dead, is purely coincidental.

Ebook ISBN: 979-8-9891172-3-9

ISBN: 979-8-9891172-2-2

❀ Created with Vellum

For all those who believe true love can conquer anything:

You have bewitched me, body and soul, and I love, I love, I love you."
- Jane Austen, Pride and Prejudice

BLOOM FAMILY TREE

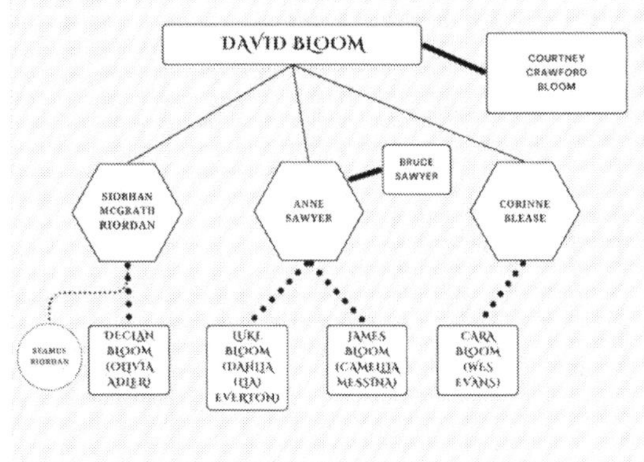

Crawford/Keller Connection

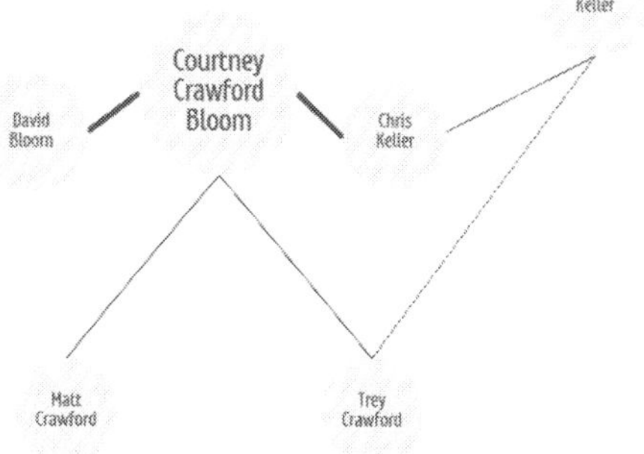

LIST OF QUOTES

(I'VE ALWAYS BEEN A LITTLE OBSESSED WITH THE ROMANTIC ERA POETS)

Poems & Quotes in See You Maybe

Chapter 2

*Sonnet 116 Shakespeare (Olivia as Rose)

Chapter 8

*The Clod and the Pebble by William Blake from Songs of Innocence and Experience (Declan)

*Love's Philosophy by Percy Bysshe Shelley (Olivia as Rose)

*She walks in Beauty by Lord Byron (Declan)

Chapter 12

*Annabel Lee by Edgar Allen Poe (Declan)

Chapter 43

*Virginia Woolf's diaries (Declan)

Chapter 50

*Wuthering Heights by Emily Brontë (Olivia)

Chapter 51

*Soul meets Soul by Percy Bysse Shelley (Declan)

The Importance of Being Earnest by Oscar Wilde

I chose this short comedic play because I've always loved it, and it plays on the trope of intentional mistaken identity for the purpose of courtship. The story revolves around two young men, Jack Worthing and Algernon Moncrieff, who both adopt the name "Ernest" to escape social obligations and pursue romantic interests—which of course leads to a series of misunderstandings and mistaken identities.

Oscar Wilde is famous for his use of wit and humor to poke at the societal norms of his time period, especially concerning marriage, class, and identity. Which I thought was apropos for Declan. One of the main themes is the importance of being true to oneself which is also seemed appropriate for Declan's character arc.

NOTE FROM KATE

Quick little back story about this series and why it means so much to me.

When my husband and I married (cough cough) a million years ago—straight out of college—we honeymooned in southern Ireland. It was an incredible trip full of castles, pubs, hikes, and history. Ever since, that beautiful place and the amazing people who live there, have always held an extremely special place in our hearts.

We returned for our twentieth anniversary, and after a few days in Dublin, we drove south hitting all the amazing little towns en route to County Kerry—possibly my favorite place on Earth. Standing next to a little stream in an indescribably green forest, (Everything you've ever heard about how green and beautiful Ireland is… Think more!) Declan Bloom first spoke to me.

My husband—aided by a few pints—patiently waited that day, as I typed furiously into my phone for more than two hours, creating all the broad strokes of the Bloom family and who they would love.

At the time, I was in the middle of another series, and it killed me that I couldn't get started right away on their story! Now, it's hard to believe their stories are finally done. Sniff Sniff.

I hope you have enjoyed the Blooms as much as I have enjoyed writing about them. These characters will stay with me forever.

There will be more books in this universe, and the Blooms will pop up every now and then. So, it's not goodbye.

Thank you so much for going on this journey with me!

XOXO Kate

CHAPTER ONE

Atlanta—Present Day

Olivia wiped her damp palms on the black pencil skirt of her suit, and took a deep breath to steady herself.

Breathe Olivia.

Anticipation fluttered wildly in her chest making her feel like she might jump out of her skin.

This is actually happening.

Olivia fought the urge to check her reflection.

Do I have lipstick on my teeth?

"Nervous, sweetheart?" Richard, her boss and former father-in-law, his face pale and drawn, asked. Normally, she'd remind him not to use the endearment at work but today she let it slide, as her eyes searched his face. Richard's treatments were taking their toll on him, and Olivia's heart squeezed with guilt, knowing her decisions over the last couple of years had added to his stress.

"Our financials are in order, and the presentation you put together looks incredible. Don't forget *they* approached *us* about XEROS," Richard reassured her.

Olivia smiled weakly. Nervous wasn't the word she would

have used. It was far too simple for the maelstrom of emotions currently wreaking havoc with her central nervous system.

Excited. Overwhelmed. Hopeful. Terrified.

Her heart pounded as she stared unseeing out the window at the cars far below. Richard strolled away from the window, his own anxiety over the meeting with Bloom Capital evidenced by his hands clutched in front of him. She swallowed a curse as the sharp smell of her ex-husband's cologne polluted the air around her.

"Yeah, Livvy." Kyle pitched his voice low, ensuring others in the reception area couldn't hear him. "Don't be *nervous*. Don't think too much about the fact that if you mess this up, you'll cost my father millions," he sneered. "His only chance to retire and live out his last days in peace entirely depends on you."

Olivia tried to shift away, hating that his body standing so close to hers immediately made her nauseous.

"So many people are counting on *you* to not fuck this up."

Olivia stiffened but refused to let his words affect her. Kyle's poison couldn't reach her.

Not today.

She *should* be worried about all of those things. If the presentation to Bloom Capital went well, and the equity group purchased Armstrong Electronics, the Armstrong family would make a fortune, and her employees would keep their jobs.

But she wasn't thinking about *any* of that.

What had consumed Olivia from the moment she received the introductory email from Bloom Capital was the realization that…

She would see him again.

Declan is on the other side of those mahogany doors.

The man Olivia thought she'd never see again after their magical week in Ireland.

"It's in the bag," Stuart Pruitt, head of the Armstrong Electronics' Research and Development Division, said confidently as he joined them. "You have nothing to worry about Olivia."

Kyle curled his lip at the man and strode to where his father was waiting. Olivia gave Stuart a grateful smile. It wasn't the first time he'd intervened when Kyle had tried to corner her.

"Bloom Capital isn't the only one interested in getting their hands on XEROS," Stuart reminded her. "We still have that other meeting in a few days." He shook his head. "But I still can't figure out how Bloom Capital and Bloom Communications are connected."

Olivia licked her lips, pleased when her voice sounded even as she explained. "Declan Bloom was the CEO of his father's media company, Bloom Communications. After his father's death, Declan formed a private equity firm—Bloom Capital."

She forced herself to focus. There was a lot more at stake than just seeing Declan again. The executives she was meeting today played in a much bigger sandbox than she was used to. Olivia needed to be flawless.

Over the last four years, Armstrong Electronics had sunk everything they had into the development of the microprocessor they named XEROS. That gamble was about to pay off. The XEROS prototype had performed beyond their expectations, and several companies had approached them about purchasing the entire company to gain control of the invention.

She inhaled a slow breath through her nose, and just as she thought she had gained control over her heart rate, the double doors swung open and an attractive woman in a sleek, red pantsuit ushered them in to the conference room.

Olivia's legs trembled as she followed Kyle and his father into the room. Her heart thudded hard in her chest as she discreetly scanned the handful of faces, searching for *him*. Olivia shook hands and heard herself returning pleasantries automatically, but her body was in an uproar. Olivia pivoted, trying to see around a tall man.

A stab of nerves hit her. Maybe he hadn't come.

The man speaking with her turned to welcome Stuart, and the world slowed around her.

Her heart stuttered.

There he was. Even more handsome than she remembered.

Declan Riordan.

No, that's not right.

Riordan was the name he'd let her believe was his—not his real name.

Olivia still remembered the shock she felt seven years ago, when she saw his picture on the cover of *Trend* magazine, and discovered who Declan *really* was. The body she'd memorized, draped in a designer suit over the headline: *Declan Bloom, CEO Super Star.*

She'd felt like a fool.

It only took a quick Google search, and staring at photographs of him longer than she'd admit even to her best friend, for her to be sure it was the same man.

As if there was any mistaking the square jaw and dark brows over his devastating violet eyes. Even on the two-dimensional, glossy cover, Declan captivated her.

Olivia didn't know why he'd given her a fake last name all those years before. To be fair, she'd let him believe her name was something different as well. However, it finally made sense why she could never find him during those late night, wine-fueled internet searches.

Olivia hadn't known she was trying to track down the man of her dreams using not only the wrong name but in the wrong country. The man she had fallen head-over-heels, soul-shatteringly in love with twelve years ago while on vacation in Dublin.

Declan sat centered on the far side of the long conference

table, one leg crossed over the other, his broad shoulders leaned back, taking up the entirety of the leather chair. The position at the table wasn't necessary. No one could deny the power Declan exuded or how his presence demanded attention even while he ignored the group from Armstrong.

Light from the window behind him highlighted his profile. Turned slightly, he listened to the man leaning down speaking quietly into his ear. Her heart flipped as a dark curl slipped over his forehead before a large hand lifted to push it back.

Olivia's feet had a mind of their own, and inched closer, only to come to an abrupt stop.

What am I doing?

This wasn't a bar in Dublin, and they weren't alone.

She stood awkwardly as people flowed around her, taking their seats. Declan had yet to acknowledge any of them. Was he being intentionally rude as a negotiation tactic? If so, it was working. The previously confident expressions on her colleagues' faces had grown wary.

"Move," Kyle hissed in her ear, pinching her hard just above her waistband as he moved past her to take his seat. Olivia didn't mean to flinch, but she was out of practice. Kyle hadn't hurt her physically in the two years since she'd walked out, limiting himself to cutting words and intimidation whenever he saw her.

His minor brutality wasn't a total shock. Kyle had been on edge lately, and she was always his favorite target. Olivia's surprise came in that he would risk doing it here, where his father might see.

Richard took the seat directly across from Declan. Kyle and Stuart claimed the seats on either side of Armstrong's owner. The two lawyers Armstrong Electronics hired filled in the other seats. Eyes turned her way, and Olivia was suddenly conscious that she was the only person in the room still standing and quickly slipped into the only open seat on their side, next to Stuart.

Around the table, people fidgeted, straightening the papers waiting in front of them, but the head of Bloom Capital, deep in conversation with the man standing to his side, continued to ignore them. The awkwardness of the moment grew, and even the Bloom Capital representatives exchanged confused glances.

Declan lifted one long finger and brushed it back and forth across his full bottom lip thoughtfully. Heat spread low in Olivia's stomach as her eyes followed the slow stroke. An image of Declan lifting his lips from her stomach and meeting her eyes with a mischievous grin appeared in front of her. She blinked as goosebumps rose on her arms.

"I'll handle it when we're done," Declan's deep voice rumbled, and her heart lurched.

It's been so long.

Memories washed over her in a torrent—that same voice whispering everything from "I love you" to absolutely filthy commands that still made her blush when she thought about them.

The man nodded and turned to go, and Declan finally gave the group his attention.

Look at me, Olivia silently implored him. Her pulse jackrabbited as she anticipated his reaction. He had to know she was here. Declan would have done the same due diligence on Armstrong as they had done on Bloom Capital.

Her picture was on the website...

Would he want to talk afterward? Maybe get a drink? Was he single?

The blogs referred to him as a bachelor, and Olivia hadn't seen a picture of him recently with one of the models normally on his arm... She'd checked.

Declan's violet gaze met Richard's, and his lips lifted in a cool smile. "I apologize. A family emergency popped up. I'm sure you understand."

"Of course," Richard agreed. "Thank you for hosting us here today. We're looking forward to sharing a full picture of Armstrong Electronics' capabilities and exploring how we can move forward in partnership."

Declan nodded.

Anxiety threatened to make her squirm, but Olivia curled her toes inside her heels, reminding herself to stay still.

Richard continued, "Let me introduce my team."

Olivia straightened, her eyes on Declan.

This is it. He will hear my name, look at me and...

Olivia's heart fell to her feet when not even a flicker of recognition crossed his face as her name was announced. Declan simply rested the same vaguely uninterested gaze on her as he had when it was Stuart's turn.

The voices continued as Bloom Capital's acquisition team was introduced, but Olivia was having a hard time breathing. Raw pain speared through her chest, and her blood thumped through her veins so hard she felt light-headed.

Declan was the love of her life, and he didn't remember her.

CHAPTER TWO

ATLANTA—PRESENT DAY

Declan had steeled himself for this moment, but nothing could have prepared him for how it felt to have *her* standing in front of him again. She was thinner, too thin, and the dark circles under her sapphire eyes spoke to long hours. Her dark hair was shorter, but the shiny waves were as beautiful as he remembered. Declan's fingers twitched. He imagined the strands would still be as soft and rose-scented as they had been the last time he ran his fingers through them.

Four years ago, when he was still CEO of Bloom Communications, Declan heard rumors of a lightning-fast microprocessor being developed by a small electronics company in Atlanta. The company didn't have a prototype yet, but he'd put them on his radar. A processer as fast as the company promised would make the streaming services that the Bloom Communications' Digital Media Division sold the best in the industry.

For a moment, when he'd opened the dossier his team had compiled on the key stakeholders at Armstrong Electronics, Declan thought he was hallucinating. He opened dozens of these folders a week—a perfectly ordinary action that rocked him to his core in seconds.

Her first name was different, but the wide smile and mesmerizing eyes, looking up at him from a nondescript vanilla file folder, were the same. Eyes he'd last seen swimming with tears in the crowded Shannon airport.

"'Love alters not with his brief hours and weeks, but bears it out even to the edge of doom,'" she quoted the passage to him with a watery smile.

"Sonnets? Have you given up on the Romantics?" he teased. Declan tucked Rose's dark hair behind her ears, unable to resist the urge to touch her one last time.

"I don't want to say goodbye," she choked out.

His eyes stung and the bridge of his nose prickled. Neither do I. *"How about 'See You?'" he joked, trying to resist the impulse to grab her hand and run back to the rental car.*

Her lips twisted in an attempt to smile even as tears slipped over her cheeks. "Maybe."

His Rose.

But Rose wasn't her name. Not her first name anyway.

Olivia Rose Adler.

After the initial shock, Declan was amused to discover she hadn't been completely honest with him either. Even with a false name, Declan could have found her at any time over the years. He hadn't tried. Couldn't let himself even entertain the thought because that way only led to pain—the what ifs and the maybe somedays...

There was no place in his life for someone like her. She deserved better.

His eyes drifted to the man sitting to Richard Armstrong's left—his son Kyle. Olivia's ex-husband. Something ugly rose from deep inside Declan. He knew she'd lived a life without him—in fact, his team's research proved she'd led an impressive one—but, seeing the evidence of that life in front of him was different.

Olivia Rose Adler, CFO, married to Kyle Scott Armstrong, VP.

When Declan saw the line in her dossier, four years ago, he'd wanted to howl—the pain so deep he couldn't breathe. She was married. He hadn't been able to bring himself to read Kyle's information. Declan preferred not to know the details of this man she'd chosen.

It was easier for Declan to think of Kyle as a nebulous entity, not a flesh and blood man that he could imagine her with. Holding her. Touching her.

Declan's jaw clenched, and he forced himself to relax.

The head of Armstrong's Research and Development Division came to his feet and nodded at a man by the door to dim the lights for the presentation. Chairs swiveled to watch the slides projected onto the far wall. Declan tuned the man out as he detailed the benefits of XEROS.

Declan already knew what he needed to know about the processer. He was *much* more interested in watching Olivia where she sat, farther down the table. Indulging himself when no one else would notice, their attention directed the opposite way.

Olivia fidgeted with her papers, and Declan could tell by the twitching lines at the corner of her lips that she was angry. Hurt.

It's better this way, Declan assured himself. Let Olivia hate him. It would be easier for both of them. Heaviness settled over his shoulders like a blanket.

No matter how much Declan wanted her, he could never have her. A connection to him would put her in danger, making her a target for his enemies. So, he would keep up the charade and pretend that she meant nothing to him even as he ached to claim her as his own. It was the only way to keep her safe.

Stuart wrapped up his presentation with an awkward science joke, and Olivia gave her colleague a smile before she stepped to the end of the table and flipped to her first slide—the financial position of Armstrong Electronics—the only piece that *should* matter to an equity firm.

Declan wasn't particularly surprised to learn she'd become the CFO of the small family-run business. Olivia was clever and quick, and he knew all too well how excited and determined she had been to be successful.

Somehow, all Olivia had achieved during those years apart almost made the pain worth it. Validation that the decision they made twelve years ago, to limit themselves to only one week, had been the right one.

Before meeting Olivia, Declan had worked hard to solidify his role in his father's media empire, needing to prove he was more than simply his father's son. He knew the position he was poised to take after returning from Ireland would require his full attention and dedication, and that left little room for a relationship.

Olivia had her own ambition. She'd finished her course work on her MBA, and when he last saw her, she was excited about starting her first job—at what he now knew was this same electronics company.

Declan rested his chin on his hand, using his fingers to obscure a smile as he listened. Stiff at first, most likely because of him, Olivia soon relaxed and moved through her presentation with ease, speaking in a clear, confident voice. She was magnificent.

Olivia parried several pointed questions from his team without hesitation, making it harder to hide his smile. He'd seen plenty of people fold under less pressure at these meetings.

She wasn't lying... *exactly,* but Declan knew from their research Olivia was presenting the data in the best possible light. His team knew it too. More than one had questioned why he wasn't going harder at the electronics company—challenging their accounting.

Armstrong Electronics carried massive debt accumulated by buying the warehouse attached to their offices to use as manufacturing space. They had also hired an army of skilled engineers and techs to develop XEROS.

Declan had a well-deserved reputation for being cut-throat in his business practices. He never bought when he could simply take, so a few on his team had asked about the generous purchase price. Declan could buy a similar company and use whatever means necessary to duplicate XEROS, but that would take time. Time was something he didn't have, because Bloom Capital wasn't the only corporation interested.

Bloom Communications' new CEO, and Declan's former best friend, Chris Keller was also bidding on Olivia's company.

The price wasn't about her.

Declan *had* to get control of XEROS. It was necessary for him in his bid to win over the Bloom Communications board and reclaim his rightful position as CEO of his father's company.

Yet, as Declan listened to Olivia speak, he wasn't thinking about getting his revenge on Chris. Instead, he was filled with a deep aching regret for what could have been.

CHAPTER THREE

Atlanta—Present Day

Stuart grinned as they walked to the elevator. As the chief developer, part of the purchase package from Declan's company had included a hefty bonus for him. Bloom Capital's offer was generous—too generous—and that had alarm bells ringing in Olivia's head.

Even if the financial snapshot was completely accurate, and Olivia knew her valuations wouldn't stand up under closer scrutiny, the number was too high. Not to mention there were far too many perks for those in management positions. Something was wrong with the situation, but she couldn't put her finger on what it was.

Olivia rubbed at her forehead, as the all too familiar throb started behind her eyes. Was she being paranoid? The pressure of the deal, seeing Declan again—it was too much.

Over the last couple of months, Olivia had argued frequently with the Armstrong board, consisting entirely of her ex-in-laws. She'd tried to explain that failure to disclose all of their shareholders was borderline fraud. Technically, they only needed to declare a list of the majority shareholders, which was composed of the Armstrong family. Only a handful of people knew that Richard, his sister, and their children, now held the minority position in the company.

Kyle, who operated as the in-name-only vice-president, argued that if one of the potential buyers challenged her reports, Olivia could always say she made a mistake.

A mistake… where she had somehow missed the twenty-six people who owned the other fifty-two percent. He was a moron.

However, because no *one* person owned over two percent of shares, Olivia finally gave up trying to convince them of the danger. After listing the Armstrong immediate family members individually, along with the percentage of stock they held, she added one line that read "two percent owners," and hoped no one noticed the 's' on the end of the word 'owner.' It was dishonest and made her look incompetent. Olivia hated it.

The morning of that final board meeting, Richard had arrived straight from one of his treatments. Clearly weak and sick, he'd made it into the office. But as they sat around his desk, he had sided again with his son with the words, "This is *his* inheritance, Livvy. His opinion matters." A not-so-subtle reminder that no matter Olivia's professional expertise, she was no longer family.

Later that evening, Olivia was the last to leave the office after spending hours perfecting her presentation. She found Kyle waiting for her by her car.

"You always have to be right," he spat, his voice dripping with venom. The civility he still gave her in the office for his father's benefit was gone, replaced by the Kyle she'd lived with for too many years. "Everyone in the room tells you something is okay, but you just *have* to be a know-it-all. Little, insecure Livvy wants everyone to tell her she's right."

He stepped into her space, his chest almost touching hers. Actively resisting her fight-or-flight instinct, Olivia's eyes slid away from the rage in his.

"My father is fighting for his life. You know the doctors aren't sure if the chemo will be enough this time. Doesn't he deserve to finish out his years enjoying what he worked so hard for?"

Her eyes snapped back to his, her own anger spiking. "We both know this isn't about Richard. This is about *you* wanting the millions you'll get for your stock."

Olivia wanted to shove him off, but she knew it would only make him angrier, and they were alone in the dark parking lot. After she left Kyle, Olivia made sure they were never alone together, and now she cursed herself for becoming complacent. Kyle barely came into the office anymore, even for meetings. It never occurred to Olivia he would exert the effort to wait for her in a cold parking lot.

Kyle barked a laugh close to her face, and she tried not to react as his hot breath covered her.

"That's what this is about, isn't it? You're acting like a selfish, petty bitch because you won't get any of the stock buyout." His eyes glinted. "You want to wreck the deal for everyone. Breaking my father's heart once by destroying our family wasn't enough. Now you want to stress him out more when he's dying. You really are a cold-hearted bitch."

Olivia swallowed past the lump in her throat. "I would have filed for divorce years ago if not for your father, and you know it."

He rolled his eyes. "Ugh. I'd forgotten about your daddy issues. Can't make your own happy, so you latched onto mine. No wonder you were such a terrible wife. You only married me to get into the family and get that promotion. Thank god, I've got a real woman now." Kyle's smile turned vicious. "And since she already has a kid, at least I know her parts work the way they are supposed to."

Every syllable sliced through her. Olivia had wanted a baby so badly. In the early days of their marriage, and when things were still good—before Kyle's true personality had revealed itself—she'd gone off birth control with no success. After she learned of Kyle's infidelity a year later, while lying naked from the waist down on an exam table, as her gynecologist wrote her a prescription for the STD Kyle had given her, they were rarely intimate again.

Olivia should have left Kyle then. She shouldn't have believed his lies, that the affair was a onetime thing... That he would change.

"Don't take shit." Grandma Rose's voice rang in her ears. She would be so disappointed in Olivia if she were still alive. But then again, she'd have to get in line.

There was some truth in Kyle's accusations, and Olivia wasn't proud of it. Richard Armstrong had been her mentor since she got her first part-time job at Armstrong Electronics in high-school, doing basic administrative tasks. She'd known him for years as her best friend Jessica's quiet, but kind, uncle.

When he offered her a position that she wasn't fully qualified for, straight out of college, Olivia felt like her dreams had come true. Richard said he saw something in her, and over the years had encouraged her to take on more and more responsibility until she was essentially running the company.

Olivia knew that a large factor in her saying yes to Kyle's marriage proposal was she wanted to be part of the family. She'd been working at Armstrong for more than five years at that point, growing in position and authority faster than she ever would have been able to at another company.

When the fireworks exploded at the company picnic, and Kyle fell on one knee in front of everyone, her overwhelming feeling was one of being trapped. If Olivia said no, she would have to find somewhere else to work, and she'd poured her heart and soul into Armstrong Electronics. She loved Kyle, or thought she did, and when Jessica began screaming "Congratulations!"

and rushed to hug her before Olivia even answered, it all felt inevitable.

Jessica knew about what happened with Declan in Ireland. He was all Olivia could think about for months after she returned to Atlanta. She'd sobbed on her friend's couch more times than she could count, missing Declan so much she thought she would die.

"If you marry Kyle, we will be family for real."

Olivia grinned. "His amazing cousin is a big selling point for him."

"So, you like him?"

"It's only been a couple of dates. He's nice."

Jessica's eyes narrowed. "Why does it sound like you're about to come up with some dumb excuse why you don't want to go out with him again, like you always do?"

"We work together, Jessica. It hasn't gone beyond a couple of dinners. We could still be friendly if we end it now. But if we keep going... What do I do when it doesn't work out? He's my boss's son."

"Don't say when. You don't know that it won't work out."

Olivia didn't look at her friend. It was hard to tell her best friend that her cousin left her feeling flat. Kyle was attractive and polite. He'd even made her laugh a few times. But it wasn't the heart-stopping feeling she was looking for... the one she still longed for.

Jessica frowned. "You've got that faraway look in your eyes again. This is why you shouldn't read romance novels. You think all those book boyfriends are real. That's not real life."

"How can you say that? Do you remember when you met Gavin?"

A soft smile crossed Jessica's face. "Fair enough. But we're not perfect, and sometimes he eats potato chips, and I want to strangle him for chewing so loudly." She waved a hand in the air. "Have you kissed him yet?"

"Jessica! He's your cousin."

Jessica waved her hand. "Meh. I'll pretend we aren't close. How did it feel?"

As people hugged her at the picnic, Olivia knew the root of

her dilemma. Jessica, like the rest of the Armstrongs, was extremely close to her family, and they would close ranks against an outsider—her.

Olivia would lose her career and her best friend if she turned Kyle down. In a daze, she'd let the excitement sweep her along, telling herself that everything was fine and that it was time to let go, once and for all, of the fairy tale she'd clung to.

Just as Olivia predicted, within months of the wedding, Richard informed her that now that she was officially family, he could finally promote her to the executive suite.

She'd smiled and convinced herself she was happy—that it was worth it. Sure, Kyle got on her nerves, and in the bedroom she usually had to finish herself, but it was a pleasant enough existence. She had the job of her dreams, a nice house, and her parents finally looked at her like she'd done something right.

Did it matter that sometimes Olivia dreamed of violet eyes, dark curls, and an Irish accent that called her Petal?

As time went on though, the downhill slide of her marriage picked up speed. Kyle no longer hid his affairs, blaming her for their lack of sex life and her inability to get pregnant. Once Kyle decided she was the problem, it only got worse. Olivia worked too much, he accused. And his favorite refrain: Olivia's success emasculated him in front of the rest of the company.

In his eyes, and her parents', she was a failure as a wife.

"You act like your job is more important than him."

"There's more to life than ambition."

"Stop being so selfish. You need to see it from his side."

"It's unnatural for a woman to not want to be home more."

"You should try harder to make your husband happy."

Soon, Olivia was to blame for anything and everything that went wrong in Kyle's life. Perceived slights became intentional insults in Kyle's world, and he was determined to make Olivia pay for them. Until the day he went too far. When she lay bruised and bleeding on the kitchen floor because the Chinese take-out she'd brought home was missing his spicy mustard, Olivia knew it was time to leave.

The elevator doors opened with a quiet whoosh, pulling her from the unpleasant memories. Everyone stepped on. But she hesitated, her stomach suddenly rolled and sweat broke out at the base of her spine. Adrenaline crash. The reality of what had transpired in that conference room for the past hour was finally hitting her.

Don't throw up, Olivia told herself, breathing through her nose as she joined the others. The elevator jerked into motion, and the momentary weightlessness as they descended perfectly mirrored her thoughts. Watching Declan, oblivious to her, had felt like falling. As if she'd somehow simultaneously become untethered from reality only to also need to be present at what could be the most career-defining meeting of her life.

For twelve years, she'd held on to the memory of that week in Ireland. Whenever things seemed bleak, or Kyle told her she was unlovable, or her mother looked at her with open disappointment that she wasn't more like her sister, she'd clung to those memories. Declan loved her, and she'd been lucky to have that connection with him. Even if it only lasted for that perfect week, it was more than some people got in a lifetime.

Now, Olivia was forced to acknowledge that Jessica was right all those years ago when she urged Olivia to move on. It wasn't real. She'd over romanticized it. Olivia rubbed at her sternum.

"You okay, Olivia?" Stuart stayed back as the others disappeared into the parking lot. The plan was to reconvene at the office to go over the Bloom Capital offer.

"I'm fine," she lied.

"You're really quiet, and you've been pale ever since the meeting started. Have you eaten today?" He peered at her through his round tortoise-shell glasses.

"No." She latched onto the excuse. "I skipped breakfast because I was nervous about the meeting."

He frowned. "You shouldn't skip meals. I see your uneaten lunch in the break room almost every day."

It was true, the stress of the last few years had taken its toll on her, but she hadn't realized anyone was paying attention.

Olivia gave him a grateful smile. "I know. Once we sell, I'm planning on a long vacation full of frozen cocktails on a beach somewhere. Completely unplugged."

Stuart snorted. "You won't last twenty-four hours."

CHAPTER FOUR

DUBLIN—12 YEARS AGO

The faces around her blurred, and Olivia felt a hand steady her when she stumbled into a group of men by the bar.

"Steady on girl," a man's voice laughed.

Olivia offered a weak smile back, but her stomach churned unpleasantly. What in the world made her think she could keep up with her flatmates and their friends? She should have stopped by the third round of shots that were handed around by the maid-of-honor, but Olivia had felt warm and happily buzzed, and she wanted to fit in.

She'd lost count after that, sipping on a Guinness that Eva—the bride-to-be who Olivia had met for the first time the evening before—insisted was essential on her first visit to Dublin.

This spontaneous trip was completely out of character for Olivia. But, with a week left before she was due back in Atlanta to start her first real grown-up job, she'd given in to her flatmate, Genna's, enthusiasm.

The mini semester she'd attended at Oxford had wrapped up a few days before, and for the first time in her entire life, Olivia's schedule was completely free. After years of working her ass off, always pushing herself to be number one at school and building her resume, her future was secure. What might be her dream job was waiting for her when she went home.

When her flatmates invited her to come with them to their friend Eva's hen party in Dublin, Olivia thought, why not? Like Genna had pointed out, Olivia needed to experience more than just classes in romantic literature while she was there. And, a classic hen party was a must.

However, Olivia had seriously underestimated the women's tolerance for alcohol. Now, as she was coming back from the bathroom, she was having a hard time spotting the group she was with. You'd think Eva's giant, fluffy veil and the sash that spelled out BRIDE in silver glitter would be easy to spot, even in a crowded pub. But, it seemed that during the time Olivia had spent in line, waiting for the bathroom, the crowd had doubled in size, and the live, folk music in the corner had ratcheted up the noise making it hard to think.

Shit! Olivia squinted, scanning the crowd for the telltale veil. There it was. Over by the back corner. She worked her way through the crowd, trying not to bump anyone's drink, her black boots already sticking a bit to the floor.

Olivia successfully reached the group without an alcohol shower and leaned gratefully against the wood-paneled wall, happy to be on the outskirts of the raucous crowd. The only people she knew were her two flatmates, Genna and Amanda, and she'd only met them when she arrived in Oxford six weeks earlier.

The women had all been friendly when she'd met them at the airport, but Olivia was careful not to refer to any by name... because to be honest, they'd begun drinking on the plane, and Olivia wasn't confident she remembered who was who.

The woman closest to her turned, her dark hair brushing Olivia's arm. Olivia was standing way too close to her. Bright, blue eyeshadow highlighted her curious eyes. "All right there, luv?"

Pull it together. Don't be the lightweight American, even if that is exactly what you are.

"Oh yeah. I'm great." Olivia frowned and moved her tongue in her mouth. The words hadn't sounded right, but the woman just chuckled and patted her on the arm and turned back to her friends. The floor swayed, and she bumped into the woman again. This time, her eyes were less friendly when they turned back.

Olivia licked her lips, and her eyes passed over the group that had, at some point, become a colored blur. Maybe she should go back to the hotel.

"Where'd Genna go?"

The woman frowned, and several of the other women were now looking at Olivia.

She cupped her hand to ear to hear Olivia better. "Who?"

"Genna."

The dark-haired woman's brows furrowed, but it was the blur in a large veil that leaned forward. "Did you lose her?"

Was Genna lost? Olivia tried to make her mouth form the words she wanted, but the room tipped sideways, and she stuck out a hand to catch herself.

"Whoa, lovey. What's your name?"

The veil leaned close to Olivia's face, coming suddenly into focus.

That's not Eva. This bride has red hair.

Olivia's cheeks burned hot, and she stumbled back.

"I'm so sorry. I should go."

She felt a hand rub her back. "Did you lose your friends? Can you call them?"

The vague panic that had formed in her chest eased. "Yes.

Good idea." But when Olivia searched through her crossbody bag, her phone was nowhere in sight.

"It's gone."

The group exchanged glances. "How about we'll have someone call you a cab?"

But Olivia's moment of lucidity was sliding away again, and her stomach rolled. Was she going to throw up?

"Where are you staying?" a woman with a turquoise bob and heavy eyeliner asked.

Olivia pulled her room key out of her purse and held it up in front of her. Someone took it from her, and she felt the cold plastic of the card against her skin as someone tucked it past her high neckline and into her bra.

"Found your phone, luv." The woman laughed, and Olivia reached up to pat her chest.

Yes, that's right. She put her phone in her bra. "What's your room number?" The voice was no nonsense, and Olivia responded without conscious thought.

"303." Something cool brushed over her arm.

"What's your name, doll?"

"Olivia Rose." She gagged, the words slurring before she got her last name out. Why did she give them her full name?

The stroking on her arm moved faster before the hand holding her forearm let go. "There you go, Rose."

"Excuse me," Olivia sprinted for the bathrooms, the line thankfully gone.

After getting sick, Olivia splashed water on her face, holding her cheeks and trying to make her face come into focus in the tiny mirror. She slumped against the wall and closed her eyes. Thumping on the outer door roused her.

What are you doing, Olivia? Don't you dare black out in a foreign country. You need to get back to your hotel. Find everyone tomorrow.

Olivia yanked the door open to the angry face of a young

woman, who shoved her out of the way and headed for a stall. "Can't lock everyone else out," the woman groused.

Thankfully Olivia spotted a chair tucked into an alcove at the back of the hallway.

I'll just sit for a few minutes, sober up, and then I'll get a cab, she told herself, sinking down and hooking her purse on the back of the chair.

Someone kicked her chair, waking her.

"You're alive. Thought ya might be dead." The young man laughed. Another man behind the first slapped him on the shoulder. The only detail she could discern, as the large male figures loomed over her, was that they both wore striped, long-sleeved polo shirts.

"C'mon. We'll buy you a drink."

"No. I'm good, thanks." Olivia wasn't sure if the words were clear enough.

They laughed, and then firm hands pulled her to her feet practically carrying her to the bar. Her feet refused to obey her brain's commands. When the two men ordered shots, Olivia shook her head and tried to step away, but one stood close behind her, pressing her up against the bar. He reeked of whiskey, and her stomach rolled.

Oh god, she was going to be sick again. Olivia put her hands on the bar and tried to push back to free herself, but a hand came to her hip, biting in as she heard the man argue with the bartender.

"Nah, mate. She's fine. We're friends."

The bartender continued to argue with them, but Olivia was more concerned that she was about to throw up on the bar. "Gonna be sick."

"Fuck off, mate. She's done," the bartender barked.

"Wanker," the man pinning her said, and then hands were spinning her, which didn't help her stomach.

"Is that your hotel room?" Someone pulled at her, and fingers brushed against the skin of her inner forearm. "Don't worry, we'll get you home." The hand that held her upright slid lower, and then slipped under her skirt brushing against her ass.

"No!" Olivia twisted away, but somehow they were at the door. Through the haze, her instincts screamed at her to get away.

"You're all goo—" The words cut off, and he was ripped away, causing her to stumble backward. He flew to the side, and Olivia saw his friend step forward and throw a punch. Then it felt like all hell broke loose, as several of the men nearby were all too willing to jump into a fight after a night of drinking.

A hard shove from the side caught her, and she slipped, her head smacking the bar as she fell. Olivia sat for a second on the floor, watching the legs and feet moving erratically around her until her stomach couldn't be ignored any longer.

Pulling herself upright with the help of the bar, Olivia stumbled to the bathroom and locked herself in a stall before her stomach revolted again.

CHAPTER FIVE

DUBLIN—12 YEARS AGO

Declan hadn't planned on staying at the pub after he left a message for his Uncle Iain. But Brian, who normally handled the door Friday nights, had suddenly bent over in agony and rushed to the toilets at the back of the building. To help his cousin out, Declan offered to fill in. He thought that keeping an eye out for troublemakers, with the chance of maybe knocking some heads together, was a welcome distraction from the anger that had been simmering in him all week. Not to mention it was a nice change from his every-day corporate life.

His mother's family, the McGraths, had built an entertainment empire across Ireland. They owned several bars and clubs in Dublin, including one in the famous Temple Bar area. The Celtic Crown was slightly off the main, and while it might not be the first stop on a tourist's pub crawl, it was frequently one of the last, and saw plenty of excitement between the locals and the tourists.

After the last week, Declan had enough anger boiling under his skin that he almost hoped he'd have an excuse to fight. So far, the opportunity hadn't presented itself. Instead, he watched the striking brunette with pale skin and red lips who had come in with a hen party a couple of hours ago. He appreciated beautiful women. What healthy twenty-five-year-old man didn't? But there was something about this girl that had his gaze returning to her again and again.

Her outfit didn't scream look at me in the way some of the other skimpy, tighter dresses around her did. But he wasn't the only one in the pub who had noticed her short leather skirt, tights and high-necked sleeveless blue top that looked like it was painted on.

Her hair was long and dark, nearly black, a tone so deep that under the twinkle lights decorating the bar, it looked almost blue as it hung in long waves down her back. She turned her head, lips parted in laughter at something the bride said, and he stared.

Declan couldn't tear his eyes away from her. His gaze followed her graceful neck each time it tilted back to down one of the many shots she and her friends were consuming.

His cousin Colum relieved him for a few minutes, and when Declan returned to his post at the door, he couldn't find her. Declan stood, his full height allowing him to glance over the heads of most in the pub. No sign of her or her friends. He shoved the pang of disappointment away.

You have bigger things to worry about than some random girl.

The next hour passed quickly as the pub filled with the cheerful sounds of a Friday night. Declan felt his muscles relax, and rolled his shoulders. The simple task of working security at the door of one of his family's many establishments was more relaxing than his life in New York. When he was in Ireland, he was Siobhan's boy, not the heir apparent to his father's billion-dollar media empire.

His cousin worked his way through the crowd, his black T-shirt stretching across his biceps, and pressed a pint into Declan's hand.

"Thanks," he said, taking an appreciative sip. Nothing tasted as good as Guinness on tap.

"How are things going with Seamus?" Declan's mood soured with the mention of his older half-brother. He might sometimes resent being sent to live in the States with his father when he was twelve, but there were drawbacks to Dublin as well. Family ties and loyalties ran deep alongside grudges.

His mother, Siobhan, was the youngest of her siblings and the only girl in the McGrath household. She had been welcomed into the family business when she was ready, but there had never been any question that the vast, powerful business the McGrath family had amassed over the last century, legal and otherwise, would pass to the eldest male heir and his offspring.

Siobhan married Oein Riordan, much to her family's dismay, when she was young and had Seamus soon after. But when her husband was killed during a robbery, it left Siobhan and Seamus in an odd position.

A McGrath by his mother, but also a Riordan by blood and name, Seamus's loyalties were even murkier than Declan's. At least, Declan's father never got into physical turf wars with his mother's family the way the Riordans and the McGraths had. When Declan was born, the result of Siobhan's relationship with the American billionaire David Bloom, the first lines were drawn between him and his brother.

David Bloom claimed his son and raised him to take over his own empire one day, whereas Seamus felt lost in the middle. Close to power on so many fronts, but no chance for his own.

The result was a resentful man who frequently saw his younger brother as a rival. Declan had little in common with his elder brother, and as time passed, he became increasingly impatient with Seamus's lack of ambition.

Declan offered him a job at Bloom Communications, but his brother had scoffed at him. Seamus would rather spend his afternoons in a pub with his Riordan cousins, talking big and making sketchy deals that would only end up getting him into trouble that Declan had to fix.

It was the reason Declan's mother summoned him home last week, and the source of yet another argument with his father. David Bloom had been furious, hating what he considered Declan's misplaced priorities. If the senior Bloom had his way, Declan would cut ties with Seamus instead of flying thousands of miles to bail his brother out of a deal that had gone badly. But what could he do? Seamus was his blood.

"Declan?" His cousin's words brought him back.

"It's taken care of."

Colum's lips pressed into an angry line. "He needs to stay away from Padraig Riordan."

Declan grunted and took a long draw of his drink.

"I'm serious. He's reckless. Cuts corners and pisses off the wrong people." Brown eyes met Declan's with a message he wanted to ignore. "Seamus is going to end up in jail or dead. No one will be able to help him then."

Declan's neck tightened. His McGrath uncles had made it clear they were done protecting Seamus. His last deal, selling guns to a dubious group, had taken place inside a McGrath establishment. There was a lot their family would forgive, but putting the legal businesses at risk by conducting illegal activities was forbidden.

"He'll bring you down with him," David Bloom said, after Declan briefed him on why he needed to go to Ireland for a few weeks.

"I'll be back when I can." His violet stare met his father's. He would not defend his decision.

Red crept up his father's neck, and he slammed his hands down on his desk. "You are my son and an officer of this company. You can't gallivant around the world paying off criminals for your brother."

Blood beat behind Declan's eyes. "Only for my father, then?"

David Bloom's eyes narrowed. "Be careful, boy. I've given you this position, and I can take it away just as easily." He snapped his fingers. "You have two brothers behind you, happy to take your place."

Declan's spine tingled, even though he knew it was a bluff. "Neither Luke nor James have any interest in working for this company, and you know it. They haven't even graduated college yet." He leaned forward, bracing his hands, arms extended on his father's wide wood desk, and let his father see his resolve.

David Bloom was a bully, and he would pounce if Declan showed the slightest weakness. "I've earned my spot in this company, but if you don't want me here anymore, say the word. I've got no problem going somewhere else."

To his surprise, his father was the first to blink. David Bloom picked up his fountain pen and scribbled a signature across the check in front of him. Declan straightened.

"Two weeks." His father held up a finger. "I don't give a fuck what is happening with your degenerate brother, or how angry your mother is with me. Your ass is in your seat in that board room in two weeks."

Declan controlled his features. Was his father saying what he thought he was saying?

David's upper lip wrinkled. "You've been asking long enough."

"You'll name me president." It wasn't a question.

"Two weeks." He returned to his papers. "Send Lucille in on your way out."

Declan stared at his father's bent head for a minute, his jaw working. It was the carrot his father had dangled in front of him for years. Everyone knew that, despite his age, Declan was making more and more of the decisions at Bloom Communications, and that this was the path always intended for him.

He didn't have any illusions that his father was giving up control. David Bloom would still be in charge as CEO, but it was the first step in handing over the reins.

"Tell Siobhan I send my love," David Bloom called, as Declan reached the door.

That was a week ago. The situation with Seamus had been easier to smooth over than Declan first thought. Once he handed over the cash, it seemed all was forgiven by the Albanians.

"I've convinced him to take a position in the States with one..."

Declan trailed off, his attention caught by something over Colum's shoulder.

She's still here.

A bizarre feeling of excitement passed through him at the sight of her, swiftly extinguished as he watched her stumble through the bar. Her eyes were owlish and she had a vaguely confused expression on her face. Declan tracked her until she joined a group on the side. He peered across the crowded pub. That didn't look like the group she came in with. But at that distance he couldn't be sure.

"He's leaving Dublin?" Colum's ginger eyebrows climbed his forehead.

Declan forced his eyes away from the beauty. "For now, at least."

Colum clapped him on the back. "Hope it works out." His tone didn't hold much hope. Declan sighed. He didn't have much either.

A cold, steady rain began, and Declan lifted the stool he was half-perched on further into the doorway. He stretched his neck, and scanned the thinning crowd.

His blood blazed white hot.

From the back hallway, the brunette was being led—more accurately half-carried—by two drunk idiots. Her head bobbled, and Declan surged to his feet and raised his hand to signal Colum at the end of the bar, but his cousin was busy talking to a customer and didn't see.

Declan's fists clenched, his body thrumming with an irrational level of rage. Any woman being taken advantage of would make him angry, but the absolute primal desire to protect *this* girl was new and slightly alarming.

Declan forced himself to stay where he was. He watched the men hold her up against the bar and felt a moment's relief when one of Colum's bartenders took one look at the girl and shook his head with a scowl.

Finally catching his cousin's eye over the crowd, he lifted his chin toward the trio. Colum frowned and immediately made his way toward the two men. The McGrath's had very strict policies on behavior in their pubs, and everyone knew it. These morons must be tourists to think they would get away with that shit here.

Denied at the bar, they moved toward the door, their speed slowed by the woman held up between them, who stumbled every few feet. One of the assholes slid his hand under her skirt, and when her face scrunched as she tried to twist away, Declan was off the stool before he realized it. Hauling the man groping her back by his collar, Declan threw him to the side as Colum roared Declan's name. Probably in a vain attempt to remind Declan to keep his head. Too late.

Fury pulsed through him as he pulled his arm back and slammed his fist into the other asshole's jaw, throwing him backward into the crowd. Pints and glasses went flying as people turned angrily, launching themselves into the brawl. Shattering glass and screams echoed as the band came to an abrupt halt and customers fled out into the rain.

A blow to the side of his head rocked him to the side, and he tasted blood. Shoving those in his path out of his way, Declan frantically searched the room.

Where had she gone? He needed to make sure she was okay. He didn't stop to ask why he had such an overwhelming urge, he just accepted that he did. The two men who accosted her were helping each other to the door... But the girl was gone.

"What the fucking hell?" Colum raged at him as he comped the people still in the bar, and shut the door, locking it. "You're lucky no one called the Gardai, and it was almost closing time. You can't fight customers."

"They were going to rape her."

"You don't know that."

"I do. She was wasted. She had no idea what was happening."

Colum shoved a hand through his short hair and surveyed the damage. "Yeah, well, she's gone now, and we're left with a right mess."

"I'll clean it up."

Colum arched a brow. "Prince Valiant is good with a broom and mop?"

"Fuck off." Declan's blood was still hot, but what bothered him the most was the feeling that he'd lost something. Which was ridiculous. He'd never even spoken to the girl.

It took him two hours to clean the bar. Colum had stayed for a bit to help, but after they'd cleared the broken chairs and swept up most of the broken glass, Declan insisted his cousin go home.

"I've got it, mate," he said, taking a garbage bag from Colum's hand. "Go home."

Declan locked the door behind his cousin and finished cleaning the bar. He was on his way to the back door with the garbage bags when he heard a faint snuffling noise. He froze, listening.

It wasn't unusual in these old buildings to have mice, but when the noise came again, he realized it was human and coming from the ladies' bathroom. He sighed. Great, a straggler.

Declan pushed the door open slowly and ducked down to peer under the stall. A pair of black boots was visible, slumped against the opposite wall.

Shit, please don't be an overdose.

He pulled at the door, but the latch was thrown. The snuffling came again.

Okay, still breathing. That's a good sign.

"Oi! Pub's closed. You need to come out."

Declan's annoyance grew when the person didn't answer. He wasn't in the mood for this shit. He slapped his palm against the door twice, the lock rattling loudly.

He heard a squeak and then a low moan. "Are you okay in there?"

A quiet voice muttered something that sounded like "worst party ever," before the boots scraped against the floor, followed by the metallic snap of the latch.

It was her. Her eyes, a crazy, deep sapphire-blue were still bleary, but she didn't seem quite as out of it as she had before. She lurched forward, gaze serious, her entire being focused on walking and staying upright.

"Pub's closed." He repeated, extending a hand to help her, but pulled it back when she just stared at it.

"Ow." She grimaced. A hand rose to the side of her head.

Declan frowned at the angry welt marring her skin. His fingers reached out, and lifted her heavy hair away from her face before he was aware of what he was doing. She reared back, and their eyes met and locked. Her pupils flared wide with alarm.

Declan swallowed a curse and gestured at her injury. "You've hit your head."

Her fingertips gingerly felt around her hairline. "I fell?" Her gaze lifted to his again, and she leaned backward as if she just realized how close they were standing. "I should go."

"Where are you staying? You're not in any shape to be wandering the streets of Dublin by yourself."

Declan was only thinking of the liability for the pub, he assured himself. She'd hurt herself on the premises. He was solely motivated by the need to protect his uncle's business from being sued, he tried to tell himself. He was absolutely *not* trying to prolong his time with her. Because that would make zero sense.

Her eyes darted to the door, but the slow tracking of her pupils showed she was still drunk, and it occurred to him she might have a concussion. Declan had his share from playing rugby, and while it didn't look serious, he didn't think she should be alone, wandering a strange city in the rain in the middle of the night.

"Here, come into the light." He caught her hand, ignoring the surge of electricity that traveled up his arm when he took her fingers in his, and gently pulled her forward. "It's too dark in here," he explained when she hesitated. "You could have a concussion."

Her face eased, and a tiny sigh slipped from her lips. His gaze immediately dropped to her mouth and the deep reddish pink color of her lips. Declan had a sudden urge to touch the full curve of her bottom lip to see if the color was natural.

"You stopped those guys earlier."

Declan looked down at her as he pulled the bathroom door open, but didn't bother answering.

She tripped in her boots as he guided her past the chairs, and he put his hand on the curve of her waist to keep her upright. Declan thought she would pull away, but when she rested her weight against him, he had to fight the desire to pull her closer.

What the fuck is happening?

While the Celtic Crown would never be accused of being brightly lit, the lights on the side of the bar were enough to see her face clearly. He tipped her chin up with his forefinger so that the light fell across her face.

She was beautiful. Even with her makeup smeared, and the now messy mass of thick dark hair tangled around her face, he couldn't take his eyes off her.

"How'd ya know?" Her slightly slurred words brought him

back as he moved a finger in front of her face. Not the most scientific of tests, but Declan thought she was okay.

Her pointer finger tapped the tip of his nose, startling him. "Answer the question."

Declan stared, his own lips twitching when a dreamy smile crossed her face. "How did I know what?"

"How'd ya know I wasn't with them?"

Declan wasn't about to admit that he'd remembered when she came in. That he'd been watching her but that he'd somehow missed when she was left behind, and that she was becoming incapacitated.

The finger poked at the corner of his mouth, and he had the inappropriate desire to close his lips over it and suck it in. "Smile, frowny face. We're in Ireland. I've never been to Ireland before."

Declan removed her hand, but didn't let go as he lowered it between them. "I don't think you have a concussion. But you're going to have a hell of a headache tomorrow."

"Are you a doctor?" Her brow creased.

"Hmm?" He needed to step back. Let go of her hand. He couldn't bring himself to do it.

"Are. You. A. Doctor?" She over enunciated the words as if he was the one off his head instead of her.

His lips quirked. Even drunk, she was adorable. "No. But I've seen plenty of concussions."

She placed her free hand on his bicep and squeezed before running her hand over his chest. Declan's stomach clenched.

"You're huge and hot. Are you a fighter?"

"Rugby." He grunted, willing his body to not react.

She doesn't know what she's doing, asshole.

"Hmmm." Slowly, she removed her hand.

Declan let out a heavy sigh. "Let's get you home."

She pouted, and the hand was back on his chest. "You could come."

Declan's eyes squeezed shut, her words sending his cock a message he knew she wouldn't mean sober. The invitation in her eyes was crystal clear, and any other time, he wouldn't hesitate to take her home and lose himself in her body for the rest of the night, but the universe clearly hated him.

He'd done a lot of bad things, but taking advantage of an inebriated woman wasn't one of them.

"You have no idea how much I want to take you up on that." Declan didn't realize he'd said it out loud until she responded.

"Then do it." Her eyes beamed at him, and for the tiniest moment, he let himself sink into them. They really were phenomenal.

"Where are you staying, lass?"

She snorted with laughter. "Lass. Isn't that Scottish?"

"Not always," Declan answered. "Are you here with friends? What's the name of your hotel?"

She looked worried for a minute, and then her brow cleared. Grabbing the collar of her shirt, she pulled it away from her body and looked back at him with a bright smile that hit him like a bolt to the chest.

"Found it!" she exclaimed happily, as she attempted to bend her arm at an angle to reach inside the tight, high neckline. She scowled. "Stupid top… can't reach." Her hands went to the hem, and she began tugging it up. He saw a tantalizing stretch of white skin before he pushed her top back down.

"You don't want to do that, lass. You aren't home yet."

She stared at him like he was an idiot. "I know. My key is in my bra."

"Oh." Was that supposed to make sense?

She tugged hard at the neckline, and he heard the distinct sound of threads popping, but it apparently gave her enough room to maneuver, and she pulled out her phone and a plastic hotel room key.

"It's like Mary Poppin's purse in there. What's that on your arm?" Declan caught her wrist and turned her arm over. "You came prepared." He laughed.

"Huh?" She peered down at the lipstick writing on her arm. "Oh! That's me." She pointed with her other hand to a smeared spot followed by the word 'Rose.' "And that," she said triumphantly, pointing to the other words, "is my hotel and room number. That nice red-haired bride helped me."

"Is that why you smell like roses, because of your name?"

Jesus. Did I really just say that?

"Rose perfume like my Grandma Rose. She didn't take shit and I don't take shit!" For some reason, that made her almost double over laughing.

"Okay, Rose. The Blackwater isn't far from here," he said, naming the hotel written on her arm. "I'll walk you back. Sit here while I finish closing up."

Declan led her to one of the low chairs, and swiftly shut off the lights and locked the doors.

When he pulled her to her feet, she slid an arm around his waist and leaned into his chest. "You smell good."

And then she nuzzled his chest. Literally *nuzzled* her cheek against him. "But you're too hard."

Blood surged to his groin.

No. Asshole. Drunk.

Before Declan realized what he was doing, he had dipped his head and pressed a kiss to the top of her hair, catching a hint of rose again.

That move alone shocked the hell out of him.

Rose sighed and leaned heavier against him, stumbling as they navigated the cobblestones in her heeled boots.

Declan ended up half-carrying, half-walking her the short distance to the small boutique hotel where she was staying.

Swiping her key card on the external pad, he pulled the door open and helped her inside, his arm around her waist.

A young man behind the desk looked up disinterestedly until he caught sight of Rose slumped against Declan.

"Good night, eh?" He gave Declan a knowing leer and then blanched when Declan leveled a blistering glare at him.

His throat bobbed when he swallowed. "Her friends came back earlier. They're looking for her."

The young man glanced at Rose. "Need some help? She's pretty out of it, huh?"

Declan didn't like the way the man's eyes lingered on the length of Rose's legs in the short skirt and shifted her body so that his larger frame partially blocked it. "My girlfriend's fine."

With another dark glare at the man for good measure, he jostled Rose a little to get her moving again. "Come on, lass. Let's get you to bed."

"About time!" Against his chest, he heard her snort with laughter. She lifted her head and looked up at him with a bright smile. "How'd you know my name was Rose?"

His lips twitched. "It's on your arm."

She lifted it and stared at the smeared red writing. "Oh yeah. That was really nice of that bride."

"*That bride?* Was there more than one?" he asked, using his free hand to swipe her card, keeping the other one wrapped around her to keep her upright.

She thought for a moment as though it were a serious question, and then nodded solemnly. "At least two."

"Hmm." Declan tried not to laugh, thankful she was at least an accommodating drunk.

Rose stumbled in front of him into the room. He flipped on the overhead light and turned to place her phone and key card on the table when he felt her fingers plucking at the hem of his shirt. His skin burned where her fingertips stroked over him.

"Take this off. I want to see."

Declan leaned away, but Rose got one hand fully underneath, her palm splayed across his stomach. Then she purred. Actually, fucking purred. A sound from low in her chest and so sultry, he was instantly, painfully hard against his zipper.

"You're so warm," she hummed, her fingers tracing over his abs.

Declan felt like a fucking inferno, but there was nothing he could do about it. He needed to stop this before he did something they'd both regret.

I deserve a sainthood, he thought, walking her backward toward the bed, as her hand continued to explore his skin under the shirt.

The back of her knees hit the bed, and she dropped like a rock. "Oof."

Declan kneeled in front of her and slowly removed her boots. He eyed her stockings, skirt, and top. She'd be more comfortable sleeping without them, but he wasn't that big of a masochist.

Reaching behind her, he caught the top of the coverlet and pulled it back. "Okay, Rose, under the covers."

She blew out a breath, her plump lips vibrating in a raspberry. "I have to pee."

Rose struggled to her feet, dropping back twice before she was able to stand on her own.

"I've got it," Rose said, when he tried to steady her. She stumbled to the door next to the bed and rested her cheek on the door jamb. "Wait here. Don't move."

As soon as she was under the covers he'd go, Declan promised himself. He heard water running and then giggles. Was she okay?

"Rose?"

The door swung open suddenly, and Declan's mouth went dry. Rose had used her time in the bathroom to pull off all of her clothes and now stood completely nude in front of him.

Look at her face, asshole.

Declan swallowed hard just before she launched herself at him, and his arms were suddenly full of soft, warm skin.

His body reacted instinctively, arms wrapping around her. His brain registered silky skin and hard nipples pressed to his chest. Electric shocks sprouted over his body, and urgent raw hunger coiled tight inside him.

No.

He lifted his hands to her shoulders and somehow managed to get her into the bed without touching anything else he shouldn't.

But... Fuck... She was perfect.

Declan grit his teeth as he pulled the coverlet up to her shoulders. Rose blinked up at him in confusion, like she couldn't quite figure out what had happened. She wasn't the only one.

His body strained against his clothing, the caveman in him wanting to rip off his own clothes and press his body against all that soft skin. His muscles tense, Declan retrieved the trashcan from the bathroom and filled a glass with water before placing both next to the bed.

"Thanks," she whispered, her eyes drifting shut.

He should leave now. The girl was safe in her hotel bed. Declan didn't belong here. Except everything in him told him to stay. It didn't make sense. He'd hadn't even had a coherent conversation with Rose, and yet he felt drawn to her.

His Irish grandmother had been full of stories about Celtic mysticism and fate, that he'd always dismissed as superstitious nonsense. For a split second before his logical brain reengaged, it struck him that the concept didn't feel so far-fetched anymore.

Declan brushed a heavy lock of hair off her forehead, and Rose let out a contented sigh.

"Goodbye, Rose," he whispered, and then did something completely out of character. Declan leaned forward and kissed her forehead, allowing his lips to linger for a minute as he inhaled her scent.

Shaking his head at his ridiculousness, Declan picked up her clothes off the bathroom floor and set them on the chair.

Why are you stalling?

A soft snore disturbed the silence, and he smiled. No more excuses. It was time to go. Turning off the bathroom light, his hand was on the door handle when he heard the first whimper. A sound so sad he couldn't help but look back.

Rose's eyes were screwed shut, her face scrunched in unhappiness. He hesitated with the exterior door partially open.

It's just a nightmare. People have nightmares.

A low, mournful sound filled the room. "Don't. I won't tell. I promise. Open the door. Please." Her voice bordered on panic, and she began thrashing under the covers.

Declan shut the door with a quiet snick. "Rose." He sat on the side of the bed and shook her shoulder. "Rose," he repeated, leaning closer.

Her eyes flew open, and for a minute she stared up at him, her gaze burning into his. "Don't leave me alone in the dark."

Was she awake, or was this a night terror?

Either way, he hurried to turn the bathroom light on, pulling the door so that a thin band fell across the foot of the bed.

"Please. Don't leave me," her soft voice begged.

Declan knew she wasn't fully present in the moment. Most likely she had no idea what she was saying, but his self-control had officially reached its limit.

Toeing off his boots, he pulled the cover back to join her in the bed. Just until she was solidly asleep, he told himself.

But when she rolled toward him, pressing her full breasts against his arm, her nipples peaking, Declan thought he might break. His cock throbbed painfully against the zipper of his jeans, and he adjusted himself while trying to think of anything but the naked woman next to him.

Nope.

He was trying to do the right thing, but Declan was far from a saint. Sitting up abruptly, he pulled his shirt over his head and then forced it over Rose's head, gently working her arms into the sleeves. Her hair looked like a tousled dark halo around her pale skin, illuminated only by the bathroom light. She pursed her lips and frowned. She was definitely awake now.

"Go to sleep, Rose."

She flopped back on the pillow and tucked her hands under her cheek. "I know this is a dream, but this is the best one I've had in a long time." She rubbed her toes against his shins. "Those are rough. Take them off."

"Not a good idea."

Seriously, he wanted a medal and maybe a fucking parade.

"Yes." Rose rubbed her feet against him. "I don't like it. Sexy dream men don't wear jeans to bed."

Her hands went to his buckle, and Declan grabbed her hands, trapping them before pulling them away. The second he let go, they were back, a stubborn expression on her face.

"If I take them off, will you roll over and go to sleep?"

"MmmHmm."

"Seriously?"

"Promise."

What the fuck are you doing?

This is a terrible fucking idea.

Declan ignored his brain, frantically telling him to stop, as he removed his pants under the covers and tossed them to the floor.

He had lost his mind. It was the only rational explanation for how he was behaving.

Declan huffed a quiet laugh and lay back down, careful to leave at least a foot of space between them. Lying on his side facing her, he watched fascinated as she gave him a sweet smile, before her thick lashes drifted shut again, casting shadows across her cheeks.

Declan watched her sleep for far longer than he should have. They were strangers. This was complete madness. But he couldn't deny that lying next to her, listening to her breathe, filled him with an odd sense of peace.

He didn't know what was happening, but as he allowed himself to close his eyes, he accepted that whatever it was… He wasn't going to walk away.

CHAPTER SIX

ATLANTA—PRESENT DAY

"Let me show you what being under the Bloom Communications umbrella means." Chris Keller beamed at them across the table at the conclusion of their meeting.

Olivia was a little surprised when the CEO of the global corporation had come to the meeting himself. He was younger than she'd expected, not too many years older than herself. His kind face and a casual attitude were the complete opposite to Declan.

She mentally frowned. Why was she comparing them?

At the end of the meeting, Chris had thrown out an invitation to attend the famous Crystal Gala in New York as his guests.

Kyle's face lit up at the prospect of a such a high-profile event. "That sounds amazing."

"It's unnecessary," Richard demurred

Kyle glared at his father.

"It would be a great chance for you to meet some of the heads of our other divisions. Show you how Armstrong Electronics will fit perfectly into our corporate family. XEROS's potential is extremely exciting."

Olivia smiled. Chris seemed earnest, but she couldn't help but hear her grandmother's advice in her ear. "Anyone who promises you everything is lying."

"We'll keep all the design functions in-house here in Georgia, but you might need to come to the corporate offices at some point. This way you'll get to know everyone in a more informal setting, and the next day I'll give you a tour of our building."

"Won't our joining you make it look like we've already accepted your offer?" Richard asked.

"Dad, this is how business is done." The muscle in Kyle's jaw ticked, and Olivia looked away.

"I understand your concerns, Mr. Armstrong, but I assure you, this kind of thing is done all the time. This deal is a little like a marriage. I don't know what your other offers look like, but Bloom Communications wants to work *with* you. And, if we are going to be working together, it is a good idea to see how well we fit." His eyes drifted to Olivia, and he smiled. She returned the smile, and Kyle scowled.

"Will your fiancée be there?" Kyle cut in.

Was he really going to act like he was jealous? Though Olivia wasn't sure of whose attention he was jealous. Chris's or hers?

Chris's smile didn't slip, but his eyes dimmed. "I hope Courtney feels up to coming. Recently she has suffered some terrible personal losses."

Olivia held her tongue, not sure how to respond. The deaths of both of Courtney Bloom's sons had dominated the news several weeks before. Local news channels had run the story multiple times a day—the macabre draw of murder and money irresistible to the public. The headlines had been lurid. *Youngest Son of Billionaire Widow Dead After Multiple Murders Revealed.*

With his characteristic lack of sensitivity, Kyle's eyes gleamed. "I read about that. How crazy is it that she's your fiancée, and her stepson is the other guy trying to buy us? *And,* the woman who shot her kid is Declan Bloom's sister-in-law."

The air in the room grew thick with tension, and Chris's jaw tightened. "It was very shocking." Seeming to shake it off, he cleared his throat and extended his hands palms up. "What do you say? Would you like to attend the Crystal Gala as my guests?"

Richard glanced at Olivia, and she gave him a small nod. "We'd be delighted."

Olivia smiled. It might be fun. She'd been to plenty of black-tie events in Atlanta, but never something as high-profile as the Crystal Gala.

"Wonderful. I'll have our jet ready on Friday morning."

Kyle beamed, and even Olivia had to admit the prospect of flying private for the first time was exciting.

Now seated in the buttery leather seats and accepting a mimosa from the flight attendant, she tried to relax. Richard wanted to wait until after Christmas to announce their decision, but Olivia couldn't help but worry that at any moment something would fall through. She couldn't truly relax until the sale was complete.

Olivia sipped her drink as Chris lowered himself into the seat across from her. She didn't miss how his eyes roved over her crossed legs, and she swung her foot. He met her eyes with an unapologetic grin at having been caught looking.

"Courtney couldn't make it?" She deliberately referenced his fiancée.

Chris's face drooped. "She flew back to New York yesterday. She didn't think she could travel and attend the event on the same day."

"This must be an awful time for her."

Chris rolled his lips in before pushing them out again with a thoughtful expression. "Those boys were everything to her. She's having a hard time... coping."

A stab of sympathy went through Olivia. Losing your children would be traumatic enough, but the circumstances and stories coming out about the crimes they had committed… had to make it worse.

"I'm trying to help her, but it's hard." Chris continued quietly. "Matt and I had our issues, but to find out Trey…" He shook his head. "I don't think I've fully accepted it. Sometimes I wonder if he..." Chris turned to look out the window at the clouds.

"Wonder if he what?" Olivia bit her lip. That was rude. This must be difficult for him. Over the last couple of days, she'd looked into the story online. One of the murders Trey Crawford, Courtney's youngest son, had confessed to, before being killed by the woman he had kidnapped, was Chris Keller's own father. There was a deeper story to all this, she was sure of it.

Chris let out a heavy sigh. "I shouldn't have said anything. I'm sorry. Not particularly professional of me." He chuckled, but his hands clenched in his lap.

Olivia smiled. "It's okay. Like you said, if we are going to be partners in a sense—"

"It's only that you're so easy to talk to," Chris interrupted.

Olivia wasn't sure what to say to that.

His eyes studied her face for a moment, then he leaned forward suddenly, his expression earnest. Olivia instinctively pushed her back into the seat. "I wouldn't have said anything. I'm trying to let it go… Camellia, she's the podcaster who killed Trey…The police insist she shot him in self-defense, but I can't ignore the connection. It seems like an extreme coincidence that Declan Bloom's sister-in-law just happened to be the one to kill Trey. The Blooms haven't exactly been quiet about the fact they think Courtney was involved in their father's death."

Olivia's eyes widened in shock. "I haven't heard anything about that."

Chris's expression faltered. "I'm sure it's just the grief talking.

It's only..." His eyes returned to the window before returning to her. Chris appeared to struggle with his words. "Do your research. You need to know who you are getting involved with."

The unease that appeared when he had gotten close came roaring back. He seemed sincere, and yet...

Her eyes cut to the other passengers. Richard and Stuart were asleep, and Kyle was flirting with the poor flight attendant. He'd be of no help, anyway.

Sensing her discomfiture, Chris leaned back, remorse written all over his face. "I'm so sorry. That was inappropriate. I like you, Olivia, and I *really* like XEROS. I'm hoping you'll accept our offer, but I worry you don't know what the Blooms, particularly Declan, are capable of."

"Declan?"

He grimaced. "People have always whispered about how Bloom Communications did business when the Bloom family was in charge. Declan might claim it was a petty move by Courtney to force him out once she inherited the stock, but the fact is, the board had grown weary of how he did business... His less than savory connections made them nervous."

"There are always rumors about powerful people," Olivia hedged, intentionally keeping her voice neutral. Her first instinct was to defend Declan, but she realized that the man she wanted to defend didn't exist.

Olivia had heard the innuendos about David Bloom and his cadre of children. After discovering Declan's true identity, Olivia had a hard time reconciling the Declan she knew—the man who recited poetry from memory while lying in the Irish sun—with the cutthroat businessman people spoke about.

"Trust me." Chris's lips twisted bitterly. "They're true. I've seen first-hand how the Bloom family operates. If you are of use to them, they can be charming, but the second they are done with you... You don't exist."

Olivia shifted in her seat, her chest tightening.

"I'm not gossiping. I'm genuinely concerned for you and..." Chris looked at Kyle and the others to assure himself that no one was eavesdropping. "I don't think you've come across Declan's type before. Not that you haven't built an impressive business, but Bloom is a global..." He rubbed his palm against his cheek and lowered his voice. "Declan and I were friends for most of our lives. Best friends, really."

Olivia's jaw dropped open.

"Does that surprise you?" He tried to make his tone self-deprecating, but there was an edge he couldn't hide.

"My father was their family doctor and a close friend of David Bloom, so Declan and I were thrown together a lot. We actually had a lot in common... Dec can be a lot of fun... when he's getting his way." He sighed again. "But the older I got, the more disturbed I was by the things I saw happening. They all do it. David, Declan, the twins, even Cara. They can turn on the charm and make you feel like you are the center of the universe, but then just as quick, they flip the switch and you are left alone out in the cold. An outsider."

Her heart ached. Chris's words hit too close to Olivia's own situation,

"I know what that's like," she said quietly, and Chris gave her a quizzical look. "Family businesses can be a tough group to break into."

His eyes returned speculatively to the other passengers.

"I imagine even worse when you *leave* the family. Our situations are similar. I pulled away from the Blooms and... That's why I still have questions about Trey and Matt's deaths. Why Courtney is having such a hard time accepting the police version of what happened..." He shook his head. "I know they claim that Camellia Messina got Trey on tape confessing, but she married James Bloom less than two weeks later. Between him and his brother Luke, they know how to work the legal system.

"Then, if you consider their sister Cara is married to some sort of computer hacker... It wouldn't be hard for them to fake a recording. Who knows how many judges and cops Declan has in his pocket?"

Olivia couldn't hide her shock. "You think they murdered—"

"No." He sagged in his seat. "I don't know. The whole situation is so hard to accept... I'm sorry, I never should have said anything."

Olivia was deeply uncomfortable with the conversation but nodded, hoping Chris would take it as a signal it was over and return to his seat.

There was clearly a lot of animosity between Chris and the Blooms, Declan in particular. She was getting a terrible feeling that Armstrong Electronics was going to end up as collateral damage in whatever war the two men were waging.

The flight attendant stopped by to let them know they would land soon, and Chris stood staring down at her for a long moment, his hand resting on the back of her seat.

"Whichever company you choose, be careful. Declan has a reputation for a reason."

Olivia gave him a bland smile, not wanting to reveal how much the conversation had unnerved her.

But as the plane made its descent into the New York area, a sudden disturbing thought hit her.

Does Chris know about our history? He said he'd been best friends with Declan. Would he have told Chris about the week together the way she had told Jessica? Was this his way of warning her not to make the same mistake? Then again, Declan didn't know her real name, and he hadn't remembered her...

"What were you and Chris Keller speaking so cozily about?"

Kyle hissed in her ear as they waited for their luggage to be put in the black SUVs waiting for them.

"He was just trying to muddy the waters of his competitors." Olivia slipped on her sunglasses even though the day was overcast.

"Right," Kyle grunted. "Don't screw this up by flirting, Livvy. It will only make you look stupid and embarrass my father. He's way out of your league. Though maybe that's your goal? To embarrass me more?"

With an intentionally bored look on her face, Olivia took a few steps away from Kyle under the guise of supervising their luggage. His fingers grabbed at her elbow, but released almost instantly, and Kyle let her move away. Olivia's heart raced, and she struggled to maintain her calm façade. She hadn't survived Kyle with her job intact for him to ruin it for her now that they were divorced.

The stress of the potential deal was bringing out the worst in Kyle. Since she moved out, and their divorce finalized, he'd been unpleasant on the rare occasion they'd been forced to interact, but Olivia suspected he was as happy as she was that their marriage was over. However, over the past several weeks, his behavior had shifted back to what it had been when they were married.

Olivia tightly controlled the air entering and leaving her lungs. She was *so* close to being completely free of him. With the buyout, Kyle would most likely leave the company to live the life of leisure he'd always wanted. Not that it would look much different from the one he led now, but it would mean he no longer came to the office, and hopefully, she would never see him again.

Once in her room, Olivia tried to settle her nerves, but she still had hours to go until the event that evening. Tea, she needed tea. Fortunately, there was a café only two blocks away, and by the time she returned to the lobby, her tea had cooled enough for her to drink.

Clutching her cup of mint tea, Olivia waited for the elevator that would take her to her floor. A petite woman jabbed at the button, balancing a drink carrier with three coffees and what looked like several individual pastry bags. Two bags slid to the side, clearly in danger of ending up on the floor.

"Argh," the woman growled.

"Do you need some help?" Transferring her cup to one hand, Olivia carefully stacked the bags in the center of the carrier so that the coffee cups blocked the edges. "Hopefully, that will hold you until you get to your room."

"Thanks." The young woman flashed a brilliant smile at her. "I volunteered to get sustenance for my sisters… Well, I guess only one is technically my sister, but I know Dahlia will be soon enough," the woman said, as the elevator car arrived and they stepped on. The young woman barely paused as she continued to speak. "I know Dahlia says she wants to wait a year, but I'm a big fan of fast weddings…" She stopped cheeks flushing.

Olivia tried to follow the woman's train of thought, but her violet eyes were distracting.

"I'm babbling, aren't I?" The woman huffed a breath that ruffled her golden hair. This woman was seriously stunning. "I babble when I'm nervous, and my anxiety about tonight is about as high as it can be."

Olivia hummed what she hoped sounded like agreement, then the words swirling in her brain slipped out. "You have the most beautiful eyes."

"Thanks. I used to hate them. My brothers used to tease that the color made me look like a cartoon character. Which is so dumb because one of them has the same—" The doors dinged open. "Is this your floor?"

"Car-bear," Olivia said, instantly wanting to kick herself when the young woman's eyes grew huge in her face.

"How did you—"

Olivia practically leapt off the elevator as the doors slid shut behind her. Rushing to her room, she fumbled with her key, splashing tea on her hand. Shutting the door behind her, she leaned her head against it and tried not to cry.

CHAPTER SEVEN

DUBLIN—12 YEARS AGO

Olivia's mouth was a desert. She glanced around the room, feeling disoriented.

How did I get back here?

This is my room, right?

Panic climbed in her throat before she let out a slow exhale of relief.

Okay, same boring landscape on the hotel bedroom wall, and there's my suitcase spilled over the floor. My outfit from last night neatly folded on the chair...

She had a vague recollection of wrestling with the shirt in the bathroom and tripping... Her hand skimmed down her body to the sore spot on her hip.

She was hurrying because...

Olivia's eyes darted to the side, triggering a stabbing pain in her temples. Inches from her face, a honey-colored bicep rested across a chiseled jaw darkened by stubble.

Holy Shit, there is a man in my bed.

Her eyes bulged as memories flooded back. The hot-as-hell

bouncer had walked her home from the bar. And then she'd taken off all her clothes.

Oh god! She silently groaned, her cheeks flaming. *What happened next?* Olivia tried to concentrate, but her head pounded painfully.

A shift of the sheets next to her brought the scent of bergamot and something deliciously male, before a large, warm hand moved under the covers and spread across her stomach. For the tiniest second, she forgot her hellacious hangover. The warmth of the hand had traveled, waking up other parts of her body.

Damn, he smelled good.

Olivia maneuvered to the side, hoping to get out of the bed without waking her unknown bedmate.

Please tell me I at least asked him his name.

Just as her left foot touched the ground, and she attempted to calculate the physics of torso movement versus blanket friction and the likelihood of waking him up, the warm hand cupping her waist tugged her back up against a firm chest. Pressing her tight against an exponentially warmer body who, by the hard length pressing against her ass, was now very much awake.

Her hormones lit like the Fourth of July, but resisting temptation Olivia cleared her throat and moved purposefully away to sit on the side of the bed, the arm that held her dropping away with a sleepy objection.

Summoning her courage, Olivia glanced over her shoulder and was hit with the most gorgeous eyes she'd ever seen. Were those real? Olivia tried not to gape, but… seriously? Men shouldn't be allowed to have lashes like that.

"Morning, lass." The deep voice, raspy with sleep, was a straight shot to the ovaries. She was hungover, not dead.

Did I have sex with him? Or worse. Did I have sex with him and not remember?

Inscrutable eyes watched her silently, and another memory

popped into her mind. Her hand crept up and found the lump on the edge of her hairline.

He'd taken on the two guys trying to carry her out of the bar. Olivia vaguely remembered falling and going to the bathroom to get away… What happened next?

Should I ask him what happened? This is going to be humiliating.

Hey, thanks for coming back to my room with me. Did we have sex? Was it good? Can I have a do-over?

Her brain began to spiral.

This is fine. Everything is fine. I'm an adult, and he didn't murder me. Clearly a drunken evening gone awry. And, so what if it's the first time I've ever had a one-night stand, and he just happens to be the sexiest man on the planet... And I don't remember getting to touch him.

Gah! Those shoulders!

He is beautiful. Like someone plucked one of those Grecian statues out of a museum, dipped it in sex appeal, and then breathed life into it. Warm, vibrant, muscular... Oh shit, he's laughing at me.

"I wish I had a camera," he said. "You should see your expression."

"I'm going to have anxiety nightmares about this moment until the day I die," she muttered.

A cloud crossed his face. "Do you have a lot of nightmares?"

"What? No."

What a weird question.

Silence stretched as the shirtless man in her bed lifted his arms and tucked his hands behind his head, impressive biceps flexing with the movement. She licked her lips. *Am I drooling?*

"Good morning," Olivia belatedly said.

A sleepy smile crossed his face and…

Are you serious? Is that a dimple?

Her eyes, defying her perfectly mature thoughts, dipped to scan his impressively muscled upper torso and shoulders.

It was insult to injury. He was seriously the hottest man she'd ever seen, and she didn't even remember sleeping with him.

A sigh slipped from her lips, and then her eyes widened in horror when his eyes lit with humor, and a smile stretched through his thick morning beard.

Olivia swung her legs over the side and fairly launched herself out of the bed. "Just… I need… I'm going to take a shower."

Olivia shut the door harder than she intended, fairly certain she heard him chuckling. Swiftly pulling off his shirt, she flung it blindly back into the room, before closing the door again.

Is he naked under the blanket? Go find out, her body screamed, but sanity had finally reasserted itself.

Turning the shower on, Olivia took her time. Hot water sluiced over her, alternately making her feel cleansed of the pub yuck and absolutely exhausted. She couldn't remember the last time she drank that much. If ever.

Stepping out of the shower, Olivia wrapped herself in a towel and struggled with what she should say. "It was a fun night. Sorry I don't remember it."

She'd taken stock of her body while she was bathing, but other than the new bruise on her hip and the lump on her head, she couldn't tell anything was different.

I'd be able to tell, right? Or is that just something people say?

Olivia hadn't been intimate with anyone in over a year. With her school and work schedule, she didn't have time for relationships.

Shouldn't I be sore or something?

An image of his enormous frame dominating her bed appeared in front of her.

I should definitely be sore.

More memories came back like her own personal slideshow of embarrassment: Throwing herself at him in the bar, him offering to take her home.

Did he try to leave?

She frowned and mentally shook herself.

I'll just be casual. Adults do this all the time.

This. Is. Not. A. Big. Deal.

But, when she stepped out of the bathroom, a question about his breakfast preference on her lips, it died on an exhale. Less than five seconds confirmed what she knew instantly.

The bed was rumpled, but empty.

Her Irish vacation fling was gone.

Why do I feel so disappointed?

Cocooned in her towel, Olivia tumbled into the bed and pulled the duvet over her head. Her last thought before drifting off again was *no one can ever know.*

"Rise and shine." Warm lips pressed into hers before pulling away too soon and the air around her filled with the intoxicating smell of coffee.

"I thought you left."

"Just to get coffee."

"Ah." Olivia took several grateful sips, trying to get her brain to fully engage and make sense of the intense feeling of relief she had at seeing him on the side of her bed.

Olivia pushed to a sitting position and studied him over the cup. He wore the same dark Henley and perfectly faded jeans as the night before. Her imagination hadn't failed her. He was the best-looking man she'd ever seen, and for whatever reason, she was entirely comfortable sitting in a towel in front of him.

Was she still dreaming?

"What's wrong?"

Olivia glanced at him, surprised. He pulled the chair in the room over to the bed, and slouched in it, resting his sock-covered, crossed feet on the foot of the bed. "You've gone all… pinchy."

"I don't know your name," she admitted.

He smiled then, eyes twinkling. "Declan."

"Right," she smiled back, "I'm—"

"Rose. I know." He chuckled. "A strange bride wrote it on your arm."

What the hell is he talking about? Oh—

"Named for your Grandma Rose, who doesn't take shit, but also you wear rose perfume because it reminds you of her."

Oh god! Should she admit her first name wasn't Rose? That she'd been so wasted a complete stranger had to write her name on her arm with cosmetics like a dog's ID tag. *'Hi, my name is Rose, and if you found me, my mommy is ugly crying.'*

She sipped her coffee to buy time.

I mean, my name is *Rose. My middle name anyway. It's not like I'll see him again.*

"Did I share any other tidbits with you last night?"

"Other than declaring your undying devotion to me as long as we both live?" He broke off with a laugh. "I'm kidding."

"You're hilarious," Olivia groused. But something was picking at her brain. Something she'd forgotten, and it was important. "Oh my god!" Her spine went ramrod straight. "I've missed my flight, haven't I? What time is it? Where's my phone? Oh my god! My flatmates must think I'm dead."

She swung her legs to the side, sloshing her coffee, only to freeze when Declan extended her phone in his large hand. "You're all good."

"What are you doing with my phone?" she asked suspiciously.

"It was lighting up constantly, so I answered them." He shrugged. "I thought you'd rather sleep than have them banging on your door at daybreak."

"You answered them? As me?" She gaped at him.

His eyes dipped to where her towel was slipping, and she tightened her hold but stayed silent.

"You really should have a password on it."

Olivia scanned through the texts, groaning inwardly.

"Where are you?"

"Where did you go?"

"Are you okay?"

"Are you coming with us?"

It was the return text purporting to be her that made her want to shrivel with embarrassment.

"I ran into a good Samaritan who helped me back to the hotel, but I need to sleep off the gallon of booze I drank. See you back home." Olivia read the text aloud while he sipped his coffee, clearly unrepentant.

"It wasn't a lie." Declan regarded her steadily.

To her surprise, she found her outrage at his audacity waging war with her amusement and so settled for rolling her eyes. She quickly regretted the movement when her headache throbbed.

"You know what you need?" Declan didn't wait for her to answer. "A traditional fry-up. It's a guaranteed cure after a night out with the lads."

"Guaranteed by whom?"

"Generations of Irishmen," Declan deadpanned, and she couldn't help a small smile.

Olivia squeezed her eyes shut, wanting to drop back into her pillows.

"As a non-native, I'm not sure that's going to work. I think I need the tried-and-true American remedy of a sports drink and a handful of ibuprofen."

The bed bounced a little as he moved his feet, and when she opened her eyes, he had a sports drink in one hand and two small pills in his other open palm extended toward her.

She snatched up both. "Are you some kind of Irish angel?"

He huffed a laugh but didn't answer. Olivia swallowed the pills and gulped half the drink before looking at him again. "I don't suppose you rescheduled my flight, too?"

Declan shook his head with a smile. "I thought I'd let you handle that. You know… if you could walk today."

"I'll live." Olivia leaned back against the pillow. "I'm just tired."

"Why don't you go back to sleep?"

Her lids were heavy, but she fought against it. "Will you stay?"

An electric current charged the air around them, and Olivia didn't dare open her eyes again. She couldn't believe she'd just asked that. She didn't even know him. But the thought of him disappearing made her sad.

Something pulsed in the surrounding air as Olivia hardly dared to breathe. She heard a rustling, and when she peeked between her lashes, she saw Declan shedding his jeans. Though to her disappointment, he kept his massive chest hidden beneath the long-sleeved shirt. "Nowhere else I'd rather be, Petal."

Olivia rolled to her side, facing away from him as he climbed into bed behind her.

He pushed her hair over her shoulder out of his face. And she would have sworn she heard him say something about 'a bleedin' saint,' but she was already half-asleep again, pulled under by the heat of his body next to her and an inexplicable feeling of contentment.

The sunlight, bright through a gap in the curtains when she opened her eyes again, told Olivia it was at least mid-day if not later. A large hand cupped her breast where her towel had slipped, and she could feel soft snores against her neck. Her body tingled, and heat pooled in her belly. But as much as she wanted to arch into his palm, her bladder made itself known, and Olivia slowly slipped from the bed.

After taking care of her most immediate needs, Olivia brushed her teeth, feeling a million times better than when she'd woken hours before.

Her stomach growled as she pulled the knee-length sundress over her head and crept quietly back to the side of the bed to watch Declan sleep.

He looked like some sort of fallen angel. The sheet covered his lower half, but his rounded shoulders and biceps strained at the fabric of his shirt. Dark lashes fanned out over tanned cheeks covered in thick stubble, the only thing softening a face that was pure masculine beauty.

Olivia sighed. Only she could come home wasted with a virtual sex god, share a bed, and still not get laid.

"Does that sound mean I need to get up?" Declan asked, his eyes still shut.

Olivia flushed, even though he couldn't see her. "There was the promise of something called a fry-up, I believe."

His lips lifted in a smile, and he rolled to his back, opening his eyes to blink sleepily at her.

"Fry-up. Yes."

Ten minutes later, they were dressed and retracing their cobblestoned route from the night before, while Olivia tried to keep her anxiety at bay. "I can't believe I lost my purse."

"It'll be at the pub," he assured her. "If not, we'll sort it out, Rose."

Not for the first time, Olivia thought about correcting him, but at this point, it was just too embarrassing. What harm could come of it?

"It was nice of you to make sure I got home safe last night. Thank you." She scrunched her nose. "I mean, if I didn't say it before. I wish I could remember if I did."

Declan flashed one of his brilliant smiles at her. "All part of the service."

Olivia was so dazzled by how the smile took him from handsome to devastating, she stumbled on the uneven cobblestones, almost falling. His large hand locked on hers, his strength righting her. But as she regained her footing, he didn't remove his hand. Instead, he interlaced their fingers, and the sense of rightness had her heart pounding.

When they reached the pub, Declan pulled the door open ushering her in front of him without relinquishing her hand.

Two people sat in a booth near the front, absorbed in a guidebook.

"Last time I leave a lazy Riordan to close up," a man yelled from behind the bar where he was stacking glasses. "You left the garbage bags by the door, you fecking eejit!"

The bartender's gaze shifted curiously to Olivia before dropping to where their hands were still connected.

"Rose thinks she left her purse here last night. Any chance it got turned in?" Declan lifted a black leather jacket off the hook by the door.

"If you'd bothered to clean up, you'd have found it and remembered your coat. But now I understand the rush to leave."

"Colum," Declan's tone warned. "Ignore my cousin. Working in a pub, he tends to forget his manners."

Some sort of unspoken communication passed between the men, and Colum broke into a smile.

"Ah, don't mind me. Is this yours?" He dipped behind the bar and emerged with her cross-body bag.

"Thank god!"

He tossed it across the bar to Declan, who caught it with one hand before handing it to her.

"I found it in the hall outside the ladies."

Olivia could feel her face heat. "Thanks."

Declan's hand was already pulling her to the door when his cousin called out again in a more serious tone, "Seamus has already been round this morning looking for you. Said you weren't answering your phone."

Declan's fingers tightened on hers for a fraction of a second. It was a small movement, but her attention was suddenly on the tension in his shoulders and the muscle ticking in his jaw.

"It's handled."

"Yeah, lad, but..."

"It's handled." Declan's voice was hard, and a shiver ran down Olivia's spine.

Colum raised both hands in surrender. "It's your brother. A runner picked up your message for Uncle Iain... He's looking for you too."

Declan didn't acknowledge the words, tugging her through the front door.

"If there is something you need to deal with..." Olivia trailed off.

Declan came to a stop and turned her to face him. "There is nothing I would rather do right now than introduce you to the best fry-up in Dublin."

She studied his face intently, noticing how his broad chest rose and fell rapidly, as if he were trying to suppress some deep emotion. Olivia couldn't explain it, but she sensed that Declan was just as eager to explore what was happening between them. The real world could wait a little longer.

"Is it far? Because I'm starving."

Gratitude flashed across his face. "Not too far."

CHAPTER EIGHT

Dublin—12 years ago

Olivia eyed the plate in front of her dubiously. The heaping plate of bacon—rashers, Declan had been quick to correct her—eggs, sausages and potatoes didn't seem appetizing. She poked at a round, dark-colored blob before glancing to Declan, already devouring his plate. "Do I even want to know?"

"The name?" His eyes gleamed. "Probably not. Eat it anyway. It'll put hair on your chest."

"Yeah, that's just what I'm after."

Declan laughed and pushed her plate closer with his fork. "Eat. You'll love it. I promise. And if you don't, I'll find you a bagel."

Olivia resisted the urge to stick her tongue out at him. A few bites later, she conceded he was correct. She didn't know what magical ingredient was in this meal, but she was hooked.

Olivia hadn't missed the fact that the café they had stopped at, after a *not* short walk, had stopped serving breakfast hours ago. But, after a few quiet words to an older woman behind the counter and a kiss on each cheek, the gray-haired woman disappeared into the kitchen, following a lighthearted cuff to the back of his head and a "cheeky bastard."

Declan selected a booth toward the back. When Olivia slipped into the seat facing the door, he'd intercepted her with a vague excuse. But she didn't miss his quick survey of the restaurant, or the fact that every time the bell over the door chimed, he looked up to see who entered.

It should have been alarming, his vigilance to their surroundings. It wasn't. There was no concern from Declan, only a simple self-assurance that made her feel comfortable and safe in a way she never had. Particularly not with a stranger.

"Why are you being so nice to me, Declan Riordan?"

His expression arrested, and she could see her own confusion at their situation cloud his eyes.

"Honestly? I don't know."

Declan shifted in his seat, clearly uncomfortable with his own admission, and she decided to take pity on him.

"Whatever the reason, I appreciate it."

Their gazes caught and held, *something* passing between them. A shiver ran down Olivia's spine. It felt like every cell in her body was focused on this moment. On the man sitting across from her. Declan's nostrils flared on an inhale, his pupils dilated, and she knew she wasn't the only one who felt it.

Her voice was slightly breathless when she blurted out, "What's the last book you read?"

She mentally kicked herself when he blinked at her. The strange intensity of the moment gone.

"*The Importance of Being Earnest.* Though technically it's a play."

"Oscar Wilde?"

"Yes."

His expression grew defensive, and she hurried to add, "I just finished *A Portrait of Dorian Gray.* I started reading Wilde when I knew was coming to Ireland. I'm a dork like that," she babbled, feeling embarrassed. "But I was hooked. Blake used to be my favorite, but Wilde has a way of just cutting through..."

"The bullshit? Yeah, he's a bit more blunt than Mr. *'Love seeketh.'*" Declan popped one of the sausages in his mouth.

Olivia knew her mouth was hanging open. "You read Blake?" Declan frowned, so she hurried to add. "I just wasn't expecting you to quote poetry. You're an onion."

Her cheeks felt like they were on fire.

Inside thoughts, Olivia

"Excuse me?"

"From Shrek." Olivia didn't think it was possible, but her face flamed hotter. She couldn't seem to shut up. "He tells Donkey that Ogres are like onions. Lots of layers."

Declan stared at her like she'd lost her mind. He was probably regretting being nice to her now.

"You... I mean... you quote Blake, read Oscar Wilde, but there's also the whole..." She waved a hand at him. "Sexy, muscly, alpha-male thing going on. You're kind of a fantasy."

My fantasy.

Olivia wanted to slap a hand over her own mouth and disappear. Could she claim to still be drunk?

While she scrambled for a way to walk back her words, Declan's lips lifted into a full, genuine grin. "Sexy, alpha male, huh?"

Olivia was convinced her mortification was going to reduce her to ash right there in the cafe. The only way through was to brazen it out. "I have eyes."

Declan dragged his tongue over his lower lip, his eyes heating. The low-level arousal she'd experienced since waking up next to him exploded into full-fledged lust. Her breath caught as she stared at his mouth, and she squeezed her thighs together against the ache.

The words "let's go back to the hotel" were on the tip of her tongue when Declan sucked in a sharp breath.

"What were your plans for Dublin?"

Olivia swallowed the words, all too aware that his thoughts weren't on the same page. "If I'd rallied earlier, I probably would have gone to see the Book of Kells or gone on the Irish Writers Pub Tour. At this point, I'm sure all the tickets are sold out for the library, and I think I should probably give my liver a break."

"I can get you in.

Olivia studied the dark curls of his bent head as he pulled several bills from his wallet and laid them on the table. "Yeah? With no ticket?"

He looked up and smirked. "Yeah."

She narrowed her eyes, trying to decide if he was serious, and decided to call his bluff. "Okay."

"Finish your food, Petal." He jerked his chin at her plate of food. "It's a bit of a walk."

A steady drizzle started on the trek back up the hill to the city centre. Declan shrugged off his jacket and insisted she hold it over her head when he noticed her shivering in the rain.

"Who told you wearing just a thin sundress would be appropriate for Irish weather?" He laughed.

"It's summer," she said, trying to keep her teeth from chattering.

"Irish summer is not the same thing, Yank." He grinned at her, rubbing her chill-bumped arms.

His words reminded her of something that had been puzzling her. "How come you don't have a strong accent, like your cousin?"

Declan's arm slipped to her waist, pulling her away from the curb as a car approached, rainwater splashing out from its tires. "I have an accent."

"You do, but it's not as thick as I would have expected."

He glanced at her from the corner of his eye. "Did you think we all sound like the Lucky Charm's leprechaun?"

She flushed. "No."

Declan chuckled, the arm around her waist giving her a quick squeeze. The heat radiating off him was unreal, and Olivia resisted the urge to cuddle closer. "My dad is an American."

"Oh."

"Here we are," he said, turning under the gate to the quadrangle of Trinity College. Declan tucked her under one of the massive stone overhangs. "Wait here. A friend of mine is working. Should be able to get us in."

Olivia bit her lip, the chill was becoming uncomfortable, and she suddenly realized what he was proposing. The ticket times were well past, and the rain had driven all but a handful of the most determined tourists from the grounds.

She was essentially a rule follower, and without Declan's grin to distract her, Olivia's brain had kicked back into overdrive. "I don't want to get you in trouble."

He pressed a quick kiss to her temple and winked before walking backward out into the rain. "Stop worrying, Rose. '*I can resist everything except temptation.*'"

"Did you just quote Oscar to me?"

"I didn't realize the two of you were on a first name basis." He grinned, the dimple in his cheek appearing.

"Yeah, we are," she shot back, but Declan had disappeared around the corner of the building.

Less than five minutes later, he returned with a short man, dressed in a suit, in tow.

"Come on, Rose. Live a little," he whispered, pulling her out of the alcove and over to a side door. Without a word, the man unlocked the door with a heavy-looking iron key and gave Declan a speaking look.

"Thirty minutes. They'll be making the rounds."

Declan clapped the man on the shoulder before dragging the door open and propelling her forward. The dim light of the hallway hit her at the same time as the faint mildew smell of old books. It was heaven.

"If I go to jail, I'm blaming you."

"You aren't going to jail."

Declan led her through several small hallways and short staircases until he pushed open a heavy, carved wooden door with a creak, and Olivia gasped.

In front of her, from floor to ceiling, and covering one end of the long library hall to the other, were the priceless books of Trinity College.

"Oh my god." Olivia's heart fluttered as she took a few halting steps forward.

Declan smiled at her, interlacing their fingers again. "Book Of Kells?"

She nodded as he led her to the illuminated manuscript displayed on a pedestal.

"They only moved it in here recently. It used to be at the top of the stairs, which would have made it more difficult. Lucky for us, they are getting ready for an exhibition."

"This is incredible." Olivia turned back to the rows of books. "Can you imagine what must be hidden in these shelves?"

"Have you always loved books?"

Declan rested his hip on a bench set in the middle of the hall as Olivia strolled down the length of the room.

"Always." She craned her neck to look at the books near the ceiling. The building's thick stone walls and the rain outside made her feel they were completely separate from the rest of the world. "I haven't had as much time to read in the last several years, but I love it. It's always been a way to escape from the real world."

"Did you want to escape?"

"Sometimes." The admission startled her.

Declan pushed away from the bench and walked toward her. "What is your favorite thing to read? When you want to escape?" His voice was hushed when he stopped in front of her.

Heat swept through her at his proximity. Olivia caught a hint of his cologne as he absently adjusted his jacket on her shoulders. Her hormones kicked into overdrive, making it difficult to form a coherent thought. "The Romantics," she managed. "Wordsworth, Blake, Shelley..."

Declan's damp curls had fallen onto his forehead, and this time when her fingers twitched, she didn't resist. He sucked in a breath when she pushed them back, and then lightly ran her nails through his hair.

Declan's eyes burned into hers, the hard planes of his face drawing tight. Olivia felt like she was drunk, even though the alcohol had left her system hours before. There was a magic to this place, and it made her bold.

She wanted him. This mysterious, complex man who she'd met by chance. Olivia knew she would regret it for the rest of her life if she didn't act on it.

Lifting on her tiptoes, Olivia pressed her lips to his. At first, she thought he wouldn't respond, his lips remaining still. But when she flicked the tip of her tongue against his lower lip, it was as if something snapped inside him. Powerful arms clamped around her waist, and pulled her hard against his body. Declan's mouth slanted over hers, his tongue stroking inside. Tasting and teasing as she moaned into his mouth.

Olivia clutched at his huge shoulders as he thrust a hand into her hair, holding her still beneath his lips. Declan's kiss was all-consuming, and filled with an urgency that left her breathless. His mouth moved with a desperate hunger, as if he couldn't get enough of her.

When his teeth scraped along her lips a shiver ran through

her. The hand gripping her waist flexed, and he pulled her even closer until he was cradled between her legs.

Adrenaline and lust pulsed through her. Olivia felt delirious, and with a gasp she broke the kiss and placed a hand over his chest. His heart thundered beneath her palm.

"I want you to take me back to my hotel now."

Thunderclouds formed in Declan's eyes, and he stepped back. Knowing where his mind had gone, Olivia fisted his shirt in her hand and pulled him back to her mouth.

"Your friend gave us thirty minutes," she said against his lips, when she lifted for air. "I need more than that."

Declan's jaw clenched twice, emotions she couldn't identify racing across his face.

"Please," she whispered.

His whole body trembled, and then her hand was in his, and Olivia was doing her best to stay on her feet as he strode for the door. The drizzle was still steady; the rain was refreshing on her overheated skin.

They were silent as Declan led her back through the streets to the hotel, her fingers securely interlaced with his like he was worried she might change her mind and pull away. It should have felt awkward, the long walk back, but with every step, she was more confident.

There was no rational reason for her to feel this level of closeness to someone she'd met less than twenty-four hours before. But Declan made her feel safe… valued. As if she was the most important person in the world. When Olivia covered their joined hands with her free one, he looked down at her, raindrops clinging to his eyelashes.

The hotel door had scarcely shut behind them when Olivia found herself spun to face him. Declan was shoving his jacket off her shoulders, his mouth crushing hers. Lips and tongue claimed her as goosebumps covered her skin, and her nipples hardened.

Olivia groaned, almost lightheaded with need, as she arched her hips against him and yanked at his shirt. Desperate to touch his hot skin.

Barely breaking their kiss, Declan reached an arm up and roughly pulled his shirt over his head, before tossing it to the floor.

Olivia's fingers scrabbled at his belt. His big hands cupped her shoulders, and his lips traveled from her mouth and over her jaw, leaving a trail of kisses. "Easy." His lips teased at the delicate skin of her ear lobe.

Declan let out a low groan when she cupped him through his jeans, filling her with a sense of power. His head tipped back, his eyes squeezed shut, panting as her palm pressed and stroked against the length of him.

"Fuck. Slow down, Petal." Declan ignored his own words, lifting her and walking the few steps to set her on the edge of the bed. Olivia reached for the hem of her dress, pulling it over her head in one movement. Declan's nostrils flared as he took in her white cotton bra and panties. She hadn't brought any sexy underwear for the trip, not expecting that anyone would see it.

Declan's reaction made her feel as though she were the most desirable thing he'd ever seen. His face taut, he placed a hand beside her on the bed, his massive chest pushing her flat. When his lips found hers, the kiss was slower. His thigh bumped hers wider, and he settled against her.

Olivia whimpered and attempted to lift her hips to grind against his erection, but Declan's weight had her deliciously pinned beneath him. Panting, she clutched at his back, her nails digging into his skin, her mouth biting down on the hot, tight skin of his chest.

Olivia had never felt this way before. She was out of control. Her whole body was on fire. The intensity of sensation was so strong she thought if she didn't come soon, she might be at real risk of heart failure.

"Wait," Declan growled against her neck as he decorated her collarbone with open-mouthed kisses. When he licked between her cleavage and pinched her nipple between his fingers hard, she bucked upward.

"I don't want to wait." Her voice was a desperate whine, and she twisted her hands tight in his hair, trying to pull him up from his exploration. "I need you in me... now."

Declan pulled one bra cup to the side, and the feel of his rough palm was almost her undoing. Her head thrashed, and her legs shook as his tongue rasped against the pebbled peak.

"So beautiful," he said, blowing cool air across her moist skin. His fingertip lazily circled the nub. "Perfectly pink. Just like your mouth," Declan's lips closed over her, tugging and sucking her into the hot moisture of his mouth.

Olivia cried out as almost painful electricity shocked her between her legs. Declan slipped a hand between their bodies and into her panties, his fingers curving over where she throbbed. He nipped at the underside of her breast with a groan as one thick finger slipped through her folds and sank deep inside her. Her legs trembled.

"Perfect." The guttural sound came from deep in his throat. "You feel fucking *perfect,* Petal."

Lifting off her slightly to pull her underwear down her legs, she felt his weight lower over her again. "Open for me."

Olivia's thighs fell apart, and she bit back a sharp cry as a second and then third finger joined to stroke and twist, curling inside, driving her insane. Olivia's body tightened into a coil. "Declan... yes. Oh my god..."

His thumb pressed against her clit, and she exploded. Declan swallowed her scream in a kiss, as a rainbow of color burst behind her eyelids. His fingers slowed, gliding in and out as wave after wave of pleasure shook her body, his lips moving gently over hers.

Pulling back, Declan stood next to the bed gazing down at her. "Your whole body turns the most delectable shade of pink when you come."

Propped on her elbows, Olivia watched as he removed his jeans and boxer briefs, shoving them down his thick thighs and kicking them away.

She tried not to stare. She really did. But if Declan in clothes was sexy, Declan naked and fully aroused, violet eyes hooded with desire, was the hottest thing she'd ever seen. He wrapped a hand around himself, stroking once, a half-hopeful, half-resigned look on his face.

"Don't suppose you have a condom?"

Olivia grinned and pointed at her suitcase. "An entire box of pink ones."

She thought he'd ask the obvious question, but within seconds Declan had found the box and rolled one on, settling himself between her thighs. He stroked his tip through her slick folds holding her gaze. "Pink is definitely my new favorite color."

"Hen party fav—" The last of the word lost. She cried out as he surged into her. He stilled for a minute, letting her adjust to the fullness.

He was so deep Olivia felt like she couldn't breathe. Declan was overwhelming. He was everywhere. His scent in her nose, his forearms framing her face—above her, inside her.

Her hips lifted to meet his relentless thrusts, the tension inside her spiraling higher with every plunge. Declan hooked a hand behind her knee, pushing it high on his back, and angled his hips so that he rubbed against her with each stroke.

Olivia's orgasm crashed over her, her body shaking as

Declan's rhythm became less controlled, more frenzied. He buried his face in her neck with a hoarse shout, as his body shuddered and finally slumped over her.

His weight was almost suffocating, but she didn't care. She ran her hands up and down his arms. He was still inside her, but it didn't feel like enough.

Declan's lips moved against her neck. "That was..."

Olivia squeezed around him, and he moaned, before slipping out of her. Discarding the condom, he returned to lie on his side next to her, supporting his head with one hand while he watched the other lazily run up and down her bare thigh.

Olivia sighed happily, the words from one of her favorite poems slipping out. *"'And the sunlight clasps the earth, And the moonbeams kiss the sea—What are all these kissings worth if thou kiss not me?'"*

His hand stopped, and she squeezed her eyes shut. *Stupid Stupid Stupid.* And just when she was sure she had ruined the moment, his palm cupped her chin, and she opened her eyes.

Declan's gaze felt like it saw all the way into her soul. With a sweet smile, he said in his low, rumbly voice. *"'She walks in beauty, like the night. Of cloudless climes and starry skies; And all that's best of dark and bright. Meet in her aspect and her eyes...'"*

He stopped, the thunderclouds back in his eyes, and he flopped onto his back an arm over his eyes. "I can never remember the whole thing."

Olivia was pretty sure that at some point on this trip she must have died, because not only did this man just give her the best orgasms of her life, he quoted Byron in all his naked glory.

"What time is your flight back to the States?"

Her heart squeezed. "My flight's at noon tomorrow, but I'm going back to Oxford. I'm not due home until next week. I'm starting a new job."

Declan was silent for a minute, and doubt began creeping into her happy bubble. Then he was up, pulling her to her feet and turning on the shower.

"Excellent. Plenty of time to finish that box."

CHAPTER NINE

Dublin—12 years ago

Declan stared at the ceiling of Rose's hotel room, partially illuminated by the bathroom light. She was stretched out like a starfish, snoring quietly. Rose was worn out, and frankly so was he, but his brain wouldn't take the hint and shut down.

Jesus. What the fuck was I thinking? Quoting fucking poetry like a lovesick puppy.

He hadn't been thinking, and that was the problem. Since he'd met her last night, it was as though she'd put some sort of spell on him. His normal, rational, logical way of thinking was thrown out the window, replaced with this other version of himself he didn't recognize. Every part of him was attuned to every part of the beautiful woman next to him.

Rose had looked up at him, her eyes soft and warm, and a poem he'd memorized for a class at prep school poured out of him.

Declan didn't know what to think. He should be worried about what it was his Uncle Iain wanted to speak to him about, or why, after just settling his debt, his brother Seamus was looking for him as well.

Today—with her—he hadn't thought about it at all. He wasn't Declan Bloom and all the pressures that came with his life. He was Declan Riordan. It had been wonderful. Wonderful and freeing to meet someone who accepted him as he was.

In the back of his mind, he heard the echoes of a warning. *Be careful. She's different. Special. You can't keep her.*

Declan knew he should listen, because after what was easily the best sexual experience of his life, his chest had swelled with emotions. Emotions that had no business being there. Rose was a tourist on vacation, and she was leaving in the morning.

The crushing feeling on his sternum meant nothing, he told himself. *But it did.* Declan had spent the last several hours exploring every inch of her body with his mouth and hands, but it wasn't enough. And it wasn't just the sex.

Being with Rose settled something deep inside him. Today, spending time with her, it had felt like all the pieces of his life that whirled with nonstop demand inside him had finally drifted into place. The constant need to stay on alert, to think five steps ahead of everyone, even his own father… had all quieted with her hand in his. He wasn't ready to let her go.

The thoughts swirling in Declan's head slowed to a stop, an audacious plan taking shape.

He frowned.

Will she think I'm a creep for even suggesting it? Am I a creep for suggesting it while letting her believe I'm someone else? If anyone in the family heard about it? If my father…

Declan scrubbed a hand over his face.

Fuck. This is a terrible idea.

One that would most likely blow up in his face. But he'd been living his life for his family since the day he was born. Was it wrong to want to take a step back from the world and be Declan for a while?

~

"I HAVE AN IDEA," Declan said, handing her the cup of takeout coffee he'd gotten while she was asleep.

Rose pushed her mess of hair out of her face, revealing a deep crease on one cheek from where she had lain on the sheet, dead to the world. She rubbed at her eyes, and he smiled.

"Hear me out before you answer."

She pushed to a sitting position, her back against the headboard, the sheet bunching at her waist, leaving her top free for him to ogle.

Rose took a large sip of her coffee and then another. "Give me a second," she muttered, slurping at her cup.

"You really have the most beautiful breasts I've ever seen." Declan grinned when she choked, and a bright flush covered her porcelain skin.

"As a wake-up call, that's pretty good." Rose's fingers toyed with the sheet, like she was going to cover herself, but then they relaxed. "What's your idea?"

Declan took her lack of self-consciousness as a positive sign. "I have a week off too." Her brow furrowed, and he rushed to explain. "I'm starting a new job in a week. It's a promotion, so this might be my last time off for a while."

"You got a promotion at your cousin's bar?" Lines appeared between her eyebrows.

"It's a family business. We all have to work our way up." It wasn't a total lie. "What would you say to us spending our last week of freedom together?"

"What?" A cautious look crossed her face.

Declan traced a finger across her cheekbone and over the shell of her ear, back along her jaw and over her lips, before cupping her cheek. He just needed to touch her, and he'd stopped trying to figure out why.

"Yesterday was..." Despite his well thought out speech, words failed him, but Rose smiled, leaning her cheek into his caress.

"I know."

"I don't know what this is between us, and I know we both have lives we have to go back to... but... We don't have to go yet. Stay with me in Ireland. I have a place in the south. We can rent a car. Go wherever you want."

Rose licked her lips. She hadn't said no right away. He felt the first bit of hope creeping in.

"Like a week in bed?" Her tone was a little too careful, and Declan lowered his hand.

"Not just that. Though a week-long sex fest with you sounds pretty damn good."

Declan felt like his heart was in his throat, and his pride was screaming at him to shut up, but instead of listening, he was honest with her.

"Last night was incredible. Fuck, that doesn't even begin to do it justice... But it's more than that. I can't explain it, and I know it doesn't make sense, but there's something here, and I know I'm not the only one to feel it."

Rose's eyes were wide, and she stared at him unblinking.

"I know any sort of future is out of the question. We live in different worlds... but one week..."

Declan held his breath. This was the most vulnerable he'd ever made himself to another human, but he didn't regret it. Didn't regret shedding the mask he wore every day. "You can trust me."

A little smile lifted her lips. "I know. I don't know how I know, but I do."

Declan's pulse raced. "Does that mean?"

"Yes, Declan Riordan. I'll spend the week with you."

"Really?"

"Yeah?" She grinned. "That sex fest sounded pretty enticing."

While Declan retrieved his things from his mother's home and rented a car, Rose rescheduled her flight for six days later out of the Shannon Airport in southern Ireland.

Taking her suitcase and putting it in the tiny backseat, he held her door open for her.

"Are you sure?"

Rose laughed. "You're making me think you didn't want me to say yes."

Declan kissed her hard on the lips. "It was the best thing I'd ever heard."

Her eyes grew misty, and Declan felt his heart thump hard. If he wasn't careful, he was going to fall in love with this girl. *That* would be a disaster.

"Where are we going?" she asked, staring out the window as they left the city and merged onto the highway.

"I thought we'd head south. Spend the night somewhere near Kilkenny. It's beautiful." Declan rubbed at his thigh. Was he nervous? What the hell? "There's, uh, a castle and some other historic stuff… if you like that kind of thing."

Rose reached for his hand, bringing it to rest in her lap. "I *love* that kind of thing."

Kilkenny wasn't far, and while Declan had never particularly enjoyed car trips, preferring his father's private jet, the hours on the road were some of the most relaxed and fun Declan could remember.

Rose put on early 2000s era pop music, singing along and teasing him until he joined in. After strolling the town hand in hand and convincing her to visit a small farm distillery, they ate dinner in a pub where Rose declared ham and cheese toasties the perfect food.

That night, when the person in the room next door banged on the wall, after the second time Rose screamed his name, and he covered her mouth with his hand, Declan realized he'd never been happier.

"This looks like it was plucked out of a storybook." Olivia's face was practically pressed to the window as they entered the scenic drive around the Ring of Kerry.

Warmth filled his chest. He'd spent the first part of his life in Dublin, and later full time with his father in Rhode Island, but this area of Ireland would always feel like home.

Her head swiveled back and forth, looking out his window, then through the windshield, before returning to her own side.

"Are you getting hungry?" Declan eyed the puffy white clouds. "The weather is nice now, but that's no guarantee it won't change in an hour."

They'd ordered a picnic lunch from a small shop in Kilkenny before they left. While waiting for it to prepared, Rose had dragged him into several shops along the high street. She had only brought a couple of outfits as her trip was intended to last just a couple of days. As she oohed and aahed, taking forever to pick out the woolen sweater she wanted, Declan was more than content to wait. She added a couple pairs of leggings, a few T-shirts, and a loose skirt to her pile before wandering over to inspect a display of teacups.

She picked up each one, her nail tracing the unique designs. When her brow wrinkled, and she put it back, he joined her. "Do you want it?"

Rose shrugged, but she chewed her lip. "It's not very practical. What am I going to do with one tea cup?"

Declan smiled. "Start a collection."

"I'm not sure I'm a collection kind of girl." Her mouth moved back and forth. "But I might like to be."

"My grandmother had a collection. Mam was furious when her mother left it to me in her will, along with the cottage. Which is crazy because my mother is a city girl through and through."

"Are you close to your mom?" It was the closest they had come to discussing anything personal.

"I'm not sure if close is the right word. My mother is a force of nature, and she likes to get her own way." Declan's lips twisted. "We have that in common."

"Who doesn't? Everyone wants to get their way."

Declan cocked his head. "I suppose that's true."

"It's only a problem if someone decides that what they want is more important than what everyone else wants. No negotiation is won without compromise."

Rose walked back to where she'd left her clothing choices with the cashier, her words leaving Declan to stare after her.

Picking up the pink, flower-shaped tea cup sitting on a leaf saucer that she'd been admiring, he hurried to catch up, reaching for his wallet.

"Let me," he said, extending his credit card.

"Absolutely not." Rose brushed his hand away, and Declan folded his fingers, obscuring the card, realizing too late that the telltale black rectangle would give him away. Bouncers rarely qualified for Black Amex cards.

Thankfully, Rose hadn't noticed. "These are for me. You've already handled the rental car and hotel." The cashier put the clothes in one big bag, her gaze bouncing between the two of them. "Besides," Rose said with a smile, "I start my big girl job soon, so I'll have extra money."

Declan blinked. Not once in his life had anyone turned down his offer to pay. Granted, Rose didn't know the truth about his finances, but something told him it wouldn't matter if she did.

"Thank you for offering, though. It's very sweet." She gave him a brief peck on his lips and turned to the door. "Our basket should be ready by now."

Declan quickly purchased the tea cup, urging the woman behind the counter to wrap it quickly, all the while keeping an eye out that Rose didn't wander back wondering what took him so long. Joining her, he dropped his smaller bag inside of hers to hide the gift.

He pulled the car over into one of the many viewing-spot parking lots. Declan lifted the basket with one hand, holding Rose's hand with the other. Finding a flat spot in the sun, Declan spread the picnic blanket over the short grass and moss, while Rose unpacked the basket. She opened two bottles of water, handing one to him.

"Back there at the shop," Declan said. "That thing you said about negotiation. That doesn't sound like an English major."

"I'm not an English major."

"I thought you said you were studying at Oxford. You know, all those writers and poets..."

He trailed off when Rose laughed. "That was for fun."

Declan's brow furrowed. "You went to Oxford for fun? Are you some kind of super nerd?"

"Probably. I am pretty smart." She pretended to dust off her shoulder, a happy laugh bubbling out. "But no, I'm not graduating from Oxford. I was a business major."

Declan shook his head. "I'm confused."

"I went to a state school on a scholarship, but I always wanted to study literature, specifically the Romantics. My graduate school has a mini-mester abroad option at Oxford. Even though the credits don't apply to my degree, it's the only way I could ever attend. I saved up so that I could do it before joining the real world." She screwed the top back on the water. "Officially, I graduate with my MBA in a couple of weeks."

"So, I was right, you went to Oxford for fun?" Declan was impressed. "And you already have a job lined up prior to graduating. Aren't you the little overachiever," he teased, but Rose's face fell and she took a bite of her sandwich.

He nudged her with his elbow. "Hey, that's a good thing."

Rose swallowed and stared out at the mountains. When she finally spoke, her voice sounded so sad he wanted to put his arms around her. "You'd think so, wouldn't you?"

"Doesn't everyone?" he mimicked her words from the shop.

Rose let out a heavy sigh and dusted the crumbs off her hands. "No. Not if they don't like what you're overachieving at."

Declan weighed his words carefully, aware the subject was touching on something painful for her. "Who?"

"My parents primarily. They don't understand why I've worked so hard to get the position I was offered. Yes, it's from a family friend, but if I hadn't killed myself in internships and graduated top of my class, I don't think he could have just given it to me."

"Parental expectations can be suffocating." He knew that better than most.

"My problem is my parents don't have *any* expectations of me beyond getting married. They aren't happy that I have different goals for myself." She lay back and bent her knees, staring at the sky. "My mother can't understand why I want a career. In her mind, a woman's life begins and ends with children. And that's great if it was what I wanted... It's what my sister wants, and she's extremely happy in her life. But it's not what I want."

"Is it a religious thing?"

She huffed a laugh. "No, that at least would make sense. I suspect it has something to do with Grandma Rose, but my mom won't talk about it."

"Grandma Rose, who doesn't take shit?" His lips quirked.

Rose rolled her eyes, but she turned her head to smile at him. "Yes."

"What does Grandma Rose, have to do with all of this?"

"My grandmother was a career woman before it was cool." Declan could hear the pride in Rose's voice. "Her husband died young, and she had to support my mom. She started out writing copy in an advertising agency, but eventually moved up until she was an executive. She wore the best clothes and always smelled like this expensive French perfume—Wild White Rose. I found it on the internet a few years ago and ordered myself some. I thought my mom was going to cry the first time I wore it—and not because she misses her mother. I don't wear it at home anymore."

Declan leaned closer, inhaling. "Is that what you've been wearing? I'm a fan."

Rose nodded. "I feel confident when I wear it. More like myself."

"Then what's the problem?" Declan rolled to face her.

"Me. I'm the problem. I think my mother embraced the whole June Cleaver thing because it's the mom she wished *she'd* had growing up. She loves to tell me how lucky I am that she is so involved in my life, but what 'involved' means to her, feels a lot like control to me.

"My choosing a different path makes her angry, like I'm rejecting her or something. She can't understand that it's okay if I want something different than what she chose. I do want kids some day, but I also want a career. I think it's worse for her because the life I want looks a lot like my Grandmother's. My mom has never been able to accept who I am. I think part of her actually hates me for being different."

A tear slipped free, sliding down her cheek, and she swiped at it angrily. "She may not be wrong. People don't like different. That fear of the dark?"

Declan nodded warily, suddenly afraid of what she would say.

"The one and only time I was invited to a sleepover was in fourth grade. I was the weird, nerd girl in class with no friends. So, when one of the cool girls in my grade, Annabelle Fisher, had a birthday, I was so excited to be invited. I only found out later, from eavesdropping on my parents, that Annabelle's mom made her invite everyone in the class."

Rose sniffed, but her eyes had dried. "It was obvious no one wanted me there. After her parents went to sleep, Annabelle suggested we play hide and seek. She told me the best place was the closet in the basement. I went along with it when she said she'd hide there too." Rose shivered, and Declan had the urge to hunt down a bunch of school-aged girls—even though they'd be adults now.

"Long story short, it was a trick. They shoved me in and locked the door. I didn't get out until my mom came to get me the next day at lunch."

Declan's mouth fell open with horror. "Those little bitches."

"Hence the fear of the dark." Rose made a face. "I was convinced there were bugs on me and that I could hear voices. I've always had an overactive imagination. It doesn't happen all the time. I'm not afraid of the dark... exactly... It just pops up when I'm feeling stressed or vulnerable. I'm guessing being black-out drunk in a foreign country qualified for my subconscious."

"What happened to them... the girls? What did your parents do?"

"Nothing." Rose sat up and began to put items back in the basket. "I don't know why I'm telling you this."

Declan caught her hands. "I'm glad you are. I want to know you. I want to know everything about you."

She stared at him, the blue of her eyes swirling with something he couldn't identify. "Will you let me know you too?"

Declan nodded. *I'll try.* "But first I want to hear what happened."

Rose shrugged. "It's really not that dramatic a story. Annabelle's parents were mortified. I was teased about it and for being a nerd all through high-school, and my parents told me I should try harder to fit in so that people would like me. Making friends still isn't something that comes easily to me."

Declan's chest ached. "But you won, Petal."

She frowned.

"You won." His voice was probably fiercer than appropriate, but he needed her to hear him. "They tried to break you and you kept going. You graduated, got your MBA, attended Oxford, and are about to start a job you are excited about, and you're only what, twenty-five? Grandma Rose would be so proud. You didn't take their shit, and you kept going."

Rose's lips twisted to the side, but he could see by the light in her eyes his words had gotten through. "Twenty-three, give or take a day."

Declan stared at her. "You're only twenty-three?"

She ticked off facts on her fingers. "Early birthday, skipped second grade, didn't exactly love high school so I graduated early, and then took college classes year round." She shrugged like she hadn't just revealed an impressive accomplishment.

"I'm having sex with a child prodigy," he laughed, only half kidding.

She snorted, rising to her feet. "Not a prodigy, just someone who had a goal."

Declan reached for her, tugging her back down so that she straddled him, one knee on either side of his hips. Propped up on his arms, he brushed her loose hair back behind her ears. "I think you might be one of the most remarkable people I've ever met."

She flushed, the color tinting her porcelain skin. Her head ducked and then lifted to meet his gaze. "Thank you."

He looked at her quizzically as she planted her hands flat against his chest.

"For listening. For seeing me."

Warmth filled Declan's chest, her words hitting him harder than they should. "I'm so glad you got drunk the other night," he joked, afraid to examine what he was feeling. It felt wonderful and dangerous all at the same time.

Her body shook with laughter, making her hips rock against him, her fingers catching in his T-shirt.

"You are ridiculous, Declan Riordan." She smiled against his lips, and then hers moved, their soft warmth gliding over his. "You make me feel like I belong just for being me. I'm not sure I've ever felt that way before."

"Neither have I," he murmured as his mouth crushed hers. His lips and teeth soon traveled down her neck and Rose angled her head to give him access to the soft spot just below her jaw that never failed to make her squirm. Her rose perfume filled his nose as he sucked on her neck, his cock turning to stone as she rocked against him.

"Ahem!" A loud voice nearby broke through his lust-filled brain, and Declan turned his head to see an older gentleman with a walking stick glaring at them.

"This is a public place." The man scowled, as Rose hid her face in his chest.

"Right. Sorry."

They gathered the rest of their lunch items, and Declan held the basket in front of his jeans. Rose had dissolved into giggles by the time he shut her car door. He rested his forehead against the steering wheel, his own sides heaving with laughter.

"I totally forgot where we were," she wheezed.

As Declan started the car and pulled back onto the narrow two-lane road, it hit him that he had too. When he was with Rose, he felt like a normal twenty-five-year-old, free to make out in public.

He grabbed her hand and held it tight, pulling their clasped hands onto his thigh. She glanced over at him, but he didn't want to talk. His need to be with her felt like it was on almost a cellular level, and that was terrifying because they only had four days left.

CHAPTER TEN

New York—Present Day

"Wow!" Stuart exclaimed, when the elevator doors opened in the lobby, and she found the rest of the Armstrong Electronics group waiting.

"I could say the same." Olivia smiled. "You all look very handsome." And they did. All three were attired in black tuxes and bow ties. "You clean up well." She kept her voice friendly, but didn't let her gaze land on Kyle. He was handsome, but Olivia knew all too well what his boyish good looks were hiding.

Richard beamed. "You've always looked beautiful in blue."

Olivia *felt* beautiful. She made it a point to dress well at work —thank you, Grandma Rose—but she didn't get the opportunity to dress up like this frequently. She had splurged on a shopping spree at a high-end boutique in Buckhead. The strapless, sapphire silk gown with buttons up the back, fit her like a glove, and the stylist had talked her into topping it with two short ropes of pearls that rested just below her collarbone.

Stuart offered her his arm. "Bloom Communications sent a car."

Tucking her hand into the crook of his elbow, she walked

with him to the exit. Olivia climbed inside the limousine, feeling glamorous and confident.

The private club where the gala took place was only a short ride away on the Upper East Side. Spotlights lit up the building's white stone façade, and Olivia shivered as she emerged from the car into the cold, New York air.

"I can't believe you didn't bring a coat. It's December," Kyle sniped at her, as he buttoned his tuxedo jacket. His eyes scanned her bare shoulders and lingered on her cleavage longer than she would have liked. "But then you always have to be different."

"Kyle," Richard reproved quietly.

Olivia ignored him, excitement building inside her. Couples dressed lavishly in gowns and furs climbed the stone steps in front of her before entering two large wooden doors flanked by torch light.

"I feel like I'm in a movie," Stuart murmured close to her ear, and she gave him a smile. "Let me." He extended his arm as she used one hand to lift her skirt to ascend the stairs.

"Thanks. I'm glad you're here. I'm feeling a bit like Cinderella right now."

"Let's just hope we don't turn into pumpkins at midnight."

Olivia giggled, Stuart's attempt to make her laugh dissolving the rest of her nerves.

Who cared if she didn't know anyone here? When would she ever attend an event like this again?

When they cleared the foyer, Olivia's mouth fell open, and she heard Stuart let out his own startled exhale.

At the far end of the marble foyer, the room opened onto a massive ballroom below. Just beyond an elaborate wrought iron landing, a dual-sided, marble staircase descended into the vast room.

Everywhere Olivia looked was candlelight. Candles of varying heights were set in heavy gold candlesticks, and multi-armed candelabras, placed atop tables lining the perimeter walls, dripped with crystals refracting the light into rainbow prisms on the surfaces below.

Reaching the railing, Olivia looked up at the massive crystal chandeliers hanging over the space, their lights dimmed to not distract from the candlelight effect.

Two twenty-foot Christmas trees decorated with white lights and ribbons book-ended the room. Arranged across the marble floor between them were elegantly set tables with crisp, white linens, silver, and crystal, surrounding tall vase-centerpieces filled with sprigs of evergreen and white roses. A string ensemble quietly played classical music in a corner.

It was magical.

With one hand on the banister and the other on Stuart's arm, Olivia carefully descended the steps, conscious of her higher-than-normal heels.

"Olivia." Chris stepped toward them as they joined the crowd. He raised her hand, and there was a moment, when his lips lingered on the back of her hand before he made eye contact, that made her wonder if he was trying to flirt with her. "Stuart."

Olivia was forced to drop her friend's arm so that he could shake Chris's outstretched hand.

"I want to introduce you to Lawrence Talbot." Chris angled his body to include an older man behind him. "He's our chief counsel at Bloom Communications. Lawrence, this is Stuart Pruitt, head of Research and Development for Armstrong Electronics."

The men shook hands. Lawrence asked Stuart something about his opinion on intellectual property rights, and Chris moved between her and the men. With a hand on the small of Olivia's back, he turned her away.

"While they're talking shop, let me get you something to drink."

Olivia cast one last glance at Stuart, who had narrowed his eyes as Chris steered her. Was Kyle right? Was Chris actually interested in her, or was this his way of trying to influence her?

"You look gorgeous tonight," he said, as they approached the bar. "I hope that's not inappropriate."

"Thank you."

"What would you like? Champagne? Wine?"

Olivia's eyes scanned the bar as the scent of pine decorations on the bar reached her nose. "Jameson and ginger ale with lime, please."

Chris raised an eyebrow at her as the bartender fixed her drink, setting it and a short glass of scotch in front of Chris. What made her order that? Nostalgia?

Because you can't stop thinking about Declan.

She mentally shook herself.

"A whiskey drinker. I thought southern girls drank bourbon."

Olivia arched a brow at him. "Southern girls drink whatever they like."

"I stand corrected." Chris watched her speculatively for a moment, his eyes dipping briefly to her breasts before meeting her eyes. "I have to admit, you aren't what I expected?"

"What did you expect?"

His gaze went to where her colleagues stood. "I thought you'd be a figurehead. Married into the family, promoted at an extremely young age…" He shrugged.

Olivia narrowed her eyes. "If you'd done your homework, you'd know that XEROS is *my* baby. I may not have the technical skill to have designed it, but it was my initiative."

"I did know that. I apologize for my assumption." Chris placed a hand over his chest and gave her his best sheepish smile. "I shouldn't have assumed that you earned your spot just because of your ex-husband."

"I'm sure you wouldn't want me to speculate that you only got the position of CEO at Bloom Communications because you are engaged to a majority shareholder."

She smiled sweetly at him, even though irritation still simmered in her blood. It was reckless, but if they were to partner with Chris Keller and Bloom Communications, she needed him to understand that, even though they were a small company, she wouldn't be steamrolled.

His expression hardened for a second, but when she didn't break eye contact, it lightened, and he tipped his head back with a laugh. He shook his head with a grin. "You are a delightful surprise. I think you and I are going to work together just fine."

She smirked at him over the top of her glass. "If we agree to your terms, you mean."

He clinked his glass against hers. "Here's hoping that you say yes." His eyes flared, and Olivia had the distinct impression that Chris was implying something else.

"Yes, to what?" a silky tone asked. Two hands with crimson nails appeared on Chris's lapels as a blonde woman in a matching red dress appeared behind him and pressed herself against his back. She would have been beautiful if not for the anger twisting her features.

"Darling." Chris's smile dimmed, but he took her hand and led her to stand next to him. "Olivia and I were just toasting to what I hope will be the newest acquisition of Bloom Communications. Olivia, this is my fiancée Courtney Bloom."

The woman glared at Olivia, her pupils dilated. Her eyes raked over Olivia, and whatever she saw seemed to make her even more unhappy. She turned and rubbed her breasts against Chris's arm.

Chris's face tightened, and Olivia downed her drink at the awkwardness.

Is she trying to mark her territory?

"Baby," she whined. "I need a drink." A muscle ticked in

Chris's jaw. "And don't you dare say a word about mixing my meds with alcohol."

Courtney suddenly raised on her tiptoes and nipped his jaw. A gasp nearby clued Olivia in that she wasn't the only one shocked by the woman's behavior.

Chris inhaled through his nose. "I wouldn't dream of it, darling." He sent an apologetic look to Olivia, but she took a sip, hoping the glass obscured her expression. "Another round please, and a vodka tonic."

Courtney continued glaring at Olivia behind Chris's back, making the hairs on the back of Olivia's neck go up. There was something off about the woman. Her eyes were wild, her chest blotchy like she was trying to stop herself from screaming.

Is she on something?

Chris took Olivia's empty glass from her hand and pressed a new one into it. "Shall we head to our table?"

Olivia happily stepped away, scanning the room for her colleagues. Behind her, she heard Courtney arguing with Chris, not bothering to keep her voice down.

"Don't think I didn't see you flirting with her. You are not going to humiliate me like this. Haven't I been through enough lately? Do you want me to snap? Is that it? Because you won't like what happens. Don't push me, Chris."

Chris murmured something Olivia couldn't hear. Several heads had turned their way to watch their progression through the room, Courtney's increasingly loud complaints providing them with a show. Olivia *really* hoped her cheeks weren't as red as they felt.

"Did you see where they put our table? It's an insult. I know they did it on purpose. They probably *asked* to sit there to torture me." Courtney's voice had risen, but there was pain in it. "All of David's spawn watching me. Mocking me after they killed my babies."

Olivia's steps faltered. *Wait? What?* Surely she didn't mean… But as they drew closer, Olivia saw one table was indeed watching them more closely than the rest.

Two identically handsome faces hardened when they caught sight of the approaching group. They and a third man were seated alternately around the table with four stunning women. Olivia instantly recognized Declan's younger sister and bit back a groan.

"Fiona!" Courtney exclaimed, and one woman lifted a perfectly manicured brow at Courtney.

"Courtney, I'm surprised to see you here tonight. So soon after…" The woman made a theatrically sympathetic face. "But I suppose everyone grieves differently. I don't think I'd be out partying so soon after my children died, but to each their own I guess." Her lips lifted in a plastic smile.

Olivia might find Courtney's behavior unpleasant, but Fiona's cruel comments were shocking. Cara and the others at Fiona's table exchanged wide-eyed looks.

"Traitor." Courtney hissed at the woman covered in diamonds. "Judas! Your father is a member of the board, and you're sitting here panting after the devil."

Olivia's gaze fell on the empty seat next to Fiona.

But before the beauty could reply, Chris gripped Courtney's elbow and said in a low tone, "You are making a scene. If you can't control yourself, go home."

Courtney wrenched her arm away. "You'd like that, wouldn't you? Hide me away while you do whatever with…" Her vicious stare landed on Olivia. "Whoever."

Thankfully, Stuart came to her rescue. "Olivia," he said, rising in his seat, doing his best not to stare at the scene unfolding. "I've been looking for you."

Olivia sank gratefully into the seat next to him. On her other side was an older gentleman with snow white hair and a haughty expression. The entire Bloom Communications' table watched as Chris maneuvered a wobbly Courtney into a seat on the far side of the round table.

Olivia was thankful for the large centerpiece that partially shielded her from Courtney's glare.

"I don't know which fool put the Blooms at a table so close to ours," the older man sniffed. "They should be fired. Unless the drama is what they are after." He turned to Olivia. "Alan Carrol, and this is Helene." A bored looking young woman next to him nodded at Olivia.

"You must be Olivia Adler. The CFO." He kept talking not waiting for a response. Apparently, her input to the conversation wasn't necessary. "I'm a member of the Bloom Communications board and an investor with Bloom Capital. So whichever bid you choose, I win."

Without another word, the older man began picking at the salad plate the servers had placed in front of each of them. Olivia met Helene's eyes and was surprised when the woman rolled hers, before opening her purse and popping a small white pill in her mouth.

Olivia's appetite had vanished but she forced herself to take several bites. She hadn't had anything since a smoothie that morning and the tea in the afternoon.

"Have you been on the board long?" She heard Stuart ask.

"Decades," Alan answered between bites, clearly uninterested in talking to any of them.

"What was all that about?" Kyle, never one for discretion, jerked his head toward the table where the Blooms were seated.

Unfortunately, from where Olivia was sitting, the family was in her sight line, the one empty seat mocking her. It hadn't occurred to her that Declan might be attending, but now seeing the empty chair… Maybe Declan wasn't coming. She squashed the disappointment that settled in her chest.

Even if he does...

He doesn't remember you.

Alan looked at Kyle for a moment, and then shrugged. "It's not a secret. That's the Bloom family. Their father, David, founded Bloom Communications. There has been a rift ever since his death when his eldest son, Declan, was removed as CEO."

"Really?" Kyle twisted in his seat to look.

"Yes. Luke and James are the twins. The brunette is James's wife." The older man's eyes cut to Courtney and Chris. "Camellia is a famous podcaster."

Was the man trying to start a fight? "The blonde with her back to us is Cara Bloom, well now Evans. She married this year as well. That must be her husband next to her."

Olivia snuck a peek at the handsome man in glasses.

Kyle squinted and then gasped. "That's Lia Everton, the movie star, right? Fuck yeah. I'd love to meet her."

Olivia felt a tinge of embarrassment before she remembered she wasn't responsible for his behavior anymore.

"Yes," Alan drawled. "Next to Luke Bloom."

"Who's the other one? She's hot." Kyle ogled Fiona, and Alan's face tightened.

"That is my daughter, Fiona." His words were clipped.

Kyle slugged back more of his drink. "So, why's she sitting over there instead of here? Aren't they like... the enemy?"

"Yes," Courtney suddenly exclaimed, having followed the conversation. "The Blooms are demons set on destroying me just because their father loved me and left me his fortune. They are horrible, horrible people. They never cared about their father. I'm the one who took care of him. I deserved it." Her voice trembled with self-righteousness.

Alan made a face. "Declan and his father had their issues, but Declan was always loyal to the company."

"You're only saying that because you want him to marry

Fiona," Courtney exclaimed. "I've heard the rumors. Fiona's telling everyone who will listen that they're practically engaged. Don't think I don't see the maneuvering going on around me. You're trying to steal what's mine and put Declan back in charge."

Olivia lost the thread of the conversation as a boulder lodged in her stomach. Declan and the icy beauty were getting married? She set down her fork, sure she would choke if she tried to force another bite past her tight throat.

The salad plates were cleared, and Olivia used the transition to escape. "If you'll excuse me a moment." She wasn't sure where she was going. The bathroom was probably as good a place as any to hide while she got her emotions under control. As she made her way across the room, her senses flared to life, and she knew she was being watched.

Detouring to the bar, she ordered another drink, even though she still had a full one left at her seat. From that vantage point, she scanned the room but couldn't find anything out of place or anyone paying her special attention.

So why did she feel like her skin was on fire? Almost as if drawn by a magnet, her eyes rose to the landing at the top of the stairs.

Mouthwatering in what was obviously a tailored tuxedo over his muscular frame, Declan Bloom stood above the ballroom. His hands were braced on the railing, and even from that distance, she could see the anger in his face. Anger directed at her.

CHAPTER ELEVEN

NEW YORK—PRESENT DAY

What the fuck is she doing here?

Olivia was absolutely breathtaking in the blue gown. Her thick hair was twisted on top of her head, with only a few curls left to caress her bare shoulders.

She stood at the bar scanning the room, and then her eyes lifted and met his. He was too far away, but he knew the sapphire of the dress matched her eyes.

A bolt of longing shot through him. Declan wanted to put her on his plane, and take her somewhere far away, somewhere she wouldn't be tainted by the ugliness that was in his world. But here she was. Despite his best efforts, his Petal was standing in the middle of the sharks.

Olivia stared at him for a minute before her gaze flicked coolly away, and he wanted to roar. As much as Declan needed to keep his distance from her—for both their sakes—he couldn't stand the thought of her giving her attention to anyone else.

Declan followed her line of sight, and ice flowed down his spine as he watched Chris Keller stride across the room to her side. Declan's hands gripped the metal railing, and he imagined it flexed a little. Something ugly and dark bubbled up as Chris bent his head to say something in Olivia's ear.

That bastard was standing far too close to her. Declan imagined Chris inhaling her French perfume, and his hands trembled with rage as Olivia shook her head at Chris with a small smile. Red mist formed at the edges of his vision as the bastard touched her *again*. Planting his hand on her back, Chris leaned in, his face almost touching Olivia's.

He is a dead man, Declan reminded himself. He allowed himself the brief fantasy of how he would do it. *I'll start with the hand that touched her and then...*

It took all of his self-control not to thunder down the steps and claim Olivia as his.

The thought sobered him.

That was the one thing he *couldn't* do. It didn't matter that every fiber of his being wanted her... If Chris knew who she was... what she meant to him... Chris wouldn't hesitate to hurt her in order to get to him. Declan would die before he let that happen.

Thankfully, with her glass in hand, Olivia moved away from Chris and headed back to her table. Declan exhaled a harsh breath and struggled to get his rage under control. He needed his mask.

Declan forced himself to take measured steps down the staircase and toward the table that his company had sponsored. He knew Bloom Communications would also have a table at the gala, and he appreciated his family attempting to put on a united front with him for the various board members and society present around the room.

It wasn't until he reached his seat that he remembered he had included Fiona in their number.

"Are you all right?" Cami, James's new wife, asked quietly as he took his seat next to her.

Declan liked his new sister-in-law, but she was entirely too observant for his comfort.

"I'm fine." He unfurled his napkin and placed it across his lap.

"You missed the salad course," Fiona's lips were smiling, but he heard the edge in her voice.

"I was working." She frowned, but he had no intention of apologizing. Better she understand now, that *if* they made an alliance, it was purely for business purposes.

Declan was conscious of the awkward silence that fell over the table, and part of him hated that it was his arrival that had dampened their mood. Things had changed over the last twelve years. After what transpired in the hours after he'd left Olivia at the Shannon airport, Declan put a part of himself in a box, never to be opened again.

It wasn't worth the pain.

Recently, over Thanksgiving in Atlanta, there was a moment when he thought things might go back to the way they had been when they were younger—before the pressure from his father and his duty to his family had hardened him.

Before he'd lost her.

Now sitting amidst the couples, the divide in his family was obvious. His siblings had moved on. They'd made new lives… happy lives, far from the lives their father had planned for them.

Part of Declan wanted to rebel too. Walk away and start over, maybe even… With ruthless will, he shut down that train of thought before it could fully form.

It was his responsibility to take care of his family, to get justice for their father, to regain the Bloom fortune stolen from them, and reclaim the business that was his birthright.

After a minute, the conversations started again, as his siblings discussed their Christmas plans. A few bites of dry chicken later, Declan could feel Chris's eyes burning into him from a seat at the nearby table, but Declan wouldn't give Chris the satisfaction of looking at him. He turned to answer Cara's question, mentally noting Olivia's location. She was smiling at her coworker... Stuart. He said something to her, and Olivia tipped her head back with a sparkling laugh.

Declan's jaw tightened, the happy sound hitting him in the gut. He wanted to be the one who made her laugh, to have her smile like that at him again.

"You can't play that card."

"I can." He smirked, laying the card down on the pile between them.

"You're cheating!" she accused, her cheeks rosy from the bottle of wine sitting on the floor next to their cards. She rose up and leaned forward on her crossed legs, and snatched up the card he'd just played.

His T-shirt rode up to expose the creamy skin of her inner thighs.

"I asked if you had any eights, and you said no. Cheaters forfeit. I win!" she crowed.

"I don't remember that," he said, trying to keep a straight face. He pretended to peer closely at her. "Are you drunk again?"

"No. You dirty cheater," she laughed. "I win." She tossed her hand of cards on the floor and shimmied where she sat, waving her hands in the air. "I win. I win. You lose," she sang.

"Oh yeah?" He dove toward her, toppling her to the rug in front of the fire, his hand cupping the back of her head before she hit the floor. His other slipped under the shirt to find the sensitive spot on her ribs that made her squeal with laughter.

"Cry mercy," he said, tickling her soft skin.

"Never!" Her face was lit with laughter.

"Darling? Did you hear me?" Fiona's manicured hand, nails painted black to match the form-fitting mermaid gown she wore, patted his lapel in a proprietary way, pulling him from the memory.

Declan looked down into her brown eyes. Fiona was a gorgeous woman, with all the right connections to help him reclaim his position. A marriage to Fiona would ensure her father's support, virtually guaranteeing his reinstatement as CEO.

"Declan." Her voice held a warning note, and he realized he had been staring at Olivia's profile. "You're taking me to the ballet this week, right?"

"No. I need to get back to Atlanta."

Fiona's red lips puffed out. "I'd hoped we would get to spend some time together."

Declan picked up his fork, forcing her to remove her hand. Fiona's pout became real, and her eyes narrowed. Declan was all too aware of his siblings watching their interaction with interest.

"You have to go already? Christmas is next week." Her lip curled. "Why on earth would you want to go to Atlanta?"

"I can think of a few reasons," Cara drawled, her eyes shooting daggers at Fiona.

Fiona's eyes flicked dismissively to Cara. "I know it's more your speed now, Cara. That's understandable." Her eyes devoured Wes, Cara's husband, and Declan thought he heard his sister growl. "You all have your own little lives now. It's sweet that you are so attached to your brother." Her hand came down on his forearm, and Declan had to remind himself not to push her away. "Isn't it past time for you to move on… separately?"

James shifted in his seat, and Luke glared at his plate. But Cara wasn't interested in being discreet. Even as her husband's hand stroked over her bare shoulder, red blotches that matched her dress appeared on her cheekbones.

"No matter how our family changes, *we*," she said, as she pointed around the table at each of her siblings, "spend the holidays together."

Fiona's smile was knife-sharp. "I know that's how you've done it in the past, but you aren't children anymore, Cara. At some point, you have to grow up."

Cara bristled, but before his baby sister could go nuclear,

Declan interjected in a soft but deadly voice. “My family will always be my priority.”

“You son of a bitch!” Courtney suddenly shouted and jumped to her feet, her chair flying backward at the table next to them. She shook off Chris’s hand as he reached to catch her.

Declan’s eyes narrowed. It looked like the reports he’d been receiving were true. After her sons' deaths, Courtney was falling apart.

“I know what you’re doing?” Courtney hissed before storming away.

“My god. She’s so embarrassing. No one is going to want her on their fundraising committees. Poor Chris.”

The entire table stiffened at Fiona’s comment.

Cara practically hummed with anger, and Declan watched as Wes massaged his wife's nape, gently stroking until her shoulders relaxed. Cara directed a glare Declan’s way, her lips pressed into a tight line.

Declan knew that his mother had let it slip a few weeks ago that he intended to marry Fiona, and that his family was unhappy about it. But it wasn’t his sister’s disappointment that was the focus of his thoughts. It was the errant and unwelcome thought that he wished he had what Cara had. What each of his siblings had found with their partners. Someone who loved him, knew what he was thinking without being told, and sought to relieve the stress. He’d had that once.

His gaze found Olivia again. Her mouth was moving, and Pruitt laughed. What were they talking about? Declan tossed his napkin on his plate.

Cara gave him a funny look and then turned her head to look over her shoulder at Olivia. *Fuck.* He was being too obvious. Cara’s eyebrows scrunched together.

“What do you have planned for the holidays, Lia?” Fiona

asked across the table. "You must be invited to *so* many Hollywood parties!"

"Please call me Dahlia, Lia is my stage name. We're on hiatus right now," Dahlia said coolly. "Cameras go up in Vancouver after the new year."

Luke threaded his fingers through hers on the table. "We plan on staying home and relaxing. We're just happy to be in the same city for a while."

Fiona blinked. "You are staying in Atlanta too? Well, if everyone is going to be there, maybe I should come down and join you for the holidays. We can all be together," she said, smiling at Declan and laying her hand on his forearm again.

He barely registered her possessive move. His muscles felt like they were locked in cement, and his skin was stretched too tight, consumed by the woman nearby. No matter how he tried, his brain continued to torture him, pulling him into the past.

"You didn't want to be home for your birthday? You should have told me, Petal. I would have gotten you a cake."

Blue eyes blinked at him, half-asleep, before she rolled to her side, pulling his arm around her. He knew she was more asleep than awake. "Home is where you are."

His lips brushed her hair, his heart shattering. "Not your family? People you love."

"I love you."

Two days left.

"Please, don't leave me," he whispered into her hair, knowing he would never be brave enough to ask when she was awake.

Declan shook his head.

Get a fucking hold of yourself.

He could see James watching him with a confused expression. Heart hammering, Declan forced himself back to the present.

"If Declan is going to insist on spending the holidays there, I guess I should sacrifice and go too."

Declan swallowed a groan. He couldn't tell if Fiona was intentionally trying to insult his family or if she simply didn't care.

"I love Atlanta," Cara bit out. She had the most history with Fiona, and while Dahlia and Cami sat ready with silent support, they knew Cara could handle the socialite.

Fiona gave her a condescending look. "I'm sure it's lovely, but it's not the same as New York." She paused dramatically, her eyes skimming over Cara with a plastic smile. "I'm sure it's perfect for your new life, Cara." Fiona's fingers dug into his arm. "Declan lives in New York. This is his home."

Luke cocked his head. "Is that true Declan? Do you consider New York your home? Not Dublin or Connecticut?"

"I'd have thought Rhode Island…" James sounded like he was chewing glass.

He gave his brothers a quelling look.

"His business is in New York." Fiona waved her hand dismissively. Declan grit his teeth. Much as he wanted to tell Fiona *exactly* what he thought of her speaking for him, Declan couldn't afford to alienate her. Or more accurately, her father sitting nearby.

"New York is a great city," he said, plucking her hand off his arm and placing it on the table. "But I can conduct my business from anywhere." He leveled a stare at her that she couldn't misunderstand. "Home is where my family is."

His chest warmed a little when Cara beamed at him, but Olivia's lilting laugh from the next table had him narrowing his eyes again. Chris said something else, and Olivia's dark curls caressed her shoulders as she laughed. He wasn't the only one annoyed. Courtney had returned to the table and was now glaring at Olivia like a serpent ready to strike.

His instincts were on full alert. Declan didn't like the way she was fixated on Olivia. Courtney had become unpredictable over the past few weeks, and while he welcomed the psychotic bitch's breakdown, he didn't want Olivia anywhere near her when it happened. His low growl drew the attention of his siblings, and they turned to look at the other table as well.

"I'm surprised they sat so close," James pointed out.

Fiona pursed her lips. "Surely that's water under the bridge by now. It's not like you all didn't walk away with a fortune."

Declan saw Dahlia turn her fork like it was a weapon, and if looks could kill, Cami's glare would have ended Fiona, but it was Cara who had him the most concerned. His sister's small stature might fool some, but her blood was Bloom through and through, and she had survived things that would have broken most people.

He needed to put a stop to this… now. Declan stared at Fiona, letting her see the fury in his eyes. "Nothing is *water under the bridge*."

More laughter came from the table next to them, and this time, he knew it was something Olivia had said from the way her ex-husband and Courtney glowered at her.

"Who is that?" Dahlia asked.

"The one who looks like Snow-White?" Cara pursed her lips. "She's stunning, but she should be careful. Courtney looks like she's going to skin her alive," Cara said, her voice a little too interested. Her eyes weren't on Olivia, they were on Declan, waiting for a reaction.

She wasn't getting one.

Fiona took a sip of her wine. "She works for some little company they're trying to buy. My dad said they brought them up here to woo them or whatever." She rolled her eyes.

"Armstrong Electronics out of Atlanta," Cara supplied, and all eyes turned to her. "What? I have Google."

Wes exchanged a look with his wife and then turned to Declan. "Isn't that the company your mother said that *you* were trying to buy?"

Everyone at the table looked at the group nearby and then back at him. He grunted and drained his whiskey.

"This fish is good," Cami said brightly, nudging James with her elbow.

James raised an eyebrow at her, but besotted fool that he was, he followed his wife's lead to change the subject.

"Gotta love a catered dinner." James bared his teeth and everyone except Fiona and Declan laughed.

Conversation was stilted as they ate. He knew his heavy mood and Fiona's presence were affecting his family, but there was little he could do to remedy it. They would just have to get used to Fiona. They would understand it was worth it in the end.

He was doing this for them.

Fiona made a few snide comments about other attendees, but when the rest of the Bloom family wasn't interested in gossiping about who was wearing what or which vacation locale was no longer au courant, she stood up.

"Excuse me for a minute, darling. I need to speak with Bianca. We're co-chairing a fashion show."

Cara got up from her seat and scooted into the one next to Declan. "Who do you keep glaring at over there? Chris?"

"Cara—"

"I'm just asking," she cut him off. "Because it seems to be every time that woman lau—"

"Cara," Declan barked.

Wes's back snapped straight at Declan's tone, and he gave Declan a hard look. Declan struggled not to roll his eyes. As if he'd hurt his sister. Though he could admit a grudging respect for how protective his new brother-in-law was.

"I'm just interested in the company," Declan said in a softer tone.

However, Cara's comments had drawn the table's attention

and now everyone had swiveled in Olivia's direction. Declan ground his teeth.

"She's a beautiful woman. Ow!" James yelped dramatically when Cami swatted him. "I can still notice when people are beautiful, even though you are the most spectacularly beautiful."

"As long as you remember that." Cami looked at Declan. "What are your chances of buying the company? It's not great they're here with Bloom Communications, is it?"

In the break before dessert, several people had gotten up, including Courtney and Fiona's father, who had been sitting next to Olivia. Declan watched as Chris moved to the empty seat next to her. Chris angled his body to fully face her, and they began speaking in low tones.

Declan's fist clenched on the table. His inability to snatch her away, hold her, claim her as his, burned like acid in his stomach.

"Declan?" Cara sounded worried.

"I'm fine."

"You look like you're about to explode?" Luke pointed out, his eyes on the couple at the other table.

Chris's eyes flicked up and met Luke's before roaming the table and settling on Declan. Rage burned through Declan's veins as a slight smirk lifted from the corner of Chris's lips.

Declan hadn't realized he was halfway out of his chair before a strong hand clamped on his arm, and his brother hissed, "Not here."

Chris's lips moved, and Olivia suddenly got to her feet, her cheeks pink, and strode from the ballroom.

What the fuck had that bastard said to make her blush?

"Easy," Luke said again, and Declan realized he had balled the linen of the tablecloth in his fist. He forced his hand to relax. His brothers looked at him with identical frowns of concern.

"What's going on with you?" James asked

"Yeah, you look like you're about to go Game of Thrones in here."

"I need a drink." Declan shoved his chair back so hard it almost fell.

Surely Olivia wouldn't fall for Chris's smarmy bullshit. He'd seen his former friend in action enough that Declan knew women found him attractive. Acid rolled in his stomach at the nauseating concept.

No. Olivia is smart. She will see right through him.

You didn't, a nasty voice in his head said.

Chris played you for a fool for years, and you never even noticed. You didn't see the monster that lay underneath his smiles until it was too late.

"Is she involved with Chris?" Luke's voice sounded close by.

Fuck. Why can't they leave me alone?

Declan jerked his eyes away from Olivia as she moved toward the back hallway, and frowned at his brother, before taking his glass from the bartender.

"No."

Twin pairs of gray eyes met his as James joined them. "Then why are you staring at her?"

"I'm not."

"You have barely taken your eyes off her since you got here?" James looked at him with a too-knowing expression. "Who is she?"

Is that true? Has anyone else noticed?

Declan stiffened. His eyes darted to Chris, but he was still seated and talking to Olivia's ex-husband.

"I need to speak to Alan."

Luke caught his arm just above the elbow, forcing him to turn back. "You don't need to marry Fiona Carrol to get Bloom Communications back. It's not worth it."

Declan narrowed his eyes at his younger brother and dropped

his gaze to the hand on his sleeve before it flashed back up in warning. Luke's jaw set, but his fingers relaxed.

They didn't understand. They couldn't. As hard as their father had been on his brothers, the pressure and intrinsic responsibility that went with being their father's heir had been his alone to bear.

It meant protecting their family and ensuring the Bloom legacy—not just for his siblings but for their children. Power equaled protection. Declan had witnessed it on both sides of his family. He didn't have the luxury of falling in love like they did.

Without a word, Declan straightened his sleeves and made his way to where Fiona and her father stood, ignoring the people who tried to gain his attention.

"Declan," Alan greeted him with a wide smile. "My daughter was just telling me you're heading back to Atlanta tomorrow." He turned an indulgent look on his daughter. "I explained that business has to come first. Those purses of hers won't buy themselves." The man guffawed at his own joke.

Declan didn't smile until he pictured what any of his mothers would say if this jackass made such a misogynistic comment in front of them.

"I know Declan has to work," Fiona simpered. "I was only hoping he would go with me to the Nutcracker this week. I'm on the board of the ballet, you know. It's important I be there. Appearances are everything."

Fiona's eyes were on his face, implying Declan should understand the importance of what she was saying. But for the life of him, he couldn't figure out why her needing to go to the ballet had anything to do with him.

"Plenty of time for that, darling," Alan patted his daughter's hand.

Like a movie, his future with Fiona played out in front of him. Fiona would be on his arm in the latest designer gown at these events, ready to wage war in her petty feuds over who might have monopolized whose stylist, and who had been selected to chair which charity committee. It was enough to make him want to hurl the ice sculpture, poised on the table next to him, to the ground.

Then a glimpse of what his life might have been, flashed in front of him, had he only made different decisions. Olivia smiling up at him first thing in the morning, her cheeks still flushed from sleep. Their children…

He shook it off.

I'm losing my fucking mind.

It didn't matter what might have been. This was the world that he lived in, and he would do what needed to be done for his family. It wasn't about the money. His brothers and sister were all successful in their own right, but the power that came with the Bloom name and fortune is what he wanted for them. What he needed to keep them all safe.

Eventually, even wielding the McGrath's influence and his brother's blood connection to the Riordans, along with the resources that came with being a Bloom, hadn't been enough, and Seamus's trouble caught up to him. But it was the power of the Bloom name that saved his brother from the worst of his consequences. His older half-brother may not have enjoyed his years in prison, but he was alive.

Which was a lot fucking better than being tortured and murdered by the people he'd double crossed, Declan thought, knowing what would have happened if he hadn't stepped in.

"I saw Armstrong Electronics was Bloom Communications' guest tonight." Declan said, ignoring both Carrols' obvious attempts to push him into declaring a commitment.

Alan's eyes turned shrewd. "Yes. Interesting group. The son is an idiot, but the rest of them seem competent enough."

"That hardly matters."

Alan pursed his lips. "True. Though as part of the deal, Chris is dangling the carrot that those who choose to stay on will still have a say in how their company is run."

"We both know that won't be the case." Declan met the man's eyes. "All he wants is XEROS."

Alan lifted a shoulder and sipped his drink. "Same as you."

But I'm not lying to her about what's on the table.

Did it matter? This was business, and there was no room for sentimentality.

Alan swirled his drink. "If Chris pulls this off, it will be hard to remove him at the annual shareholder meeting… regardless of…" The man's eyes went to his daughter, and Fiona smiled at Declan. He ignored his sudden nausea. Alan continued, "Any connection between us. My shares won't be enough to push you over. You need this to win the battle to sway the other board members to your side."

"I'm not concerned."

"Good. Ah, here is your beautiful sister. Cara, it's been a long time. I hear congratulations are in order."

Cara smiled at Alan, but Declan could see that her eyes were troubled. His brows immediately drew together when she tucked an arm through his. Cara couldn't stand networking, and she hated these formal social events. She wouldn't interrupt unless it was important.

"Thank you," Cara said, with a radiant and false smile that reminded Declan of all the years she had attended these events for their father. "I'm sorry, but I need to steal my brother for a minute."

Fiona's lips tightened, and she barely concealed her scowl. Declan turned his shoulder to her.

"Of course," Alan interjected, to diffuse the tense moment. "Fiona, your godmother is here. We should say hello."

Not waiting for them to walk away, Cara tugged Declan to the side, away from the small groups of people, and turned her back to the room.

"Who is she?"

Declan, more than a foot taller than his sister, immediately located Olivia at her table. "Who?"

"Oh my god! Do you think I'm stupid?" Cara rolled her eyes. "I don't even have to look over my shoulder to know *exactly* who you are looking at."

Declan tensed. "I don't have the first clue what you're talking about. Are you pregnant? Is that why you're being emotional?"

"If we weren't in public, I would punch you in the face."

"You couldn't reach if you had a stool."

"Yeah… well… there are plenty of sensitive parts that I can."

"Not very lady-like Car-bear."

"Who said I was a lady?"

His eyebrow lifted. "I suppose if years of Swiss boarding school couldn't—"

"You aren't going to distract me, Dec," she interrupted. "Who. Is. She?"

Declan sighed. His baby sister had grown into a confident adult, and while normally he'd be proud of her assertiveness, right now he wished she wasn't so observant.

"Who is who?"

"Olivia Adler."

Declan blew out an exasperated breath even while his stomach clenched. "You just gave me a name, so obviously you know who the woman is."

"That's not what I mean, and you know it." Cara's eyes sparked. "Who is she to *you*?"

"I'm trying to buy her company."

"Bullshit."

Time for redirection. "Fine. I wasn't going to tell all of you this, but… Olivia Adler's company has developed a device that can increase streaming speeds ten times over. If I acquire it before Chris does, several key Bloom Communications' board members have assured me I will have their backing at the annual shareholders' meeting if I call for a vote of no confidence. I will become the CEO of Bloom Communications again."

"And Fiona? She's part of the deal? Because of her father?" A soft, disappointed puff of air escaped her lips. "Declan, you aren't really thinking about marrying her just to secure her father's voting block, are you?"

That was exactly what he was planning on doing, but he didn't like how the disappointed look on his sister's face made him feel.

"There is nothing official yet, but yes, I think Fiona would be a suitable—"

"Suitable?" Cara cut him off again. It wasn't lost on him that there were only a handful of people in the world who would dare do that. Half of them blood related and the other half were their spouses—and Olivia.

"I don't remember you asking my opinion or advice when you married your ex-con roommate after only knowing him for a few months."

It was an awful thing to say, and the hurt on Cara's face made Declan instantly regret his words. His sister's mouth snapped shut.

"Cara—"

"Don't. Wes is *nothing* like Fiona."

"I know. I didn't mean it the way it sounded."

She sucked in a breath. "I know you didn't. I also know you are being mean because you are trying to get me to back off because you're hiding something."

If she only knew.

"I won't, Dec." Her expression was fierce. "Not when it comes to your happiness. You aren't alone."

Declan sighed and looped an arm around his sister's shoulders, giving her a side hug. "Everything is fine, Car-bear. You just need to trust me."

She pulled away from him, and the look in her eyes made his stomach sink. "I do trust you, Declan. Someday, you are going to trust me enough to tell me why a woman you claim is just a business associate knew who I was and my family nickname by the color of my eyes."

Declan's heart stopped. "What?"

"We shared an elevator this afternoon. She was nice."

Declan bit the inside of his cheek to hide his reaction. This was bad. Really bad. If Olivia told Cara about Ireland...

"Don't get involved in my business, Cara." He intentionally used the low menacing tone that worked so well on most people, but his sister snorted, before turning to walk away. She stopped and turned back.

"I just met her again in the ladies' room. Courtney had cornered her." Cara's expression was grim. "Courtney noticed how much attention Olivia's drawing. And not just from Chris."

"What happened?" he snapped.

Cara cocked her head. "See. That's not the reaction I'd expect over a business associate."

"You know as well as I do how sick Courtney is."

"She was just being a bitch. Olivia handled it fine, and Courtney left. Nothing homicidal." Cara winced. "Poor word choice."

For the next ten minutes, Declan made the rounds, but he couldn't focus. He couldn't pull himself from the past, and it was an almost minute to minute struggle to not look in Olivia's direction.

"Can I have some of your asparagus?" He speared the vegetable off her plate before she granted permission. It had only been three days. How was it he felt like he'd known her forever?

"Seeing as how it's already on its way to your mouth, it's a moot point," she teased. "But back to the question. Favorite childhood cartoon."

Declan chewed, thinking. "I was always partial to He-Man, but I think it was mostly the sword."

"'By the power of Greyskull'..." Rose giggled as she recited the cartoon's tag line.

"My little sister loves the Care Bears. It's almost a fetish."

Rose choked on her beer. "How old is she?"

They were seated on the floor around the scarred table in front of the fireplace. He'd offered to drive back to town to go to the pub, but Rose wanted to cook. She teased him the entire time, forcing him to help prepare the meal. He couldn't remember the last time he'd enjoyed one more.

"Eleven going on thirty," Declan groused. "Too pretty for her own good." His lips lifted, and he took a sip of Rose's beer, having finished his own. "Her eyes are like mine... and our dad's... but they are so much brighter. And she's so fucking sweet." He chuckled. "Doesn't matter who our father brings into our lives, Cara welcomes them with open arms. With her purple eyes, Luke started calling her Share Bear, which of course evolved into—"

"Car-Bear," Rose laughed. "I'm sure she loves that."

She'd remembered. One comment from one conversation, twelve years ago. Declan's chest ached, and it felt like he couldn't draw a full breath.

You can't have her. She deserves better.

Declan made his way back to his seat, his thoughts too unsettled to even pretend to make polite conversation. Fiona was waiting for him, a brittle smile on her face.

"Where have you been? You left me with your family."

In fact, he'd left her with *her* family, but he wasn't interested in arguing.

Their table had rearranged so that Cara, Dahlia, and Cami sat next to each other, their heads bent close in an intense conversation. After a moment, Cara leaned over to Wes and whispered something. Wes looked over his shoulder at the table next to them and nodded.

"Are you all planning a covert operation or can we all play?" Fiona turned her head to look where their attention had gone, and she snickered. "Is she drunk? This is why they shouldn't let just anyone into these events."

Declan told himself not to look, but it had the same result as if he told his heart to stop beating. His head swiveled, body tingling and nerves jumping, as he watched Olivia slowly come to her feet at the table next to them. She tottered on her heels before he watched her back expand with a deep breath.

His narrowed glance went to the glass in front of her before it returned to her. Her ex-husband rose, and came to Olivia's side taking her elbow just as Chris also reached for her. The two men exchanged words but Declan couldn't hear them through the rushing in his ears and the pounding of his heart.

He was going to fucking lose it if that asshole didn't take his hand off her. And Declan wasn't sure he cared any more.

Olivia was blinking slowly as though she wasn't fully aware of what was happening around her, but he'd seen her face crumple when her ex touched her.

Declan's hands shook as he clenched them into fists, trying to hang on to his control. His lungs constricted barely easing when Kyle removed his hand.

Slowly, appearing to concentrate on every step, Olivia stepped away from the two men and maneuvered between the tables using the seat backs for support.

His pulse raced and he clenched his jaw, fighting the urge to charge after her. The intense need to protect her was painful to resist.

"Wow," Fiona laughed. "That's mortifying."

Declan ignored her, his entire existence focused on Olivia's elegant form as she reached the stairs.

She's fine. She's here with her coworkers. They'll help her. They are her family.

His eyes searched her table and then scanned the room. Where the fuck was her father-in-law or even the one who mooned after her?

Olivia had one foot on the lowest step when she paused, swaying slightly. Everything in him screamed to get up. The desire to make sure she was safe beat in his blood, and it took every ounce of his willpower to keep him in his seat.

You can't. There are too many eyes here.

His brain whirled as he searched for a solution.

She's drunk. It's fine. It's not the first time she's been drunk in the last twelve years.

Which was quickly followed by frustrated fury as he wondered who'd brought her a sports drink the next morning. Who'd taken care of her?

It should have been me.

Declan had almost convinced himself that she was all right, when he registered the change on Chris's face. His expression was calculated as he trailed after Olivia to the steps.

Declan's lungs felt like they were on fire, and his heart thundered against his ribs. He couldn't let...

"Go." Declan heard Wes say, and in unison, the three women rose and hurried after Olivia. He wasn't the only one observing what was happening. He dragged air into his chest, ignoring the looks his brothers were casting in his direction.

"Where are they going?" Fiona asked, staring after the women as they hurried to catch up to Olivia and Chris as they reached the top of the stairs.

Declan blew out a breath. It was going to be okay. His sisters would make sure Olivia got in a car, and then when she got to her hotel...

"Excuse me." Declan stood abruptly, avoiding eye contact with his brothers as he headed for the stairs. Their footsteps thudded close behind as he took the stairs two at a time.

What the fuck was he doing?

Still, his legs carried him forward. He would just make sure she got in a car...

In the foyer, he saw the trio of women surrounding Chris, blocking his exit. From the look on Cara's face, she was arguing as she tried to take Olivia's arm. Olivia was limp, her entire weight sagged against Chris, her head lolling to the side.

Chris had one arm wrapped around Olivia's waist, his hand on her ribcage far too close to her breasts. Declan's vision tunneled, and all he heard was the blood in his ears. He snarled when a muscular arm caught him, pulling him to a stop, barely registering Wes and Luke rushing past him to join the women.

"I don't know what's going on, or who she is to you, but you look like you are about to dismember him," James hissed in his ear. "And I can't let you do that in public. Pick a time, and I'll be by your side. But *not here*."

Declan twisted in his brother's grip, trying to shake him off, but James's grip tightened. "Wait. Let us help you. They won't let Chris hurt her. If you were thinking straight, you'd know this is the wrong play."

Declan was conscious of his chest rising and falling, the need to commit violence strong, but through the murderous haze, his brother's words seeped in. James was right.

"Get your fucking hands off me."

James glared at him, but his grip lessened. "Breathe. He's leaving."

Declan shook him off, torn between wanting to go after Chris and murder him for trying to take an obviously incapacitated

Olivia home, and rushing to where the girls were attempting to get Olivia to walk to the door. Luke stretched out his arm to wrap around Olivia, and with an audible crack in his mind, Declan's control snapped.

His long legs ate the distance between them, and ignoring the shocked looks of those around them, he swept Olivia up into his arms. Declan had a fleeting sense that he was making a huge mistake, but the instant Olivia's body relaxed into him and her head rested against his shoulder... everything inside him settled.

Could he really be blamed for lowering his nose to Olivia's hair.

Her familiar scent—Wild White Rose—filled his senses.

Declan ignored the curious looks as he strode swiftly toward the waiting SUV and gently placed her on the back seat, before climbing in and pulling her into his arms.

CHAPTER TWELVE

County Kerry, Ireland—12 years ago

Not twenty minutes back on the road after their picnic, Rose had spotted a waterfall in the distance, and since Declan had already discovered he couldn't say no to her if it put a smile on her face, they had parked and hiked to the top.

"Why would you ever leave here?" Rose asked, as she gazed out at the green hills. "No offense, Dublin is great, but this is..."

Declan drew her to stand in front of him, his arms looped loosely around her waist and kissed her temple. "I wish I could stay down here forever," he admitted. "I never feel like myself as much as I do when I'm here."

He rubbed a cheek against her hair, his nose filling with her scent. It was addictive, and for a moment, he wished he could freeze this perfect moment in time.

Dusk was falling by the time they made it back to the car.

"We'll have to stop at the pub for dinner," Declan said, as they approached the outskirts of the town closest to his house. "I don't have anything at the cottage. I thought we'd get some pre-made meals, but someone wanted to hunt for a pot of gold," he teased.

"If ever there was a pot of gold, it was in that forest," she insisted. "The air was green. Green! Air isn't supposed to have a color. It was definitely a sign that fairies were nearby."

"Uh huh." He rolled his eyes playfully. "Like any self-respecting fairy would show themselves to a tourist."

Rose stuck her tongue out at him over the roof of the car. Declan shook his head and led her across the street to a pub. Each time the door opened lively Gaelic folk music spilled out into the night.

"How do you feel about fish and chips?"

"I thought that was a British thing."

Declan widened his eyes in mock horror and said in a dramatic whisper. "Better not say that around here. You'll get us run out of town."

She mimed zipping her lips shut, and he laughed.

"Maggie's Hearth has the best fish and chips in the world." He stuck his lower lip out and batted his eyes. "You don't want to be responsible for me being barred for life, do you?"

"Never."

He winked and led her into the small building, choosing a table in the back while she visited the restroom to wash her hands.

"House special and a pint of Harp, please." Declan was already salivating in anticipation of his all-time favorite meal.

"And for your wife?" the young server asked, as she glanced at Rose returning.

"She'll have the same." Declan didn't know why he didn't correct the woman's mistake, but like everything else this week, he went with what felt right.

"I take it you've been here a lot," Rose said, as the server returned with the beer.

He lifted his chin in thanks before taking a sip. "Not as much as I'd like. I try to get back here at least once a year, but it's getting harder with work."

The young woman returned with two steaming plates.

"Best fish and chips?" Rose lifted an eyebrow.

"Without a doubt," he said, before proceeding to educate her on the virtues of salt and vinegar over tartar sauce.

They laughed and talked as they ate, but as they were finishing their meals Declan noticed several people in the pub continuously looked their way. When the older woman behind the bar caught his eye and smiled, cocking her head toward Rose, his stomach sank.

Fuck. What was he thinking bringing her here. He'd been coming to this pub since he was a child.

He swallowed a groan. And he'd let the server think they were married.

"All done?" he asked, pulling several bills from his wallet, and tossing them on the table.

Rose looked at him quizzically and grabbed her last two fries. He practically dragged her to the door. He needed to get out of there… fast.

If someone says something, she'll know I lied about who I am.

Not that he was afraid she would be unforgivably angry about the different name. That misunderstanding could be explained. It was how she would feel finding out he was actually Declan Bloom: prep school graduate, billionaire heir apparent, and Irish mafia adjacent, rather than Declan Riordan who was free to laugh and talk and love…

"Was that Maggie?" she asked, swallowing her last bite.

"Who?" Declan opened her door, looking over his shoulder to see if anyone had followed them onto the street.

"The lady behind the bar. The one who made you look like you'd seen a ghost."

Declan started the car. "Well, if it had been Maggie, I would have. She's been dead for years. That was her daughter, Claire.

She doesn't like me," he lied. When Rose gave him a funny look, he knew she didn't believe him.

By the time they pulled up to the cottage, Declan had relaxed. Odds were the server wouldn't remember the whole *wife* thing, and his mother hadn't been to the area in years. And if it became an issue, he would do what he'd been trained by his family to do—control the situation by hitting harder and faster at whatever came at him.

"Wait for me," Declan said as he pulled to a stop, rocks crunching under his tires. "It's dark. I don't want you to trip."

Rose peered through the windshield at the faint outline of the roof. There was no light except for the moon above, and for a split second, Declan worried Rose wouldn't enjoy the simplicity of the cottage.

He unlocked the front door, and told her to wait while he turned the lamps on. The second the space was illuminated, she gasped.

"I love it." Bright eyes scanned the small room. The cottage consisted of one main room with a fireplace and a tiny kitchen, complete with a traditional Aga along the wall, and two small bedrooms.

In the glow of the lamps, Declan tried to see it as she would for the first time. Hard white plaster walls, rough-hewn timbers along the ceiling, and small windows that framed the hills of the Ring of Kerry. A chintz sofa and a faded wing-back chair, along with a small, scarred wooden table in front of a stone fireplace, were the entirety of the furnishings. He'd never bothered to update the kitchen because he was never there long, and the idea of cooking for one was mildly depressing.

"Your grandmother's collection." Rose spotted the rows of tiny decorated cups hanging from hooks beneath the kitchen cabinets.

"These are beautiful." She lifted one down.

"I think some might have been my great-grandmother's." Declan shrugged. "I should have paid more attention to the stories."

Rose inspected each cup, taking down another in the shape of a rose sitting atop a white saucer.

Her lips twitched. "Coincidence?"

No. None of this feels coincidental.

"She didn't like to travel, so she always asked one of her sons or my mother to bring her cups from wherever they went."

"You inherited it from her?"

He nodded. "I think she understood how much I needed this place. The excuse was my mother was the only girl."

Rose frowned. "What about your brother, Seamus?"

Declan froze.

"At the Celtic Crown, your cousin Colum mentioned him."

He ran a hand over the top of his head. "You don't miss much, do you? To answer your question, I don't know why she left me the cottage instead of him. Most of the other grandchildren got money." *A lot* of money and the reins to the empire his grandmother and grandfather had built of bars and restaurants. But he couldn't tell Rose that.

"After my grandfather died, she came here to live full time. She said she didn't want to live in their home in Dublin without him."

At the time, he'd thought it was ridiculous, but now... Declan was already having a hard time imagining what life would look like without Rose in it. Maybe it was a mistake to have brought her here. Where her presence would linger long after she was gone.

Declan carried in their bags and retrieved the small cup he'd purchased for her. "It's not much, but you seemed to like it."

Her eyes glistened as she gently unwrapped the tissue paper protecting the fragile cup. "I thought maybe as a souvenir..." He gave her a crooked smile, feeling suddenly, uncharacteristically unsure. "So, you could remember..."

"I love it." Her smile was a little watery. "But I will never forget."

~

"TELL me about this job you're starting." Declan wanted to know, but he also didn't. He hated the thought of what was taking her away, but her eyes lit up every time she mentioned it, and he wanted every bit of information he could get about Rose—it was all he'd have to remember her by.

"It's not that it's so exciting," she said, slightly out of breath after their climb up the hill. She leaned against the wall of the ruins to catch her breath. "But there is incredible opportunity to grow and actually make a difference within a company. I'm really lucky. Richard, that's my friend Jessica's uncle, is really taking a chance on me."

Rose's gaze grew vacant as she stared back the way they came. The constant drizzle hadn't dissuaded her from exploring, though they were somewhat protected now by the stones. Her head was haloed by dark frizz, and Declan didn't think he'd ever seen anything more beautiful.

"I can't let him down. It's too important."

"To succeed?" Declan asked, moving closer. Her cheeks were pink from the exertion, and he had the sudden urge to kiss her.

"Yes. I have to prove that—"

"It was all worth it," he finished for her. Her surprised eyes met his, and for a moment he thought he could drown in them. Rose nodded.

"I get it. You want to prove to everyone that the sacrifices you made had a purpose."

If anyone in the world could understand that drive, Declan

could. He lifted a hand, and ran the back of his fingers down her cheek. "You will. You'll be a star. I have no doubt."

"I sound arrogant, don't I?" She sighed.

He shook his head, suddenly fascinated by the drops of rain still clinging to the tendrils and smoothed her damp hair back off her face with his hand. "You sound like someone with ambition. Be proud of that. You have a goal, and you shouldn't let anything or anyone get in the way."

Her breath caught as his thumb dragged across her bottom lip, pulling it to one side.

"I don't think I'm better than anyone. That's not what it's about." Rose watched his mouth hovering inches above hers. Her lids grew heavy, and her pupils dilated so that the irises looked like midnight. Declan settled his hips against her, using his weight to press her into the wall. Her nipples hardened against his chest, and he let out a low growl of satisfaction.

"Is it okay if I think you are?" Declan's teeth caught her lower lip, and then his tongue stroked over hers slowly, taking time to taste her.

Rose moaned into his mouth, her arms wrapped tightly around his shoulders. When he finally broke the kiss, they were both breathing hard, and she cast a quick glance around to ensure they were still alone.

But when her gaze returned to him, he saw her eyes were worried. "It'll probably be so boring compared to…"

Understanding hit him. God, she was adorable. "Being a bouncer?" Declan's lips quirked up, and her cheeks turned scarlet.

He laughed, and braced his hands on either side of her head, and gave her a little of the truth. "I'm not really a bouncer."

"Right." Her voice was slightly breathless, and her hips arched into him.

"I was only helping my cousin that night."

"Mmhmm." Rose slid her hands around to cup his ass, pulling him toward her. Lust shot through him like a lightning bolt, and he crushed her mouth with his. He kissed her until he couldn't breathe, and she wore the dreamy expression he'd become addicted to.

"Technically, I work for my father."

"Oh." She lifted her head slightly off the wall. He wanted to smile as she blinked, trying to follow the conversation, but his own body was screaming at him to sink into her heat and lose himself.

"Family businesses are good," she said huskily, and then planted her lips on him. This time, her urgency fueled his, and he was done teasing her.

Declan gripped her thighs and lifted, pressing her back to the stone wall of the ruin. Rose wrapped her legs around his waist, and when he rolled against her, she let out a needy whine, her hands tangling in the hair at his nape.

Pleasure zapped down his spine, and he felt his body grow almost painfully hard.

"Does he own a bar like your cousin?" Rose gasped as his lips found the pulse at the base of her neck and sucked.

"What?"

"Your father… oh god… yes, like that." She cried out, as one hand found her breast and squeezed, rolling her nipple between his fingers.

"Never mind," she panted as she ripped at his zipper, letting out an exhale when she wrapped her fingers around him. Her other hand frantically tugged at his waistband, but her own legs locked around his hips impeded the progress.

Lowering her feet to the ground, Declan's jeans and boxer briefs fell to his feet, and then her hand was back. Declan's chest heaved and his thoughts fractured, as her nails stroked him gently from the tip of his cock to the base, and back again. Her fingers worked over him, and his mouth fell open as he gasped for air. Declan was certain Rose could ask him anything she wanted... Hell he'd tell her state secrets if he had them.

Rose's breath caught when he dipped his fingers into her leggings, and his brain almost short circuited at the feel of her, hot and wet, grinding against his hand. He pushed the fabric roughly to her ankles.

"Declan... please... I need." Her hands reached for him as he lifted her again. She leaned back slightly, and ground against him. Declan slid his hand between them to circle the sensitive bundle of nerves.

Rose whimpered and tilted her hips, causing the tip of his erection to nudge her entrance. His eyes rolled back at the sensation of her slick scalding flesh sliding against his cock.

Reality hit him.

Fuck, we're out of condoms.

Declan had intended to stop at the shops, but Rose saw the castle ruins on the hill from the car window...

His brain melting down, Declan struggled to form words but her hips gyrated, and he slipped past her entrance, her body eagerly welcoming his. He groaned through gritted teeth, ordering his body to stay still.

"Rose, baby. I don't have anything."

She circled her hips, his hands supporting her weight. "I know I'm supposed to care, but I don't think I do," she whimpered, and moved so that he slipped in another inch.

"I've always worn condoms. Always... but..." All the blood that had rushed to his cock was impeding his normal brain function.

We can't do this, his brain reminded him, even as he tried to rationalize it. He'd never had unprotected sex, not once. He trusted Rose when she said she hadn't been with anyone in a long time... but there was always the chance...

An image of Rose, her belly swollen with his baby, filled his mind, and he groaned, his body drawing up tight. *Not helping.*

"Plans, Petal," Declan gasped, trying to pull back. "You have big plans."

"Fine."

Declan had never heard such an unhappy sound, but then in direct opposition to her agreement, she locked her ankles behind his back and pushed up, sinking him almost all the way inside her.

"Fuck!" The word hissed out of him at the feel of her with no barrier. Rose gripped him like a vise, and when she moved again, his body reacted, flexing his hips to sink the final length.

"Yes," Rose moaned, and opened her eyes to stare into his.

"You're a witch." He reached between their bodies to circle and press against her clit. "It's the only explanation."

A light sheen of sweat covered his body as he struggled not to give in to what his body was screaming at him to do.

"I'm so close," Rose panted, her nails digging into his shoulders. "Please."

A better man than he would tell her no, and he tried. He really did.

"I can't come in you, baby. Ah!" He gasped when she rolled her hips against him.

Rose's lids were heavy, and her tongue slicked across her lower lip before a wicked smile covered her face. "Then you'll just have to come somewhere else."

Fuck. Did she really just say that?

With a groan, Declan gave in to primal instinct, one hand thrust in her hair to prevent her from hurting herself when she threw her head back against the rough wall as his hips pistoned into her.

The muscles around his spine contracted as he drove into her, his mouth covering her cries as he found the rhythm that drove her wild.

"Perfect," he grit his teeth, clinging to his control. "You feel so fucking perfect."

A sharp cry tore from her throat, and Declan kept moving as she rode the waves of her pleasure.

Her eyes glazed, Rose unhooked her ankles and lowered her feet to the ground. Not breaking eye contact, she sank to her knees in front of him, and Declan barely had time to whisper her name like a plea before her mouth was on him.

"Jesus," Declan hissed out a harsh breath, and fisted one hand in her hair as the other gripped at the stone wall in front of him for stability, while her lips and tongue drove him out of his mind. His breath came in short pants, and he forgot where he was. Who he was. His face tipped to the sky as his release ripped through him.

When his brain re-engaged, Declan bent, holding her leggings so that she could step into them, and slowly drew them up her legs. He held her face in his hands, his tone reverent. "You are everything I've ever dreamed of."

Rose blushed, but her features were soft.

"I'm serious." Declan stared into her eyes, wishing he knew how to put into words what she meant to him. "I love you." He hadn't meant to say it like that–a bald statement while they were both still breathing hard.

Rose took his hand in hers with trembling fingers. "I love you, Declan."

Declan lowered himself until he was sitting with his back against the wall, and he tugged her down until she straddled him, their chests pressed together, feeling her heart beat against him. She lay her cheek on the top of his shoulder and sighed. "I really, really love you."

His ribs crushed around his heart as he stared at the ruined walls rising above them. All Declan could do was wrap his arms around her and hold her close, their heartbeats slowing to the same pace.

"I really, really love you too."

"It's dumb to be so sad, isn't it?" Rose sniffed. *She's crying*. The pain in his chest was so sharp Declan thought for sure it had cracked wide open.

"Then I'm dumb too," he said, burying his nose in her hair, ignoring the stinging in his eyes.

Rose hummed against his chest. "We need to enjoy the time we have. Right?"

Declan swallowed past the lump in his throat. "Right." He held her closer. *"And we loved with a love that was more than love, I and my Annabel Lee."*

Rose was quiet for a moment. "Morbid. Isn't he talking about his dead girlfriend in that poem?" she asked dryly. "Why is it always the women who have to die? Bambi's mom, Dumbo's mom, and now you're quoting Edgar Allen Poe?"

He smiled, hearing the humor in her voice. "You might need to study some more, Petal. Dumbo's mom doesn't die."

CHAPTER THIRTEEN

New York- Present Day

"I see what you're doing," a shrill voice accused, when the door to the bathroom where Olivia had taken refuge from Chris's flirting was pushed open.

Fantastic. So much for hiding.

Courtney stalked toward her, the woman's nails suddenly biting into the tender skin of Olivia's upper arm.

"What do you think you're doing?" Olivia yanked her arm back, causing the glass in her hand to slosh dangerously. Worried about spilling it on her dress, she set it on the counter and took a step back.

Courtney Bloom's pupils, far too dilated to be natural, glittered with malice. "I've watched you all night. Flirting with all the men. Laughing at all their jokes… making everyone look at you. You think just because they want your company, they're interested in a nobody like you?" The woman sneered. "They're not. He would never be interested in someone like you." Tears welled in the woman's eyes.

"I'm not flirting with anyone. I'm here for business only." Olivia kept her voice even, slightly concerned by the woman's unpredictable behavior. I'm not the one you should be upset with, your fiancée is, Olivia wanted to say. When Chris had taken the vacant seat next to her, Olivia hadn't expected him to take such a flirtatious tone. But Chris was slick. There was nothing in his words she could object to, but his tone and the way his eyes kept dipping to her cleavage made his intention clear. But was he seriously interested in her or was it part of his negotiation tactic. Did he think she was so inexperienced his attention would make her vote for his company's bid?

"Liar! The only reason you're here is because you're hoping to fuck Chris. I know it! And don't think I haven't seen the looks you've been sending Declan. Are you hoping to spread your legs for him, too?" Courtney was shouting at the end.

Behind Courtney, the bathroom door opened, and Olivia grabbed the distraction to duck into a stall and shut the door. It might have been cowardly, but she didn't see any other option. The woman was crazy.

"You little bitch." Courtney spit out, apparently finding a new target. Olivia peeked through the crack in the stall door and recognized the newcomer.

"Give it a rest, Courtney," Cara said in a bored tone. "You know everyone can hear you in the hallway, right?"

Olivia felt her face heat.

Declan's sister heard? Maybe I can hide in here for the rest of the night.

Courtney's face turned purple, and she opened her mouth to spew more venom at the young woman, but Cara simply ignored her and entered a stall.

Olivia leaned against the stall wall and buried her face in her hands.

This deal is cursed.

A hand slammed on the stall door, making it rattle, and Olivia jumped. "I hope you're not stupid enough to think he's actually interested in you. Chris loves me, and I fight for what's mine."

Heels clicked across the marble floor and then silence. Had she left? Just when Olivia thought it might be safe to emerge, she heard a muttered "Bitch." Then the heels continued across the floor, and the door slammed.

Her legs shaking, Olivia exited the stall and washed her hands. Grabbing her drink, she took several large gulps. If ever there was a time to get numb.

"Are you okay?"

Cara's reflection joined hers in the mirror.

Olivia forced a smile. "Yes, thank you." She dried her hands and reached for her drink again. "I'm not flirting with Chris." She wasn't sure why she felt compelled to explain.

"I know." Cara grimaced. "Courtney's nuts. I'd say ignore her, but in reality, watch your back."

Olivia choked on her drink.

"I know Declan is going to be pissed that I'm getting *involved*." Cara made air quotes. "He can deal. You seem like a nice person." Her eyes were serious when they met Olivia's. "Chris and Courtney aren't what they seem."

Olivia tipped her glass up finishing the drink, hoping to buy time and think of an appropriate response. Chugging a cocktail probably wasn't the best one.

"I'm just here for the party."

Cara watched her with a small smile but held her hands up in surrender and moved to the door. Olivia wouldn't deny she was curious about Declan's younger sister. She remembered how much he cared for and felt responsible for his younger siblings.

Cara's hand was on the door handle when she asked, "How do you know Declan?"

"We met last week about a potential deal to buy the company I work for." Olivia was pleased her voice came out even.

"Hmm. It's just the two of you can't keep your eyes off each other when you think no one else is looking."

Olivia's face flamed. Was she that obvious? Quickly followed by—Was Declan looking at *her*?

Her stomach rolled unpleasantly. Definitely shouldn't have chugged that drink. "I think I'm probably watching everyone. A lot of networking opportunities," she finished lamely.

Olivia picked up her clutch from the counter, and tucked it under her arm. "It was nice to meet you, but if you'll excuse me, I don't want to miss dessert." Olivia took two steps forward, and the world tilted. She blinked as her hand caught the lip of the bathroom counter, and her vision wavered before Cara's concerned face came back into focus.

"Are you all right?"

She nodded, but kept her mouth shut, feeling nauseous. On her way back to the table, Olivia mentally counted her drinks.

I only finished two drinks... but I've been stressed and haven't eaten much.

By the time she made it to her seat, the world was fuzzy. Stuart was gone, and so was Richard. Courtney still sat next to Kyle, both of whom glared at her reappearance. At least she *thought* they were looking at her. Her brain felt like it was trudging through mud.

She took a few bites of the cheesecake in front of her, but it tasted weird. Her head felt heavy, and she was suddenly exhausted. It had been a long day. I'll just close my eyes... She jerked, eyes flying open when Stuart laid a hand on her arm.

"Olivia?"

"Mm-hmm." She smiled at him feeling better. Actually, she was feeling pretty good. The nausea and blurred vision had disappeared. Everything around her seemed a little brighter, and a delicious floaty feeling took over her arms.

She licked her lips. "Where is Richard?"

That didn't sound right. "Richard," she repeated slowly, but her words sounded slurred even to her ears. Courtney laughed across the table, making Olivia's head swivel. The world took a few seconds to catch up.

Stuart frowned at her. "He's waiting in the car. I'm going to head back to the hotel with him. Maybe you should come with us."

"Yes, go." Courtney said, a dark smile on her face. "You don't belong here."

Olivia's temper sparked. "No thank you, Stuart. I'm going to stay a little while longer. I'll get my own car."

That sounded normal.

"Okay." Stuart looked unsure. "Call me if you need anything."

Olivia forced herself to eat several more bites of the cake before the world tipped again and she lost her grip on the fork. It clattered loudly against the china plate.

Shit, am I drunk? Breathe through your nose, Olivia.

She planted her hands on the tabletop, to ground herself, trying to absorb how solid the table felt. It didn't work. She needed to leave before she passed out.

Olivia concentrated on rising slowly, but the table blurred in front of her again, and Olivia waited for it to clear before moving.

"Classless," Courtney said loudly. "Why is she even here?"

If Olivia didn't feel so ill, she'd be embarrassed. She wanted Declan with such a sudden intensity, she thought she might cry.

No! What the hell?

She shut down the thought immediately.

You haven't needed him for twelve years. You don't need him now.

Chris's voice was in her ear. "Let me help you."

He sounded genuinely concerned, but Olivia wanted to get away. Be by herself and forget this night had ever happened.

"Fine. I'm fine." If she kept her sentences short, he might not hear how drunk she was. "Going to make a call."

Before she could step away, the scent of Kyle's cologne filled her senses. She flinched back as he caught her elbow, his grip pinching more than helping steady her. He chuckled, but Olivia knew she was the only one there that heard the furious undertone in it.

Panic bubbled in her stomach and clawed up her throat. Not Kyle.

What had Dr. Turner said? When the panic came, she was supposed to count… use her senses… Find five... But her mind betrayed her, and she couldn't focus on anything.

"My wife never could hold her liquor. I think it's time for us to go home."

She sucked in a breath, and both of Chris's faces frowned. "You're our guest here tonight. Stay. I'll make sure your *ex*-wife gets back to her hotel safely."

Olivia sensed rather than saw the testosterone battle over her head, but Kyle's fingers loosened, and she didn't want to wait and find out who the winner was.

Stairs. All she needed to do was get to the top of the stairs and then get a taxi.

Olivia glimpsed the hard lines of Declan's face as she maneuvered past his table. Her face tingled, and she felt like she was breathing through sand. She managed the first step without a problem. A slight bit of her panic abated. Almost there.

A powerful arm came around her waist a little too tightly as she stumbled, and a fresh wave of nausea won against the panic.

"Slow down, beautiful," Chris said. "I'll take care of you."

She shook her head. One curl was stuck to the side of her face.

Sweating? Really?

"I'm okay."

Chris's arm was unyielding as he propelled her up the stairs and toward the front door.

"No." Olivia tried to make her voice firm, but it was barely more than a whisper, and now the panic was back. The world had become a massive swirl of color, and alarm bells rang faintly in her head. But no matter how she tried, she couldn't get her brain and body to communicate at the same time.

"I'll get you back to your hotel."

Olivia struggled to form words, but darkness was closing on the outside of her vision, and her breathing was shallow. What was wrong with her?

"Here you are." A feminine voice sounded brightly nearby, and then a different, smaller pair of hands wrapped around her biceps, a soft floral scent wafting over her.

"Cara." Chris's arm tightened around Olivia, but the grip on her biceps didn't relent and the forward motion stopped. "Olivia isn't feeling well. I'm helping her home."

"Well, we're here now."

"Old friends from the ladies' room," another feminine voice said. Someone jostled Olivia, and the tight band around her waist loosened.

Olivia had the vague sense that tomorrow, when she remembered being at the center of a tug of war in this luxury lobby, she'd be mortified, but all she felt was relief when Chris's body moved away.

"Besides, I think Courtney needs you. She didn't sound happy when you rushed out. I'm sure you don't need another scene after all the bad press lately. And, escorting an incapacitated woman to her hotel isn't great optics. Don't you agree?"

Even through the fog in her brain, she heard the bite in Chris's voice. "Olivia, do you want to go with them?"

Olivia nodded and licked her lips. "I'm so sorry."

"No need to apologize, Olivia." Chris chuckled, but there was no amusement in the sound. "I'll see you tomorrow for the tour."

"Sleaze." Olivia heard someone say, but she was more concerned with keeping upright as her legs threatened to buckle completely underneath her.

"Don't feel well," she whispered.

"Shit. Have you got her, Dahlia?" Hands tightened, and someone else was pressing into her.

"Yup. Let's get her to a car."

"She was completely sober in the bathroom twenty minutes ago," Cara said, as they made slow progress across the marble floor.

"Look at her eyes," another voice said. "I think she's been dosed. I wouldn't have thought that likely at one of these events, but you never know."

"Should we take her to the hospital?"

"No. Please," Olivia muttered, not sure if she was making sense. Not sure she was even awake. "Need my bed."

Where am I?

"I don't know, depending on—Cara! She's slipping."

One moment Olivia was falling, and the next she was weightless, pressed tight against something hard. Massive arms tucked her close, and she rested her cheek against the smooth fabric. His voice rumbled, and she nuzzled closer, the familiar sandalwood and bergamot smell instantly relaxing her.

"I had a bad dream," she whispered, trying to force her eyes open. "You were—"

"Hush," Declan said, as he adjusted her in his arms.

She'd tell him tomorrow. Olivia let the darkness pull her under. The last thing she remembered was being placed on warm leather and a voice whispering into her hair.

"I've got you, Petal. You're safe."

CHAPTER FOURTEEN

COUNTY KERRY, IRELAND—12 YEARS AGO

"Your tone was weird earlier." Rose said, as they lay in bed later that night, his body curled around hers.

"When?"

"At the castle. When we were talking about your job."

"I wasn't really interested in conversation."

She sent an elbow back lightly into his ribs. "Don't be annoying. I meant before."

"You're a bad influence on me," Declan teased trying to distract her. "I never thought I'd ever fuck in a National Heritage site."

"Nice try." Rose's tone grew serious. "Do you want to work for your father?"

Declan stirred. "Why would you ask that?"

She lifted a shoulder. "It was just your face, or maybe your tone of voice. I don't know. It just seemed like maybe you didn't."

"That must have been some tone of voice if you got all that. I was thinking about how to get you naked… not about work."

"Don't do that. Don't pretend I don't see you. If this time together is all we ever have, let's at least be honest with each other." She hugged his arm, where he held her under her breasts. "I'm leaving in less than forty-eight hours."

Declan fought the urge to deny the inevitable racing toward them.

"And while it's terrified me to be honest with you, I know this will likely be the most special week of my life."

Rose shifted and rolled to face him. The light was low but he could make out the glow of her eyes. "I'm in love with you, Declan Riordan. I'm leaving, and we won't see each other again. Let me in."

Declan felt like his heart had seized in his chest. He couldn't breathe. But she wasn't done. Rose was so much braver than he'd ever be.

"I know you," she said quietly. "I know you on a level that doesn't make sense, and I also know that for some reason, you are terrified to tell me about yourself. You've been holding part of yourself back this whole time. I promise, nothing you say will change how I feel."

She snuggled into his chest, tucking her head under his chin, and his arms closed firmly around her, wishing he never had to let her go.

"Even if I don't know your details, I know *you*," she whispered. "But I'd really like to know the details."

In the darkness, her voice contained infinite sadness when she said, "Maybe I'll see you someday across a crowded room..."

Declan shook his head, his throat clogged with emotion. "Not likely. Two different worlds, Petal."

"Okay." Her voice was resigned. "Then, if I'm never going to see you again, why can't you be honest?"

"I don't talk about myself." Declan could feel a tension building inside him. He wanted to tell her. He really did, but a lifetime of self-protection was hard to break. "I told you about my brothers and sister, about my childhood dog, about how I love to read the classics. That's not something anyone else knows," he offered, hoping it would appease her, but knowing it wasn't what she meant.

"There is something you're holding inside. Who is safer to tell than someone you'll never see again?"

Declan was silent for so long, she sighed. "I'm sorry, I shouldn't push. Let's just enjoy our time."

He shook his head, his thoughts racing. "You didn't. You're right." His fingertips stroked up and down her spine as much to comfort himself as her. "It's hard to talk about, because it never occurred to me, until you asked, that it *was* something to talk about. Until I met you, I'd never really thought about whether I *wanted* to follow my father into his business."

He rested a cheek on the top of her hair, breathing her in, waiting for the peace that always came when she was in his arms. "It was never an option," he admitted. "My brothers, they haven't had the same expectations put on them."

Rose lazily dragged a fingernail through the hair on his chest.

"Then there are my parents. Believe me when I tell you that *both* of my parents are extraordinarily strong willed, and they were of one mind when it came to my future."

Declan rolled to his back, his arm securing her against his side. Rose slung a thigh over his and rested her cheek on his chest.

"They never asked what you wanted to do?"

"Hardly," he scoffed. "Given the choice, I would have stayed with my mother and cousins, but no one asked me. I was shipped off. My father wanted me, and my mother agreed. So, off I went."

Rose made a tiny noise of distress, and he chuckled. "It wasn't so bad. I have a nice life. I have my siblings. When they aren't irritating the hell out of me, they are my favorite people in the world."

"But no one asked what *you* wanted?"

Declan twisted a lock of her hair around his finger, her questions making him feel things he didn't want to. "I'm the oldest."

"That's not a reason. Primogeniture went out with smallpox." Rose tried to lift her head to look at him, but he tugged on her hair to keep her in place.

Declan wasn't sure he could be so open if she looked at him. "Not even close to accurate, but I appreciate the support," he said wryly.

"Just because you're the oldest, you don't have to do what your father wants." Angry air huffed across his skin, and he stifled a smile at her defense.

"My parents are difficult, but they aren't ogres."

But for all the privilege, his father's way of life was a cage.

For all of them.

"He wouldn't understand if you told him you wanted to do something else?"

Absolutely not. His father had made it clear, a long time ago, what Declan's priorities should be, and David Bloom never cared if he drew blood with his words. His no-holds-barred approach to getting what he wanted, even with his children, was effective.

Declan respected it. Hadn't he learned to be the same?

The last time any other path for Declan had been discussed, he was twelve years old, and he informed his father that he wanted to be a professional rugby player. Declan was big for his age and fast. The coaches for his Irish school team said he had real potential.

David Bloom's eyes pierced Declan over the formal dining room table where they always ate. Declan had arrived the day before to spend the summer with his father. "You are a Bloom, and my eldest son. It is your legacy to take over this company."

In a rare show of defiance, Declan folded his arms across his chest, determined for once to tell his father how he felt. "I don't want to."

David Bloom glowered at him in silence for several minutes, but

Declan didn't budge. Slowly, his father's expression shifted, and a proud smile lifted his lips. "You're a lot like me, boy."

Despite his anger, pride swelled within him. His father never gave praise. "I hope so."

Declan saw how people responded to his father, his strength... his power. People respected his father. Feared him.

David Bloom set down his wineglass and regarded Declan seriously. His voice was unusually solemn. "It's imperative that you remember that family is everything. Blood is everything. Individual desire is selfish. A weakness."

Declan eyed him warily. This was new. Typically, his father didn't approve of what he saw as Declan's misguided loyalty to his blood in Ireland.

"You have three younger siblings, and they need you. They will need this company. I won't be here forever, Declan, and as my son, you will be the head of the family."

"Luke or James..."

"I have no doubt they'll be successful in their own right, but you *are my heir."*

Declan felt like the walls were closing around him, even while he was simultaneously thrilled that his father was speaking to him like he was a grown man.

His father cocked his head, and almost as if he'd read Declan's mind, he continued. "The twins are only eight years old. What makes you think they have the makings of the kind of leader Bloom Communications will need?"

"What makes you think I do?" Declan shot back.

Approval flickered in his father's eyes. "Your little brothers are smart. Extremely smart, and there is a toughness in them... but they are their mother's sons."

Declan narrowed his eyes at his father. He knew his father still loved Anne, and Declan easily understood why. Even after Anne ended the relationship with David Bloom and moved the twins to Atlanta, she had remained a loving and nurturing mother to Declan and treated him the same as her biological sons. He loved her too.

"Don't misunderstand me," his father's voice was sharp. "I respect the hell out of Anne, but she's soft. She didn't want this life, and that will always factor into how Luke and James view my business. My blood runs through their veins, but that softness will always be in them. You don't have that."

Declan's brow furrowed, but he didn't argue. He understood what his father meant. Siobhan was anything but soft. His mother loved him fiercely, but in the world she grew up in, there was no room for weakness. Growing up, even as an adjunct member of the McGrath family, he'd understood that at a young age. The mantra of both sides of his family was family loyalty above all else.

"Be proud of who you are." Declan sat up straighter. "You want to take care of your family, don't you?"

"Yes, sir."

"They'll need looking after. I'm not a young man, Declan, and this company will be turned over to you earlier than it would normally be."

Declan's alarm must have showed because his father chuckled. "I'm not sick. But the majority of my life is over. You are the future of this family."

"You might fall in love again," Declan said. "Maybe you'll meet someone like my mother... have another child."

David Bloom's expression changed, and Declan felt like a door had slammed shut. "I won't fall in love again, and I'm happy about that. I love each of my children and their mothers, but it's important for you to remember that love is weakness."

Declan was tempted to roll his eyes. His father loved women and was infamous for his many relationships.

"I'm not talking about sex. Or even companionship," his father snapped, further cementing Declan's belief that his father knew everything. "I'm talking true, soul-deep love. It will be a draw on your energy.

A hold that will make you question your decisions. Blunt the killer instinct necessary to survive in our world."

David Bloom drew in a breath, looking as though he'd surprised himself as much as Declan with his words.

A week before term was to start in Ireland, at the end of summer, Siobhan informed Declan that he would live permanently in the United States with his father.

"Are you all right?" Rose placed a palm on his chest, pulling him from the memory.

Declan hadn't thought about that night in years. No surprise why it came to him now. "My father is harder on me than he is on my brothers, but I understand why. I can take it. Most of the time, I relish the challenge. The battle between us."

"What about your sister?"

"Cara?" Declan thought for a minute. "Her mother is… fragile. I think my father has a hard time differentiating between the two of them." He laughed. "He doesn't know her as well as he thinks. Cara can be terrifying… not that I'd ever admit it to her."

Declan felt her smile against his bare skin, and she pressed a kiss to his ribs. "I think it's wonderful how much you love your family."

"I would do anything for them," he admitted.

Rose yawned. "I'm jealous. I would like to be loved like that."

Her words were light, and he knew she didn't mean them to be the dagger to his heart that they were.

"I love you, Rose. I know it's crazy for us to be saying it so quickly. But I do."

Declan felt dampness trickle down his side. He squeezed his eyes shut, determined not to fall apart along with her, because if he thought too closely about losing her, he would.

"I love you too, Declan. It's just bad timing," she whispered, her voice a little broken. "I wasn't saying it was your fault." She suddenly sat up and looked down at him. "We both have these big plans…" Her voice broke. "I just wish it didn't hurt so much."

Declan reached up and pulled her mouth down to his, tasting the tears on her lips.

"I know, Petal. If there was a way…"

"Maybe someday, right?"

"Right."

They could both cling to that, however unlikely it was.

CHAPTER FIFTEEN

New York—Present Day

Olivia shifted, trying to force her favorite weighted blanket off. It was too hot. The blanket moved again, and scent enveloped her, even as crisp arm hair rasped against the bare skin of her belly.

She knew before she opened her eyes who it was, but what she couldn't figure out was how it had happened. Cracking her eyes open an inch, she saw Declan's face, slack with sleep on the pillow beside her.

Olivia held still, the surrealness of the situation hitting her. Without moving her head, she saw by the early dawn light coming through the crack in the curtains that she was in her hotel room.

How had she gotten back here? Olivia scanned her memories for some explanation. There was the gala, eating dinner, Courtney accusing her of hitting on Chris… but then everything else was a blur.

There were only flashes of scenes in her brain. Hazy faces, dark quiet shifting to noise, the cold porcelain of the bathroom floor under her knees, someone stroking her hair…

Somehow, she was back in her hotel room, and Declan was in bed with her. His heavy arm was thrown across her bare stomach and a leg was thrown over hers.

Oh my god!

Fabric pulled across her chest when she tried to move away, and she realized she was wearing an oversized T-shirt. The only skin exposed was where the fabric had been pushed up. Even though her brain was trying to tell her something was very, *very* wrong with this situation, her body didn't seem to care.

Her hormones had fixated on his massive, bare chest half-draped over her and the large hand resting next to her face. Declan was even bigger than he had been as a younger man. Her eyes greedily traced the ridges of definition on his chest and the outline of the heavy muscles in his arm. Heat pooled in her belly, and she fought the urge to turn further into the embrace.

What is wrong with you? He's an arrogant ass who didn't even remember you. Did we have sex?

No. She remembered how it felt after Declan had been inside her.

A shot of lust between her legs made her want to curse.

Really, Olivia?

Her head ached as she tried to force the memories back. Olivia studied Declan, noting the differences from the last time she'd been this close to him. Her fingers tingled with the desire to trace his strong cheekbones, the slight scar near his temple. His nose was different. Slightly flattened across the top, like he'd broken it since she'd last kissed him.

The heavy, dark stubble covering his jaw was the same, and a memory of how Declan would wake her with the delicious scratch of his beard against her inner thighs rolled over her, making the insistant needy pulse between her legs turn into a sharp ache.

She was being ridiculous. She'd pined after this man for more than a decade, while he had completely forgotten.

And yet, with his face relaxed in sleep… the thick fringe of lashes hiding those mesmerizing eyes… This was the Declan she knew. Not the angry, cold man she'd encountered recently.

The hand by her head came down, skimming lightly over her breasts before coming to rest on the curve of her waist. Olivia could feel him thickening against her, and when he flexed his hips into her, a cascade of heat flooded her body.

Olivia bit her lip to stifle her response. Declan's lips twitched, quirking up slightly in his sleep.

He was waking up.

This was going to be beyond awkward. Were they destined to only connect when she was drunk?

She should probably slip out of the bed, put some clothes on, reinforce the distance between them. Maybe she should leave the room.

But before her limbs could obey her brain, his face inched closer on the pillow, and his nose nuzzled into the hair by her ear, and she heard him whisper, "Petal," before his firm lips closed over her earlobe and tugged.

Olivia melted.

The hand on her waist pulled her closer, rolling her until she cradled his erection, and he pressed hard against where she throbbed. His hips began to move in a slow steady rhythm, sending pleasure spiraling through her body.

She should put a stop to this now. Figure out what happened last night. But desire turned out to be more powerful than her rational brain.

Declan's stubble scraped over the soft skin under her jaw before he dipped lower to leave hot, open-mouthed kisses under her ear, trailing down her neck and back up again, until his mouth found hers. Olivia opened beneath him, welcoming the stroke of his tongue against hers.

"So sweet," Declan groaned into her mouth. His hand slid to

the curve of her ass, pulling her tight against him. "You always taste so sweet."

Olivia smothered a moan as he pulled her leg over his hip, and ground his hips into her core. One hand cradled her head, holding her still, while the other dipped between her legs, sliding under her panties and through her slick heat.

"Fuck, Petal. You're soaked," Declan groaned against her lips before delving in again, claiming her mouth.

Her hips rolled up, seeking more. One thick finger stroked inside, his thumb pressing in firm circles above. The sensations he elicited were too much, and the moan she'd been holding in escaped.

At that moment, Olivia didn't care why Declan was there. She needed him.

"So eager." He chuckled darkly when she undulated against him. "So fucking perfect. Always."

Declan's head lifted with a smile, and then his eyes opened.

Olivia knew the exact moment Declan came fully awake.

He froze.

The look of horror on his face was all that kept her from pleading with him not to stop. It felt like an eternity that they stayed like that, their bodies pressed together, Declan's fingers still deep inside her, his erection pulsing against her stomach, hot and hard. His chest rose and fell, and it felt like every muscle in his body tensed.

Olivia refused to look away. Declan's eyes were almost amethyst with passion, but more than that… He *knew* her.

She'd bet her life on it.

Declan sucked in a ragged breath, and her heart twisted when the walls came down behind his eyes, shutting her out. Then, as if she were a bomb that might explode if he moved too fast, Declan slid his hand away and rolled to his back on the bed beside her.

Olivia instantly felt cold and tried to ignore the heavy press of tears and the anger building in her chest. She didn't understand the game he was playing, but she thought she might hate him.

Without a word, Declan sat up, swinging his legs to the side of the bed, his head in his hands.

"You remember."

The sculpted muscles of his back drew taut, straining against his skin.

"I heard you." The room was quiet, the thick glass of the window shielding them from the sounds of the city below. "You called me Petal… when you were waking up."

A tremor ran through him, and Declan pushed to his feet, quickly stepping into his pants, fastening the belt, and reaching for his white dress shirt draped over a chair, all while keeping his back to her.

Olivia sat up. Looking down, she realized it was Declan's white undershirt that she was wearing. Her eyes found her dress crumpled on the floor.

"Why did you pretend not to know me?" She wanted to sound unaffected, but even she heard the hurt in her voice. Declan shoved his arms into his dress shirt and began doing up the buttons without looking at her.

Her anger skyrocketed.

Is he going to pretend like I'm not here?

"Did we fuck?" Her accusation seemed to shock him, and he faced her, his hands frozen on the buttons only done half way.

"You think I fucked you while you were unconscious?" There was a dangerous note to his voice, and in anyone else, she might have used caution.

Not Declan.

"No," she admitted. "But I don't remember how I ended up here."

"You drank too much," he said, and then the corner of his lips lifted the tiniest bit. "Some things never change." Then he scowled. "Though I would have thought you'd have learned your lesson by now. What would have happened if I hadn't been there?"

Olivia's face heated. "I didn't… or at least I don't think I did."

Declan seemed on surer ground now that he was angry. "Does this happen a lot? You get drunk at business events and go home with any man available?"

Olivia gasped, and her temper ignited. "Fuck off. I only had two drinks."

Declan huffed a disbelieving breath and sat to tie his shoes, leaving the rest of his shirt hanging open.

"You didn't answer my question."

With jerky movements, Declan scooped up his tuxedo jacket from the chair.

He was going to leave without talking to her.

Asshole!

"How about an easy one? Why am I in your shirt? I need to know what happened to me last night?" A bit of her fear must have translated because, with a heavy sigh, Declan's shoulders dropped, and he turned back.

"You got sick." He glanced toward the bathroom.

Olivia blanched.

This is just getting better and better.

"You said you couldn't breathe, so I had to rip your dress off."

"You *ripped* it off?"

A ghost of a smile teased at his lips. "Too many damn buttons. After… I put you in my shirt."

Her gaze fell again to Declan's chiseled chest, still visible through the partially buttoned shirt. Colors on his chest peeked from where the edges of the shirt moved. He has a tattoo!

Olivia licked her lips. *Why is that so hot?*

"Why did you stay?"

Emotions warred in his face. "I guess I was worried you might actually stop breathing." His arm swung wide in frustration, pulling the edges of his shirt and jacket further apart, and bringing the ink on his skin into full view.

The air in her lungs seized, and her gaze zeroed on the image. Olivia surged to her knees to get a better look, and Declan's eyes dropped to his body to see what had gotten her attention. He cursed and pulled his tuxedo jacket closed, blocking her perusal.

"When we met in that presentation, you pretended like you had never seen me before. Why?" Her voice shook, but she couldn't tell if it was from pain or anger.

Declan's voice was ice cold. "Would it have helped if I'd announced to your colleagues and my own that you and I fucked on vacation a lifetime ago?"

Olivia's eyes narrowed. "That's not what it was, and you know it."

His face hardened. "It was a long time ago. From what I remember, we had a nice enough time."

"Nice enough," Olivia scoffed. "Is that why you have a fucking *white rose* over your heart?"

A muscle ticked in Declan's jaw. "I have a tattoo. It has nothing to do with you."

"Reeaallly." She drew out the word mockingly. "You're going to stand in front of me and pretend that's not about me?"

Olivia felt like she was in a tornado of emotion. A tumultuous mix of relief, pain, and anger. It *hadn't* all been in her imagination. Declan *had* loved her too. It was there for anyone to see.

Declan slowly buttoned his shirt, obviously trying to prove he was unbothered. "Thinking back, I believe that is what you said your name was. Rose, right? We both had our small deceptions." He shrugged and tugged at the cuffs of his tuxedo jacket. "I'm sorry to disappoint you, *Olivia*, but my tattoo has nothing to do with you."

"Declan—"

"Do you honestly imagine you were the first woman I've lied to about who I am?" His expression was so unyielding he looked like a completely different person.

Olivia felt the first touch of uneasiness. "But you called me Petal just now."

"Why do you keep calling me that?" Olivia asked, as Declan ran a fingertip from the swell of her breast to a peaked nipple and across her cleavage to give attention to the other breast.

"Call you what?" His eyes followed his finger's movement as they lay on her hotel bed in Dublin.

"Petal."

Declan lowered his head and sucked the tip into his mouth, before blowing cool air across it, making it instantly pucker.

"Because my fair-skinned friend..." He grinned at her before returning his attention to her body. "You are my perfect white rose." His fingers traveled lower to circle her belly button. "And I knew this beautiful skin would be softer than a petal. I was right."

He slid down her body, kissing his way past her stomach and over her hipbone, before dragging his nose up through her center, making her arch her back.

"A sweet." His tongue licked over her, making Olivia cry out. "Delicious." Another lick, firmer this time. "White rose."

Declan sighed. "Olivia, you weren't the first, and you weren't the last. It's just what I call women. That way, I don't need to remember so many names."

Olivia was suddenly very conscious of the fact that she was sitting in a hotel bed, wearing a T-shirt she had no memory of putting on, while Declan stood fully dressed, looking down at her as if she were a foolish child.

"Our brief encounter means nothing. It was a lifetime ago. Is it going to be a problem, Ms. Adler, or are you capable of being professional?"

Olivia swallowed hard, shoving the pain lancing through her

into a box deep inside and locking it away. She had come too far and endured too much to let him ruin her career.

She brushed her hair back from her face and met his stare with one equally impersonal. "Not at all. Thank you for making sure I got back safely. This won't happen again."

Something flickered across his face but was gone before she could identify it.

"Good."

Then the door shut, leaving her in semi-darkness. She flopped back against the pillows that still smelled like him, with an arm thrown across her eyes.

How is this my life?

A sudden need to use the bathroom had her up and moving. Olivia pushed the door open, reaching for the light switch, only to realize it was already on. After taking care of her bladder, she washed her hands, bracing for what she would see in the mirror. However, the smeared mascara and caked makeup she'd expected weren't there. Her face was clean.

"What the hell?" Olivia leaned closer to the mirror to inspect her face, but her first glance had been correct. No makeup.

Her gaze fell to the trash can. She reached forward and picked up one of the still somewhat moist makeup-remover toilettes that almost half filled the bin. She looked from the paper-like product to her reflection, and then to the light on above her, realization dawning.

He took my makeup off and left the light on.

Even though it wasn't full morning yet, Olivia didn't bother trying to go back to sleep. After a quick online search, she booked a ticket and sent a text to Richard and Stuart, and a separate email to Chris, saying she wasn't feeling well and would see them back in Atlanta. She tried not to worry too much about how badly she'd embarrassed herself in front of their potential buyer.

But what consumed her thoughts was Declan.

He was lying, and she couldn't understand why.

Three hours later, when she was supposed to be meeting her co-workers for breakfast, her phone dinged with a text from Stuart.

Stuart: You're going home?

Olivia: Yes, family emergency and not feeling great. See you Monday.

Following the flight attendant's instructions, Olivia shut her phone off, leaned her head back against the seat, and pretended to sleep all the way back to Atlanta.

CHAPTER SIXTEEN

New York—Present Day

Declan leaned against the wall outside of Olivia's hotel room, hoping that if he could control his breathing, it would also ease the ache in his chest.

Too close.

He'd been seconds away from making a catastrophic mistake. The urge to pound on her door, force his way back in, and drive himself into her body until she screamed was almost unbearable.

The look on her face when he said she'd meant nothing to him…

He was a bastard, and this was exactly why he had to stay away from her.

Declan inhaled a deep breath through his nose and let it out slowly.

Olivia wasn't an option for him.

His jaw ticked as he made his way back to his apartment in the city. He was furious with himself. He should have expected Chris's interest in her. Not just because she was a beautiful, impressive woman, but because Declan now knew that Chris would do anything to secure his position at Bloom Communications.

~

DECLAN'S PHONE was practically exploding from where it sat on his desk.

Cara: Declan! Are you alive?

Luke: He hasn't answered any of my texts.

James: Brady talked to him yesterday. He's still breathing, even if he's ignoring us.

Cami: Interesting. Last I saw him, he was carrying a 'business associate' across the lobby like some sort of romantic hero.

Luke: <laughing emoji.>

Dahlia: Don't be an ass, Luke. I'll tell your family about all the sweet things you do for me.

Luke: That's because I am an amazing boyfriend.

James: Modest too

Luke: Why should I be modest?

Cara: It's a virtue?

Wes Evans has removed himself from the chat.

Cami: Did Wes leave?

Wes Evans has been added to the chat.

Cara: Nice try. There is no escape.

Wes: I don't need to know all of this. You can fill me in later.

Cara: You better not leave again.

Luke: No marital spats in the group text

Cara: Are you guys all still coming over this weekend?

Cami: Yes!!!! Can't wait. You promised holiday cocktails.

James: Has anyone other than Brady actually seen Declan since last weekend?

Luke: Nope. If he's dead, I get the 968 he has stored in Connecticut.

James: Then I call dibs on the Spider.

Cami: Isn't that a two-seater?

Luke: Yes. Why?

Cami: No reason.

Cara: <wide-eyed emoji> Are you trying to tell us something?

Cami: No.

Dahlia: Oh my god! ARE YOU GUYS HAVING A BABY.

James: Not today.

Luke: WTF

Cami: I'm not pregnant. Stop tormenting your family.

Cara: Declan

Luke: Declan

James: Declan

Declan: Shut the fuck up.

Cami: He lives!

Declan: I'm working. See you at Cara's.

Declan swiped his thumb across his phone, setting the family group chat to *do not disturb*. He knew he'd given them a lot to talk about after the way he'd stormed out of the Crystal Gala with Olivia in his arms, but he wasn't sure what he was going to say to them. Declan had never behaved like that in his entire life.

The desire to take care of Olivia, to protect her, had been impossible to resist. He hadn't thought... just reacted. Declan rubbed at his forehead.

It was a risk he probably shouldn't have taken. But during the car ride to her hotel, when Olivia had smiled hazily up at him, Declan couldn't bring himself to leave her. He could rationalize it was because she was so out of it she needed to be watched, but it didn't explain why he'd held her hair back while she was sick. Or why he slipped his undershirt over her because he was worried she would be cold, or why he used her makeup wipe thingies to take off all of her makeup.

"Are you coming to bed this year?" Declan laughed from the bed.

The door to the bathroom stood open, and he could see the tantalizing length of her long legs under his T-shirt as Rose stood, using some sort of cloth to take her makeup off.

"Two seconds. I just need to get this off."

Declan flipped back the top of the coverlet as she tossed something in the trash can and turned to him with her glorious smile.

"You know, you'd save a lot of time if you didn't wear makeup."

Rose planted a knee on the bed and leaned toward him, her breasts hanging free in his shirt, her heavy, dark hair enveloping him in her rose scent.

"Still would have to wash my face. You don't want me to be a gross old hag someday, do you?"

His heart twinged. "You'll be the most beautiful one-hundred-year-old around," he said, letting his brogue roll his Rs. Rose giggled as she straddled him, the heat of her against his cock drawing an instant response.

"It's all about prevention," she breathed before lowering her lips to his.

"Armstrong Electronics sent some questions," Cecile said, striding into the temporary Atlanta offices. Declan grunted. He would have been surprised if they hadn't.

Cecile hesitated, and Declan glanced up from the papers in front of him.

"Did you want them now?"

"No."

She had been with him long enough to know there was no point in questioning him. Declan would look over their questions, but he had no intention of answering until after Christmas. "Leave them on my desk. What time is your flight?"

"Seven o'clock. I'll be back on the twenty-eighth, and I'll be available on my cell if you need me. Todd is leaving soon, too."

Declan nodded. Working for him was a 365-day kind of job, but he compensated his employees well for their dedication.

"This deal is what I'm focusing on. There won't be any movement before then. Enjoy your holiday."

"Do you need me to arrange anything for you?"

He glanced up, and Cecile arched a perfect eyebrow. "Do you need me to send anything to Ms. Carrol?"

Shit. He'd forgotten about Fiona. A weight descended on his shoulders, and a vision of sapphire eyes flashed in front of him. He gripped his pen and mentally shook it off.

"Yes. Something nice. Not jewelry."

"Her personal shopper mentioned she's been eyeing the new Hermes bag."

Declan grunted. He should have known Cecile would be two steps ahead of him.

"Great." He returned to his work, listening to Cecile's heels tapping across his office and the shutting of the door.

After a moment, he flipped the file shut and leaned back in the chair, scrubbing a hand across his eyes.

He couldn't concentrate. No matter how hard he tried to will his mind into submission, it kept returning to the other night. It was as though the seal on the vault of memories he'd shut away years ago for his sanity had broken. Now, he couldn't think of anything *but* her.

Declan groaned. He'd called her Petal. *Idiot.*

He looked around the offices he'd leased for his time in Atlanta. They weren't nearly as luxurious as his offices above Water Street in New York's financial district, but they suited his purposes. He hadn't been lying when he told Fiona that all he needed for work was a phone. Most of what he did these days was put the deals together.

He could move to Atlanta… His siblings were here, and soon there would be nieces and nephews. His mood soured as he looked down at the folder Cecile had left on his desk.

But so was she. Declan couldn't live in the same city as her and not have her. It was hard enough being on the same planet now that he'd seen her again.

He wasn't that big of a masochist.

But once the deal was done… and Chris and Courtney dealt with… maybe…

No. He forced himself to ignore his emotions.

If he regained his seat at Bloom Communications, he would need to live in New York, and her job was here.

Not to mention if someone from his past who felt wronged ever came looking.

She was safer away from him.

Declan stood, loosening his tie as he shuffled the files on his desk into a neat stack. He wouldn't be getting any work done tonight, and the skeleton staff he'd brought to Atlanta had already returned to their families for Christmas.

Declan had always loved the holidays, the time with his family… but everything was different now. When his father died two years ago, and Courtney inherited his father's fortune, Declan had wanted to challenge the will immediately. He knew her first step would be to remove him from his position as CEO at Bloom Communications, the company he'd given his entire life to.

And of course, that was exactly what she'd done, before cutting them all off. The money hadn't been a hardship for Declan or his brothers. They each had money they'd either earned or received from their father throughout their lives to build their own fortunes. But losing status and money had devastated Cara, only twenty-four at the time. His jaw clenched again as he remembered everything his sister had gone through.

Cara may have moved past it, happy in her marriage and new career, but Declan wouldn't rest until he'd gotten revenge.

He punched a number into his phone. "Progress report," he barked, not bothering with a greeting.

"Merry Christmas to you too," Brady drawled.

Declan narrowed his eyes as he paced across the office to stare down at the street below. He wasn't in the mood to put up with the man's antics.

Brady was the twins' friend, not his. Declan didn't need friends; he needed answers. He let the silence draw out between them, begrudgingly acknowledging that Brady wasn't easy to disconcert.

It was one of the reasons Declan hired Brady's security firm rather than his normal security team. He had put the younger man in touch with Vincent Menardi, former head of Bloom security, and tasked them both with looking for the prostitute who had survived Chris's drunk driving accident. Declan needed that woman's testimony as leverage.

Brady might come across as carefree and nonchalant, but Declan had learned, when it came to his job, Brady was deadly serious.

A heavy sigh sounded on the phone. "With all the fancy education you Blooms got, someone should have spent money on a finishing school. You guys are cranky as shit."

"Noted."

"We used the name Vincent gave James—Abigail Sanders, the alias Vincent set up for her after the accident—and tracked her to New Orleans, where she got a job as a dancer, but after a few months she disappeared again. There are other Abigail Sanders in the US, but none of them matches her description or background."

"Do you think she's dead?" Declan's brow furrowed in concern. That would be disastrous. He needed the woman alive to uncover the details of what happened almost four years ago, when Chris, driving Declan's car, had killed a prostitute who worked for Courtney's escort service. Declan bitterly recalled how Courtney and Chris had framed him, using the threat of turning him over to the police to blackmail his father into marrying Courtney.

The familiar knot tightened in his stomach as he remembered how his father had believed Courtney's lies, thinking Declan had been the one driving. Though Courtney's son Trey had manipulated photographs to incriminate Declan, it still hurt that his father hadn't trusted him enough to ask.

The old anger surged through him. David Bloom had been a stubborn man. Vincent, loyal to the Blooms and convinced Declan was the driver, had arranged for the surviving escort to be paid off. But now knowing the truth, Vincent was eager to help.

There was no statute of limitations on murder. Even if they couldn't prove Chris was the driver during the fatal accident, it should be enough, along with everything else, to convince the board to reinstate Declan as CEO.

CHAPTER SEVENTEEN

Atlanta—Present Day

The week since returning from New York had not been pleasant. Richard and Stuart had bought the story that she had suddenly become ill, but Kyle wasted no opportunity to jab at her. When Jessica called to say she was in town for the holidays, Olivia had been excited to reconnect with her old friend.

Olivia held her coat tightly around her as she made her way toward the restaurant door with an odd mix of anticipation and anxiety. The two women hadn't sat down, just the two of them, for years.

When they were married, Kyle didn't like her meeting Jessica alone, probably concerned that Olivia might reveal what was happening in their home. As time passed, their old telephone marathons grew shorter and shorter, replaced by texts and memes.

It hadn't been a problem until Jessica learned Olivia had left Kyle and hadn't told her the truth about them living apart for over a year before Olivia filed for divorce. Jessica claimed she understood that Olivia was trying to protect Richard while he was ill, but Olivia got the distinct impression Kyle had done a better job of swaying his family to his version of their marriage.

The hostess seated her, and Olivia draped her coat over one of the chairs. She toyed with her water glass and ordered a peppermint tea, not sure why she was so nervous. Jessica was late, but that wasn't a surprise. The steaming mug was placed in front of her just as Jessica bustled in.

Her chestnut hair was shorter than the last time Olivia had seen her, and though a wide smile stretched across her face, Olivia imagined she saw a tinge of something forced around the edges. Olivia came to her feet, but instead of the usual tight hug, Jessica gave her a half-hug and an awkward pat on the back.

"It's so good to see you. It's been way too long." Jessica shrugged out of her coat, but paused before she lay it on top of Olivia's. Her face pinched slightly as she stroked one hand down the cashmere. "This is nice."

"Thanks." Olivia wanted to joke she'd found it on sale like they used to, but something in Jessica's tone kept her silent.

"Do you want some tea?"

Jessica wrinkled her nose. "I'll have a glass of Chardonnay, please. Make it a large one." She let out a little laugh as the server walked away. "It's mommy's day out. I'm sorry I'm late. You know how kids are... Right when I'm ready to walk out the door it's, 'Mommy, where's my shoe' and 'Mommy, Clementine is breathing on me.'" Jessica laughed before sobering. "I'm sorry I didn't mean..."

Olivia smiled back, ignoring the old hurt that spiked in her chest. "Nothing to be sorry about. I love hearing about your kids."

"Pfft." Jessica rolled her eyes and took a sip of her wine. "Not nearly as exciting as your life. High powered CFO jetting off in a private jet to a black-tie gala." There was that edge again.

"It's not all it's cracked up to be, trust me." Olivia reached for a piece of bread and slathered it with butter, even though her appetite had disappeared.

They ordered their food, and Jessica ordered another glass of wine before she made a face at Olivia. "I've been patient… now tell me *everything*."

Olivia fiddled with her tea bag, not meeting her friend's eyes. "It's been really busy. Everyone at the company is excited and nervous about the offers. I think we know which way we're going to go—"

"Ugh!" her friend exclaimed. "Not that. Don't get me wrong, I'm pretty excited about the payout I'm going to get for my stock. Things have been tight lately with me staying home with the kids, so this buyout is a godsend. Who knows? Maybe I'll even buy a fancy coat like yours." She scrunched her nose. "Maybe not. I have a feeling that coat isn't kid friendly."

Olivia managed a smile. Was she looking for jabs where there were none?

"What I want to hear about is Mr. 'Hold on to the Headboard and Scream My Name.' It must have been crazy seeing him again. I googled the company when Uncle Richard told me who the buyers were… I almost passed out when I saw the picture. I thought the name sounded familiar."

A knot formed in Olivia's stomach, but she forced her face into a neutral expression. An unintended perk of her life with Kyle. She'd learned to mask her emotions. Call it instinct, but something was off between her and Jessica, and Olivia wasn't sure she trusted her anymore.

"He didn't remember me." Olivia shrugged and gave a self-deprecating laugh.

Jessica set her wineglass down, her mouth hanging open.

"I wasn't expecting anything," Olivia hurried on, "but it's pretty mortifying." She had no intention of telling Jessica about what happened in New York or that she was convinced Declan was lying.

"Wait? So, he didn't remember it the same way? What did he say?"

The knot in her throat grew. "No. As in, *didn't remember me,* didn't remember me."

Jessica's brow wrinkled, but there was something in her expression that made Olivia uncomfortable. "What did he say when you told him?"

"Nothing. I didn't say anything. It was a business meeting. Perhaps, the most important one of my career. I wasn't about to say, 'Hey, I guess you don't remember me, but I told you my name was Rose twelve years ago, and we fucked like bunnies across southern Ireland for a week.'"

Jessica winced. "Yeah, I can see how that would be awkward." She took another sip of wine. "I always knew the guy sounded too good to be true. And when we found out he'd lied to you about who he was..." Her frown deepened. "It won't affect the sale, right? I know that sounds callous considering he basically peed on your fantasy, but you know what's at stake with this." Jessica leaned forward. "For my uncle, I mean. You won't let your hurt pride get in the way of the deal..."

Olivia felt sick. Jessica had been her best friend, her only friend really for most of her life. The person she'd confided in and cried to in the months after she returned from Ireland. She knew what that week had meant to Olivia.

Intense loneliness swept over her. Olivia had thought if anyone would understand how difficult this situation was, it would be Jessica. But the day Olivia filed for the divorce, was the day their relationship changed. "Of course not," she said smoothly.

Jessica must have registered her cool tone because she grimaced. "I'm sorry. I'm an asshole. You created a whole fairy-tale memory around this guy, and to find out he was just using you for sex—"

"What are you talking about?"

Jessica stared at her, lips in a firm line. "Liv, I love you, but ever since you came back from Ireland, you've been obsessed with this guy. You almost didn't marry Kyle because of it."

"Yeah, what a tragedy that would have been."

Jessica's lips pressed together until they almost disappeared. "I'm not saying my cousin is flawless, but you never gave him a real chance. You never let him into your heart because you had this imaginary man who was 'perfect.'" She rolled her eyes. "How could any real man compete with that?"

Olivia gripped her tea cup, slightly surprised that the handle didn't snap off in her hand. "You know that's not why we got divorced."

"I know. I remember. He wasn't nice to you… hurt your feelings."

Embarrassed and ashamed of what her personal life had become, Olivia had hidden the worst of it from the world, but she had no idea this was how her friend felt.

"It was a bit more than that."

Jessica's eyes softened. "I know. Kyle told us about how not being able to get pregnant affected you… the marriage."

Hurt and disbelief slammed through her.

"It's understandable," Jessica continued. "I know how much you wanted a family, how much your mom and sister were pressuring you… and I was having kids…"

Olivia's heart pounded in her chest, and her lips tingled.

As if from a distance, she heard Jessica say, "Marriage is hard. God knows, half the time I want to kill my husband."

Color and noise rushed back in, and Olivia could hear her own harsh breathing.

"Did you know he gave me an STD?" Olivia blurted out. Her

voice was too loud, and out of her periphery, she saw people glancing their way. Her cheeks heated, but she was too enraged to care. She was tired of hiding Kyle's bullshit for the sake of saving face.

"I found out he was cheating when the doctor handed me my prescription. That was a fun moment. Kyle didn't even deny it, though he was sorry that time. He claimed the affairs he had later were *my* fault because I *embarrassed* him at work. I apparently didn't make him feel like a man."

Olivia shook her head, ignoring Jessica's pale cheeks and wide eyes. "Like an idiot, I *still* stayed. I thought I could fix it. I wasn't about to be a failure at marriage, not after..." She didn't need to tell Jessica about the pressure Olivia's family put on her to get married and start a family. "I tried for years!"

Jessica's embarrassed fidgeting broke Olivia from the spell she was under. She bit her lip, ordering herself not to cry. She'd been about to reveal more than she'd ever told anyone. Olivia cleared her throat and reached for her purse.

"Goodbye, Jessica."

Can this line move any slower? Olivia groused to herself, checking the time on her phone. Normally she didn't mind lines, but she was already running late after meeting with the board that afternoon. Using work as an explanation for why she was late would only lead to a lecture from her mother.

She should be relieved that the decision was finally made. Her vote hadn't mattered in the long run as the decision to go with the Bloom Communications offer was unanimous. But Olivia couldn't shake the feeling that Declan would not take losing lying down.

Over the last few days, Olivia had done some research online, and reading between the lines, she thought she had a pretty good handle on where the animosity between Declan and Chris came from. Only the notification of leadership change had been reported in the business pages. It was in the gossip blogs that she learned all the nasty details about what happened after David Bloom's death.

It was obvious the two men were looking to destroy each other, and she hated Armstrong was caught in the middle. However, on paper, the decision was straightforward. Chris's offer was better, not only because the purchase price was higher, but because Chris had readily agreed to add the stipulation Richard wanted—that all the current employees would be retained.

They had sent the same stipulation along with their questions to Bloom Capital, but Declan hadn't deigned to get back to them. Richard was eager for it to be over.

The woman in line in front of her stepped back suddenly and bumped into Olivia, causing her to lose her hold on the three bottles of her mom's favorite wine that she had cradled in her arms.

Shit! Olivia frantically fumbled for the bottles as her purse hit the ground, but one slipped through her fingers. Before it could smash on the floor, a tanned hand shot out and caught it, just as the scent of sandalwood and bergamot hit her. By the awestruck look on the other woman's face, it was exactly who Olivia feared it was.

The woman practically leered as she gave Declan a detailed once over. "Your reflexes are amazing. Are you a professional athlete?"

"No."

The light in the woman's eyes only dimmed slightly. "Well, you're certainly good with your hands."

Did she just lick her lips?

Despite herself, Olivia bristled and considered accidentally hitting the woman over the head with one of the bottles.

"I think this is yours." Olivia wanted to ignore him, but Declan nudged her with the bottle. Olivia turned just enough to take the bottle, refusing to look at him.

"Thanks." Her purse still sat on the floor. Thankfully, it had landed upright. As she tried to figure out how to gracefully hold the bottles while also picking it up, Declan bent again.

He was standing too close, and it was playing havoc with her body. Her skin prickled. She was burning up.

The woman in front of them wasn't happy being ignored. "Such a southern gentleman."

Olivia was proud of herself that she didn't laugh outright. Declan's chest brushed against her back, her temper making her heartbeat pick up its pace.

Or, at least she told herself it was her temper. He was trying to intimidate her, but little did he know, she'd promised herself years ago that she would *never* let a man make a fool of her again.

Olivia pivoted, elbows out, but instead of forcing Declan to take a step back as she intended, Olivia practically bounced off him, while he barely budged, even when her elbow collided with his abdomen.

Which made her angry.

The situation was made worse when his hands immediately shot out to steady her, before he plucked the bottles out from the crook of her arm with one of his large hands and tucked them into the same arm where he still held her purse.

"Let me help you with these." He had the audacity to smirk at her. "You seem a bit unsteady."

If looks could have killed, Declan would be laid out on the floor in front of her. Dead.

"I'm fine. Thank you." Olivia said through her teeth, as she reached to reclaim her bottles. But Declan had them so snug between his bicep and forearm, nothing less than a fight was going to get the bottles back.

"That's so sweet of you."

Olivia gave the woman credit. On the outside Declan looked like a dream. It wasn't until later you found out it was all a lie. After all, hadn't she agreed to a week with a stranger in a foreign country after only eighteen hours and some mind-blowing sex?

"Succubus," she muttered.

The woman's forehead creased. "What?"

Declan's lips twitched. "Pretty sure that has to be a female."

Olivia turned the full force of her glare on him. "Have you seen your eyelashes lately? They're longer than most women's" She turned to face forward again, only to realize he was still holding her wine and purse.

Damn it! He makes me crazy.

The line moved forward, but their line mate still gaped at them. "I would kill for eyelashes like that."

It was Olivia's turn to smirk. "My point exactly."

The woman looked horrified. "Not that it's feminine on you… I mean, you are very masculine… I mean…" The woman looked like she wanted to fall through the floor.

"Thank you." Declan sounded pained.

Good.

"The line's moving." Olivia lifted her chin to indicate the woman should move up. She was being rude, but really? This was the last thing she needed tonight.

"In a hurry?"

"Yes," she bit out.

"I'm not."

Why did he sound so friendly? She looked suspiciously at him over her shoulder.

"I'm heading to my sister's for Christmas cocktails," he added.

"That's sweet. I'm Vanessa, by the way," the woman said, clearly not willing to give up. "I'm close to my family too."

"Maybe we should swap places." Olivia said with a tight smile. "You two probably have a lot in common."

The woman's eyes lit up, but Declan spoiled her escape by saying. "But I have all your stuff."

"You could just hand them to me." Olivia bared her teeth at him, pretending it was a smile.

A mischievous light shone in his eyes, and for a second, she forgot to breathe. Because he looked like *her* Declan.

"Where is the chivalry in that, Rose?"

Olivia ground her teeth.

Vanessa frowned. "Oh, you know each other."

"No," Olivia said, at the same time Declan said, "We work together."

"No, we don't, and we never will."

The light disappeared, along with his playful expression. "Explain." He snapped, his expression darkening.

Eyes rounding, Vanessa spun and took a few steps closer to the person in front of her.

A stabbing pain started behind Olivia's right eye. She shouldn't have said anything. It wasn't like her to make mistakes like that. This is *his* fault, she thought, scowling.

"Your board said they would let us know of the decision the week after Christmas." Declan's tone sent chills down her spine as he slipped into full billionaire boss mode.

"*Let you know,* not make our decision." Olivia rubbed at her eye. "Look, I shouldn't have said anything, but I guess it doesn't matter now. The board voted this afternoon. We will be accepting the Bloom Communications' offer."

Declan's jaw worked back and forth, and his eyes turned black. "We haven't given our response to the questions you sent over."

The pain was spreading to her temples, a viselike grip that would soon have her entire skull at its mercy. "I am aware. Bloom Communications responded within an hour of receiving them. Richard felt it showed how much they cared."

She sighed. Declan was making her tense, and her neck muscles contracting weren't helping stave off what was shaping up to be a killer migraine.

"To be honest, it all came down to employee retention. You were upfront about the fact your plan included the elimination of positions. Richard wants his company to live on, not be stripped down to be sold again."

The muscle in Declan's jaw ticked. "So, this *isn't* personal? This isn't because I didn't remember things the way you did."

Olivia shook her head, and then immediately regretted the movement when her eye twitched. "My god, your ego!" She rubbed at her temples. "You honestly believe I would tank a deal, for the company I've dedicated my entire adult life to growing, because you hurt my feelings?"

He tilted his head. "Did I hurt your feelings?"

"Ma'am," the annoyed voice of the cashier cut through their tension.

"Right. Sorry." Olivia stepped forward but refused to acknowledge Declan when he put the bottles and her purse on the counter.

The first bout of nausea hit her as she pulled her credit card from the reader, snatched her bags, and with a terse Merry Christmas, bolted from the store as a second cashier rang up Declan next to her.

She had to get out of there. Between what she knew would be an awful evening with her family and running into Declan, Olivia had reached her limit.

Freaking anxiety-induced migraines. Her body constantly failing her made Olivia feel weak. But she didn't slow her pace until she reached the safety of her car. She grabbed for her door handle, the remote key unlocking the door.

Declan's large hand appeared next to hers, and he pushed the door shut, crowding her against the car. Furious energy rolled off him in waves.

Her stomach tightened into a knot, and a vise tightened around her lungs as panic began its crawl through her veins, and her head throbbed.

She breathed deep through her nose. "Step back." Her voice wasn't nearly as strong as she'd intended. He didn't budge. "Now."

Abruptly, he stepped back, and Olivia turned to face him. Declan's face was blank, but his eyes were concerned as they scanned over her. She held a hand out for him to keep his distance. He looked from her trembling hand, suspended in the air between them, back to her face, his mouth turning down.

"I didn't mean to scare you."

"Then you shouldn't accost women in parking lots." Olivia said, leaning into her anger. "I know you are upset—"

"Chris is going to gut your company. *He's lying.* Bloom Communications has no need for an electronics development company. All he wants is XEROS, and he is only saying what you want to hear in order to get it."

"The employee retention clause will be in the contract." Olivia ignored the rising pressure in her head. These were the same arguments she'd given the board, but had been ignored.

Olivia had been fighting for months… years, really. She was exhausted.

"There won't be any employees to retain if he shuts the doors. You can't trust him."

"And I should trust you? That's a bit like the pot and kettle, isn't it? You'll say whatever it takes to get what you want, too.

Chris *might* be a liar, but I already *know* you are one." Olivia took a deep breath. "Look, it's done. This is over."

"The fuck it is," Declan growled.

"The board voted."

Declan's lips parted, probably to argue, just as a fiery arrow of pain lanced across both eyes. His expression changed in a heartbeat. "Are you okay?"

"I'm fine. You gave me a headache with your stubbornness. I'm late for my parents, and I know you have somewhere to be as well."

Olivia forced herself to meet his eyes. This was it. There was no reason for her to see him again.

The tightness in her chest intensified but it had nothing to do with her anxiety. "Goodbye, Declan."

He stared at her silently as she yanked open the door and tossed the wine into the passenger seat. As she pulled away, she saw him still standing in the same position watching her.

CHAPTER EIGHTEEN

Atlanta—Present Day

"I can't believe you brought your own whiskey." Cara glared at him. "You knew I had special holiday-themed cocktails."

Declan eyed the miniature candy canes decorating the green, sprinkle-covered rims of martini glasses containing a suspicious milky liquid.

"Pass."

She turned her scowl on Luke when he asked, "What did you call this, again?" He held up the glass to inspect its contents.

Cara narrowed her eyes. "Santa's Little Helper."

James snorted, and Cami took a sip. "It's delicious, Cara. Ignore them."

"They're great, baby." Wes squeezed his wife's waist and pressed a kiss to her temple.

Declan resisted the urge to make a rude comment. He'd already seen Wes hide his beer behind a poinsettia plant.

"Did you see all the trees? Cara has been decorating every spare minute she has." Wes angled his head at the small tree in the kitchen.

A Christmas tree in the kitchen. Whoever heard of such a thing?

"These are so cute!" Dahlia lifted one of the miniature ornaments to examine it. "But your Star Trek tree in the living room is my favorite."

Luke, James, and Declan exchanged looks, and Luke rolled his lips in to hide his smile. Declan hummed.

"Have you always been such a huge fan?" Cami asked.

James coughed to cover his laugh.

Cara squared her shoulders and rounded on her brothers, but Wes held her tight and pulled her back into his side. "She'd never seen it before she met me. An immediate convert." He smiled indulgently down at his wife.

She crossed her arms with a huff, and then looked evilly at her brothers. "Curling up with my hot new roommate was all the incentive I needed."

Luke pretended to gag.

"You loved it," Wes said.

"I loved something." She waggled her eyebrows, and the other women laughed as Wes's cheeks flushed.

Declan looked around the room. He was genuinely happy for his siblings, even if the glimpse of what he would never have made him want to run.

He frowned, Olivia's face in the parking lot flashed in front of him. He shouldn't have cornered her, but her reaction seemed too extreme to come from being startled.

She'd been shaking, and he'd seen the pain in her blue eyes. Now that he thought of it, she seemed off even before the parking lot.

Olivia clearly had a severe headache, but Declan couldn't shake the feeling that something else was wrong, and it drove him insane that he didn't know what it was. He wanted to grab her, pull her close, ask what it was and then do whatever was necessary to fix it for her.

But he couldn't, and she wouldn't have told him anyway.

Might have something to do with you showing up again and acting like a heartless bastard.

"What has you frowning so darkly over here?" Dahlia asked.

His expression cleared. "Work." It was true. He was still irritated that Armstrong had already voted, but it didn't matter. On the car ride to his sister's, he'd put his back-up plan into action.

"I bet it's Snow White," Cara said, joining them. "How is she?"

"How would I know?" He gave his sister his best shut-the-fuck-up look.

Dahlia gave him a funny look. "Declan, you swooped in like a superhero and carried her off. We didn't hear from you for days. No one is buying that there is nothing between the two of you."

"It's business. She was drunk, and you three..." He lifted a brow to include Cami as she sauntered up. "Were going to drop her. I was trying to avoid a scene."

"Mm. Yes. You carrying her like a bride over the threshold... That definitely didn't cause a scene. Besides, she wasn't drunk."

Declan glared at his sister. "Thanks for your expert analysis."

"I'm just saying I've never seen anyone go from upright to incoherent that fast. Except in Ibiza."

"She wasn't on drugs," Declan snapped. "Olivia has a low tolerance for liquor."

"How do you know that, if you just met her?" Cami asked.

"Stop glaring at my wife," James all but snarled, coming to Cami's side.

She patted James's chest. "I'm a big girl. Besides, I think it's kind of sweet how defensive Declan is getting over this."

"That's it. I'm leaving."

"Don't be so grouchy," Cara said. "We discussed it. We think someone slipped her something. Maybe roofies? I was talking to Olivia right before, and she was fine."

"Seems like an unusual venue to drug a woman." Dahlia frowned. "She was with coworkers, right… oh!" Her green eyes widened. "Chris *was* awfully determined to take her back to her hotel."

Declan's blood boiled as rage consumed him. He wanted to hit something… hard.

"That would be a pretty obvious move for Chris. He's more of a snake in the grass than an obvious creep." Cara squinted. "Now, Courtney, on the other hand." She sucked in a small breath. "That bitch."

"What?" Declan barked, and out of his periphery he could see Wes glare at him.

Cara made a face. "I may or may not have been eavesdropping on their argument in the ladies' room. Courtney was completely unhinged, accusing Olivia of trying to sleep with Chris and even you." She cut her eyes to Declan. "I told you I wasn't the only one who noticed how you were watching her. Anyway, Olivia's drink was on the counter unattended."

"Valium or another benzo would do it," Cami mused. "If Courtney had something like that in her purse, she could have put a few pills in Olivia's drink. It would act almost the same as a roofie, except it would have made her sick, not just incoherent."

Three pairs of female eyes swung to him, and Declan was well aware that his brothers and Wes were listening.

"Was she sick that night?" Dahlia asked, her voice a shade too innocent.

"How the fuck should I know?"

"Watch your tone," Luke growled.

Declan rolled his eyes. "If they are going to gang up and try to bully me, then I get to treat them like the bratty sisters they are."

When Dahlia and Cami beamed at him, he blinked. "What?"

James's arm encircled Cami's shoulders with a grin. "He doesn't get it. There's no use trying to make him understand."

Declan wondered if Olivia's headache was contagious, because his family was making his head pound. "Understand what?"

"You called them your sisters." Cara poked him in the side.

He lifted his brows. "And that's what has you all staring at me like I sprouted a second head?"

"You can't really blame us," Luke teased. "You don't really exhibit human emotion that often."

"Fuck me." Declan closed his eyes. "I need more whiskey if I'm going to deal with all of you."

"While you're making yourself another drink, let's talk about what's important," Cara began. "Do you have a tree yet? I can help you decorate your hotel suite if you like. Also, if you were serious last week about relocating to Atlanta, I'd love to help you house hunt..."

"Kill me now," he muttered, doubling the amount he normally poured.

Luke extended his glass, and Declan splashed a liberal amount into it. "Your date was pretty pissed when you disappeared."

"I know." He'd gotten several angry texts and a phone call the next day about how he'd embarrassed Fiona by disappearing. What could he tell her? She hadn't even crossed his mind that night.

"I know you have a plan. You always do," Luke said, taking a swig of his drink. "But that woman is a truly horrible individual. Cara told us stories from when she and Fiona were in the same social circles. I'm not talking about the normal bullshit either.

"Did you know she put a young woman in the hospital for spilling a drink on her at a party? Fiona broke a vase over her head, and kicked her repeatedly in the head. Or that there are rumors about her helping cover up more than one sexual assault for male friends?"

Declan inhaled sharply. "No, I didn't know that. I'm assuming her father kept it quiet?"

"You know how that shit works in your world."

He did. It's what he was trying to protect Olivia from. But what did it mean if someone from that world was already coming after her?

CHAPTER NINETEEN

Atlanta—Present Day

"This is going to be epic," Kyle crowed. Stuart beamed, and Richard leaned back in his seat, a peaceful expression on his face, his hands folded in front of him on the table. Olivia wished she could share their satisfaction with the final deal that had been struck with Bloom Communications, but her nerves were strung tight.

This will be over soon. Kyle will be gone, and life will calm down.

"I'm going straight to the dealership. There is a Lamborghini I want to order," Kyle continued, already mentally spending his new fortune.

Chris Keller had been extremely generous, and the purchase included large signing bonuses to each of the C-suite execs and most of the management level employees.

Olivia should be happy. So, why did it feel like the other shoe was about to drop?

One word.

Declan.

Olivia had seen the way Declan and Chris looked at each other at the gala. And how Declan's mood had instantly turned when they ran into each other the week before Christmas and she mentioned the board had voted. It was more than just professional rivalry. The competition between the two men was personal and had everything to do with Declan's desire to regain his family's business.

"What's wrong with you?" Kyle's sour expression appeared in front of her. "This is a time to celebrate, and you look like the miserable bitch you are." He leaned closer so that her nose was filled with his cologne, and she fought the urge to gag. "One of the best things about this deal is that I won't have to see your frigid ass at the office every day."

"Kyle. Come sit by me." Her former father-in-law called, and when Kyle turned to face his father, his features were arranged in a smile. Richard's eyes landed on her face, and Olivia forced her lips into a smile.

She hadn't hidden the truth from the older man for so many years to let him know now just what a monster he'd raised. What was the point?

Melissa, her receptionist, popped her head in the door of their third-floor conference room. "Bobby just texted from the first floor. They're in the elevator."

This was it.

Olivia nodded at the lawyers who were placing the packets of documents in front of each chair. Kyle's eyes gleamed, and Olivia took a deep breath, letting it out with a slow exhale.

Stuart patted her on the arm as he passed her to take his seat. "You did it, Olivia! It all worked out for the best."

She nodded, wishing she felt the same happiness and relief the rest of the people in the room were experiencing.

Relax, Olivia. All that's left are the signatures.

She discreetly shook out her hands and gave Melissa a nod. With a grin, her receptionist opened the doors wide, and a phalanx of Bloom Communications representatives strolled into view.

The look of triumph on Chris's face was undeniable, and it only made her nerves draw tighter. This deal was too good to be true. Neither of the bidders had pressed her about the valuation or asked for a demonstration of a prototype.

It didn't matter, Olivia assured herself. Her employees would keep their jobs instead of being laid off as Declan had proposed, and Richard could spend his final years fishing on the lake.

If Chris or his colleagues were surprised to see so many employees lining the walls, they didn't let it show. This was a big day for Armstrong, and several people had asked to be there to witness the transfer.

"It's lovely to see you again, Olivia." Chris smiled.

"You as well. I'm glad we could come to an agreement so easily."

Olivia took a seat next to Kyle at the end and scooted her chair slightly to the right so that she wouldn't risk brushing his arm.

Kyle was right about one thing. Not being forced to interact with him anymore was a definite perk of this deal.

She could finally, fully, move on. The weight on her chest eased.

The lawyers went through the terms one last time, and the standard mutual congratulations and symbolic back-slapping ensued.

"Olivia is owed the lion's share of the credit for where we are," Richard spoke up surprising her. "It was her vision and determination that brought XEROS into reality. We wouldn't all be sitting in this room together if it weren't for her. She will be an asset to Bloom Communications."

Olivia's heart swelled, and to her embarrassment, her eyes stung. Richard hadn't mentioned anyone else on the team individually. It was the closest she'd ever come to a paternal figure essentially saying they were proud of her.

Chris nodded. "Absolutely. I'm looking forward to working…" He paused and something flit in his eyes. "Very closely with Olivia."

Nerves started in her stomach. On the surface, his words were appropriate, and his expression was bland—so why were her alarms going off?

Olivia shook herself. She was being paranoid. Not every man had a hidden personality.

Kyle scowled. "Great. If we're all done telling Livvy what a precious unicorn she is—can we make it official? I've got a date with my dream car."

Chris reached for the pen laid by the side of his folder but dropped it when the conference doors flew open, hitting the walls with a bang.

"What the fuck?" Kyle yelped.

"This meeting is over." Declan, looking far too handsome, stood in the doorway, his impeccably-tailored suit accentuating his broad shoulders. She swallowed as a dark smile appeared, making him look exactly like the dangerous predator he was.

Declan's announcement had been for the room, but his eyes were only on Chris, who had stood abruptly at the interruption, his chair shooting backward.

"It's over, Declan. I won. There is no need for theatrics."

Olivia was paralyzed as the energy in the room shifted. The hostility between the men was so tangible she could imagine them pulling out broad swords and going to battle right there.

Declan took two long strides past Chris, completely dismissing him. The look of rage on Chris's face was frightening. Melissa, flanked by two large men, stood in the doorway wringing her hands,.

"I'm sorry, Olivia. They wouldn't listen. I told them you were in an important meeting..."

"It's all right, Melissa."

"Mr. Bloom this is hardly—"

"My apologies." Declan cut Richard off in a tone that made it obvious he wasn't sorry. "This meeting is over."

He turned a wintry smile to the Bloom Communications lawyers. "Lawrence, Paul. Armstrong Electronics is no longer for sale."

The men looked nervously between Declan and Chris, who stood, nostrils flared, chest heaving beneath his suit, looking as if he was going to attack at any second.

"Mr. Bloom... Declan... I understand the implication this has for you... but we have a deal in place. The majority shareholders have approved the terms—"

"Incorrect, Paul." Declan turned a wolfish smile on the man. "The majority shareholder of Armstrong Electronics is not interested in selling. Frankly..." His voice was full of silky threat, and the man visibly shrank. "I'm disappointed you didn't do a better job vetting the key stakeholders."

"What are you talking about? Of course, we want to sell!" Kyle shouted, but Stuart's brow wrinkled, and with a sick pit in her stomach, Olivia knew what was coming.

"It's too late." Chris took a step toward Declan, his hands curled into fists at his side. "I beat you. I know it's hard for you to accept since you've been handed everything your entire life but I've been ahead of you for every move. You lose." He came within inches of Declan, his eyes blazing with open hatred.

One of the men by Melissa took a step forward, but Declan lifted his hand without looking away from Chris, and the man stopped moving.

If she didn't know him so well, Olivia would have thought Declan was unmoved by Chris's words, but she saw the lines of his face twitch before a smile of savage satisfaction spread across his face.

"You will never win against me, Chris. Under normal circumstances, you wouldn't even be worth competing against. And let's be honest..." The smile widened. "This was hardly a competition."

"Say what you want," Chris spit, "I won. I'm buying this company, and there is *nothing* you can do about it."

Declan turned his back to Chris and addressed the rest of the room, his face inscrutable. "I have acquired the majority share of Armstrong Electronics."

"That's impossible," Kyle insisted, his face turning red. He gestured between Richard and himself. "Between my father, and myself, along with my aunt and cousin, *we* control the majority. It's *our* company."

Olivia felt sick.

She'd warned them, but she'd failed to make them understand.

Richard had lost his company, and it was her fault.

"No, you don't, Kyle." Olivia licked her lips and breathed past the boulder currently in her lungs. "Over the last few years, Armstrong sold off small amounts of shares to raise the capital necessary to expand our manufacturing and testing abilities. Twenty-six sales in two percent increments, to be exact. Fifty-two percent of the company."

Stuart blanched, and Kyle shook his head slowly, his face bewildered. "No. Dad..." His voice trailed off. Richard's face had grown pale, and he swayed in his seat, bringing Olivia to her feet.

"Get him a glass of water," she commanded Melissa.

"I'm fine," he waved his hand in the air, as he studied the two men squared off across the table. His eyes rose to Olivia's, and her heart clenched at what she saw. "Could he have bought them all? Is that even possible? Why wouldn't they tell me they were selling? My family..."

Olivia didn't know *how* Declan had secretly maneuvered all the small family stakeholders into selling him their shares, but she didn't doubt he was capable of it.

"It's entirely possible." She struggled to keep her face blank. Olivia could hear the concerned murmurs from the employees behind her. No matter how she might be falling apart inside, she couldn't let them see.

"But... But what does that mean for us?"

Olivia spared her ex-husband a glance. *Now* he asked questions? Up and down the table, the murmuring among the people at the table and other members of staff who had come to witness the signing grew louder.

"Prove it." Chris snapped.

"I've already sent the lawyers representing Armstrong copies of my shares and proofs of sale."

One lawyer pulled out his phone and began punching furiously at the screen. His quiet groan was almost lost under Declan's next sentence.

"But for now... I'd appreciate it if anyone not currently employed by Armstrong would get the fuck out of my conference room."

Chris's jaw worked, and for a second, his eyes went past Declan and then to Olivia, before glaring at Declan.

"This won't get you what you really want. I'm still the CEO," he hissed. "And I will *destroy* you before I see you in that seat again."

"Vincent," Declan called, and a man with a close-cut buzz and stocky build appeared in the doorway. Chris turned white. "You remember Vincent Menardi, my father's head of security, don't you, Chris? He and I have been having some illuminating conversations lately. The things I've learned..."

A dangerous light flashed across Declan's eyes, and his voice was hard when he addressed Chris. "Now that I know... I promise everything will be back as it should be. Very soon."

Chris's throat bobbed, but he reclaimed his composure. "Vincent is a disgruntled former employee. No one will believe anything he says."

Declan flicked an invisible thread off his crisp, white shirt cuffs and said, in a voice that lifted goosebumps on Olivia's arms, "Enjoy your life while you still have it."

"What?" Chris scoffed. "Are you going to have one of your goons shoot me? Here in the middle of a conference room."

For a few seconds, no one in the room breathed.

"Of course not." But before the room could exhale, Declan continued with such menace in his voice the air in the room crystallized with his icy words. "When the time comes, I fully intend on keeping that pleasure for myself."

The Bloom lawyers blanched, as Chris's eyes narrowed. But before the men actually came to blows, the lawyers were up and tugging on Chris's arm.

Chris suddenly relaxed his posture and rolled his shoulders before letting out a harsh bark of laughter. "Your arrogance will always be your downfall, Dec." He tugged at his lapels, straightening his jacket. "Gentlemen, ladies."

His eyes lingered on Olivia before he turned and strode from the room, leaving the Bloom Communications' entourage to hastily gather their belongings and hurry after him.

Declan turned to face the group, a harsh expression on his face. The crowd of bystanders watched wide-eyed, clearly unsure how this change of events would affect them. Nothing in his expression boded well for their future.

Bitter acid roiled in Olivia's stomach. What did it mean for all of them? The payouts and bonuses they'd all expected wouldn't be coming now. Declan didn't need to give them anything. He'd outmaneuvered them all, and she feared he would make good on his promise to dismantle the company.

He had no use for any of them. All he wanted was XEROS for his revenge.

Olivia's temples pulsed as her anger built. She had built this company as much as Richard, and she'd be damned if she sat back and watched Declan destroy everything she'd spent the last decade of her life devoted to.

But what can I do?

A woman, who Olivia recognized as Declan's—actually, she had no idea what Cecile's job title was—entered the room dressed in an immaculate blue dress. With an impassive face, she distributed folders to each person at the table before stepping back to stand with her back against the wall.

"I'm sure this comes as a surprise, but as you are all gathered here, it's the perfect opportunity to explain how things will be in the future."

Declan's gaze landed on her, and Olivia realized to her surprise she was still standing. She tried to read the expression in his violet eyes, but a wall had come down.

This man was a stranger.

"If you will be seated, we can begin."

Olivia didn't move.

"Be seated." His words lashed out, but she refused to break eye contact and slowly lifted one eyebrow.

Fuck him, if he thinks he's going to intimidate me.

Declan's expression softened a fraction. "Please."

Stuart tilted his head, his expression worried. "Olivia."

"Sit down," Kyle hissed, but Olivia felt as though her feet had been nailed to the ground.

Declan's mouth opened to say something else, but Kyle reached out and yanked her wrist, causing her to instinctively jerk back, freeing herself. "Sit down, Livvy." Kyle's eyes blazed at her, but he lowered his hand.

Acknowledging silently to herself that her stubbornness wouldn't help, Olivia finally moved, but when she lifted her gaze, she saw Declan watching Kyle with a terrifying expression.

"I've provided proof of my ownership," Declan began, as Olivia slid into her seat. "Now that I own a majority of the company out-right, it changes things."

"But the deal you offered is still good, right?" The desperation in Kyle's voice was obvious.

How had she not seen how truly stupid he was before she agreed to marry him?

Declan blinked at him. "There is no deal."

"But—" Stuart looked pale.

"This is your fault!" Kyle turned a furious face to Olivia, and she struggled not to react. "You told him about the shareholders," he accused. "You'd do anything to get back at me."

Richard put a hand on his son's back. "It's not Livvy's fault." His face was haggard.

Olivia stared at Declan. She had thought she understood who Declan was now—that there was some echo of the man she'd loved—but she saw clearly that she'd underestimated him and the danger he posed.

CHAPTER TWENTY

ATLANTA—PRESENT DAY

Declan hadn't missed the momentary fear in Olivia's expression when her ex-husband reached for her, before she quickly masked it. Several pieces came together in his mind forming a very ugly picture. Only a lifetime of control kept him from pulling out his gun.

But if what he suspected was true—Kyle Armstrong's days on earth were numbered.

"What does this mean?" Stuart asked. "For the company?"

Declan spared a glance at the balding man, but didn't answer. His gaze slid back to Olivia. Her color had returned to normal, but the look on her face was enough to cool the violence simmering inside him.

Olivia looked like she was planning a murder of her own. His, if the death glare she was giving him was any indication. For some reason, that made him want to smile. Her Grandma Rose would be proud.

"Are you going to dissolve my company?" Richard Armstrong asked in a quiet voice.

"Not entirely. However, there will be massive restructuring."

"You mean eliminating divisions," Olivia said.

Declan gave a small nod. Her eyes flashed fire at him as gasps filled the room. "Yes."

It wasn't the way he would have preferred to let the Armstrong Electronics employees know, but it was done now, and there was no point in dwelling on it.

He lifted a hand to silence the murmuring and exclamations that filled the room. "My team will work closely with the Armstrong leadership to determine where changes will be most effective. Generous severance packages will be given to anyone who is determined to be redundant."

"Redundant. I suppose that determination will be based on your educated analysis of a company you just discovered." Olivia's voice dripped with sarcasm, and pride flared in Declan's chest even as the other people on her side of the table widened their eyes.

She wasn't going to give up without a fight.

He was looking forward to it.

"First of all," Declan pinned her with a hard stare, but Olivia didn't wilt as so many typically did. Her chin tipped in challenge.

It might be the sexiest thing he'd ever seen, and he pressed his lips together to prevent the smile that threatened.

"I've had my eye on this company and XEROS for almost four years."

Olivia's lips parted slightly as she registered what he said. He'd known where she was years ago, and Declan saw the pain in her eyes before it was hidden again. Declan wanted to throw everyone out, and kiss those rosy lips. Tell her it would be okay... He cut the useless thought off at the root.

No one, not even Olivia, could know how he felt about her.

"Second," he continued. "I hope this board will work closely with me to adequately assess the *true* financial state of your operation." Declan saw the second the barb hit, and Richard shared a look with his son.

Olivia cocked her head. "Will you listen? Or is this a game you're playing to get rid of us with no fuss? Tell us what we want to hear, and then do whatever the fuck it is you have had planned this whole time?"

"Shut up. What is wrong with you?" Kyle snapped, and then turned to Declan with a chuckle. "I apologize for my wife. She's just surprised and spoke without thinking. You know how women are."

Blood thrummed in Declan's ears. How had he not known? He'd let Olivia down. Was the truth about their marriage in the dossier he had refused to read for his own selfish reasons? If it was, he would never forgive himself. He should have done a better job of making sure she was safe and happy even if it wasn't with him.

"Ex-wife."

Kyle blinked, confused. "What?"

"Olivia is your *ex*-wife."

Kyle's mouth rounded in an O, and then his expression turned cunning. His eyes raked over Olivia in a way that made Declan want to grab Kyle's tie and slam his face into the table repeatedly.

"I see." The man's insinuating tone made it clear to everyone in the room what he was implying.

Slashes of red appeared on Olivia's cheekbones.

"You see what?" Declan kept his tone even, but anyone with half a brain could sense the dangerous threat vibrating off him. A silent warning to back off and find cover before Declan ripped him apart.

Apparently, Declan had given the man too much credit because Kyle shrugged and then smirked. "I heard about you and Livvy in New York. You helped her back to her room, right?"

A couple of giggles sounded from the employees standing

along the wall, and Stuart stared at Olivia with such a hurt look that Declan filed it away as something to keep an eye on.

"Kyle," Olivia hissed.

"What? It all makes sense now. Did the two of you cook up this plan together? You told him about the minority shareholders. Did he pay you, or did you cut a deal to keep your job and screw over me and my family in the process."

"Enough." Richard rose to his feet, briefly resting his weight on his hands before pushing straight. "Olivia has worked hard for this company." He grimaced. "We all have. Are you keeping the current leadership in place?"

"No. Cecile will notify each of you over the next couple of days. After your interview, I'll make my decision."

"You want us to interview for jobs we already have?" Kyle looked stunned.

Declan ignored him. "Cecile, find a space in this building for us to work. I want to be settled by the end of the day at the latest."

"You're taking an office here?" Olivia sounded appalled.

Declan looked at her over his shoulder as he strode from the room. "Of course."

When the door opened thirty minutes later and everyone filed out, they seemed surprised to find him still there. Declan wasn't concerned about the dirty looks thrown his way or the panicked questions he'd heard through the walls. He'd faced far more dangerous adversaries than a disgruntled engineer.

He wasn't sure why he'd waited after dismissing Cecile, Vincent, and Brady's two men. Declan hadn't brought security with him because he genuinely believed he needed protection from Chris. He was more than capable of taking care of himself, but the show of power had been helpful. What had Chris called it? Theatrics? His former friend knew him well. Too well.

Everyone else had left, and only Olivia still lingered at the table while she typed on her phone. She was furious and worried, and even though Declan instinctively wanted to wrap his arms around her and soothe any concerns, their discord suited his purposes perfectly.

After Kyle's outburst, more eyes would be on them. Declan needed to tread carefully. He knew it was a mistake to wait for her, but apparently he couldn't help himself from creating an excuse to talk to her. To spend a few more minutes near her.

He leaned against the doorframe, watching until Olivia finally looked up, her lips were compressed into an angry line. Her eyes blazed sapphire with her fury as she strode toward him. But if she thought he was going to step aside, she'd forgotten who he was.

"We called several of the family members you bought shares from. You grossly overpaid for all of them."

Declan bit back a smile when Olivia crossed her arms across her chest. She was beautiful when she was angry.

"I did."

"Why?"

Declan lifted an eyebrow. "Because I could."

"Pfft. That's an asinine answer. This is some sort of sophomoric pissing contest with Chris Keller."

His name on her lips immediately dissolved Declan's good mood. He drew to his full height, towering over her, and Olivia tilted her head back to maintain eye contact.

"You don't care if you destroy my employees and their families?"

"Business is brutal."

"*Business.* Right. What about the Armstrong family members who still hold shares? A hostile takeover means they have to wait until you sell Armstrong Electronics to get their money. Not everyone has time for that."

Declan wondered why she cared so much. They weren't her family anymore, and from what he'd learned from her divorce decree, she hadn't been granted any of the shares Kyle possessed.

"That's up to them. When word gets out that a premium was paid for the other shares, it will boost the worth of their own—at least for a short period. If they're smart, they'll find a buyer."

"That doesn't help the employees who don't own stock but do rely on this job to pay their bills."

Her impassioned voice and flushed cheeks had his body at odds with his brain. Olivia was making valid points. Professional points. But all Declan's body cared about was getting his hands on her. Pushing her against the wall and taking her mouth.

Olivia's growl pulled him out of the fantasy, and she moved to stalk past him. Declan caught her hand, and he dipped his head close to her ear. He kept his voice low so only she would hear. "Maybe, I'm just not done with you yet."

CHAPTER TWENTY-ONE

ATLANTA—PRESENT DAY

Olivia fought against the intense heat Declan's words sent cascading through her. She resisted the urge to close her eyes and savor the way his warm breath, against the delicate skin of her ear, brought her body to life.

Calling on her anger, Olivia snatched her hand out of his and shoved at his immovable chest. "Don't pretend this has anything to do with me. You wanted this company for your own reasons, and we both know it."

"You have no idea what I want, or the lengths I'll go to get it." His eyes flicked to her mouth.

Her heart hammered as her body swayed toward him, betraying her. She had to get away from him before she did something really stupid—like beg him to kiss her.

"I think we both know no one gets everything they want."

Raw need flared in his face before it disappeared just as swiftly.

Olivia didn't understand the game he was playing, but if he wanted to play games she intended on winning. She lifted on her toes, bringing herself closer so that their lips were almost touching, and her breasts brushed against his lapel. Declan's breath hitched, and she bit her lip to keep from smiling.

"I'm going to fight you for every single one of my employees," she whispered.

Declan's chest moved against her breasts with every heavy breath, sending a bolt of electricity straight to her core. His eyes darkened to amethyst and Olivia was thankful for the layers of clothing that prevented him from feeling her nipples harden. For an agonizing moment, they stood pressed together before he stepped back. Then, almost as if he couldn't help himself, Declan tucked the hair that had fallen from her French twist behind her ear.

"I'm looking forward to it, Petal."

Olivia thought she did a good job hiding her trembling legs as she walked back to her office. Her body thrummed with frustrated arousal, the ache between her legs almost unbearable. Her plan to torment Declan had burned her just as much as it had him.

She didn't have time to dwell on it though as she made her way through the building. Every few feet, one or more concerned employees stopped her.

"My wife just had our baby." Denise from accounting twisted her hands in front of her, her eyes anxious. "We need my health insurance."

A few of the long-time employees had tears in their eyes.

"I'm too old to get a job somewhere else."

"My wife's salary alone won't cover our mortgage."

And the one that cut the deepest, "You are going to fix it, right, Olivia?"

She gave each one what she hoped was a reassuring smile,

even though she had little hope at the moment. Over and over, Olivia repeated the same phrases, "I'm going to do my absolute best," and "I'm sure the severance packages will be enough to cover any interim bills."

She'd make sure of it. Olivia wasn't sure how yet, but she wasn't going to let Declan destroy this company.

By the time she closed the door to her office, she felt like she was suffocating.

What if I can't fix it? What if because I agreed with the rest of the board to take the Bloom Communications offer, I doomed these families? What if...

The pressure in her chest grew painful, and nausea swirled in her stomach as her vision fuzzed. She pressed a damp palm hard against her chest, and tried to focus on her breath that was coming in short, fast bursts.

Not now, Olivia. Get it together. You don't have time for this.

She dropped into the black velvet office chair, slipped her heels off, and curled her toes into the carpet.

Breathe. Her burning lungs fought her.

After a few minutes, when she no longer thought she would hyperventilate, Olivia forced her eyes open and began the coping exercise her therapist had taught her to control the panic attacks.

Consciously using each of her senses she forced herself to concentrate: soft carpet under her toes, the silky material rubbing over her arms, the sound of her breathing, the wind picking up out the window, voices outside her office, her cellphone gripped in her hand, the chip in her red nail polish, the poinsettia in the corner.

The weight on her lungs eased a little as she brought the world around her into focus. A few more controlled breaths and she lowered her hand, grateful that she'd made it to the privacy of her office before the attack had gotten really bad.

Intellectually, Olivia knew there was nothing to be embarrassed about. She no longer saw Dr. Turner regularly, but the therapist had helped her understand that the panic attacks and anxiety-induced migraines came from years of living in a perpetual state of fight or flight in her home.

Olivia didn't have them for months at a time, but she didn't need to look far to see what had brought them back. The stress of the last few months had been extreme, and Olivia hadn't been eating or sleeping well. Add in Declan's reappearance...

Her heart finally slowed to a regular pace, and with a shaky exhale, Olivia slipped her shoes back on. Freaking out wouldn't solve anything.

Conversation buzzed outside her door and she knew everyone was worried, wondering if they were still employed. Olivia couldn't promise them anything yet, but she *could* make sure her numbers were bulletproof and do her best to advocate for them.

Would it be enough?

Over their last few interactions, there had been moments Olivia saw glimpses of the Declan she remembered: taking care of her in New York, teasing her in line at the liquor store... But it was almost as though those pieces had slipped out against his will, and the weakness angered him.

A knock sounded on her door, and Olivia sighed, lifting her hands off her keyboard.

Melissa stuck her head in the door, eyes wide. "Richard has left for the day."

Olivia frowned. Why was that something she needed to know? Richard rarely worked full days anymore.

Her receptionist bit her lip. "Um, Kyle is storming around screaming downstairs. What do you want me to do?"

Olivia stared at her for a second before making a decision. "Nothing. He's not my biggest problem right now." Melissa started to close the door, but Olivia called her back. "Can you send out an office wide memo for me?"

"DID YOU FUCK HIM?" Kyle snarled when she came out of the ladies' room late that afternoon.

"Go away." Olivia moved to brush past him in the hallway, but his hand clamped hard on her wrist, wrenching it up between them as he stepped into her space. She could smell the alcohol on his breath, and her stomach twisted. Kyle and liquor were never a good combination, and the knowledge that they were likely alone in the building, because she'd sent everyone home early, sent fear spiraling through her.

"Let go of me." Olivia tried to keep her voice firm, but it came out breathy and she hated herself for it.

After two years, why did he still have this effect on her? She had no problem standing up for herself with anyone else.

Instead of moving back, he used his grip to shove her backward, and her head bounced against the wall.

Kyle's eyes glittered. "I saw the way he looked at you. Did you fuck him in New York? Did you come up with this plan to screw me. Was that your plan all along?" Tiny bubbles formed at the corners of his mouth, and Olivia's throat closed.

His chest slammed hard into hers, pinning her to the wall, making it hard to breathe. As much as she wanted to be brave, her eyes slid away. "Kyle—"

"Tell me the truth!" He roared in her face, his body shaking like he might lose control.

This is not good.

"I was just as surprised as you were today." Olivia hated her mollifying tone, but she needed to get away from him. Sober Kyle was bad enough, he never did anything that left a mark. Drunk Kyle was a totally different story.

"Did. You. Fuck. Him." His eyes narrowed, and he pushed his face even closer, his hot breath on her face making her want to throw up.

"Of course not."

Kyle leaned his head back and stared into her face. Olivia held perfectly still, ashamed that he could still elicit this reaction from her.

He smirked. "You tried though, didn't you? I saw how you were staring at him during the gala. I saw how drunk you were. Stumbling up the stairs... You made a fool of yourself."

Olivia didn't defend herself. It would only make things worse. Kyle gave her arm a vicious twist before letting go and stepping back. Olivia let out her breath slowly, not wanting him to see how terrified she'd been.

"He rejected you, didn't he?" He gave her a quick once over. "Been there done that, right?" Kyle's laugh was cruel. "Jessica told me all about how that guy played you. Had you spreading your legs like a whore after you met him in a bar. Lied about who he was." He adopted a falsetto. "*Be nice to her, Kyle. This is hard for Livvy. She really had a thing for this guy, and he didn't even remember who she was.*"

Olivia felt the blood drain from her head and ice spread through her stomach.

Jessica told *him? Why?*

The betrayal sliced deep.

"You should see your face," Kyle snickered, thrilled by her pain. "You are *so* pathetic. Do you really think Declan Bloom would want a cold fish like you? He's a billionaire. He's probably had even more top shelf pussy than me. Good for him though that he figured out quicker than I did what a loser you are. Maybe we should compare notes."

Don't respond. Don't say anything.

When Kyle saw he wouldn't get the response he wanted, he feinted toward her, and when Olivia lifted her hands to protect her face, he laughed again. "You always thought you were so much better than me. So much smarter than me. Look at you now. What your parents always said is true. Your desperate need to be the center of attention is why you're so miserable—why you were such a failure as a wife and a woman. Pathetic," he spit.

Olivia swallowed hard, hoping the pain from each of his barbs lacerating her heart didn't show.

She knew her parents had never understood her. They hadn't even tried to hide their disappointment and disapproval when she told them about her divorce.

"Is your job really more important than your husband? I read that stress can cause infertility. Maybe you should take some time off. Kyle can provide for you. He loves you."

Olivia hadn't bothered to explain herself. She'd learned early on that any complaints she had about her marriage would always be turned back on to her.

She'd caught her parents looking at her sometimes like she was a changeling. Some alien species swapped in the crib for their sweet, biddable baby. Or, in her mother's view even worse... another version of her own mother.

Kyle jabbed a finger in her face, dragging her from her thoughts. "You better not do anything to fuck with my money, Livvy, or I promise you *will* be sorry."

Long after he was gone, and she'd locked her office door, Olivia sat at her desk and trembled.

CHAPTER TWENTY-TWO

ATLANTA—PRESENT DAY

The first interview of the day was with Richard Armstrong. It had been the man's company, and it seemed appropriate to start at the top and work down. Arriving at the building that morning, Declan kept his face turned forward, refusing to give in to his desire to search for even a glimpse of Olivia.

The need to see her burned inside him, but after the scene yesterday, he knew it would draw unwelcome attention if she were the first person he called for an interview. Declan forced himself to be patient.

The older man sank into a chair in the conference room where Declan had set up temporary operations. He received no pleasure taking this man's company from him, and because he knew how Olivia felt about him, Declan was prepared to be generous.

"As I'm sure you imagine, I don't need another CEO at this company."

"I figured."

"However, in a gesture of—let's call it good will for what

you've built—I'm prepared to offer you two-thirds of my original offer for your shares, in exchange for today being your last day."

Declan watched surprise skate across the man's eyes. It wasn't a secret the man was ill, his time on earth limited. Declan might be a bastard, but he wasn't *that* big of a bastard. Not to people who didn't deserve it, Declan amended in his head.

"Are you going to fire everyone right away?"

Declan shook his head. "No. The bones of this business are good, and some of the products in your development pipeline are interesting. It will take some time to fully assess the potential. However, you have bloated overhead, and you're over-leveraged. In order to make Armstrong Electronics attractive to future buyers, cuts will need to be made."

"The XEROS development required it."

"XEROS has been developed. You don't need all the research staff or technicians any longer."

Declan flipped through the pages in front of him until he found the one he wanted and slid it across the table. "The executive compensation and perks packages are ridiculous. Particularly based on what I can see regarding some of those executives' performances."

Richard scanned the page with a frown. "Those retreats were necessary for team building."

"But only the board went? Aren't you all family?"

"Ky—I thought it was a good idea. It's what all businesses do."

"The country club membership for your son? His shooting club membership? A brand-new Porsche as a company car?"

"It's important to network." The man didn't sound as if he believed what he was saying.

"What exactly does Kyle do here?"

"He's the vice-president."

Declan stared hard at the man. Nepotism was common, but

Declan couldn't find anything that weasel did to warrant his job title.

From what Brady had discovered over the last eighteen hours, Kyle spent most of his time either on the golf course or fucking his girlfriend in his office.

"He oversees... You aren't thinking of getting rid of him?" Richard looked shocked.

"Some of your C-suite will have to go. What are your thoughts on Stuart Pruitt?"

The older gentleman gave his feedback as Declan jotted his notes.

"And your CFO? Olivia Adler?" Declan looked up from the financial reports in front of him. "Some of the reporting is... creative."

"Olivia is not dishonest." Richard's voice was firm.

Declan had zero doubts about Olivia's honesty. He leaned back in his chair and rubbed a finger across his lip. He was curious. Olivia was smart. Too smart to have put the company at risk the way she had.

"It was her decision to fund the company by selling small blocks of stock to your extended family. Those sales ultimately put your company at risk for takeover. Olivia sold over fifty percent, which meant you and your immediate family lost your power."

Richard coughed and shifted in his chair. "That wasn't entirely her fault."

"Olivia is the CFO. Things like funding and ensuring a solid financial foundation are her responsibility."

Declan waited for the man to defend his former daughter-in-law. To advocate for her to keep her job the way he had for his son. He had yet to see why the man had inspired such loyalty from Olivia for all these years.

"Yes, but it was a group decision. We faced some obstacles in securing funding through traditional methods for our expansion. Olivia suggested approaching a venture capital group, but we've always been a family company. I wanted only family to own stock." His mouth twisted bitterly. "I guess I overestimated family loyalty."

"Olivia doesn't own stock."

The older man squared his shoulders. "No."

"Wasn't she married to your son until recently?"

"Yes, but she was never given stock in her own name. She never even took our last name, and then she chose to leave our family." The man glared at him. "I allowed her to stay in her position here because she is loyal to this company, even if not to my son." Self-righteousness rang in the man's tone, and Declan stilled.

Cecile seated next to him must have noticed, but other than a quick glance, she ignored it. For a moment Declan considered rescinding the offer to buy the sanctimonious bastard's shares. "As she is not a family member, would you object to her position being eliminated?"

Declan kept his face blank as emotions warred on Richard's face. "No, if it is between her and Kyle, I don't object."

Hurt for Olivia surged in him. Declan knew how excited Olivia had been about this job and how she felt about this man. Declan vowed she would never find out how easily Richard Armstrong had abandoned her.

Declan kept his disgust to himself, but when the door closed behind Richard, Cecile snorted. "What an asshole. That woman has essentially run this entire company for years." Cecile had read the same scouting reports he had. "And he *allowed* her to keep her job. Do you think he's an idiot or just a misogynist piece of shit?"

Declan arched a brow at her.

"Sorry," she grimaced. "It's unfair, and it pisses me off."

Declan closed the file folder in front of him and held out his hand for her to put a new one in it.

"Who's next?"

The meeting with Stuart Pruitt held no surprises. Declan assured him that, as the head of Research and Development, he would be kept on for the time being. However, unlike Richard, Pruitt defended Olivia... strongly.

"They forced her to do it," he said bluntly. "She was still married to Kyle, and Richard had just gotten his first diagnosis. Olivia is phenomenal at her job." He met their eyes. "But with the family dynamic component, she was put in a bad spot."

"If you were deciding who to keep from the board, would you choose Kyle or her—"

Stuart didn't wait for him to finish the question. "Without a doubt, Olivia. She works her ass off for this company. We wouldn't even have XEROS if it weren't for her."

Declan didn't like what he suspected was the man's infatuation with Olivia, but the fervent defense of his girl saved Stuart's job.

His girl. Fuck me. Pull yourself together.

When the door clicked shut behind the engineer, Declan drew in a deep breath. Kyle's interview was next, and Declan would need to keep his composure. The man's astonishing arrogance wouldn't make it easy.

It was clear from the moment Kyle Armstrong sat down, he viewed the questions as perfunctory, believing his position at the company was safe.

Declan had decided it was best if Cecile conducted the majority of the interview, not trusting himself or his temper. Every time he thought about the look on Olivia's face when this fucker grabbed for her, he wanted to destroy something. He sucked in another breath ignoring Cecile's curious look.

Kyle's answers were bland until Cecile began asking about the other executives.

Kyle shrugged. "Olivia is nothing special. I mean she's nice enough, but *forgettable* if you know what I mean." He sent a sly look at Declan that made the hair on the back of his neck lift and his pulse pick up. He had really hoped he'd get through this meeting without violence...

"You're recently divorced, so perhaps that wasn't a fair question," Cecile said, making a note.

Kyle made a face. "Not that recently, and we were separated for a year before that. I've already moved on. She does an okay job, but her position is mainly because of her connection to me."

Declan wanted to bury his fist in the man's smug face. Repeatedly.

Cecile adopted a surprised expression. "Stuart Pruitt had excellent things to say about her."

"That's because he's in love with her," Kyle scoffed. "He's been sniffing after her for years."

Cecile's face wrinkled with distaste, but Kyle didn't seem to notice. Declan could feel his anger approach the boiling point. This asshole had been lucky enough to be her husband, to have the chance at a life with her…

Declan forced himself to relax the clenched fist on his thigh.

"Don't get me wrong," Kyle leaned forward to rest his elbows on the table. "She's not bad to look at, but she's just," he trailed off and gave Declan a leer. "You know what I mean. Nothing special."

Cecile closed her notebook with an audible snap. "Okay, I think we've got everything we need."

A haze of red had taken over Declan's vision, and he was having to exert every ounce of self-control not to beat the man senseless.

Kyle slapped his palms down on the table and pushed his

chair back. “Great. My dad mentioned you were going to buy out our shares. When do you think I’ll get that check?”

“You aren’t getting anything.”

Kyle’s face fell. “What? But my dad said…”

“I will be buying your father’s shares, but I don’t need yours.” Declan kept his tone even. “Your services are terminated. You have one hour to clear out any personal belongings from your office. I’ll be moving in this afternoon.”

Declan could feel Cecile’s surprise next to him, but she was too professional to show it.

“You can’t be serious.”

When Declan continued to stare at him in silence, Kyle’s face turned an unhealthy shade of red. “Is this about Livvy? Is it because I know the truth about you and her?”

Olivia had told him? Declan had two options. He could pay the fucker off, or he could kill him. He knew which option he preferred.

“I have no idea what you are referring to.” Declan’s voice was deathly cold.

But Kyle showed more spine than he expected. “Oh, come on. I get that it’s probably a little awkward to run into a vacation fling after so many years. But there are no hard feelings that you slept with my ex.” Kyle chuckled, but his eyes were hard. “But I imagine it will be difficult for you to keep her on, right? Optics and all that.”

So, that was his game. Kyle was out, and he wanted to make sure Olivia was too.

Declan could sense Cecile’s growing anger, but she wisely kept her mouth shut.

“I’m not sure where you heard that story, but you are misinformed.”

Kyle raised his eyebrows mockingly, demonstrating his

complete lack of self-preservation instincts. "I don't think so. Of course, I'll keep my mouth shut provided you buy my shares."

Declan was seconds away from snapping him in half.

"I'm not paying you for your shares, and you should count yourself lucky that I don't decide to tear your entire life apart, piece by piece, for your pathetic attempt to threaten me." Declan stood, and Kyle's eyes bulged, only belatedly realizing his mistake.

"This isn't the end of this," he blustered, but he practically ran from the room.

"What a sleazeball," Cecile muttered. "Proves even smart women can get fooled by a pretty face."

Declan barely heard her. Seething with rage, his heart thundered in his chest. He needed to calm down, get his head on straight. He stretched his fingers from where he'd had them clenched on his leg.

Kyle was a liability. Who would he tell? Would the story get back to Chris?

He knew Cecile was waiting for him to comment on Kyle's accusations, but she also knew better than to question him directly.

"At least she came to her senses eventually," Cecile mused.

Declan grunted and snapped the folders in front of him shut. He made a show of looking at his watch. "Let's break for lunch and reconvene at two. We have two more senior executives this afternoon."

Only when the door shut behind her did Declan allow his eyes to slam shut, and he exhaled hard. He picked up his phone and placed a call. "I want a man on Kyle Armstrong. Where he goes, who he sees, what fucking brand deodorant he prefers."

Declan waited only long enough for Brady to answer in the affirmative before ending the call. He hesitated for a moment, and then quickly typed out another text. Feeling slightly calmer, he grabbed his keys.

It would be fine. He could keep her safe.

CHAPTER TWENTY-THREE

ATLANTA—PRESENT DAY

Olivia stared at the text message on her phone, reading it for the fifth time.

Unknown: meet me at Riverwalk Park in 20 min. D.

"Olivia," Stuart repeated. "Did you hear me?"

"Yes," she said absently. "Kyle is throwing a tantrum in his office."

Stuart frowned at her. "Are you okay? You're suddenly flushed."

"I'm fine. It's just stress."

His features relaxed. "I think you are going to be kept on. I explained to the Bloom Capital team how important you are, so I wouldn't worry about anything Kyle said."

Olivia supposed she should have expected it, but thinking of Kyle's accusations the night before, she was suddenly nauseous. "What did he say?"

Stuart sighed. "That's what I was trying to tell you. Sue heard him on the phone. They fired him. He has less than an hour to get out. He's down there screaming it's your fault and some other stuff, but it's not important."

His face turned red, and Olivia swallowed a groan.

Stuart's voice was a little gleeful when he added, "No compensation for his shares, either."

Her phone buzzed in her hand.

Unknown: A response is required. D.

"Thanks for letting me know, Stuart, and I really appreciate your support. Hopefully, between the two of us, we can salvage something." Olivia wiggled her phone in the air. "I forgot I have an appointment, but let's touch base at the end of the day, and I'll let you know what they say in my interview."

DECLAN SAT on top of a picnic table facing the river. His white shirt sleeves were rolled up despite the bitter afternoon, exposing his powerful forearms. He was so handsome he made her teeth ache.

He turned to watch her approach, and her steps slowed. Declan had on the hard, impervious mask he seemed to always wear, but she could see the tension in his eyes.

"What's wrong?"

He didn't bother to deny something was. "You told your ex-husband about Ireland."

Her stomach dropped. "I only ever told one person. My friend Jessica. Apparently, she told Kyle when she saw him at Christmas. They're cousins."

"You should have told me," he snapped.

"I only found out last night when Kyle confronted me about it."

A vein in Declan's neck pulsed, and his jaw turned to granite. "What did he do?"

Olivia kept her expression carefully neutral, resisting the urge to hold her wrist. Thankfully, it was winter and long sleeves easily covered the bruises. She wasn't interested in revisiting the moment, but Declan needed to know what he could be facing.

"I don't remember his exact words. Just that Jessica told him we had a fling a long time ago, and that you didn't remember me. He wanted to know if I had used our previous relationship to sabotage the deal."

Declan's shoulders squared, and his chest lifted in a controlled breath. "It's important that no one thinks you have any influence over me, or believes that week meant *anything*. You mean *nothing* to me. I don't know you."

The searing pain lancing through her took her breath away, and when he flinched, Olivia knew he'd heard her gasp. Declan's eyes widened for a brief moment, and she saw what looked suspiciously like grief cross his face before his mask snapped firmly back in place.

Her throat ached, and she stared past him at the rushing water, determined that he not see how his words devastated her.

Her chest cracked as his next words shriveled what was left of her heart. "I told you in New York it was just sex, a lifetime ago. It has no bearing on anything in my life now." His words were harsh, and she couldn't understand why he was being so deliberately hurtful.

"You tattooed me over your heart." Olivia wished the words back as soon as she said them.

His throat bobbed as he swallowed. "That was a drunken mistake made a long time ago. And I've already explained to you, it means nothing.

"You can believe what you want. Spin it into some kind of grand, romantic gesture if it makes you feel better." His head bowed for a moment, and the cold winter wind cut through her coat. "What do you want it to mean?" Declan rasped and lifted his head. "That I got a tattoo because I wanted to be with you, and the pain was unbearable because I couldn't… So, I found the one way I could keep you with me. By permanently carrying you on my body."

Olivia's eyes flashed to his, and she saw the truth and raw pain there before he could hide it. She shook her head. "I don't know why you are saying whatever you can to hurt me. If that week wasn't real, if it truly meant nothing, you wouldn't bother, Declan. You are working so hard to make me doubt what I know… for me to accept that I imagined the whole thing… It only reinforces what I *know* is true."

Her breathing evened out, and she welcomed the chill numbness taking over her body. Numb was always better than pain.

"You're right about one thing, though. Whatever it was, it's over. It's the past. But it *meant* something, and nothing you say…" Her voice was dull as the words trailed off.

Olivia was suddenly exhausted. She was tired of fighting. For too long, it felt like she was fighting on every front of her life, and she was tired. There were more important battles that needed her energy than this.

"I see you, Declan. No matter how much you wish I didn't. You can hate it all you want… But I *know* you."

"You don't know me," he practically shouted, shooting off the picnic table and taking the two steps that closed the distance between them. He grasped her shoulders lightly, his voice almost desperate. As though he was *willing* her to agree with him. "One week. It was only a week."

Olivia refused to look away. Later, she could marvel at why she didn't have the same reaction to him as she did to Kyle. But deep in her soul, she knew Declan would die before he physically hurt her.

Torment swirled in his violet gaze before he shuddered, appearing to shed the persona he'd been hiding behind. "Petal, I can't tell you why. Who I am… what I need to do… You aren't safe if you are connected to me."

"What does that mean?" she whispered. Declan let his forehead fall forward and rested it against hers.

She longed to put her arms around his waist and hold him close. Olivia didn't know what was going on, but whatever it was, it tortured him, and despite the way he had hurt her, she wanted to take his pain away. "You can trust me, you know that."

Declan pulled back an inch to meet her eyes before his hands lifted to cradle her face. "I know, but you shouldn't trust me. I'm not the man you think I am. In the office, we have to be strangers. Do you understand? You can't look at me the way you do."

Her spine stiffened. "I don't look at you any type of way."

His hands dropped from her face, and he put distance between them before saying matter-of-factly. "We are going to be working closely together over the next couple of months. You are good at your job, but if you can't keep it strictly professional, then it might be best if you give your notice now. You need to forget about what happened before."

His emotional whiplash was killing her. "All I care about is protecting the company I've built. There won't be a problem with us."

"Good." He shoved his shirt sleeves back down and reached for his suit jacket. Without another word, he strode away to the parking lot.

Olivia sank onto the picnic table, tears pricking at the corner of her eyes. It wasn't supposed to be like this. She wasn't sure which was worse, Declan not remembering her, or admitting he did, but still not choosing her. Her mouth filled with a metallic taste, and she realized she'd bitten the inside of her cheek until it bled.

Fine. Olivia stood, pressing her fingertips to catch the tears that threatened to fall.

It really was over.

CHAPTER TWENTY-FOUR

Atlanta—Present Day

The door to the conference room was open when Olivia stepped off the elevator. Cecile sat on Declan's left, her expression curious before she masked it. From the way everyone told her Kyle had raged as he was escorted out, Olivia was pretty sure most of the company assumed she was sleeping with Declan.

Olivia set her leather portfolio on the table in front of her. In the hours since she'd met Declan in the park, she'd locked away her emotions with steely resolve. This was now strictly business.

"What is your goal for Armstrong Electronics?" Olivia asked as she took her seat.

Cecile looked startled by Olivia's preemptive strike and sent a sidelong glance at Declan. Olivia ignored it. Only the man across the table interested her. The corner of his mouth lifted before it smoothed into professional blandness.

Silence descended over the table, but Olivia refused to blink first.

"We are—" Cecile's mouth snapped shut when Declan turned his stare on her.

"The purpose of these interviews and our activities over the next few weeks will be to assess the company's general health. After that, we will make the necessary decisions regarding the future of Armstrong."

"You must have a goal in mind," she said, archly. "Bloom Capital aggressively sought to gain control of us. Why would you do that if you didn't already have an end goal?"

"*Aggressively*?" Declan's brow quirked.

"You overpaid for the shares necessary to gain the majority. Almost twice what you initially offered, and you accomplished it in secret, over a span of a few days." Olivia's lips lifted, but there was no humor in her smile. "I'd say that qualifies as aggressive."

"I'd call it determined rather than aggressive." Declan paused. "You've never seen me aggressive."

Olivia hid the shiver the silky promise in his voice sent through her.

Strictly business, Olivia.

"Determined implies a goal, doesn't it?"

Cecile cleared her throat. Olivia suspected Cecile wasn't used to someone challenging Declan so openly. Particularly when they were supposed to be defending their job.

Good.

Declan stared at her, tension crackling in the air between them. She wasn't the only one who noticed. Declan didn't move, but Cecile shifted uncomfortably in her chair.

"I have many goals. None of which you currently need to be aware of. Now, if you've finished, perhaps we should begin."

"Of course," Cecile murmured, opening the file in front of her. "Ms. Adler."

"Please, call me Olivia."

"Not Livvy?"

She saw instantly that Declan hadn't meant to say it out loud. His eyes dropped from hers, and he tapped his pen on the table.

"I prefer Olivia."

"Olivia," Cecile continued. "You've been with Armstrong for twelve years. In that time, you've risen from project manager to CFO. Some of your colleagues credit you as responsible for the growth of the company over the last six. Specifically, the XEROS program."

Stuart.

"I certainly can't take all the credit. One of the wonderful things about Armstrong is we have so many long-term employees. They're *loyal*." She put an extra emphasis on the word. "I didn't develop XEROS. That credit belongs with Stuart and his team. He brought me a prospectus, and I saw future value in it. All I did was find the funding to put an infrastructure in place so XEROS reached its full potential."

"Your method of funding put the ownership of Armstrong in a precarious position, which ultimately led to where we are today. What was your basis for that decision?" Declan challenged.

"It's been suggested the decision wasn't one you favored, but one the board insisted on," Cecile added.

Olivia wasn't sure why the woman was trying to help her, but the dark glare Declan turned on Cecile made it clear he wasn't happy about it. Cecile didn't even flinch.

"It's true that it wasn't my first choice. However, at the time, we didn't have a prototype, and without one, the more traditional lenders wouldn't touch us. Without a significant influx of cash, Armstrong couldn't afford to acquire the space or equipment, nor hire the technicians we needed, to make a prototype. That was the fundamental basis of my decision."

"Why not approach a venture capitalist?" Declan asked.

Olivia saw in his eyes he already knew the answer. Was he looking to see if she would throw Richard under the bus? "A venture capitalist would have wanted a majority share for the amount of money we needed. The core Armstrong family would have lost control of their company. The board thought, by offering small amounts of shares to extended Armstrong family members, we could raise the money we required, without lessening the ownership position. There was a risk they would band together as a power play, but it was unlikely." *Until you.*

"Do you stand behind the decision?"

"I'm the CFO," Olivia's voice was firm, and she matched his cool stare. "It was my risk analysis that led to the decision, and I stand behind the information we had at the time."

It was an answer without being an answer. Pointing fingers now was a waste of time. Cecile gave a brief nod and wrote something on the paper in front of her.

Olivia curled her toes to keep from fidgeting and concentrated on keeping her hands relaxed in her lap. Seconds ticked by as Declan studied her. After almost a full minute of the standoff, Olivia's irritation got the better of her, and she lifted her chin slightly.

Declan's lips lifted in what looked like a genuine smile. "I'm looking forward to working with you, Olivia."

That's it?

"I'd like to talk about the other employees—"

He gave a slight shake of his head. "That's a subject for another day."

Olivia bit her lip to stop herself from arguing.

"I'll be taking over Kyle Armstrong's office." He glanced at Cecile. "Put Olivia down for Monday." His eyes returned to her. "Bring your current financials."

"You have them already."

He lifted a brow. "Not the creative ones."

Olivia could tell Declan thought he was going to catch her off guard with the request, but she had been working on the more detailed reports since the failed sale the day before. "Of course.

Would you like them today, so you have time to review them before our meeting?"

She bit the inside of her cheek to keep from smiling at the startled look on his face.

Declan might think he'd won, but he was wrong.

CHAPTER TWENTY-FIVE

ATLANTA—PRESENT DAY

Surprisingly, despite the numerous angry messages Olivia received from Jessica over the weekend, and her nerves over meeting with Declan on Monday, Olivia slept better over the weekend than she had in months.

The disastrous meeting with Jessica before Christmas, and her parents' unpleasantness when she'd cancelled plans the night of her headache, followed by the conversation with Declan in the park had flipped a switch in her. Olivia was done worrying about how other people felt about what she did. She had a job to do, and that was what she would focus on.

"How could you do this to us, Olivia?" Jessica's voice had vibrated with hurt when Olivia answered the phone Friday, after leaving her meeting with Declan and Cecile.

"I didn't do anything. I was blindsided, along with everyone else."

"Kyle says you knew, and that you had him fired because you are still upset about the divorce."

Olivia held on to her temper. "For the last time, I left Kyle because he is a horrible person. Full stop. He got himself fired because it took Declan two minutes to see Kyle is incompetent."

Jessica huffed an angry breath. "Right. It has *nothing* to do with your ex-boyfriend stealing the company from my family."

Olivia swallowed the bitter words that surged to the tip of her tongue. There was no point in arguing. "What is it you want me to say, Jessica?"

"He bought out Uncle Richard, but he won't buy Kyle's shares. What is he planning to do about mine and my mother's shares?"

"I honestly don't know. We have our first real meeting on Monday. I suspect, like most private equity firms, he's going to position Armstrong for sale."

"How can you be so cold? Don't you even care about what's happening?"

Olivia's tone was sharp. "Of course I care, Jessica. My entire *life* is this company. However, my most immediate concern is for the employees who depend on their paycheck every week, not someone who thought they held the golden ticket for something they never worked for. Find an outside buyer for your stock, Jessica. It's all you can do."

"You won't ask him to—"

"I have to go. Goodbye, Jessica."

Olivia wasn't sure if Jessica had reported their conversation back to Kyle, or if he was simply being vengeful, but he had clearly called her parents as part of his smear campaign. It was no surprise they took his side.

Waking up late after a good night's sleep, Olivia was making herself pancakes when her caller ID lit up with her parents' number. They called her so rarely, Olivia picked up instantly.

It was a mistake.

They must have clutched the phone between them to share because they both interjected their opinions, often speaking over each other.

"Is it true you *slept* with your new boss?" Her mother whispered the word.

"No."

"Kyle said—"

"Kyle is my ex-husband, and I'm your daughter. Why are you still talking to him?"

"You threw away your vows. That doesn't mean *we* have to kick him out of our lives. He was a part of our family."

Olivia snapped. *"I'm* a part of your family. I'm your *child,* but you always side with him."

"Don't speak to your mother like that," her father boomed.

"Olivia." Her mother was using her you're-having-a-temper-tantrum voice. "You've always been stubborn, and you like to get your own way. Have you considered how your actions have hurt the people around you? I'm not sure you ever gave your marriage a chance. A husband needs—"

She'd heard it too many times before. "I don't have a husband."

"Who's fault is that?" her father snapped.

Olivia bit her tongue. "Fun chat. Let's do it again in a few months, like usual."

She didn't feel an iota of guilt when she hung up on her parents and powered her phone off for the rest of the weekend.

Olivia was surprised to find Declan alone on Monday when she joined him in his office. Part of her hoped Cecile or another member of his team would be there to serve as a buffer. Olivia rolled her shoulders back. Not a problem. She could take whatever Declan threw at her.

"Olivia." Declan greeted her with an extended arm, inviting

her to sit in one of the chairs facing the desk. Her stomach flipped as her eyes skated over his face.

God he is beautiful.

"I got the reports you sent. They are..." His eyes scanned down the papers in front of him. "Detailed."

"If we are going to find things to cut, you need the complete picture. There are a lot of expenditures that are unnecessary."

Olivia's plan was to cut as much non-personnel overhead as she could, wherever she could, in order to protect jobs.

A long finger rubbed his lower lip, and Olivia caught herself following the motion while he read. Biting the inside of her cheek was a quick, painful reminder to ignore how he made her body feel. Olivia opened her portfolio and extended the file she'd brought with her. "I have a list of suggestions for what would be easiest to eliminate."

Declan's gaze rose from the file he was reading to the file in her hand. His eyebrows lifted, and Olivia swore he was trying not to smile as he took it from her hand. She recognized the expression. It was the way his eyes lit up right before he laughed.

Olivia hardened her heart.

"You came prepared."

"Always." She kept her voice flat.

A mischievous expression stole across his face. "I shouldn't be surprised since you're such an overachiever."

Olivia willed herself not to respond, and after a moment, his expression grew resigned. If Declan thought he could use her feelings to gain an advantage over her by evoking that memory, he was mistaken. She wasn't a twenty-two-year-old anymore, and he wasn't the man she'd shared that confidence with.

His teeth caught the corner of his lower lip and sucked it in as his eyes ran down the page, lines appearing between his brows. Olivia dug her nails into her palms to keep her face impassive as her pulse picked up speed.

Stop staring at his mouth.

"I have questions." The furrows between his brows deepened.

She bet he did. In the paperwork provided to their potential buyers, Olivia had done her best to bury various accounts the Armstrong family used to write off personal expenses. Instead of breaking them out into itemized accounts, she'd put most of them under general operating expenses.

Declan used his pen to point at one of the lines and then frowned and tapped another one.

"On the summary report given to the buyers were the umbrella terms we flowed various expenses through. Expenses Kyle and his father deemed *important* for business. I've broken down the categories on today's report," she explained.

Declan read the list aloud, shaking his head in disbelief. When he got to the end, his eyes met hers, and Olivia grit her teeth. He didn't understand the pressure she'd been under. Declan lifted the paper in the air, his expression making it clear he thought she'd lost her mind.

"Are you telling me you've written off his various social and club memberships, as well as season tickets to all the Atlanta teams, dinners, trips..." An astonished laugh escaped.

"Yes." Olivia gave him a curt nod.

Declan drew an X over the entire section. "Well, this is easier than I thought it was going to be. Any more of your ex-husband's personal bills I should know about? Another family and kids somewhere? A mistress or two?"

Olivia sucked in a harsh breath, and Declan's eyes widened.

"I didn't mean..."

"This list is comprehensive of the easy expenses we can safely dispense with." Her voice could have frozen a volcano, and Olivia intentionally kept her language formal.

"Olivia—"

"If you will sign this..." She interrupted him, extending

another piece of paper. "I will stop payments on these memberships today."

Declan stared at her for a minute, his eyes troubled. Olivia pinched the paper harder, making sure her hand didn't tremble. Heaving a sigh, Declan took the paper, and after a quick perusal, scrawled his signature across the bottom.

"Hopefully, these savings will safeguard at least a few positions."

Declan inclined his head. "It's definitely a start."

"People are worried," Olivia pressed. "If we offer them some assurance…"

"There won't be any layoffs for at least thirty days."

Hope flared in her chest, but Declan's next words snuffed it out. "However, they *will* come. Those on the XEROS team, in fabrication, design, and support, should start circulating their resumes. They will most likely be the first to go."

Olivia's eyes narrowed. "That's almost fifty people. You need them."

Declan twirled his pen between his fingers. "XEROS will be manufactured at a company I own in Ireland. The tax benefits make it a more attractive option."

Olivia's lips parted in shock. She knew he would try to lean the company down to make it attractive to a buyer, but to hear the dismantlement would start so soon was disheartening.

"Declan, there must be—"

"A companywide memorandum will go out today. Those who choose to leave now will be offered a more generous package than those who wait until it becomes necessary to eliminate their position. Though everyone will be offered something." Declan's expression softened the tiniest amount. "I'm not trying to ruin people's lives. This is business."

Frustration and anger had her shaking as Olivia pushed to her feet. "You said I have thirty days to change your mind."

Declan let out a long exhale through his nose. "That's not what I said."

"It's what I heard." With that parting shot, Olivia turned on her heel and stalked to the door.

"Olivia." Declan's voice stopped her at the door. "Thanks for…" He held up the paper files she had delivered to him, and despite herself, her cheeks heated.

"What's this?" A worn, thin paperback dropped on her stomach. Olivia set her e-reader on the bed next to her and picked up the thin volume. "This is the book you just finished?" Her eyes lifted to his.

"You said you hadn't read it." Declan shrugged.

"I'm not sure I took you for a physical book kind of guy." Declan lifted his eyebrows. "You strike me as more of a techie." Olivia lifted her device and wiggled it in the air.

Declan dropped onto the bed next to her. "Nah. I'll always prefer the analog route when it comes to reading."

"Really? Why?"

He shrugged. "I pay more attention if I'm touching it." He gave her a sly smile as he ran a finger down her bare arm, drawing goosebumps.

Olivia wanted to snap that she hadn't given him paper copies on purpose… but she had. Now, she was furious with herself.

A young man appeared in the doorway, his eyes going from Olivia to Declan.

"I'm sorry to interrupt, but you have a phone call."

Olivia watched irritation wash over Declan's expression. "Not now, Todd."

"I'm sorry. She is insistent."

Declan's lips turned down. "My sister?"

"It's Fiona Carrol."

Olivia's stomach twisted unpleasantly.

Declan is marrying another woman.

I'm just someone from his past who temporarily works for him.

She needed to remember that. And, she told herself, the pressure in her chest had nothing to do with jealousy.

Liar.

CHAPTER TWENTY-SIX

ATLANTA–PRESENT DAY

Declan knew he shouldn't look forward to his meeting with Olivia as much as he was. If he were smart, Declan would leave someone else in charge here and go back to New York.

It was only because Chris was still lurking around, he told himself. Declan hadn't been happy to learn, that instead of packing up and returning to New York, Chris had leased a condo in Atlanta. His instincts told him Chris wasn't done fighting, and with Olivia's ex running his mouth, Declan couldn't leave Atlanta until he knew she was safe from Chris.

Olivia had kept a perfectly professional demeaner during their meeting, which shouldn't have bothered him—wasn't that exactly what he wanted? Yet, he couldn't resist the urge to provoke her, to make her smile at him the way she used to. Now, Olivia was leaving even angrier than when she'd arrived.

The door opened, and his assistant stuck his head in, surprised to find Olivia standing close to the door. "I'm sorry to interrupt, but you have a phone call."

"Not now, Todd."

The young man cleared his throat. "I'm sorry. She is insistent."

Declan's lips deepened into a frown. "My sister?"

"It's Fiona Carrol."

Olivia's shoulders stiffened, and Declan cursed silently, knowing she'd recognized the name.

"Sounds important." Olivia clutched her portfolio to her chest and slipped past his assistant.

Declan wanted to stop her, to find a legitimate reason to keep her there. There wasn't one.

He waved an angry hand dismissively at Todd, who closed the door behind him. Declan settled himself at the desk, taking a moment to rein in his annoyance. Olivia angry with him was a good thing, he reminded himself.

"You must be busy," Fiona complained when he finally picked up the handset. "You aren't answering your cell phone, and I've been trying to reach you."

"I am."

There was a pause. Normally, he would attempt to be at least a little friendly, but right now Declan struggled with being civil.

"I'm so sorry to interrupt you," she said icily.

Declan swallowed his distaste. The tentative agreement he had come to with Alan Carrol hadn't bothered him before. Now, seeing Olivia again… The concept of tying his life to Fiona left a bitter taste in his mouth.

Declan pushed the thought away. It didn't matter how he felt about it. Without her father's support, it would be exponentially harder to secure the votes he needed to become CEO again.

"Did you need something?"

"Can't I call because I miss you?"

"You never have before."

Fiona chuckled. "That's true." Another pause. "I didn't realize you were planning on staying in Atlanta for so long. My father assumed you would be back by now. Wasn't your meeting last week?"

Declan knew there had been talk in certain circles. Those who witnessed him carrying Olivia out of the gala hadn't hesitated to share the gossip. However, since Declan didn't know how to explain his behavior that night, even to himself, he wouldn't bother to try.

"It's an unusual situation. This company is going to require a bit more of a hands-on treatment than I expected." An image of his hands on Olivia's silky skin flashed in his mind, and he inwardly cursed his unfortunate choice of words.

"Mm." Fiona wasn't interested in what Declan did professionally. The concept... the power he wielded... Yes... What it entailed... No.

Declan's thoughts drifted, and he tuned out Fiona's voice.

Olivia understood what he did. They spoke the same language, and he loved that she wasn't afraid to challenge him.

"I've arranged for dinner this Saturday with Tracy and Tomas." Fiona's voice came back to him at full volume, pulling him from his thoughts.

"What?"

"Tracy recommended Inferno," Fiona continued without pause. "She and Tomas have been there before."

Declan's brain scrambled to play catchup. *Who the fuck were Tracy and Tomas?* Declan mentally ran back over what Fiona had said.

"Tomas doesn't have a game this weekend, so we don't need to worry about his curfew."

Declan's mind finally supplied the information. Tomas Davros was a professional hockey player, who played for Atlanta's new franchise team, and Tracy, his wife, had been in school with Fiona.

Declan had zero interest in having dinner with two strangers, but he focused on the only important bit of information. "You're coming to Atlanta?"

Silence.

"Yes." Fiona's words had a distinct bite to them. "Have you heard a word I've said? I'm coming for Tracy's baby shower."

The muscles in his neck eased. Fiona wasn't coming for him. Declan supposed the least he could do was spare a night to keep her father happy. "Saturday night."

"My father said you've leased a condo."

The comment sent up a red flag inside him. "Did he?"

He hadn't yet, but he *had* contacted a real estate agent.

Fiona's father was an investor in Bloom Capital, but not someone who was involved with operations. There was no reason he should know that Declan was still in Atlanta. Which meant Alan was having him watched, and that pissed Declan off.

Ever since his father's murder, the sharks had circled. Waiting for the misstep that would take Declan down and leave an opening for someone else. His jaw clenched. Fiona's next question didn't help his mood.

"How long are you planning on being there?"

Declan didn't answer. Their relationship wasn't one where Fiona should feel comfortable asking Declan something like that. In fact, they barely knew each other despite Fiona's efforts to make them appear like a couple.

"I know you have that shareholder meeting coming up… Things need to be settled before then."

She trailed off and Declan's irritation grew. If Fiona imagined she could blackmail him into giving her a ring, she was dead wrong.

"Let my assistant know what time and where dinner is."

Fiona hesitated before she spoke again. "Everyone is talking about what you did with that drunk woman at the gala, Declan. I was able to spin it that you felt responsible for her because you wanted to buy her company. That she's just a nobody who drank too much, but you need to be more careful. Appearances are everything in our world."

Declan's blood boiled. "You did what?" He didn't bother to hide the anger from his voice.

Fiona didn't back down. "You and I have reputations to protect, and you making a fool out of both of us is unacceptable. We are getting married." Her voice suddenly lightened. "We will be very happy together, as long as you don't push me. I don't care if you fuck a dozen, drunk sluts before we're married. But after... If you touch another woman, I *will* do something about it."

The rumors Luke shared with him flashed in Declan's brain, and rage swept through him. "I'm sure you aren't stupid enough to threaten me, Fiona. You won't like the result."

Fiona laughed. "Don't underestimate me, Declan. I may not be able to get to you, but I promise I'll ruin anyone who touches what's mine. See you Saturday," she trilled, and then hung up.

As much as Declan wanted to blast the woman, he couldn't. Not while he still relied on her father's votes. Declan sat for a minute trying to calm his breathing, but the more he replayed the conversation in his head, the angrier he became.

She was threatening Olivia. Maybe not directly, but it was clear she knew something was going on. And if she did... who else?

CHAPTER TWENTY-SEVEN

ATLANTA—PRESENT DAY

The halls were quiet as Olivia made her way to Declan's office, her nerves already jumping beneath her skin. The last week had proven to be her own personal blend of heaven and hell.

Over the past several days, she and Declan had two more meetings, and both times, Cecile was there. As hard as Olivia tried to stay impervious to Declan, the magnetic pull, that had existed between them from the moment they met, drew her. Olivia couldn't stop thinking about him, and that was a problem.

Once the memo about severance packages had gone out, many employees grabbed the opportunity. Olivia admitted it was a generous package. More generous than it needed to be, which only furthered her confusion over Declan.

The hard, dangerous man she'd watched battle Chris Keller in the conference room was hard to reconcile with the man who made sure her employees weren't left empty-handed. Declan wasn't soft by any means, but he also wasn't the monster she needed him to be in order to protect her heart.

Olivia had witnessed Declan be harsh and exacting, but she'd yet to see where he wasn't fair. Most importantly, he didn't automatically dismiss her ideas out of hand as she had expected.

She had been shocked when Declan agreed to implement an invoice tracking and accounting software system she'd been trying to convince Richard to buy for years. Olivia thought he would balk at the expenditure for a company he planned to sell, but after listening to her argument, he'd simply asked a few questions. Apparently she answered them to his satisfaction, because he turned to Cecile and instructed her to take care of it.

"Why do you look so surprised?" Declan asked, his enigmatic eyes on hers.

Olivia licked her lips, her eyes following Cecile as she left the room. "I didn't think you'd be interested in spending money on improvements."

"You made good points."

Olivia was flummoxed. She wasn't used to decisions being made so easily. Typically, she argued for months, if not years, to get anything substantially changed. Richard was stuck in his ways, and his favorite answer was, "but this is how I've always done it."

"Thank you."

Declan smiled, and her heart stuttered at how it transformed his face. "You don't have to thank me, Olivia. It is a sound recommendation that adds value to the company."

Warmth spread through her chest, and she smiled back at him before collecting her things. Olivia almost wished Declan would fight with her, so she could keep her focus on the company. To her dismay, Olivia realized that she looked forward to their meetings and enjoyed working with him.

She was going to end up with a broken heart all over again.

Earlier that day, Declan found her in the small second-floor kitchen. Olivia had just prepared her midmorning cup of tea when Declan materialized in the doorway. Stuart, animatedly updating her on his team's breakthrough on a design, was oblivious to Declan's arrival. But Olivia was aware immediately. She always was.

"So, this is where all the good snacks are," Declan observed.

Stuart's eyes widened, almost as if he couldn't reconcile Declan in their tiny employee kitchen. Olivia didn't blame him.

Declan sucked the air out of the room.

Dressed in a suit that cost more than her mortgage payment, Declan strolled toward the counter, inspecting the various glass jars full of snacks. He lifted the lid off one and pulled out a pack of cookies.

"This is a nice perk," he said, tearing open the plastic wrapper with his teeth. "Is this something you've always done?"

Olivia's eyes followed the action, and she swallowed hard as heat flowed down her spine to settle between her legs. She dropped her gaze to the teacup to hide her reaction, but not before she caught the glint in Declan's eyes. He knew exactly what he was doing to her.

"That's all Olivia," Stuart enthused. "She always makes sure there are treats in here for all the employees."

Declan glanced over at the rest of the selection. "What are these pink ones?" Declan plucked a package of candy out of a different container.

Stuart's nose wrinkled. "Those are pure sugar. Too sweet for me."

Olivia choked on her tea, watching in fascinated horror as Declan placed the small candy on his tongue. When he gave a small hum of pleasure, the sharp ache between her thighs intensified, and her breasts tingled. Olivia abruptly turned away, her face flaming.

"Pink is definitely my new favorite color."

He was trying to kill her.

"The pink ones are definitely my favorite," Declan said in a low voice, and she held in a gasp as he repeated the words in her head.

Was he remembering too? Had he said it on purpose?

Stuart made a comment about Declan's sweet tooth, but Olivia had no idea what he actually said. She was too busy holding on to her composure and not melting into a puddle.

Slowly, Olivia turned back. Declan's heated gaze met hers, and her heart beat in a slow, heavy rhythm, matching the need pulsing in her core. She couldn't tear her eyes away.

Stuart walked toward the counter to top off his coffee. "Did you want some coffee, or are you a tea drinker like Olivia?"

Declan's gaze dropped to her cup and then flew back up to catch hers. Air locked in her throat at his expression.

"Very pretty. Is that a flower?" Declan's voice was husky.

Stuart grinned, not picking up on the buzzing energy suddenly filling the room. "Isn't it pretty? It's your favorite, right, Olivia? Or at least it's the one she brings in the most often." He chuckled. "She has an entire collection of them—rotates which ones she brings in."

Shut up, Stuart.

A muscle in Declan's cheek fluttered, but Stuart continued. "I really like the one with the hibiscus flowers she got in Hawaii." Stuart watched Declan expectantly.

"It's lovely." Declan's voice was bland, but his eyes burned into hers, sending her temperature skyrocketing.

"I always thou—"

"Stuart," Olivia's said, sharper than she'd intended.

Color-tinged Stuart's cheekbones. "Right. I better get back. I'll send you a summary of what we talked about, Olivia." He darted a quick peek at Declan. "Hopefully, it will help."

"He's in love with you." Declan glanced at the door where Stuart had disappeared.

"Don't be ridiculous, we're friends. He's worried I'm going to get fired. I think he's trying to humanize me."

Declan's eyes touched again on the cup he had given her before saying, "I need to push our meeting until this evening, if that's all right."

Olivia hoped the slight tremble in her hand wasn't obvious as she lifted the teacup to her mouth. "Of course."

Get a grip, Olivia! Control yourself.

"Is seven o'clock too late?" Declan hesitated, the look in his eyes making it clear he wanted to say something else but was holding back.

Olivia roughly cleared her throat, breaking the intense moment, and made a beeline for the door. "Great. See you at seven."

Was she a coward? Yes. Was she also in danger of spontaneous lust-fueled combustion? Also, yes.

HOURS LATER, as she made her way to Declan's office through the darkened hallways, Olivia wanted to kick herself. She shouldn't have agreed to this meeting alone.

It will be fine, Olivia. Just do your job.

Olivia had brought Stuart's report with her, hoping that if Declan saw there were other possibilities for Armstrong Electronics, he might hold on to the XEROS team to use for further development.

His outer office was dark, but the overhead lights in Declan's were on.

See, nothing romantic. Nothing intimate.

Olivia stopped in the doorway, mesmerized by the scene in front of her. Declan sat on Kyle's black leather sofa with his knees spread and elbows resting on powerful thighs. Dark curls had fallen over his forehead, and his hair was rumpled as though he'd been running his fingers through it. Open takeout boxes littered the granite table in front of him, surrounded by stacks of paper. Declan's brow furrowed as he read a piece of paper in one hand.

He'd removed his suit jacket, and her mouth went dry at the defined muscles his tailored white dress shirt did nothing to hide. His sleeves were rolled to his elbows, revealing powerful fore-arms, and when he reached for another paper on the table, his shirt pulled tight across his flat stomach.

Cruel and unusual punishment, she thought, as an intense wave of heat swept over her. Olivia squeezed her thighs together against the ache at her core, resisting the urge to fan herself. Being physically close to him this week had wreaked havoc on her nervous system. Declan was overly careful not to touch her, but more than once she'd caught him watching with a hungry expression on his face that sent her hormones into overdrive.

"Hey," Olivia said from the doorway, and Declan's gaze rose to hers, a swift smile covering his face before he caught himself.

"I got us some food." He gestured to the containers on the table. "I thought we'd eat while we work."

That smile. Olivia's heart lurched.

Forty-five minutes later, her feelings for Declan were decid-edly different.

Declan's expression was grim as he shook his head and frowned at the report. "I'm sorry, Olivia. I don't see any way around it. We need to cut the entire division."

"That's fifty families." After sitting next to Declan on the sofa, her patience and nerves were on their last legs. One hand was balled into a fist next to her, and Olivia was irritable and unset-tled. Her skin felt like it had shrunk over her body, and she was acutely aware of Declan's powerful presence and raw masculinity inches away.

Why does he have to be so stubborn?

Declan's bicep flexed under his shirt as he ran a hand through his hair. Olivia tried not to squirm.

"It doesn't make sense to keep it. There isn't another design that is close enough to needing a prototype. They are essentially sitting there, doing nothing."

"Stuart's progress report said they'd be ready to start on a prototype by early March."

"He says that, but being realistic, it could take longer." Declan's eyes were sympathetic, which for some reason made her angry. "Best case is at least two months. That's too long."

The subtext of what he was saying hit her. "You're planning on selling before two months."

It wasn't a question, but the answer was written all over Declan's face. "I said no one before thirty days. I never promised anything beyond that."

Her brain scrambled. It's too soon, a voice screamed in the back of her mind. But was her gut reaction because she was losing the company or Declan?

"What if you didn't sell?" Olivia blurted out.

Declan sighed, and something unidentifiable crossed his face. "Olivia, I wish—"

"What if we manufactured XEROS ourselves? That's all you really want out of m… us. What if I can make the case that it's more beneficial to manufacture XEROS in-house?"

Declan's eyes met hers. The violet depths clouded with resignation and regret. Olivia pressed her lips together in a tight line, hoping it would hold off the panic growing inside her.

It will all be gone in less than two months.

He shifted to face her on the sofa, and Olivia glared down at the reports on the table, refusing to look at him. A hint of his cologne wafted over her, and Olivia suddenly wanted to cry.

There has to be a way.

Olivia knew the moment Declan stormed into the room last week that this was coming. The company would be gone. *He* would be gone again.

“Olivia,” Declan murmured, his voice soft yet insistent. “Olivia.” He repeated her name, this time with more command gently turning her jaw toward him with his pointer finger.

Sparks traveled from his fingertips through her body even after he lowered his hand. Olivia inhaled a slow breath through her nose and raised her gaze to meet his. Her heart lurched at the understanding she saw there.

The brave face she'd maintained for the last few years faltered. “I can't let them down. Everyone is counting on me. If I hadn't allowed us to get into this position, we could have manufactured XEROS ourselves. I should have made Richard listen to reason, reined in Kyle...”

Olivia trailed off, years of frustration roaring to the forefront of her brain. “I shouldn't have tried to scale so quickly. We didn't have the infrastructure in place, but I was convinced I would eventually make them see... but they were...”

“Idiots.”

“I was going to say stubborn.” Olivia rubbed a hand over her forehead, a dull headache starting behind her eyes. “The reality is, *I* let this business get over-leveraged, followed by a hostile takeover, and now hundreds of families will lose their income.” Olivia hated that her voice cracked on the last word.

Declan scooted closer, until his thigh pressed against the side of hers, the heat of it searing through her skirt. “This isn't all on you. You were one vote. I've seen how this company was organized. Even though there is a nominal board, it was essentially completely under Richard's control.”

Mortified, Olivia felt tears prick at the corners of her eyes. She would *not* cry.

“One of the first things we did was scrub the computers. I've seen all the emails… the projections, your proposals… all things that might have saved this company if Richard had listened to you. Not to mention, you were basically saddled with doing the job of COO as well. I have yet to see anything Kyle accomplished other than spending money. This is business. Sometimes it doesn't end the way you want."

"This isn't just business to me. I've given *everything* to this company."

Declan wrapped an arm around her shoulders, and she curled instinctively into his side.

"Olivia," he breathed. His free arm wrapped around her, a large hand splayed across her back.

Olivia didn't know how long they sat like that— Declan cuddling her against him. She didn't want to think about how unprofessional it was, or how embarrassed she would be when it was over. She simply accepted the comfort he offered. Olivia closed her eyes, and let her head relax against his strong chest.

Just for a minute, she would let herself pretend—that they were still Declan and Rose, and her heart was safe with him.

Lips brushed the top of her head, and Olivia burrowed deeper as his fingers gently stroked down her hair.

"I know how business works," she finally acknowledged. "I just can't believe after everything, I failed them."

"Ah, Petal," Declan whispered, his cheek pressed hard against her hair. "I understand. More than anyone."

Declan pulled back to gaze at her then, and a couple of the tears she'd kept at bay slipped down her cheeks. His lips caught one and kissed its trail back to the corner of her eye. Olivia's breath caught.

"You've worked so hard," he said against her temple. "This isn't your fault."

Olivia's eyes fluttered closed at the sensation of his lips on her skin, but it was her own gasp, as his lips found the spot beneath her ear, that brought her back to her senses.

What am I doing?

Olivia pushed Declan away, and practically jumped to her feet. "Manipulating me by being nice won't make me stop fighting for my company."

Olivia knew she wasn't angry with him, but it was easier to hide behind that emotion, than admit how she really felt.

"You show up and ruin people's lives. People I care about. And you think, with a few sweet words and kisses, you can make me give up?" Her chest heaved as she glared down at Declan, her heart pounding with more than anger.

Declan pushed to his feet, muscles tight, standing so close she could feel the heat rolling off him. "You think I kissed you because I was trying to manipulate you?"

Olivia folded her arms tight across her chest, her pulse skittering frantically. "You're the one who accused me of not being able to stay professional. So, what was that?"

Declan's eyes glittered, his nostrils flared. His battle for control played out over his features, and she couldn't resist jabbing him again. "You made it abundantly clear that what we had is over. You don't get to play these games with me."

Declan's hand shot out to catch her wrist, yanking her against his chest. Violet eyes flashing, he crushed his lips to hers, his tongue sweeping into her mouth. A guttural groan vibrated through him as he buried his hand in her hair. Olivia arched her back, and Declan's hand flexed on her hip before sliding lower, curving over her ass.

Olivia thrust her fingers into Declan's hair, moaning as desire flooded her body. It had been so long since she had felt his mouth on hers. Too long. Declan's heart hammered through the smooth fabric of his shirt, its hectic pace matching her own. She rolled her hips against his hard length, desperate for the friction they both needed.

"You taste so fucking sweet," Declan rasped, as his mouth traveled to her jaw, nipping and kissing until he reached the pulse point fluttering madly in her neck. Jolts of pleasure shot through her when he set his lips over it and sucked. His grip held her tight as she ground her body against him.

"I can't get enough of you. Can never get enough," he growled, his mouth moving across her collarbone before dipping to the scooped neck of her sweater. "I dreamed of this skin."

Olivia cried out, her head thrown back when he released her hair and kneaded her breast, rolling her nipple through her thin sweater. Need rushed through her body at dizzying speed, and her fingers twisted in his hair pulling his mouth back to hers.

Declan kissed her like he couldn't get enough. The heat of his mouth devoured her. His tongue and lips claiming her, consuming her.

A tiny fission of unease snuck through her arousal, telling her to slow down. Because Declan *was* consuming her. It happened every time she was near him. Olivia forgot about the world around them. There was only him and the way he made her feel.

But most importantly, she forgot that Declan didn't truly want her—not really. He'd made that clear.

Olivia pulled back, bringing her hands up between their bodies to push him back.

Her breath came in ragged, choppy gasps. "No." Declan's eyes were wild, almost black with arousal. "No," she repeated.

Chest straining against his shirt as he tried to catch his breath, Declan's arms fell away, and she instantly felt the cold of his loss. His hair was in disarray from where her fingers had tunneled through it, his face flushed. Her body ached with the need to press against him again, to put his hands back on her body.

"I can't do this. I won't let you use me again."

Declan recoiled as if she struck him. "I never used you."

"First, you pretend you don't know me, then you tell me you remember but it meant nothing. Finally, you say it meant something, but it's over, and I need to keep our interactions professional. And tonight..." Her voice broke. "You kissed me like you never wanted to let me go. I am not a toy, Declan. I don't exist only when you feel like playing with me. I deserve more than that. I *have* to let you go," she whispered.

Olivia avoided his gaze as she straightened her top and tucked her hair behind her ears. She couldn't look at him. Couldn't risk him seeing how fragile she really was. Olivia drew in a deep breath and forced her gaze back to his face. "We work together, and you're getting married."

The muscle in Declan's jaw clenched once, twice, and on the third flex, Olivia watched the walls slam shut in his eyes. She wanted to beg him not to go, but she bit her lip instead.

Declan's face hardened. "You're right. This was a terrible mistake," he said stiffly. "It won't happen again."

A sharp burn took root behind her sternum. She was the one who stopped. So why did it hurt so much to hear him agree with her?

Olivia turned to go, but Declan caught her hand at the last second, drawing her to a halt. They stood in silence, their hands linked, but when she looked back over her shoulder, Declan wasn't looking at her. His head was bowed, eyes fixed on the carpet in front of him. The air was heavy between them, and the ache in Olivia's chest spread until it was hard to breathe. Declan squeezed her fingers and then released her hand, turning his back to walk to his desk.

Olivia was grateful she made it to her car before the sobs fought their way free.

CHAPTER TWENTY-EIGHT

ATLANTA—PRESENT DAY

Olivia was irritable the next morning as she made her coffee, cursing when she missed her mug and splashed the hot liquid on the marble countertop. She wiped up the spill in short, angry swipes. Then, with pursed lips and a dull headache, she tucked her laptop under her arm and carried it and her coffee to the screened porch overlooking the river behind her home.

One benefit of tossing and turning all night was, somewhere around three a.m., inspiration struck her. Olivia scrolled through her notes as she sipped her coffee, slowly feeling like herself again. When her phone rang on the table next to her, a flare of alarm shot into her stomach when she saw the name displayed.

Why is Chris Keller calling me?

They hadn't spoken since the scene in the conference room the week before.

"I owe you a huge apology."

Olivia blinked at his greeting. "Good morning."

"Sorry. I should have led with that." Chris's voice sounded different. Almost sad. "I've recently become aware of something, and I wanted to call you right away. The night of the gala…" He sighed. "When you weren't feeling well…"

Olivia's cheeks flamed. She only had the vaguest of memories of Chris after leaving the ballroom. "I'm not sure what happened. I'm sorry if—"

"I'm the one who should apologize to you. I feel responsible for what happened."

What does that mean?

"Maybe I should have insisted on taking you back to your hotel, but Cara and the others were adamant. I thought it might be more appropriate for women…"

Olivia's shoulders slumped, humiliation making her queasy. "You did the right thing. I'd blame it on jet lag, but we didn't change time zones." She joked, but even to her ears, it sounded flat.

"You have nothing to apologize for." Chris's voice was so serious, the hairs on the back of her neck lifted. "You saw Courtney that night…"

Where is he going with this?

"She's not in a healthy mental state right now." Chris let out a heavy sigh. "I don't know how to tell you this, other than to just say it. Courtney apparently thought you and I were involved more than professionally. She put a couple of her Xanax pills in your drink while you were both in the bathroom."

"What?" For a beat, Olivia wondered if she had finally fallen asleep the night before and was dreaming. "She drugged me?" Olivia tried to wrap her head around the concept.

"I'm so sorry. If I'd known how out of control her behavior had become… No, that's not an excuse. I should have realized she'd completely lost it. I feel terrible. It's why you were so lightheaded. I only found out this morning."

Olivia wasn't sure what she was supposed to say. "But… Why…"

"She's really struggling with her sons' deaths. Those boys were everything to her. Losing them broke her." He sniffed. Was he crying? Despite her anger, Olivia felt a tug of sympathy for him. It wasn't his fault he was dating a crazy person.

"It's only been a little more than a month, and at first, I thought her behavior was a result of the initial shock, but it seems to be getting worse. She's erratic, mixing her medications and alcohol, the paranoia... But I never dreamed she would do what she did to you."

Another heavy sigh sounded through the phone. "I wanted you to know as soon as I heard." Chris paused. "Look, I know the deal didn't work out the way either of us anticipated, but I have a lot of respect for your abilities. I'd like to help you find another position... as an 'I'm sorry.'"

His abrupt change of topic stunned her, but Chris continued when she didn't speak. "I'm familiar with how Bloom Capital does business. Declan will strip down Armstrong and sell it. It's unlikely the new buyers will have a place for you."

"What are you suggesting, exactly?"

"Let me take you to dinner tomorrow night. You would be an asset to any company, but Bloom Communications has so many subsidiaries, I'm confident we can find the right fit within our network."

"That's not necessary." Olivia wasn't sure what to make of the offer. On the surface, it seemed harmless, but she didn't trust him. She turned his offer over in her brain, but Olivia couldn't figure out what he wanted from her. Was he worried she would make a complaint with the police? He must realize it was too late for that.

"Please. At the very least, let me buy you dinner as an apology for what Courtney did." When Olivia hesitated, he continued. "I know you've worked at Armstrong for your entire career, and while you accomplished some impressive things, it wouldn't hurt to build your network as you consider your next position."

Olivia took a deep breath. As much as she hated it, Chris was right. "All right," Olivia reluctantly agreed, before she had a chance to second guess herself. If her new plan didn't work, her employees wouldn't be the only ones looking for a job.

Three hours later, Olivia gave Todd the barest of nods as she strode past him to Declan's door.

Todd's face folded in confusion. "Did you have a meeting?"

"I only need five minutes."

He looked uncertain. "Um, I'll check."

"No problem, I'll be quick." Cecile and Declan looked up in surprise when she swung the door open. Declan's eyes were immediately wary.

"I want to present a proposal to keep the manufacturing in-house."

Cecile darted a glance at Declan. His expression was impassive. "We've discussed this—"

"That's not entirely true. You told me you have a plan to manufacture overseas, but nothing has been set in motion. I'm asking that if I present you a detailed proposal will you genuinely consider it."

"You shouldn't waste your—"

"Will you consider it?" she interrupted.

The muscle in his jaw ticked. "One week."

"Perfect." Olivia gave a nod to Cecile before spinning on her heels and marching from the room, not smiling until the door shut behind her.

The next night, Olivia chose a simple, black knit dress that tied at her side, and gold jewelry. It was only one step up from what she might wear to the office, because Olivia wasn't interested in giving off any mixed signals. She already had enough of that from Declan.

Chris smiled and opened the car door when her rideshare pulled up to the curb in front of the restaurant. "Thank you for coming."

Olivia was grateful that, although the restaurant was clearly upscale, it wasn't romantic. The lighting had already been dimmed for the evening, but the tubes of neon running over the velvet-covered walls gave the place a more casual feel. Olivia followed Chris and the hostess to one of the small tables in the middle.

"I've only been here once before," Chris explained. "But it was good."

"Do you spend a lot of time in Atlanta?"

Chris wasn't doing anything that would normally make her uncomfortable, but her guard was up. Between his desire to buy Armstrong, and his fiancée drugging her, Olivia suspected there was more to this dinner than just trying to help her professionally.

"More this past year than before. Wine?"

"Yes, please."

Chris ordered a bottle for the table. "You took a car, so I figured it was safe." He leaned back in his chair, his posture casual, and Olivia's shoulders relaxed. Was she being paranoid?

Olivia gave him a wry smile. "Wine is welcome. It's been an interesting week."

"I bet." He chuckled. "How's it going?" His palms flashed up in surrender. "Nope. Forget I asked that."

Olivia took a sip of the chilled wine their server poured into her glass. "It's all right. For the most part, it's been exactly as I expected."

"It's a shame. Armstrong has a solid design base. I really think it would have been an asset for us. Oh well, you win some, you lose some."

Olivia hummed a sound of agreement, but she wasn't

buying it. Chris had been ready to come to blows over this deal. Despite his friendly expression, Chris's eyes were shrewd. Did he think she would give him inside information on XEROS?

Just as Olivia was regretting agreeing to the dinner, Chris changed the subject, asking her about her professional history. Eventually, the easy small talk and glass of wine had her relaxing again. Chris didn't ask a single question about Declan and seemed to be sincerely interested in her career.

The server placed their dishes in front of them, and after taking a few bites of her snapper, Olivia returned to the reason she'd agreed to meet Chris.

"I'm not sure a corporation as big as Bloom Communications would be a good fit for me. How much of a difference could I make? The thing I love about being at Armstrong is I can see first-hand how what I do affects our operations."

Chris nodded. "I can understand that. We have literally hundreds of subsidiary companies. I'll make inquiries if you'd like? Do you want to stay in the tech field?"

"Not necessarily. If I'm going to make a change..." She shrugged and then bit her lip. "Chris, I appreciate this offer. It's extremely generous... But to be clear, I don't expect any special favors."

"Because my fiancée drugged you?" Chris grimaced. "It's not that. I like you, Olivia, and I think you are going to do big things." He grinned. "Networking is a bigger part of my job than you'd imagine."

"You aren't responsible for what Courtney did," Olivia reiterated.

Chris sighed. "Our relationship has essentially been over for a while, but I didn't want to end it while she was having a hard time. She's at a *spa* getting some much-needed rest." He made air quotes around the word.

Olivia wasn't sure if *spa* was code for rehab or a mental health facility, and as curious as she was, it was none of her business.

"I hope she gets whatever help she needs."

Chris set his fork down with a sigh. "I should have known it was getting bad when she had that damn necklace made."

"Necklace?"

"Courtney sent the ashes of her husband and sons to one of those companies that make faux diamonds." Chris made a face. "She said she wanted to carry them with her all the time. She's saving the rest of the ashes to have made into earrings at some point."

Olivia winced. "That's…"

"Macabre? I agree. I might understand if it was only her children, but David? Theirs wasn't an epic love story. They were married less than a year."

"I've never lost anyone close to me, so I don't know how I'd react," Olivia said diplomatically. "If it helps with her grief, and it's not hurting anyone..."

Chris stared at her for a beat. "That's incredibly generous of you… considering. I sound harsh, don't I?" He rubbed a hand over his jaw. "I'm just worn out from the last year… all the gossip. Courtney and I got involved soon after David died, and then life seemed to snowball from there."

Olivia hid her expression with her wine glass. Why was he sharing this with her? They weren't friends.

Chris's sad expression suddenly shifted as he watched something behind her. Her back to the entrance, Olivia twisted to look as the hostess walked past them, leading an extremely tall man who looked vaguely familiar, followed by a heavily-pregnant, redhead. However, it was the couple in their wake who made her stomach drop.

The air changed around her, almost as if it were manipulated by the angry energy emanating from the two men as Declan walked past Chris. Olivia swallowed hard at the black fury in Declan's face when his eyes met hers.

Chris blew out a breath, bringing Olivia's attention back to him, as Declan sat at his table across the room. She could see Declan's glower out of the corner of her eye. "I hope he doesn't take this out on you," Chris muttered.

Olivia shrugged, burying the emotions crashing through her. "Why should he?"

"Declan has an unreasonable hatred of me."

Chris adopted a sorrowful expression, but Olivia saw through it. Her years with Kyle taught her to always be conscious of body language, because it was more honest than anything else. Olivia immediately clocked the trembling fist on the table.

"I'm not sure when it changed," Chris said. "I told you before how I had distanced myself from Declan. When I started having my own success, I wasn't his sidekick anymore, and he didn't like it."

Olivia shouldn't ask. She couldn't trust Chris's rendition of what happened between the men, but she was curious to learn more about Declan's life in the years they were apart. "Did you have a falling out over something specific?"

Chris twirled the stem of his glass between his fingers. "No. Declan changed when he became the president of Bloom Communications. He was young, too young in a lot of people's opinions, but David wanted Declan there as his bulldog. But Declan didn't want to work *with* his father."

Chris huffed a quiet laugh. "Declan doesn't work *with* anyone. Declan does what Declan wants and expects the rest of us to tug our forelocks and say thank you. Things didn't turn into what they are now until we began competing over Armstrong. Well, that and the Bloom Communications' board chose me over him."

Chris didn't hide his self-satisfaction as well as he thought. Olivia reached for the wine bottle to refill her glass, but Chris beat her to it, lifting the bottle. To her shock, one of his hands covered her fingers where she held her glass as he poured the wine.

"I was worried I might spill it," he said by way of explanation.

Olivia managed a tight smile, but almost like a sunburn, the back of her neck heated, and her chest grew tight. She didn't need to look to know Declan was watching her.

"It's sad really," Chris mused. "He destroys all of his relationships. Declan battled with his father over the company, and when David stepped down as CEO, there was no one to check Declan's ego."

He sipped his own wine. "It surprised me to see his siblings in New York with him. He hasn't managed to maintain those relationships either."

Olivia frowned. "I met his sister, Cara, in New York. They seemed like they were getting along."

Something flickered in Chris's eyes. "Being a good liar is imbedded in their DNA." He looked thoughtful. "In fact, the last time I was in this restaurant, I was with Cara."

Olivia's mouth fell open. "Really?"

"Last spring. Even then, I was trying to help Declan. I thought we were still friends."

Olivia kept her expression blank as she did some rapid mental math. Wouldn't Chris already have been involved with Courtney last spring? That didn't sound like he was interested in being *friends*. Was his story self-serving because of his arrogance, or because he had an ulterior motive in inviting her here tonight?

Unaware of where her thoughts had gone, Chris continued. "Declan was worried about what was happening with Cara. She had been in the press after her father's death…"

Olivia had a vague memory of something about nude pictures of the socialite being sold to online tabloids.

"Cara is like a little sister to me. I watched her grow up," Chris said sadly. “All the Blooms were like family, but when they were cut out of the will, they wanted someone to blame.” He drained the last of his wine and reached for the bottle. “I guess because I was one of the witnesses to the will, some of the resentment toward their father spilled over to me. Then when I started seeing Courtney...”

Chris made a face. “I know it’s probably hard to believe, but because she and my father were friends, we spent time together, and I saw she wasn’t the monster the Blooms portrayed her as. She was their step-mother—the only woman their father ever married—and I’m sure that stung. Particularly when he left his fortune to her. But she’s misunderstood. Courtney has her problems, but she isn’t evil.”

“I don’t know why I’m telling you all this.” He reached forward and clasped her hand where it lay on the table, his eyes warm. “You’re really a good listener.”

Olivia forced herself not to yank her hand free, instead she slid it slowly out from under his.

A loud exclamation had both of their heads swiveling in the sound’s direction. The pregnant redhead was being helped to her feet, an uncomfortable look on her face, and she made the pained sound again. The man with her put his arm around her waist for support as Fiona waved goodbye.

Across the room, Fiona’s eyes collided with hers, and Olivia almost recoiled from the malice on the woman’s face. A calculated smile lifted Fiona’s lips, and she grabbed Declan’s jaw, turning his face to hers before she kissed him. Olivia’s stomach wrenched.

Olivia turned back to Chris and tried to concentrate on what he was saying, but all she wanted to do was run away. She felt like a fool.

“Is everything all right? You’re a little pale,” Chris observed.

Olivia seized the excuse. “I’m going to run to the ladies’

room." She gave him a polite smile before she grabbed her purse and slipped through the tables, avoiding a glance in Declan's direction.

She found the small bathroom at the back of a dim hallway. The purple, velvet-covered walls of the anteroom matched the rest of the restaurant, with another door leading to the toilet. Olivia tossed her clutch onto a large ottoman in the corner.

Her body was feverish, and the pressure in her chest made it hard to breathe. Declan was going to marry that woman. Olivia didn't believe he loved Fiona. She knew what Declan in love looked like, but he was going to marry Fiona anyway. All that mattered to Declan was getting his father's company back.

Sensation pricked behind her eyes, and she ran her wrists under the cold water, trying to bring her temperature down. Drying her hands, Olivia pulled the outer door open, only for a large body to push her back into the room. Sandalwood and bergamot filled her nose, setting her nerves on fire again.

Before she had a chance to even gasp, Declan reached behind him to flip the lock and backed her against the velvet wall. His chest heaved hard against her, his eyes burning black into hers.

"You are trying to torture me, is that it? Or do you *want* me to kill him?"

Olivia's blood ignited, and her nipples peaked at the raw expression on his face as he trapped her against the wall. "I don't know what you're talking about."

His fingers bit almost painfully into her hips. "You're on a fucking date with him," Declan growled.

"What if I am?" Olivia tilted her chin back. It was reckless, and she knew she was playing a dangerous game, but she didn't care. She wanted Declan to feel as out of control as she was. "You're on a date too."

A gravelly sound came from low in his chest, and when her tongue flicked out to wet her lips, Declan's eyes fell to her mouth.

"If he touches you again, I'll cut off his hands." The threat rumbled from his chest into hers.

It should have frightened her, instead it gave her an almost feral satisfaction.

"And I won't even care that it ruins everything I've planned. It will be worth it," he said against her lips. His foot slid between hers moving her legs apart, as his hips thrust her harder into the wall.

"Why? It's in the past, isn't it?"

Olivia bit back a moan as she rocked her hips into him, the movement scraping the buttons of his black dress shirt along the bare skin exposed by her neckline. She was deliberately taunting him, and Declan's eyes flared, his fingers gripping tighter, holding her still against his rigid length.

"Why do you care?" Olivia breathed into his ear before she closed her teeth on the sensitive flesh and bit down.

"Because you're mine." Declan's snarl ripped from deep inside him.

In a flash, his hands were on her hem, shoving up her dress until it bunched around her waist. He grasped her thighs with his large hands and lifted, using his full weight to pin her to the wall.

Olivia surrendered to the sensations coursing through her body and her legs wrapped him, as his mouth slammed into hers. Declan kissed her like he was angry… like he was desperate, and her body responded instantly to the intensity.

Olivia whimpered when he rocked hard against her, his erection rubbing against the seam of her panties until she cried out. She didn't care that they were in a restaurant bathroom, or that other people were waiting for them. Olivia didn't even care that he'd broken her heart. She wanted him inside with an almost painful desperation.

Declan's hand slipped inside her dress, palming her breast roughly. His thumb brushed her puckered nipple, as her hands yanked at his belt. There was no teasing, no drawn-out pleasure. Only frantic need that they both raced to satisfy.

Declan angled his torso back to slip a hand between their bodies and his thumb stroked over her clit. "Declan!" she cried.

He pulled her lace panties to the side until she heard the delicate fabric rip. Olivia whimpered as two long fingers sunk inside. She clenched around them and heard him growl with approval.

Declan buried his face in her neck as he rocked harder against her, his thumb rubbing firm circles over her clit, and his fingers curled inside.

"You're drenched," he groaned into her neck. "You feel so fucking perfect. *Are* so fucking perfect."

Hot breath panted against her jaw when she shoved his pants down to pull him free. She stroked his length, relishing the hot silky skin before lining him up with her body.

"Petal." Declan's pupils were blown wide when he lifted his head to stare into her eyes.

"If you don't fuck me right now, I'm going to lose my mind," she gasped, sliding him back and forth against her over-sensitized skin.

A primitive look crossed his eyes, and then he surged into her with one hard stroke, covering her mouth with a large hand when she screamed. Declan didn't wait for her to adjust to him, his pace almost savage as he thrust inside her.

Olivia clawed at his shoulders, and soon her legs were shaking, and stars erupted behind her closed eyelids as she fell apart. With a muffled shout in her shoulder, she felt Declan find his own release.

Heart still pounding, Olivia opened her eyes, reluctantly coming back to awareness. Declan's forehead rested on her shoulder, his ragged exhales feathered across her bare collarbone. For a minute they stayed joined together, as they both struggled to steady their breathing. Slowly, Declan set her feet on the ground, and tugged her dress together, as he tucked himself away.

"We didn't use anything." Declan's voice was gruff, but it didn't sound like he was sorry. "You're the only one I've ever… I would never put you at risk like that."

"I know." And she did. Deep inside Olivia knew Declan would always protect her.

There was an odd expression on his face. "But there is always the risk of—"

"No risks taken." Olivia swallowed past the lump in her throat the words immediately caused. She wasn't about to tell him it was unlikely she could have children, and that one slipup wasn't likely to result in a baby when eighteen months of trying never had.

His brow furrowed, and for a second an emotion that looked a lot like disappointment crossed his eyes. Declan stroked the back of his knuckles down her cheek.

"What are we doing?"

Declan sighed, and pulled a handkerchief from his pocket, folding it into a square. "I don't know. I forget everything when I'm with you."

His words, so close to her own thoughts, made her heart flutter. "We can't keep doing this," Olivia said. "I might not really be on a date, but you are."

"It's not a date." Declan's eyes captured hers with a sudden intensity. "Until that stunt she just pulled, I'd never even kissed Fiona. This is a business arrangement."

"Does she know that?"

Declan didn't answer, his eyes tracing over her features. Then to her shock, he reached under her dress with his makeshift pad to gently clean her tender flesh. She sucked in a breath, and his eyes flashed to hers with concern. "Did I hurt you?"

Olivia shook her head, her heart thudding. For a beat he

studied her, and then tossed the used handkerchief in the trash can. Bending, he retrieved the remains of her panties from the floor, and tucked them in his pocket.

"This isn't the time or the place for this, but you're right. We need to talk. Really talk. I thought I could..." He stared at her for a minute, and then Declan curved his hand around the back of her neck and pulled her in for a hard kiss against her lips before retreating to the door, his mask sliding into place.

"We need to get back." Declan paused, his hand on the lock. "I'm not playing a game, Petal." His voice was low, his eyes deadly serious. "If that bastard touches you again, you will be able to count the breaths he has left on one hand. Which would be unfortunate, because I have plans for him."

Olivia's brows drew together. "Plans?"

Declan gave her a grim smile. "Yes, but as usual, you've turned my entire world upside down." Then he flipped the lock and was gone.

Olivia took a minute to press her hands to her flaming cheeks, and then another to repair her makeup, but there was no hiding her flush or her dilated eyes.

When Olivia returned to the dining room, she couldn't resist a peek at Declan's table. To her surprise, Fiona was at the table alone, and if the death glare the woman was currently sending her was any sign, Fiona suspected what had happened between her and Declan.

Olivia should probably feel guilty that she'd just had sex with the woman's date in the bathroom, but she didn't.

"Why do you care?"

"Because you're mine."

And Declan was hers.

Chris's expression was rigid when Olivia sat down. "Are you all right? I was getting worried."

Olivia gave him a wan smile. "I'm sorry. I'm not sure the food agreed with me."

She didn't know if he believed her, and she didn't particularly care. Her mind and heart were in an uproar, trying to make sense of what was happening between her and Declan.

Chris looked at Declan's table and to the back of the restaurant, his jaw clenching. Olivia lifted her purse, setting it in her lap as she reached for her wallet. The least she could do was pay for half the meal.

Chris waved his hand in the air when she pulled out a credit card. "I invited you." His gaze fell on her red purse. "O.R.A.?"

Olivia replaced the card in her wallet. "My initials—Olivia Adler," she said, not wanting to get into the subject with him. Olivia wanted out of the restaurant so that she could go home and dissect what had just happened in private.

"What's the R for?" Chris lay several large bills on the check.

"Rose."

Chris's hand hovered over his billfold, and then his eyes slowly lifted to look at her. "Rose? That's a beautiful name."

Olivia murmured her thanks, barely registering his comment. Where the hell had Declan gone? As the minutes ticked by, and Declan didn't appear, the server collected the bill, and Chris's posture relaxed.

"Do you need a ride home?"

Olivia looked up from her phone. "Thank you, but I ordered a car."

Declan entered the restaurant at the same time Chris and Olivia reached the front door. His phone was pressed to his ear as though he'd stepped outside to make a call. His violet eyes were laser focused on Chris standing so close behind her, but only inclined his head slightly to her in an arrogant nod.

"Olivia," he said, without a single hesitation in his stride.

CHAPTER TWENTY-NINE

ATLANTA—PRESENT DAY

Fiona's scowl was scorching when he rejoined their table. "Darling." Fiona lay her hand on his forearm, and Declan did his best not to wince.

Why had he never noticed how much she touched him before? Was Olivia right? Did Fiona not understand the nature of their relationship?

"You were gone so long," she said.

"I had to take care of something."

"Something or someone?" Fiona's directness surprised Declan. Her nails briefly dug into his sleeve. "I noticed you and *that woman* disappeared at the same time."

"Fiona," Declan warned.

Fiona jerked her hand away, and then flung her fork onto her plate with a loud clatter. "I'm not a fool. You have been staring at her all night. This is the second time you've behaved that way."

Declan didn't spare her a glance, lifting his glass and taking a slow sip of whiskey. He set the glass down before speaking. "How is my interest, or lack of interest, in another woman any of your business?"

Fiona gasped. Declan was being harsh, but she had tried to put on a show all night for her friends, and he was tired of it. Her falsity was more grating than normal, and Declan knew the entire reason behind that was Olivia.

Olivia, who had just left the restaurant with Chris Keller. His mood darkened. "I played along tonight because you've obviously told your friends we are a couple, but I want to make something clear. Our merger is not a sure thing, and your threats are making it less likely to occur."

Fiona's face turned red. "You are acting like an asshole."

"I *am* an asshole," he bit out. "You should think about that. *If* we marry, that won't change. We both know what this is. Don't pretend I've ever told you differently."

"Are you fucking her?"

Declan finished his whiskey in one shot. He didn't bother to ask who she meant. "I work with Olivia, but even if I were, it has nothing to do with you. Just like whoever you are fucking has nothing to do with me."

Fiona tapped her nails against her wineglass. "I've never seen you like this"

Declan sighed. "Like what?"

"I've watched you cycle through countless women, never dating anyone more than a few times. But I saw how you couldn't keep your eyes off her in New York, and then again tonight. It's different. We are getting married—"

"Last I checked, I haven't proposed."

"Quit the games, Declan. I know how your family feels about me, but I also know you need my father's vote. This arrangement is mutually beneficial."

The whiskey in his belly turned sour. Fiona was right. Without her father's support, Declan would have a hard time swaying enough shareholders to get a majority vote. But for the first time in his life, he was wondering if it was all worth it.

CHAPTER THIRTY

New York—12 years ago

Declan was six whiskeys deep when Chris clapped him hard on the back.

"Welcome home."

Declan kept his gaze on the tumbler in front of him, as his best friend hopped onto the next stool.

"How the hell did you find this place?" Chris asked, looking around the dim room barely lit by neon beer signs on the wall.

"No one knows me here."

Chris smirked. "That's for sure. What are you wearing? Did you piss off the housekeeper, and she burned your clothes?"

Declan wore the same jeans, T-shirt, and boots that had been his uniform for the last week. The last thing to let go of. One last hold to the past before he forced himself back into the slick designer world he was bound to. He snorted. Pathetic.

Declan shot the remains of his drink, and the bartender immediately filled it without a word.

Chris peered at him. "Are you okay?"

"Grand," he slurred slightly.

"You look like you're ready to rip someone apart." Chris's

expression changed. "You aren't planning on getting in a fight, are you?"

Declan picked up his glass between two fingers and dangled it in front of him. That actually sounded like a pretty great idea. Maybe physical pain would finally be the thing to dull whatever devastation was happening inside of him.

He glanced at the other patrons in the bar, hoping someone would give him an excuse to give into the storm that raged in his blood.

"Dec, I was kidding." Chris looked worried.

Declan sighed. There were times Seamus's hot-headed, hit-first-think-later company was preferable. His brother *never* shied away from a good fight and would understand if Declan took on every fucker in the place.

He bared his teeth at the glass before tipping it up again. Then again, Seamus's penchant for poor decisions was exactly why the pain rooted deep in his soul would never go away.

"Why don't we go get something to eat?" Chris shifted to get up.

"No," Declan tapped the counter, and the bartender refilled his glass.

"You're too big for me to carry out of here." Chris chuckled, but his worry rang through the sound.

"I didn't ask you to."

"Dec, you're my best friend. I'm not leaving you wasted in some dive bar. C'mon. Let's go back to my place. You can drink yourself senseless there." He glanced at the bottle still in the bartender's hand. "Something that isn't going to poison you."

Declan had been drinking steadily for the last few days, anything to quiet his thoughts—the knowledge of what could never change. His mind swam in whiskey, but somewhere in his liquor-soaked brain he knew Chris was right.

He sat up straighter and pulled a wad of hundred-dollar bills from his wallet. He held them out, and when the bartender reached for them, Declan plucked the whisky bottle out of his hand and stood.

"Passing out in a bar would be *irresponsible* for a man in my position." Declan huffed a laugh before heading to the door.

"Hey!"

Declan heard Chris making excuses to the angry bartender, as he pushed open the door to the parking lot and blinked at the sudden light.

"Fuck. Is it still daytime?"

"What the hell is wrong with you?" Chris groused, jogging to catch up to him. "What the fuck?" he exclaimed, when Declan slumped against the top of Chris's small sports car, and the whiskey bottle banged the window.

"Sorry." Declan managed to seat himself in the low-slung seats, even though he had to fold his body in half to get in. He unscrewed the top of the bottle and took a long swig as Chris pulled out onto the road.

"Why aren't you at work? I called your office yesterday, and they said you hadn't come back yet."

"Tomorrow. I told them tomorrow." Declan didn't want to talk about work. For the first time in his life, it didn't interest him in the slightest.

"Drink with me," Declan slurred when they reached Chris's apartment. He tapped his bottle against the drink Chris poured for himself from his own bar. "Slainte."

They drank in silence for several minutes before Chris retrieved a bottle from the bar, poured himself another, and placed an empty glass in front of Declan. Gulping the last of his bottle, Declan set it down with a clatter and sighed when Chris immediately filled his glass.

"Did something happen in Ireland?"

Declan locked his back teeth against the image of laughing,

sapphire eyes and a perfect smile currently torturing his brain. He closed his eyes and rubbed his head.

"Are you going to be sick?"

"No." The weight of what he'd lost sank onto his chest, the pressure unbearable. "Is it your dad? I know he was pissed about you going to Dublin," Chris said carefully.

Declan snorted but shook his head.

"Did Seamus's problem not work out?"

Declan didn't share with either Chris or his siblings exactly what his brother had done before he left. He wanted to talk to Rose. He could tell her anything.

But he couldn't.

She was gone.

He was alone.

"Dec?" Chris hesitated. "I get that you don't like talking about your family in Ireland, but… I'm going to be honest…. You look awful. Literally the worst I've ever seen you." He took a breath. "We've known each other for a long time. I understand more than most about the pressures of your life."

Declan squinted at his friend through blurry eyes. Chris was right. Because of Dr. Keller's relationship with David Bloom, and their own friendship, Chris had a front row seat to the toxic dysfunction of the Bloom family.

"You can trust me," Chris said quietly, eyes earnest.

Declan still hesitated, staring at his friend. Finally, he heaved an enormous sigh. "It all went to shite." He took the glass and leaned back on the cushion, resting the glass on his knees. His eyes focused on the dark amber liquid. "You know about my mother's family... the bars. What you don't know is there are other less legitimate sources of income… more complicated branches of their business."

Chris's forehead wrinkled. "I don't think I understand."

"Guns, drugs, protection, smuggling… you name it. If there is a way to make money, the McGrath's have a piece."

Chris's eyes grew huge on his face. "Do you mean like the mob?"

Declan leveled a look at his friend, not answering the question, and took another sip. "Seamus's father's family is in a similar line of work... but not at the same level."

Chris's brows knit. "Was that the trouble he was in?"

"Seamus has never had a proper position in either family. Between him and his cousin Padraig, they've pissed off all kinds of important people. I was there to bail him out again, but it wasn't enough this time. I suppose I knew inevitably the lines would blur for him, and he'd be more of a front-line soldier." Declan gulped his whiskey to drown his anger at his brother's stupidity.

"What are you saying? If he is a member of the family, why doesn't he have a position?"

"My mother is the youngest of seven, so she was never involved with the true day to day of the business. Seamus's father was close to the Riordan action but not a decision maker. Seamus has had a hard time reconciling the two sides of his blood." Declan huffed a sad laugh. "He so desperately wants to make a name for himself. Now he has."

When Chris opened his mouth with another question, Declan took another gulp. "Only Seamus could have fucked it up this bad and ruined me along with him."

"You aren't making any sense."

"Seamus used our uncle's name, and brokered..." Declan waved his hand, the whiskey making the words hard to find. "An agreement. But our uncles cut him loose after his last disaster, and the Albanians figured out Seamus was promising something he couldn't deliver. Not the kind of people you want angry with you."

Declan rubbed absently at the ache in his chest. "I wasn't

supposed to be there, but at the last minute, Padraig had food poisoning, and Seamus thought I'd work as a stand in."

"You just have to stand there," Seamus begged. "I need your size. Spread those shoulders of yours and look menacing. It is a simple exchange."

"Seamus, you said you'd take the job—"

"Please." His brother interrupted. "Don't make me go alone."

Every fiber in his body told Declan it was a bad idea. The exact thing his father feared. That his loyalty to his Irish family would put the Bloom Empire, and his own life, at risk. But raw and reckless from leaving Rose only an hour before, and faced with his brother's panic, he caved.

It would be better if he were there, he'd rationalized. Seamus had a temper, and easy as the exchange was supposed to be, Declan might need to remind his older brother to stay calm.

The drive north to Dublin had given Declan time to think. Looking at his watch, and knowing Rose's plane was taking off, his heart rebelled at the idea of her being gone.

Why couldn't they be together? What was the point of being Declan Bloom if he couldn't have whatever he wanted? He'd find Rose, explain his deception. They would make it work. He would keep her.

It was obvious something was off the minute they entered the empty pub that night. The Albanian contingent was already there, but so were three Russians, easily identifiable by their tattoos.

His body on high alert, Declan met the eyes of the youngest of the Russians, easily ten years younger or more than his companions. There were no visible tattoos across his knuckles, so Declan wasn't sure what his position in the group was. Intelligent gray eyes met his, and in that stare, Declan saw the same unease he felt.

Ten minutes later, when the Albanian who had been speaking with Seamus, suddenly turned and plunged his knife between Seamus's ribs, it took them all by surprise.

Declan had been in his share of fights, both in the family pubs and on the rugby pitch, but it was the first time his life hung in the balance.

One heartbeat, he was pulling his brother back away from the knife before the next strike could connect. On the next beat, pain blazed across his ribs, and his gun was out and firing. Before the man's body hit the ground, someone yelled in a thick Russian accent, "No witnesses."

Then mayhem.

The next part of the nightmare Declan clearly remembered was the older Russian barking orders, and the younger man shoving Declan toward the door. Declan looked over his shoulder, but Seamus, hand clutched to his side, met his eyes with the hardest look Declan had ever seen on his older brother's face.

"Run, Dec. Go home. You were never here."

It wasn't until they ducked into an alley several streets over and leaned against a brick wall, panting heavily, that Declan realized his companion had blood all over him, and that his own side was dripping.

"You're in trouble now." Declan heard the young Russian say casually through the buzzing in his ears. The Russian flexed his hand and then wiped a bloody palm against the brick. He cast an eye over Declan. "I haven't seen you before?" His perceptive eyes studied Declan. "You aren't a soldier." He cocked his head. "Are you a Riordan?"

Declan shook his head. "I was doing my brother a favor."

"Me too... sort of..." He snorted, and then stuck out a blood-stained hand.

"Alexei Kovalyov."

"Declan Bloom."

An hour later, Declan sat in a windowless room listening to one of his uncles give him instructions while a woman stitched the wound on his side. The overall message was simple: Never speak of what happened. Albanians believe in blood feud, and if they found out his involvement, they would kill everyone connected to Declan.

His uncle explained in a disgusted voice that Seamus had taken responsibility for Declan's kill shot. Seamus was only saved from retribution by the fact the Albanian struck first. That, along with a hefty bag of cash, would keep the head of the Koci family happy. It was also helpful that, like Seamus, Dituri Koci was operating without family permission.

Seamus would survive.

As his uncle spoke, it occurred to Declan that he should feel some sort of remorse about killing the man, or for the others who had died in the pub. He didn't.

The only thought ricocheting through his brain was: he'd truly lost her now. A vicious reminder that his life wasn't the same as hers. The thought that a connection to him would bring her unhappiness was enough to make him ill. How long before his father's cutting remarks, or the sharks that he dealt with, turned her love to resentment? She deserved so much more than what a life with him would be.

His uncle continued to catalog all the things Declan needed to do and not do to safeguard himself, but his heart only heard one thing.

She's gone.

"Holy shit!" Chris's exclamation yanked Declan from his thoughts. His eyes were wide. "Are you saying you kil—"

"They erased my presence." Declan's lips twisted, aware he had just done what his uncle had drilled into him was the most important thing he *not* do. "Seamus might have done it for me, but Uncle Iain knew it meant that I owed him." Declan slumped, staring morosely at his drink. "Even with the money my father paid, I'll never be free of them now."

He exhaled a sharp breath and tipped his head back to rest on the top of the sofa. "I almost had it all," he whispered. "A fucking dream right at my fingertips."

"Huh?"

Declan raised his head, surprised that it felt ten times heavier than it normally did. The room swam in front of him. "Hubris. I'm Declan Bloom. I can have anything." A laugh broke from him that sounded suspiciously like a sob. He roughly cleared his throat, eyes stinging. "Leaving her in that airport is easily the hardest thing I've ever done. God, the look on her face. We'd agreed... She has dreams... By the time I was halfway back to Dublin, I'd convinced myself that it could work. I'd tell her who I really was. We would make it work. There is no way that the universe would deliver a love like that, only to wrench it away." His voice cracked.

Declan lifted his glass, almost missing his lips, and finished the drink. "I'll never be free of this legacy... my father's, my mother's, and now my own. Because while the Albanians have made peace with the McGraths, if they were ever to find out the truth..."

"Who are you talking about?"

Declan blinked at Chris, his lids suddenly too heavy to hold open. "Rose. My beautiful, perfect Rose."

The next day when he woke on Chris's sofa, he found his friend watching him from the stool in the kitchen. Declan sat up with a groan, his stomach and head objecting to the upright position.

"Coffee?" Chris sipped from his mug. Declan swallowed past the nausea and shook his head.

He didn't think he'd ever drank as much as he had the night before. Declan scrubbed his hands over his face.

"Thanks for letting me stay last night. I better get home and get cleaned up."

Declan pulled his boots on and headed for the door. He never lost control like that, and beneath the alcohol still roiling in his belly was the sense of foreboding. He shouldn't have told Chris about Rose.

"No problem. It sounded like you needed a friend." Declan's hand was on the doorknob when Chris spoke again. "I'm glad you told me about Rose. I'd started to think you were incapable of falling in love."

Declan managed a tight smile before shutting the door behind him. *Fuck!*

Making a call from the car, Declan had enough time for a quick shower before the doorman called to notify him that his guest had arrived.

Two hours later, he was on his way to the Bloom Communications headquarters, ready to return to life. On his chest, under a protective plastic bandage, was the white rose he'd just had inked above his heart.

Declan might not be able to have Rose in his life, but he would carry her with him forever.

"See You."

"Maybe."

CHAPTER THIRTY-ONE

ATLANTA—PRESENT DAY

Olivia hadn't seen Declan since Saturday night and she wasn't sure how she should handle what happened between them in the bathroom. Would he bring it up? He said they needed to talk. She really hoped he didn't mean at the office.

He had been out of the office for the last few days, and now that it was time for her proposal presentation, she wasn't sure if she was thankful or nervous that Cecile wasn't there in the office with them. Declan had given her one week, and she was pleased with what she had created so far.

"If you look at the figures I've pulled together," Olivia said, "we can offset much of our cost with the new manufacturing tax credits program Georgia passed in their last legislative session."

Declan looked thoughtful. "This plan requires a significant capital investment. Your facility isn't currently equipped to manufacture XEROS."

Olivia stepped forward. At least he was listening and hadn't told her to get out of his office… yet.

"That's true. However, if you look at the projections over the first two years, not only would you recoup those initial costs, you'd increase revenue by controlling your supply chain."

"That assumes I want to hold on to this business for two years."

"Even if you don't, you could put those projections in front of any potential buyer. Also, with intellectual property theft being such an issue lately, keeping the designs in-house means you can more tightly control it. XEROS is only valuable if it hits the market a year or more ahead of our competitors."

Declan was quiet for a minute, studying the papers. He picked up his pen and made a few marks. Hope flared in her chest as she bit her lip to keep from asking what he thought.

He set the papers down, but when he lifted his gaze, it stopped on her mouth.

Sparks sprang up all over her body at the look of pure lust on his face, and she released her lip. Declan dragged in a breath and raised his eyes to hers.

He shifted in his leather chair, his voice gruff when he finally spoke. "I'll look over your proposal again. There might be a compromise somewhere. Continue your research, particularly the legislative aspects, and get back to me."

Surprise held Olivia silent for a moment. But any goodwill vanished when he raised one of those supercilious brows. "Is there something else?"

Declan's tone made Olivia want to rip his head off. "Not at all," she said, with a saccharine smile. "Have a *fantastic* day."

Before she could get up, the phone on his desk buzzed. Declan ignored it at first, pushing the button to silence it, but when it immediately buzzed again, he growled.

Todd's voice was loud through the receiver. "Mr. Menardi and Mr. Worthington are waiting to talk to you. They are expected." Todd continued, "But you have another visitor as well."

"Who?"

"Ms. Carrol."

Olivia kept her face carefully blank.

"She can wait."

Todd must have lowered his volume, because Olivia couldn't decipher the next part.

"I'll make some calls and reach out to a few congressional representatives and see what assurances I can get," she said, when Declan ended the call.

The office door opened and two men strolled in before she'd crossed the office. Olivia recognized the older man from the day of Declan's takeover. The other man was younger, closer to her age, with laughing eyes and an open expression.

As they strolled past her, the younger man gave Olivia an intentionally obvious once over, before shooting her a cocky smile.

"Brady," Declan snapped, drawing the man's attention.

Brady came to a stop, pivoting back to Olivia. He extended his hand. "Brady Worthington, Investigator Extraordinaire." He jerked a thumb towards the other man. "That's my new partner Vincent Menardi, but you don't need to remember him."

Olivia took his hand, her lips twitching at the harmless flirting.

Vincent looked between Declan and Brady, his mouth turning down. "Brady," he rumbled.

With an exaggerated sigh, Brady let go of Olivia's hand. "Alas, duty calls."

Then he winked, and she almost burst out laughing. It was obvious he was more interested in irritating Declan than flirting with her. But the question was… Why had he thought it would bother Declan?

CHAPTER THIRTY-TWO

ATLANTA—PRESENT DAY

Declan exhaled and tightened the cord holding his temper in check, reminding himself that Brady was goading him on purpose. The man was walking a very thin line. "What have you found?"

Brady glanced at Vincent. "Mind if I go first?" Vincent shrugged. "I've located your missing witness."

Declan sat forward, anticipation fizzing through him.

"I haven't made the approach yet." Brady frowned. "It's a delicate situation. She has a family now—husband and two kids. It's possible no one in her current life knows about her past. I don't know how willing she's going to be to come forward and admit that until five years ago she worked as a high-end prostitute."

"I'm sure we can come up with some form of persuasion," Declan drawled.

"I know this is important to you..." Brady's voice was uncharacteristically harsh.

Declan smothered an annoyed sigh. "I only meant everyone has a price. A mortgage to pay off, college education... Figure out hers and give it to her."

Brady's posture relaxed slightly, his voice back to its normal, casual tone. "Do you want me to put feelers out? Speak to her? My guys can be pretty charming when they want to be."

"I don't know how susceptible she'll be to charm," Vincent pointed out. "She was pretty traumatized the night of the accident. It might be better if it's me. I'm the one who helped her get away."

Brady snorted. "Right. I'm sure that didn't involve *any* threats about keeping her mouth shut."

Vincent slowly turned his head to stare at Brady, but didn't bother to deny it.

Declan leaned forward, bracing his elbows on the desk. "I'll go."

The other two men glanced at each other.

"You aren't exactly warm and fuzzy," Brady observed.

"She won't buy warm and fuzzy. This woman survived as a sex worker for Courtney's escort service. That can't have been easy. She's probably better at sniffing out liars than you are."

He steepled his hands on the desk in front of him. "It has to be me. I'm the other person whose life changed forever that night. She might respond to that." He smiled at Brady's dubious expression. "I can be charming."

"Said the spider to the fly," Brady muttered, but shook his head. "You're the boss."

The younger man wasn't happy about it, but Brady's feelings didn't factor into Declan's decision. Shifting topics, he asked, "Has Wes made any progress?"

The two men standing in front of him exchanged another look, and when Vincent shifted his weight from one foot to the other, Declan narrowed his eyes.

"Yup. We did a test run." Brady nodded.

Declan didn't take his eyes off Vincent. "What?"

Vincent hesitated. "The peanut is... unhappy."

It took every ounce of Declan's restraint not to roll his eyes. Vincent had broken hundreds of laws, domestic and international, not to mention bones, in service to the Bloom family. However, when it came to Declan's baby sister, the man was a marshmallow.

"She's worried that if the hack is discovered, the authorities could trace it back to her husband."

Declan grit his teeth. "I told Cara I wouldn't let anything happen to him. Wes will not go back to jail."

He knew his sister wasn't happy about Wes being involved, but his new brother-in-law was an extremely skilled hacker, though these days he used his talents in a strictly legal capacity. When he offered to help, Declan hadn't hesitated. "How does Wes's app work?"

Brady retrieved a cell phone from his pocket and set it on the desk in front of Declan before explaining. "Essentially, once the app is pulled up, someone simply needs to place the copying phone within nine inches of the target phone they want to clone. Wes said it can access everything cont—"

"How long?" Declan didn't care about the details. "How long for it to copy the new passcodes to my father's estate?"

"One minute. Provided there isn't extra firewall protection."

Declan glanced up from the phone with a frown. "And if there is?"

"Two to three minutes. Wes is confident his app will crack whatever defenses Chris's phone has installed."

Declan nodded, satisfaction surging through him.

They were so close.

"After, I'll send one of my guys to—"

"No." Declan cut him off.

Brady's brow creased, but Declan saw by the look on Vincent's face, the older man understood Declan's intentions.

"Even with the codes, it's going to require a certain amount of skill to slip in and out undetected." Brady was persistent.

"I'm not worried about that." Declan pushed the phone back toward Brady. "I have no intention of hiding that I was there."

Brady scowled. "He could go to the police."

"He won't. There would be too many questions. Particularly if I find my father's urn. Besides, I know the house better than anyone." His face darkened. "It was my home. I have the best chance of getting in and out before security is alerted.

Brady looked at Vincent, but the man's expression didn't change. Vincent knew it was pointless to argue with Declan.

"Last place I saw the urn was on the fireplace mantel in your father's study. It's been almost two years. She might have moved it," Vincent added.

"If it's in the house, I'll find it." Cold promise rang in his voice. "If my lab discovers thallium present in the ashes, we will have what we need to overturn the will. It's proof my father was murdered. Between Trey's recorded confession to Cami about Chris ordering the thallium..."

"That won't hold up in a court of law. It's hearsay." Brady grinned at Vincent's dumbfounded expression. "What? I know things."

Declan stared at the man. He didn't explain that he only needed someone to officially open a case in his father's death. A few favors called in, along with some well-placed bribes. Declan had no doubt he would get the ruling to set aside his father's last will.

However, Declan was also sure that Brady would report back to his brothers if he said anything like that. Luke and James might *suspect* the lengths to which Declan would go, but he didn't see any reason to add to the family tension. He didn't want his family involved. The risk would be his alone.

Declan pushed to his feet. "How soon can you get me the cloned phone?"

"How's Rhodes undercover?" Brady asked Vincent.

"Excellent."

"I'll tell him to get on a flight. Tomorrow night soon enough?" Brady looked at Declan. "By the way. Your invoice is going to have a new name." He grinned. "We're now Elite Security Solutions, and our rates have gone up."

"You're working together?" That surprised Declan.

After David Bloom's death, Vincent sold his services as a mercenary. It was hard to imagine the man behind a desk. "You're going to settle in Atlanta?"

If he hadn't been watching the man's grizzled face so closely, Declan would have missed the faint red that appeared on his cheekbones.

"Getting too old for the field."

Brady laughed, clapping the man on the shoulder. "He wants to play Grandpa when your sister has kids. Let me call Rhodes and get him in motion."

When Brady stepped away, Declan watched the red deepen in Vincent's face, and for the first time in a long time, Declan was caught off guard. The former head of security was protective of Cara, and to Declan's surprise, the idea of Vincent taking on a role in their family didn't bother him the way he would have expected.

Over the last year, Cara had to confront the truth about their father, and Declan was aware she still grieved for the man she thought he had been. Then again, David Bloom had always been different with his youngest. Cara deserved another father figure in her life, and Vincent would look out for her, even at risk to himself.

Vincent watched him warily, waiting for Declan's reaction.

"She'll like that."

Relief flashed briefly across the man's face, before his regular stoic expression slid back into place.

"Rhodes is in South Carolina, so he can be here in a few hours. He's going to make the approach at that country club Chris joined."

"He seems to be making a home for himself in Atlanta," Declan growled.

This was the worst possible scenario. Declan didn't want Chris anywhere near his family or Olivia, because things were going to get worse before the final confrontation. He didn't want Chris to have easy access to the people Declan loved. Especially when Chris realized how he'd been outmaneuvered.

"It might be a temporary membership," Brady hesitated, and then pulled a stack of papers from a folder and handed them to Declan. "Yesterday's report on Chris, complete with photos. He's hanging out with your girlfriend. My operative said they looked very… cozy."

"I know Olivia had dinner with him last Saturday."

Brady's eyes flickered, his only acknowledgement of Declan's severe tone. "I meant Fiona Carrol, your *other* girlfriend. The one waiting to talk to you on the other side of that door. She's the one who has Luke and James so pissed off. You are marrying her, right?" Brady smirked, and then said, "Olivia, huh?"

"My private life is none of your business," Declan snapped.

Brady narrowed his eyes. "I don't give a fuck about your private life. I'm giving you the report you paid for."

Declan ground his teeth. "What was he talking to Fiona about?"

Brady's posture was still tense, but he let it go. "I'm not sure. They were sitting at the clubhouse bar."

His heart rate picked up. "Fiona is a member of the club, too?"

Brady shook his head. "She was there on a guest pass. The only other item of interest is Olivia's ex-husband joined them for several drinks." Brady's lips quirked. "My guys saw each other in the parking lot which doesn't normally happen for us. Anyone else at the club you want to add to your account?"

Jackass.

Ice curled in Declan's stomach. The three of them together was not a coincidence.

Were they comparing notes? On him? On Olivia?

Fiona was swiftly becoming a bigger problem than Declan expected. The animosity between Chris and himself wasn't a secret, and Fiona wasn't stupid. What was her angle?

"Keep an eye on Chris." Declan paused. "If you and Vincent have joined forces, does that mean you are offering body work?"

Brady cocked his head. "That's our plan. Do you need a bodyguard?"

Declan's lips firmed. Could he put someone on Olivia without her noticing?

No, not only would she see through it, Declan couldn't justify the need for protection.

Not unless Chris had figured out Olivia was Rose.

"No." The word felt like razor blades in his throat.

"Okay, let us know."

"I don't care how late it is. If your guy gets what he needs from Chris's phone, bring it to me immediately."

"Got it." Brady gave him a mock salute.

Declan turned to Vincent, refusing to rise to the bait. Brady was as annoying as his little brothers. "I'll need a plane that can't be traced back to me."

Vincent nodded. "Not a problem. I'll have one on standby."

"Are you going to tell your brothers?"

Declan turned his gaze on Brady. "Your contract is with me, not my siblings. I don't care how close you are with them, you would be wise to remember that."

Brady's jaw flexed, and his eyes glinted angrily. Something

much more cut-throat replaced his normal carefree expression, and Declan realized there was a lot more to this man than the insouciant devil-may-care attitude Brady presented to the world.

"Business is business," Brady gritted out.

The man didn't drop Declan's gaze, and his respect for the security specialist climbed. "Good."

Raised voices sounded through the door, drawing all three men's attention.

"This is unacceptable," a shrill voice shouted.

Brady grinned. "Sounds like our cue to leave. *One* of your girlfriends needs you"

The door slammed open, and Fiona strode in, not sparing a glance for either man standing in front of the desk.

Declan ignored her even as his temper threatened to run free. "Inform me as soon as you get what I need."

With a curt nod, they left the room.

"I can't believe you left me waiting." Fiona spat at him. "Do you know how humiliating that is?"

Declan leaned back in his chair, gazing at her with her hands on her hips. "I was in the middle of something."

"I'm your fiancée," she practically screamed. "You were in here with her *again*."

"Olivia works here." Declan kept his tone mild, but inside he was moving dangerously close to the edge of his temper. He wouldn't tolerate *anyone* saying something negative about Olivia.

Fiona must have read the message in his eyes, because she suddenly backed down with what he suspected was supposed to be a sweet smile. "I'm sorry. I was excited to see you, and I'm not known for my patience." She giggled, but Declan didn't miss the anger still burning in her eyes.

"Do you need something?"

Her smile thinned. "I wanted to have dinner with you this week."

"You said you were in Atlanta for a baby shower? That was a week ago."

Fiona waved a hand in the air. "I extended my stay. Tracy's on bed rest now but she introduced me to some of her friends, and it turns out Atlanta has a lot more to offer than I expected." Her expression turned sly. "I assumed you'd be happy about that. Isn't it a good thing that I like it? You said you wanted us to have a home here, near your family."

Declan grunted. The idea of sharing any home with the woman was repugnant. It was time to adjust his plan.

"I'm going out of town."

Fiona frowned. "Where are you going?"

Declan lifted an eyebrow.

"Fine," she snapped, before flouncing to the door. "You have to make more of an effort, Declan. I can't make this relationship work by myself."

Relationship? Was the woman actually insane?

Declan picked up his phone. "Todd, can you have Cecile come to my office as soon as she is free?"

Time for Plan B.

CHAPTER THIRTY-THREE

ATLANTA—PRESENT DAY

Brady gave her another smile as he released her hand. Olivia was positive that grin had gotten more than a few women to do whatever the handsome man wanted. But all Olivia cared about was the angry energy rolling off Declan—and how satisfying she found his jealousy.

Olivia closed Declan's office door behind her and pivoted to find Fiona raging at Declan's assistant. "I've been waiting because of *her*?" Fiona's long nail stabbed in Olivia's direction.

Todd's expression was blank. "Ms. Adler is the CFO of Armstrong Electronics. These are normal business hours."

Olivia bit the inside of her cheek to hide her smile at the not-so-subtle jab. By the angry growl, Fiona hadn't missed it either.

"You should be careful how you talk to me." She drew herself up to her full height. Olivia admitted the woman was an impressive sight. High heels and a short Chanel suit screamed privilege, but Todd was unfazed.

"I apologize if I said something to upset you."

"Once I'm Mrs. Bloom, I promise *you* will be the first thing I get rid of," the woman hissed.

Olivia attempted to slip from the office in order to avoid a confrontation, but Fiona's words about being Declan's wife made her stumble. Fiona stepped in front of Olivia, blocking her exit.

Olivia swallowed a groan and squeezed her fingers so tightly into her palms they stung.

You are at work. Don't let her get to you.

Olivia coolly met Fiona's eyes.

"You think he's interested in you, don't you?" Fiona sneered.

Olivia lifted one eyebrow. "I think Mr. Bloom is interested in my stewardship of this company."

"You're not the first, you know." Fiona stepped close enough to fill Olivia's nose with her heavy perfume.

Olivia decided to play dumb to defuse the situation, all too conscious of Todd seated inches away, and of the thin walls of their offices. For years, she had feared her coworkers would hear the things Kyle said to her.

"You think because he's fucking you, it means he cares." Todd made a choking noise, but Olivia held her ground, refusing to look away. "He is going to be *my* husband. *I* will be Mrs. Declan Bloom. *I* will live in his home, sleep in his bed, wear the jewels he buys me, and be at the absolute top of society. *You* are a nobody whore," she hissed. "Declan will forget about you all over again."

"Ms. Carrol." Todd attempted to intervene.

"Shut up. Don't you dare speak to me in that tone." The woman's eyes flared. "With his ring on my finger, I will get the respect I deserve. From you..." She speared Todd with a glare. "And from his clingy siblings."

Olivia's temper ticked up even while her brain told her the woman had said something important. Something she needed to pay attention to.

Fiona grabbed Olivia's arm, her long nails making crescents in her skin. "I know all about you. I see what you're doing. Panting after Declan like you're in heat." Fiona's face turned red, and from the corner of her eye, Olivia saw Todd stand. "You fucked him in Inferno's bathroom, didn't you?"

Olivia's cheeks heated.

Fiona's lip curled. "Play the whore for him. It wouldn't be the first time you did it to get a job. Kyle told me all about how you pursued him to get a promotion here. He doesn't want you anymore, and soon Declan won't either."

Olivia looked at the woman's left hand wrapped around her forearm. "That might be true, but I don't see a ring on your finger. Sounds like you are getting ahead of yourself."

Fiona gasped and thrust her face close enough that Olivia could pick out the almost nonexistent pores on the woman's face. "Stay away from him, or I *will* make you sorry."

"That's going to be hard, considering we work so closely together." Olivia gave the woman a stiff smile. "Speaking of, I have more important things to do than listen to your tantrum. Though it's been... entertaining."

Fiona spluttered, and Olivia stepped around her.

When Olivia reached her office, she propped her elbows on the desk and breathed deeply for a minute, wishing the socialite's words hadn't stuck with her.

What *were* she and Declan doing? Their connection burned as hot as it always had. But did he still plan on marrying Fiona? He'd said they weren't a couple, but that didn't mean he would choose Olivia.

A FEW DAYS LATER, Olivia stopped by one of the local bakery cafes to pick up a basket of pastries. Stuart and his team had been working practically around the clock to get closer to a prototype of the new design, and she wanted to reward them.

Olivia turned from the counter and saw Declan's sister Cara

waving at her wildly from a corner booth. Seated with her, Olivia recognized Dahlia and Cami. Olivia hesitated, but other than being openly rude, she couldn't think of an excuse to escape.

"Good morning," she said brightly, hoping it covered her nerves. The last time she saw these women, she had collapsed in their arms. Olivia shifted the large basket.

"We saw you standing over there and wanted to say hi. Small world." Cara laughed.

Olivia's body relaxed. "I'm glad I ran into you, too. I wanted to apologize for what happened in New York. I made a fool of myself, and I really appreciate the three of you stepping in to keep a bad situation from getting worse."

"It wasn't that bad," Dahlia said, from under a black baseball cap pulled low over her eyes.

"Thankfully, I don't remember most of it."

Cara scooted to the side of the bench seat and patted the open space. "Sit down for a minute. I wanted to ask you something." Her panic must have shown, because Cara's face softened. "Please."

Slightly terrified by what Declan's sister might want to talk with her about, Olivia sank onto the seat. She placed the basket of pastries on the table but left her coat on. "I only have a few minutes. I need to get to work."

"How is it going?" Cami asked, her eyes inquisitive. "James said there was some kind of surprise ending to the deal you were brokering."

Olivia wasn't sure how to respond to that. "We're thrilled to have been acquired by Bloom Capital."

Dahlia gave her a sarcastic look.

"At least it's keeping Declan in town for a while," Cara said. "It's been nice knowing he's around, even if we don't see him much."

"He's been a lot more involved than I anticipated," Olivia agreed.

"What's he like to work with? Does he issue edicts and then growl when you aren't fast enough?" Cara asked, laughing a little.

"It's been…" Olivia screwed her mouth to the side. "I'm trying to think of the right word."

"Complicated?" Dahlia supplied.

A laugh escaped Olivia. "Yes! Then again, if Declan's involved, I can't see how it could be anything *but* complicated." The words slipped out before Olivia realized, and she cursed herself as the women exchanged looks.

"I'm sorry, I didn't mean that as a criticism of your brother, I—"

Cami grinned. "Sounds about right."

"Declan is the most complicated human on the planet," Cara agreed.

"And stubborn," Olivia muttered, and Cara burst out laughing. "You *have* gotten to know him pretty well."

"We've been working on the restructure together."

"That can't be easy," Cami observed.

Olivia shrugged. "It's been a challenge. There haven't been any massive layoffs yet, but it's only a matter of time." Tension prickled in her spine. "Entire divisions. Everyone is working hard to hold it off for as long as possible. I usually bring them muffins on Fridays, but I thought they needed extra ones this week." She gestured to the basket. "Morale boost."

Cara scrunched her nose. "That's tough. Declan must be making you miserable. I can't believe he's going to fire all those people. That seems harsh even for him."

Her words startled Olivia. "Declan has actually been extremely fair. He didn't get rid of anyone right away, so people could start looking for jobs, and he's also offered an extremely generous severance package. Really, it's more than we would have gotten from someone else. Declan's good at what he does, and this is business. He has his own investors to answer to." Olivia realized she sounded defensive, and her cheeks flushed. She was all too aware the women were smiling widely at her.

"I should go. Thank you again." Olivia slipped from the bench, but as she bent for the basket, Cara leaned forward and sniffed her.

"What scent is that? Sorry," she gave a rueful smile. "I noticed it in New York. Occupational hazard. I'm always looking for new scents for my natural skin care products, and you smell delicious." Her nose scrunched. "Is it rose?"

"Thank you. It's rose based, but it's definitely not all natural. I have no idea what they put in the perfume."

"What's the name? If I had a bottle, I might be able to identify more of the notes," Cara said, her face serious.

"I order it online," Olivia explained. "It's French—Wild White Rose."

Cara gaped at Olivia making her uncomfortable.

"You still with us, Cara?" Dahlia asked.

Cara shook her head slowly, her lips slightly parted. "What? Yeah, I just… remembered something."

Olivia grabbed her chance to leave. "It was nice to see you ladies again."

She was almost at the door when Cara called her name. "You just met Declan, right?" Something in Cara's tone made Olivia's steps falter.

"Uh, huh." She gave a wave over her shoulder and escaped out into the cold. Olivia couldn't shake the look on the young woman's face as she drove to the office. Cara had stared at her like Olivia was the answer to a riddle she'd been struggling to solve.

~

Olivia glanced out her office window at the darkening sky and decided to leave work early. She'd wrangled an invitation to an event where she planned on speaking with several state senators about potential tax credits if Armstrong were to expand into manufacturing. As she crossed the lobby, Declan pushed the glass doors open letting the bitter wind blow in with him.

"You're back." Olivia ignored how her heart leapt at the sight of him. It *definitely* didn't mean she had missed him the last few days. Declan's tan cheeks were pinked with cold. "Looks like the temperature dropped out there," she added lamely.

With Declan out of town, they still hadn't talked about what happened at Inferno. Had too much time passed? Had they missed their moment again?

Declan's eyes skated over her face, his expression focused, as if soaking her in—as if he'd missed *her* too. "It's freezing."

They stood staring at each other in silence, the air pulsing with the electric current that always existed between them.

Declan cleared his throat. "Are you leaving for the day?"

"I'm going to corner some politicians at a fundraising event." She gave him a half-smile.

He squinted at her. "Okay?"

"Tax credits."

Understanding crossed his face, his features easing. "Ah."

They only stood a few feet apart, but the gap between them seemed so much more impossible to cross than just a few short steps.

"I should get going before traffic becomes a nightmare," she finally said, breaking the spell they both were under. "Do you have plans?"

Why are you asking that? He's going to think you are fishing for information about Fiona?

It was the truth.

"I have dinner with my family."

Relief washed over her.

"I ran into your sisters this morning."

Declan briefly closed his eyes. "They tried to interrogate you, didn't they?"

"Only a little." Olivia held her thumb and forefinger an inch apart. "They were very nice. Curious about what working with you is like. Cara mentioned how happy she is that you're in town."

Declan's whole body exhaled an irritated sigh. "She wants to house hunt."

Olivia's eyes widened. "You're considering living in Atlanta?"

"There are a lot of people I care about here."

Was he only talking about his family? Traitorous hope flared in her chest. Was she one of the 'people?'

It was on the tip of her tongue to ask, but before she embarrassed herself, a voice close by said. "Looks like it going to pour out there."

Both of their heads swung toward the other person in the lobby. Olivia hadn't realized they weren't alone. The man standing by the window shook his head. "Rush hour is going to be a disaster."

Olivia angled her head to the darkening windows. "I'll see you in the morning."

Declan opened his mouth to say something, then hesitated. His shoulders rolled back, and his chin lifted. "Drive safely," he said, before swiftly striding away.

Olivia's chest ached. What used to be so easy between them was now painfully awkward, and the reminder of what they'd lost cut deep. As she walked to her car, she wondered if this stilted distance is all they would ever have.

CHAPTER THIRTY-FOUR

Atlanta—Present Day

"How did it go?" Siobhan asked.

The expectant faces of his family, gathered around the wide island in Cara's kitchen, all seemed to hold a collective breath.

"I couldn't find it." Frustration swelled in him again.

"Damn it! You looked in the study?"

He leveled a look at his mother. "Of course, I did. The room hadn't changed at all. It was a time capsule."

Declan didn't share how he'd imagined the faint scent of his father's cologne and cigars still lingered in the air. The same cologne they now knew Chris and Courtney had used to poison David Bloom.

Conscious of the fact that security guards patrolled the estate and could discover him any minute, Declan didn't indulge in the nostalgia. The moment he stepped over the threshold, onto the royal blue carpeting his father loved, years of memories washed over him.

The last time Declan had been in the room was for the reading of his father's will. As soon as the terms were explained,

Courtney ordered her new security team to remove all of them from their home.

Declan quickly searched the study and all the other main rooms before moving to the bedrooms upstairs. The urn wasn't there.

Declan didn't tell Cara that her bedroom, still full of many of her belongings on the day of the will reading, had been emptied.

Anne, Luke and James's mother, slumped in her chair. Her husband, Bruce, squeezed her shoulder and stroked a hand over her back. "I really thought this was going to work," Anne said.

"As far as we know, the bitch threw them out." Siobhan glowered.

"We'd have heard if she had a memorial... I mean, she wouldn't just... would she?" Cara's fearful eyes sought Declan's.

Cami put her arm over Cara's shoulders and gave her a side hug. "At this point, I think Courtney might be capable of anything. Look at the two absolute psychopaths she raised. But if she disposed of the urn, Trey would have mentioned it when he was spilling his guts to me. He would have praised her for planning ahead." Cami's lip curled.

James rubbed a hand over his jaw. "That's true. On the tape, he bragged about how brilliant his mother was. So, most likely, the ashes are still out there... somewhere. We just don't know where."

"You should have Vincent follow her. Maybe there's a safe deposit box or something," Cara suggested.

"She'd need a big box to fit a whole urn in," Luke responded.

"She might have put the ashes in a plastic bag." Cara persisted, narrowing her eyes at Luke.

Siobhan turned to face Declan. "What's happening with the lawsuit all those charities and former employees filed? The ones who were also excluded under the new will.

"That was my other news. As of yesterday, the courts have frozen all the assets that they could identify as having been distributed under the will. Most of it was still in the accounts and trusts our father set up. I don't know why Courtney didn't immediately move the funds, but it was a break we needed. It's also a good sign that the court thinks there's an argument to be made that the last will was a fake."

"The only evidence we have is two taped confessions—Dr. Keller's and Trey's—but neither one is admissible," James argued. "You can only twist a judge so far Dec. Even one of *your* judges is going to have to point at some case law to support his decision. Courtney will appeal, and this will never be over."

"But there *are* two confessions." Dahlia's brow furrowed. "That has to count for *something*."

Luke shook his head, his expression grim. "Not really. There were no third-party witnesses to verify the statements."

Siobhan slammed her glass on the counter. "This is unacceptable." She pointed a finger at Declan. "Something has to be done."

Declan inhaled slowly through his nose. What did she think he'd been doing?

"Without the thallium to prove he was murdered, Courtney is going to get away with it." Cara stared morosely out her kitchen window.

"She is not going to get away with anything," Declan promised. "Neither of them will. I would have already dealt with both of them, except I want the Bloom fortune and shares back."

James's jaw was tight when he asked, "What's the next move?"

"The annual shareholder meeting. I'm going to call for a vote of no confidence to have Chris removed as CEO. The young woman—the surviving witness of the car accident—has agreed to go to New York and tell her story. Between that and the two taped confessions, the board shouldn't hesitate to remove him."

"Excellent," Siobhan beamed.

"That doesn't mean they'll choose you," Luke pointed out.

"I'm going to offer them a streaming device that has the potential to explode their bottom line at no cost." Declan braced himself for the comments he knew were to come. "One of the largest shareholders has promised me support."

Cara's lip curled. "You mean you're selling yourself to Fiona Carrol's father."

"The topic is not open for discussion."

"But—"

"No." The word snapped like a whip into the already tense air. Declan looked at his brothers. "I appreciate everyone wants to help, but it's time for you all to step back. I'll handle it from here."

James immediately began shaking his head. "I told you before, I wanted us to do things legally—"

"I tried it your way. It didn't work," Declan said icily.

James's jaw worked. "I *also* told you that when the time came, and if the justice system didn't work, I'd be there with you." His eyes locked onto Declan's. "He was my father too."

"Ah, that's lovely," Siobhan said.

"Siobhan. You realize what they aren't saying, right?" Anne frowned.

Siobhan kissed Anne on the cheek. "I understand *exactly* what they are talking about."

Anne pressed her lips together unhappily but didn't say anything else.

"I know you think because you're the oldest, you are responsible for all of us," Cara said softly. "You never let us get too close because you've convinced yourself that you're protecting us. I appreciate it… everything you do for us. But, Declan, you are *not* alone, and I don't want you to do something you might not be able to live with."

Cara's meaning was clear on her face, and emotion swelled in him. He hoped she never discovered the things he had done.

What he was more than happy to do again, to protect the people he loved.

Striding to where she stood in front of the sink, Declan pulled her into a tight hug. "Thank you, Car-bear. I'll be fine. Promise." He pressed a firm kiss to her head, and when he pulled away, he avoided his brothers' eyes, afraid of what they would see in his. He wasn't about to tell them that this wasn't even going to be the first time he'd killed someone to protect his family.

"Not to change the subject, but we ran into your *friend* this morning at breakfast." Dahlia drew the word out meaningfully.

Fuck me. Declan mentally thanked Olivia for giving him the heads up.

"Olivia was buying muffins for the office, which we..." She exchanged looks with Cami and Cara. "Thought was really sweet. We like her."

Declan's jaw clenched.

"Who is Olivia?" Anne asked, looking confused.

"She's the CFO of the company Declan bought here in Atlanta." Cara's smile was suspiciously innocent. "Olivia's kind *and* smart, not to mention stunning. You'd like her, Anne."

"Cara," Declan's voice promised retribution.

"Watch your tone." Wes glared darkly at him from where he'd been observing silently.

"I'm definitely missing something," Anne's eyes bounced between him and Cara. "Is she *not* those things, Declan?"

"Olivia is extremely intelligent," Declan said through gritted teeth. He wasn't about to fall into the trap of mentioning how beautiful Olivia was.

"She smells absolutely incredible," Cara added in an off-hand tone, but Declan felt her eyes boring into him.

"Did you sniff her?" Siobhan teased.

"She did actually," Dahlia snorted.

Luke shook his head. "Who raised you?"

"Olivia didn't mind. She told me where to find it on the internet. It's a French perfume—Wild White Rose. Apparently, she's always worn it." Cara's eyes were still on Declan, and she'd over enunciated the name of the perfume...

The pressure in his chest grew. There was no possibility Cara knew about Ireland. Yet the way she was looking at him... The others in the room were picking up on the tension between them.

"Her perfume is important, why?" James frowned at his sister.

Declan stared back at Cara, unblinking. Silently imploring his sister to not reveal whatever it was she believed she knew.

Cara's face cleared. "It's not important. I just thought it was interesting. I might order some."

Declan's shoulders relaxed, as Wes kissed his wife's cheek. "Don't even think about doing away with my honeysuckle, you little weirdo."

Cara tipped her head back to smile at her husband. "You love that I'm a weirdo."

"I do," Wes agreed, kissing her on the lips this time.

"Gross," James muttered.

"Didn't we put rules in place about what forms of affection are allowed in front of us?" Luke folded his arms over his chest.

"Shut up." Dahlia pinched his side. Luke laughed and leaned down to kiss her.

Anne beamed at the happy couples, but Declan could feel his mother watching him.

Fantastic.

Declan was the first to leave, and his mother walked out with him.

"Are you sleeping with her? Is that what your sister was insinuating? How will that affect things between you and Fiona?" Siobhan asked. "If Bloom Communications is what you want, don't let yourself get distracted this close to the end."

"When have I ever allowed myself to be distracted?" Declan demanded. "When have I *ever* let my personal wishes get in the way of what needed to be done for this family?"

Siobhan's face was troubled. "*A stór,* if this isn't what you want any more, you don't have to pursue it. It's all right to let it go."

Declan's blood simmered, and he reminded himself not to shout at his mother. "I am rightfully the CEO of Bloom Communications. I was *raised* to be the CEO. *You* made sure of that," he hissed. "It's a little late to ask me what *I* want. What I want has never been a factor in *anything*."

His mother's eyes grew wide. "Perhaps I made a mistake sending you to live with your father. I wanted you away from the troubles at home, and your father convinced me... But maybe it was the wrong choice. If you honestly believe that you never had a choice... that it was all you could ever do..." His mother clasped his arm. "*A chroi,* there is more to life than work."

Angry frustration buzzed inside him. He wanted to explode.

How could she say that to him now... After a lifetime of reminding him of his *responsibilities*.

Keeping a tight rein on his anger, he bit out, "That would have been great to hear years ago. It's too late now." Declan opened her car door.

"It's never too late. I want you to be happy." To his horror, his mother's eyes glistened. Declan had never seen his mother cry, and he instantly felt guilty.

"I'm Irish. Tragedy is in my blood," Declan deliberately misquoted Yeats as he kissed her forehead.

"You're only Irish when it suits you," Siobhan said tartly, and then slammed her car door.

When Declan turned to walk to his own car, he found Cara, arms wrapped around her stomach, waiting for him.

"Go inside. It's freezing out here, and you don't even have a coat on."

"It's her, isn't it?" Cara's voice was so solemn, chills ran down Declan's spine.

"Who?" He infused the word with as much menace as he was capable, warning her not to go there, but Cara wasn't intimidated. She never was by him.

"You don't remember telling me, do you?"

Declan's heart raced, and he forced his breath to stay even. "Telling you what?"

Cara closed the distance between them, and he saw the goosebumps on her arms. She was shivering. "Go inside, Car-bear. It's too cold."

"Then tell me the truth quickly." Violet eyes identical to his sparkled up at him. Cara softened her voice. "You told me a story —about your tattoo." Her gaze fell to his chest where his heart had stopped beneath the flower she couldn't see. "The only time you *ever* mentioned it."

Declan's ribs closed tight over his lungs.

"You were drunk," Cara continued, oblivious to the panic roaring to life inside him. "Extremely drunk. It was about four years ago. Do you remember?"

A vague memory stirred. Cara trying to push him into a seated position, threatening to call Mrs. Woodson, their father's housekeeper.

Four years ago. The day he'd seen Olivia's picture in the file and discovered she was married. The last kernel of hope that he had held on to crushed. She loved someone else. She'd made a life with someone else.

"See you."

"Maybe."

He'd gotten blackout drunk with no memory of how he'd ended up back in his room at his father's estate. *Fuck!* Cara had been there.

"I have no idea what you're talking about." His voice sounded weak even to him. "I don't remember."

"You do." Cara was firm. "Declan, you were lying on the floor of the library with books scattered around you. I was home from college, and I found you because you were singing and reciting poetry at the top of your lungs." Her lips lifted at the corner. "I didn't even know you liked poetry."

Her humor disappeared just as quickly as it came. Declan waited barely breathing, terrified of what Cara would reveal next.

"You told me that if I ever fell in love, I needed to do whatever it took to protect it. To keep it safe. Because, and this is a direct quote, Declan—'True love only comes around once in a lifetime.' I was more than a little freaked out seeing you like that.

"You were always so in control, and I could see how devastated you were. I didn't know what had caused it or what to do, so I teased you about all the models I'd seen you with. I'll never forget that moment... You ripped open your shirt and showed me the tattoo. You pointed at it and told me you had lost your wild white rose. You kept saying it over and over. 'I've lost her forever. My wild white rose.' I've never seen anyone look so sad, Declan. It breaks my heart to think about it even now."

"Cara," Declan choked out.

She shook her head hard. "I know you. You're going to deny it and say that you don't remember."

"You said I was drunk." Declan heard the desperation in his voice and grabbed for his control. "It doesn't mean anything. I might say anything when I'm drunk."

"That's not true." Cara shook her head again, her eyes flashing. "On the rare occasions you get drunk, you tell stories and laugh. It's the only time you ever let go. This was different, Declan."

"What do you want from me?" The ache in his chest grew,

creating a hollow, concave space where his heart should be. Reminding him of all the things that he would never have.

"I want you to admit it. It makes total sense now… The way you looked at her in New York, the way you swooped in and carried her out. How many times in life do you think someone is going to say those words—Wild White Rose—to me?"

"You don't understand."

"You should have—"

"Cara!" Her eyes snapped to his. "You can't mention this to *anyone*. Including your husband."

Cara's face folded. "I don't understand. If Olivia is the woman you were talking about, why—"

"I can't tell you." Declan covered his face with one hand. "I can't tell you why, Cara. Just trust me."

"You can talk to me," she said, reaching out to hold his free hand. Her fingers felt like ice against his. "I can help."

Declan pulled his hand free and dropped the other with a long exhale. "You really can't."

"You have always taken care of us, always been there when we needed something. It's time you let us return the favor. We love you."

Declan kissed his little sister on the forehead. "You've grown into a remarkable woman, Mrs. Evans. I'm proud of you."

"Olivia?" Cara persisted.

"Is my past. Some things can't be fixed."

Cara took a step back, and Declan was surprised by the recrimination on her face. "The Declan Bloom I know has never given up on something he wanted. If Olivia is who you want, don't waste your chance to have her. If this is about Fiona, we will find another way to get the company back. Someday you're going to face a choice—yourself or what you think you still need to prove to our father."

She whirled and entered the house, slamming the door

behind her. Declan stared after her, his breath rapid puffs of white in the frigid air.

A small ember of hope took flame inside him.

Was there a way he and Olivia could be together?

Would he still be able to keep her safe if everyone knew she was his biggest weakness?

CHAPTER THIRTY-FIVE

ATLANTA—PRESENT DAY

Olivia kicked off her heels and tugged her blouse loose from the waistband of her skirt. Political schmoozing wasn't something she enjoyed, but the progress she'd made at the event excited her. It was an election year. The prospect of touting a new manufacturing facility in their district was something more than one candidate was interested in. Smiling to herself, Olivia celebrated her success with a huge sushi order from her favorite restaurant.

Pouring herself a glass of wine while she waited, she stood in front of the floor to ceiling windows that looked out onto the river. Her house lights illuminated bits of her backyard, and she could make out the dark shapes of bare trees swaying in the wind.

Olivia loved this house. The moment she saw the listing, she knew she had to have it. She'd rented a condo for a year before her divorce was final, not wanting to buy anything Kyle might try to claim.

The second the ink was dry on the divorce decree, Olivia purchased the house. It was too large for only her, but she loved the privacy of the riverfront lot. The house was at the back of her neighborhood, at the apex of a cul-de-sac. The long, steep driveway sloped down toward the garage, giving her front door privacy from anyone driving by. It was her tucked away piece of heaven.

Olivia had just set the wine bottle on the marble kitchen countertop when the doorbell rang. Already tasting her spicy tuna roll, she took the few steps from the open concept kitchen to her front door, setting her wineglass on the entry table.

She should have checked the door before she opened it. Instead, expecting to scoop up a bag from the ground, she wasn't prepared for the shove that sent her reeling backwards into the house. She only saved herself from falling by catching the wood spindles of her banister. Kyle kicked the door shut behind him, his face contorted with rage. Terror skidded down her spine. His pupils were huge, his eyes terribly bloodshot, which could only mean he was drunk or high. Neither was good.

"What are you doing here?" Olivia's stomach knotted as the fear took hold of her body. Run you idiot, her brain screamed, but she felt paralyzed.

It had been two years since the last night of her marriage when Kyle had attacked her, but her body remembered. She immediately tried to think of ways to appease him—to calm him down.

"You stupid, fucking whore," Kyle snarled at her. Olivia backed up, only to trip over the heels she'd left on the foyer floor. She landed hard on her tailbone, and a sharp stab of pain ricocheted up her back.

Kyle loomed over where she lay on the floor, his fists bunched. The muscles in her body tensed, prepared for the kick she was sure would come. "You've made a fool of me."

Olivia licked her lips. "Kyle, I don't know what you're talking about." She lifted her hands, anticipating a blow, when one of his fists moved. "Tell me what's wrong. Why are you so upset?"

"Like you don't know," Kyle sneered. "You thought you were going to get one over on me?" Kyle waved his arms wide, and then halted, his gaze scanning her home. "Did he pay for this, or is this how you spent my money?"

Leaving her on the floor, Kyle stalked past her into her kitchen. Olivia let out a breath and scrambled to her feet. She weighed her options. If she ran for the door, he'd catch her for sure, and then it would be worse, and her phone and keys were in the kitchen with him. The panic tightening her chest made it hard for her to hold on to any one thought for more than a few seconds.

Not now, Olivia. You can't lose control.

Kyle stood in front of where she displayed her teacup collection on tiny hooks. With a finger he set one swinging. Olivia winced as the china clinked loudly against the cup next to it. "I can't believe you still have this crap."

Olivia inhaled and exhaled slowly through her nose. She needed to stay calm. The only way she was going to get through this unharmed was if Kyle *wanted* to leave. It had to be his idea.

"Kyle," Olivia asked, her voice as soft as she could make it. "Can you tell me what happened?"

Kyle looked over his shoulder at her, but he seemed less agitated than when he first barged in. He continued to rove through the kitchen and into the adjacent room with her sofa and television.

Olivia inched toward the foyer. Kyle stopped at the large windows for a beat before spinning to face her. "This is nicer than my place. Did you spread your legs for it?"

"No."

The word reignited his anger. Kyle's long legs quickly brought him to her again. "You think you won, don't you?"

In her haste to get away, Olivia misjudged her steps, and her back hit the wall instead of taking her into the foyer. She'd cut off her own escape route.

Olivia was shaking, and shame crawled over her that she didn't stand up to him. Kyle's nostrils flared as his chest rose and fell. She'd never seen him this enraged. Her head fuzzed as her throat closed, her heart hammering wildly in her chest.

Olivia, you can do this. Focus.

Her body didn't care what her brain wanted her to do, and she struggled to keep a smile on her face. "I could pour you a glass of wine, I-I poured myself one."

She swallowed hard when his hand clamped around her arm, and he thrust her toward the island and the bottle of wine.

His laugh ricocheted off the walls. "You're going to offer me a drink? After you got wasted and fucked yourself into a job. Whatever happened to, *'You drink too much, Kyle.' 'I don't like how you act when you drink, Kyle.'* Now, suddenly you're going to offer me one?" Kyle grabbed the neck of the wine bottle and slammed it into the counter. Wine and glass shards flew. "You fucking, traitorous bitch."

He turned and in one movement his arm swept her collection of tea cups off their hooks and into the air. She gasped and squeezed her eyes shut as they shattered all over the counter and onto the floor. Kyle grabbed her shoulders and shook her so hard her teeth snapped together. "Look at me."

Olivia's heart pounded in her chest, but she pried her lids open only to see Kyle's evil smile inches from her face. "Oops."

"Kyle, don't," she breathed. Olivia wanted to scream at him to get out, but the moment she had always feared would come had arrived. There was a different light in his eyes tonight, and he looked close to completely losing control.

For most of their marriage, Olivia made excuses for Kyle's mental and verbal abuse. It wasn't as if he hit her all the time, she'd rationalized to herself. Until the night he'd punched and kicked her repeatedly. Olivia had lain on her kitchen floor wondering how her life had gotten to that point. She'd walked away the next day and foolishly thought the divorce would keep her safe.

"You've ruined my life. He had me banned from the club!"

"I had nothing to do with that." Olivia forced herself to meet his eyes.

"They made me leave. They actually came up to me and told me to leave the premises—in front of everyone!" Kyle's shoulders bunched, and he suddenly thrust her away from him to prowl her kitchen, ranting. "You made him do that, didn't you? You don't want me to be happy." He rounded on her again. "What did you tell him about me?"

"I didn't tell Declan—" Her words were cut off when Kyle's hand wrapped around her throat. He drove her backward until she felt the cool metal of her refrigerator against her back.

"How dare you say his name to me?"

Olivia clutched at his hand, bright spots appearing in front of her. Kyle's eyes were black, and Olivia wasn't sure he even realized where he was.

She reached up and yanked on his hair. Her arms felt leaden, but the momentary pain appeared to get through to him. His expression changed, and his hand fell from her throat. Olivia sucked in gulps of air, her throat burning.

Kyle bent double, his hands on his knees, and wailed. "Why do you make me act like this, Livvy? I loved you, and you ruined my life."

"It's not ruined, Kyle," she rasped. "I have a plan that will keep the company open. It'll keep the stock price up, and then you can—"

The first blow skimmed her jaw, followed by a second to her mouth that spun her around. Her fingers caught the cool marble counter as Kyle started shouting. "There you go, again. You always have to prove how you're going to save the day."

Her eyes watering and face throbbing, Olivia forced her eyes open. The answer appeared in front of her. She didn't risk a glance back before she grabbed the handle and yanked the large knife free from its block. Bracing her back against the counter, she raised the knife in front of her.

Kyle stood with his eyes shut, gripping tufts of his hair. "You ruined *everything*."

"Get the fuck out of my house." The words weren't as forceful as Olivia hoped, but when Kyle's eyes popped open, they went from her face to the knife pointed at him and back again.

Olivia could taste the blood in her mouth, and her face and neck were on fire.

"What's this, Livvy? You're going to fight back now?" His eyes dipped to the knife, a cocky smile on his face. "Your hand is shaki—"

If she hadn't been so frightened, Olivia might have enjoyed the comical expression of shock on his face when she lunged, burying the knife in his side.

Kyle didn't drop immediately, like she expected. He let out a sharp cry and then his arm shot out and he wrapped her hair around his hand. "I'm going to fucking kill you."

Then the hand was gone, and Kyle staggered to the side, knocking into the counter as he stared down at the knife. "Stupid bitch," he whispered. Olivia watched in frozen horror as Kyle stumbled to the front door and out into the night.

Shaking, Olivia waited precisely five seconds before sprinting to the front door, ignoring the stinging pain in her feet as she raced across the broken porcelain. Flipping the lock and panting hard, she pressed her palm hard against her chest.

Oh my god. What if I killed him?

What if he calls the police? I'm going to jail!

He attacked you, her rational mind chimed in, but no one believed her before...

Kyle's family had deep ties in the city. There was no guarantee... and the humiliation of everyone knowing what she'd been hiding. People saw Olivia as a high-powered female executive. Strong. Assertive. Hell, she'd even spoken at a local high school and served as a mentor for young girls...

Now everyone would know she was a fraud. She wasn't strong. She'd been weak and afraid for so long.

Shame, deep and dark, pulsed through her.

I should have left years ago.

I never should have married him.

Olivia walked back to the destruction of her kitchen and bit her cheek hard at the sight of her teacups in a million pieces. She pulled her phone from her purse and stared at it. It wasn't 911 she wanted to call. It was Declan. She stifled the sob that rose in her throat. Grandma Rose would be so disappointed in her.

Slowly, Olivia set the phone down, and avoiding the mirror on the wall, she grabbed two ibuprofen before she began to clean.

I'll get a better security system. Maybe get the dog I've always wanted. I can handle this—if I don't get arrested tonight.

An eerie calm came over her. The fallout of her pressing charges would be worse, she told herself. Olivia could file for a protection order—or try, anyway. She had no proof it was him and no documentation from any of the prior times. Even then, Kyle would ignore a piece of paper. And if it ever got out, it would only enrage him further. How could she face everyone at work when they knew her secret?

Kyle wouldn't get close to her again. She'd make sure of it—If he was still alive, that is.

Olivia's legs shook as she climbed the steps to her room. I should lay out some clothes, she thought, in case the police come. Her mind felt oddly disconnected, and if she hadn't been so grateful for the numbness, Olivia would be worried. She'd stabbed her ex-husband. She should feel *something.*

Later that night, after she'd cleaned the cuts on her feet and her lip, Olivia rubbed arnica cream into the bruises on her face. She couldn't get Kyle's eyes out of her mind. Tears slipped down her cheeks, stinging her broken skin, as she curled into a ball under the covers. She wasn't sure what exactly she was crying for… The pain? What happened? What would come? Or, what would never be?

CHAPTER THIRTY-SIX

ATLANTA—PRESENT DAY

Declan poured coffee from the communal pot into a nondescript mug. Todd had looked at him strangely the first time he'd returned to his office with a cup of coffee from the employee kitchen. Normally, he would demand Todd go to a coffee shop, rather than drink the overcooked coffee from an employee lounge. But Declan liked the idea of accidentally running into Olivia when she made one of her many cups of tea throughout the day.

By eleven, Declan noticed the small pink teacup with the green leaf saucer was still sitting in the same place as when he came in early that morning.

Did she have a meeting out of the office? Declan scowled. He was acting like a teenager, hoping to get a glimpse of his crush. Frowning, he went back to his office and tried to concentrate. Olivia had a scheduled meeting with him in an hour. He could wait an hour, he thought, tapping his pen restlessly against the desk.

However, thirty minutes later, Todd appeared in his doorway. "Mr. Bloom, I'm sorry to interrupt. Ms. Adler won't be able to make it to your meeting today. She apologizes for the short notice."

"Why not?" Declan ignored the disappointment spiking in his chest.

"Melissa, her receptionist, said Ms. Adler caught that flu going around. She will most likely be out for several days."

Declan's brows drew down. "She's so sick Olivia already knows she'll be out for several days?"

Todd stared at him like he wasn't sure how to respond. Declan scowled when his assistant shut the door. He rolled his shoulders, hoping to shed the unpleasant feeling inside him. He stared unseeing at an email and twirled his pen between his fingers.

Olivia was sick. And alone.

The urge to check on her was overwhelming, and Declan didn't question why he didn't even try to resist.

"I'm not feeling well either." He tossed the comment over his shoulder as he strode past Todd, slipping into his coat. "Clear my calendar for the next few days. I'll be available on my cell phone." Declan paused and turned back. "Find out the best restaurant within ten miles for soup and bread, and place an order for chicken soup. Text me the address." He would have sworn Todd smiled, but that would have been completely out of character for his assistant.

Pulling into Olivia's driveway, Declan smiled as he took in the Tudor style home. With a giant container of chicken soup and the still-warm bread in his hands, Declan rang the doorbell with his elbow. A buzzing drew his gaze to his feet where a takeout bag was surrounded by flies. Dread sent an icy trail down his spine. He jabbed her doorbell again.

After several minutes of silence, Declan rang the bell a third time, his pulse picking up speed. Something was wrong. Ears straining, he thought he heard movement from inside the house, but he wasn't sure. Declan frowned and stepped back, looking up at the facade as if he could see inside. He walked down the steep driveway to peer into the windows set high on her garage door. Concern had his heart pounding when he saw her BMW parked inside.

Is she too sick to come to the door?

The dark clouds above finally delivered on what they'd been promising, but Declan ignored the freezing drizzle. This time, he followed the doorbell with several hard knocks with his fist.

"Go away, Declan, I'm sick," Olivia's muffled voice sounded through the door.

"I heard." Declan hesitated for a moment, wondering if he was making a fool of himself. When he heard she was sick, he wanted to see her. Now, standing on her doorstep uninvited, his hands full of food, he had his first doubts.

"I brought you food."

"It's not a good time, Declan." Something in her voice had his intuition pinging. His eyes fell to the bag of takeout covered in ants at his feet. A knot formed in his stomach. That bag had clearly been sitting there for a while.

"Let me in, Olivia. I won't stay if you don't feel well enough. I just want to make sure you're okay."

The silence stretched, and he scowled at the door. "It's not like I haven't seen you sick before. It's raining, and the bread is getting cold. You aren't seriously going to risk ruining fresh bread, are you?"

Still nothing. Declan's concern turned to a full-fledged alarm.

Why wouldn't she open the door?

"Just open the door. I want proof you're actually sick and not shirking your responsibilities." Declan forced a chuckle, but she didn't answer.

"Open the door," he demanded in a hard voice, and he swore

he heard her sigh through the wood. "Open the fucking door, Petal, or I'm going to kick it down!"

Her security system beeped, and then the deadbolt turned. But when the door swung inward, Olivia swiftly turned away from him to type in the code to rearm the system as he shut the door behind him.

She wore a thick terry-cloth robe, and with her back to him, Olivia waved an arm toward the kitchen visible through the doorway.

"Thank you for the food. You can put it on the island." Her voice sounded scratchy.

Something was off.

Why wouldn't she face him? Did Olivia think he cared if she had a red nose and dark circles under her eyes? She could be covered in measles, and Olivia would still be the most beautiful woman he'd ever seen.

Declan followed her hunched shoulders the few short steps through the doorway that opened into a spacious kitchen and living area. He took in the space with a glance, and his breath caught.

Massive dark wood beams soared above the twenty-foot great room walls, which were painted a soft, creamy off-white. A deep camel-colored leather sectional faced the enormous fireplace, with a television mounted above the mantel.

Olivia fussed with something on the kitchen counter, and Declan stepped further into the room. There was a thick, knit blanket thrown over one arm of the sofa, and a book lay face down on the small side table. A small, distressed wood table sat in front, displaying a stack of poetry books next to a candle. A wingback chair, placed beside the sofa, was upholstered in a muted floral fabric, and pillows with a matching print were strewn on the floor and over the sofa.

Declan licked his lips. Had she intentionally chosen the pieces to mimic those in the cottage, or had something deeper drawn her to recreate a place where they had been so happy?

His throat ached, and Declan laughed to cover the feelings crashing over him. "Still reading Blake, huh?" Declan picked up the open book.

Olivia's head was bent, hands braced on the island as she stared at the food he brought. But she didn't respond to his teasing the way he hoped.

"Sorry, I know you're feeling lousy." Declan shifted on his feet. *Why won't she look at me?*

"Can I make you a cup of tea?"

Olivia sniffed, and if possible, her stance stiffened. Declan joined her in the kitchen and placed his hands on the opposite side of the island, imitating her pose.

"Do you need medicine? I can go—" His heart wrenched at the unmistakable sight of a tear splashing on the marble, swiftly followed by another, and then a steady flow. He rounded the island to her side, but she shook her head violently, her thick hair swishing side to side. Declan's chest cracked open as hers heaved with silent sobs.

"Ah, Petal. Tell me what you need. I'll do anything." Declan reached to pull her into his arms, but she flinched away, turning her back again.

An alarm rang loud and riotous in his brain, and his stomach clenched. "Petal... Baby... What's wrong?"

Declan saw her shoulders rise and fall with a shuddering breath, and then Olivia straightened and turned to face him.

The world stopped on its axis, and his breath seized in his lungs. Every cell in his body screamed in denial. Her blue eyes were glossy, but the tears no longer fell. Declan instantly registered her swollen, split lip and the bruises on her face.

Pain like he'd never felt before split his ribs, and the monster inside him howled for vengeance. Olivia maintained eye contact with him, her wet eyes daring him to pity her. He raised trembling hands to lift the sides of her hair away from where she had shielded the swelling and bruises on the side of her face.

Calling on every ounce of his control, Declan kept his voice low. He didn't want to frighten her with the violence raging inside him. A chill dark emotion settled over him.

"Who?"

Olivia's eyes slid away. "No one. I slipped, coming down the steps. I'm embarrassed for anyone to see me."

"You can either tell me, or I can figure it out. It's up to you."

She scowled at him. "This is none of your business. I fell. It's not a big deal."

Declan couldn't completely hide the tremor of rage in his voice. "Someone hurt you." Declan stopped as bile rose in his throat at the words, and he swallowed hard. "I need you to tell me who it was."

"Leave it alone, Declan. I didn't ask you to come here. Don't show up now, acting like you have some right to my life because we fucked a lifetime ago." Her voice broke as she threw his words in New York back at him.

The cord on his self-control was becoming dangerously frayed. Declan hadn't lied when he said he would do anything for her. And what she needed right now was for him to pretend to be human—to be the man she needed—deserved. Even if he wasn't.

"You don't owe me anything," Declan agreed. "I'm the one who let you down. I'm sorry."

Olivia blinked at him, his words clearly not what she'd been expecting.

Declan kept his voice calm, even though the tempest inside him was storming almost beyond what he could contain. "You were at that political event last night." He set his jaw, grinding his teeth to keep from yelling. "Did one of those bastards do this?"

He was going to destroy whoever it was. He didn't give a fuck who it was or the influence they had. They were a dead man.

"Declan, I don't want to talk about this."

"There is a time element, baby. There could be other consequences if..." Declan choked on the words.

Olivia's eyes widened. "He didn't rape me. He was angry about being thrown out of his country club and thinks I've ruined his life."

The truth dawned on Declan with crystal clear clarity, immediately followed by the knowledge of what he was going to do to her ex-husband. Declan clamped down on his control. "This isn't the first time Kyle hurt you, is it?"

She blanched.

"Olivia?" But her expression had become frighteningly blank, as though she'd retreated to a place she wouldn't let him follow. Fear scored painfully through his veins.

Declan took a step back and inhaled a deep breath. "You're right. This is your business. If you don't want to talk about it, we don't have to."

Olivia's eyes shifted, watching him warily as he pulled the large container of soup from the bag.

He forced his jaw to unlock. "Where are your pots?"

Olivia didn't answer at first, so Declan turned toward the cabinets, so that she couldn't see his face, couldn't see the monster that had slipped its leash. He was going to peel Kyle Armstrong's skin from his body an inch at a time.

"Bottom cabinet next to the stove," Olivia said quietly, and Declan exhaled a heavy breath.

Revenge would have to wait. Right now, Olivia was all that mattered, and he needed to take care of her. Declan didn't understand why Olivia was protecting the man, but he wouldn't push.

Not yet, anyway.

Declan busied himself emptying the container into a sauce

pot and turning on the flame. Plucking a wooden spoon from the ceramic container on the counter, he stirred the heating liquid. Slow even circles while he reined in his temper.

The last thing Olivia needed right now was his anger after facing… His stomach turned over at the thought of her alone and afraid with that bastard.

"You don't need to do this, Declan."

"I know."

There was a pause. "Why are you here?"

He stirred the soup.

One circle, two circles… Breathe.

Why was he there?

"Declan?" Olivia's voice was barely above a whisper, and like the final piece of a puzzle, his life snapped into place. Declan exhaled a long, slow breath, and for the first time in over a decade, he felt the vise around his chest ease.

"Because this is where I belong," he said simply, not turning around.

Olivia's breath hitched audibly.

Declan didn't regret the words.

He should have kept her safe. The whole reason he'd walked away from her, broken both of their hearts, was to keep her safe. Protect her from him and the monsters in his world.

The whole time she'd been alone with a different kind of monster.

Declan closed his eyes, regret and fury coursing through him. "I'm sorry," he whispered.

"What?"

Declan turned to face her, his eyes locked on hers. He saw the hope and vulnerability reflected back at him, and hated himself for being the reason she ever doubted how he felt.

"Do you remember telling me that maybe someday we would find our way back to each other?" Eyes wide, Olivia's lips parted, but she nodded. Declan's lips lifted. "Someday is today."

Olivia stared back at him, frozen. Declan swallowed over the lump in his throat. "I know you might not be ready to jump back in. I have a lot to make up for, and it will take a while for you to trust me again... to forgive me."

Tears slipped from the corners of her eyes, and her cheeks were pink. "What about Fiona? You're engaged."

Declan shook his head with a smile. It felt like blinders had fallen off of him, and for the first time, he saw his life clearly. "No. We're not. She planned on using me the same way I was going to use her, but I never actually asked her." Declan knew how cold it sounded. But if Olivia chose him—if she gave him another chance—she needed to understand who he was now.

A tremulous smile tipped her lips. "I guess I should feel bad for her." Olivia's smile widened, then winced, bringing her fingers to her wounded lip. "But she is a *super* bitch."

"My sister agrees with you," Declan said wryly.

"Wise woman."

"Please don't tell her. She's a bit too full of herself these days," Declan joked, determined to keep the mood light, but relief filled his body at an alarming rate, making him slightly lightheaded.

"Bowls?" he asked, when the soup bubbled.

Olivia pointed at a cabinet and moved to the refrigerator to retrieve a slab of butter.

"Is that Irish cream?" Declan eyed the dish.

She lifted a shoulder. "It's addictive."

Olivia sliced the bread and slathered the pieces with the Irish butter while Declan filled the bowls and carried them to her kitchen table.

Aware of Olivia's every careful movement, and how she limped a little across the room, his rage coiled tighter inside him.

Olivia raised her spoon and winced at the first swallow, her hand rising to her throat before dropping it again. The neckline of her thick robe had shifted, and he could see the unmistakable outline of bruises in the shape of fingers across her porcelain skin.

Declan must not have done as good a job hiding his response as he thought, because Olivia lay her hand over his white-knuckled grip on the spoon.

"It's okay."

His jaw worked. Fuck, now she was comforting *him*? Declan mentally added a few more hours of pain to what limited time Kyle had left.

"It's not," he managed in a strangled voice. "But you don't have to talk about it."

Olivia set her spoon down and stared at him. "I don't want you to think I am some kind of victim. Like I'm weak and can't protect myself."

Declan's mouth filled with the metallic taste of blood, and he released his tongue. "I would never think you are weak, because you aren't. He is a bully and a coward. None of that is a reflection on you."

Her lips pursed, and two lines formed between her brows. "It wasn't always like this. I left after he really hurt me. We kept the separation hidden for a year, but I knew—"

The spoon bent in Declan's hand as he struggled to fill his lungs. "After he *really hurt you*?"

"I'm trying to explain." Olivia's shoulders slumped. "When it got physical, I mean… really physical… I left. I knew it would only get worse from there. He was starting to lose control."

"What does *really* physical mean?" Declan's voice vibrated with suppressed fury. The fact she believed there were degrees broke his heart.

Olivia sighed. "It's in the past."

"It's not in the past." The tether on his self-control snapped.

"He assaulted you *last night*. It's been two years since you left him. *Fuck.*" Declan ran a hand over his face as a realization hit him. "You have had to work with him every day. Why didn't you leave Armstrong?"

Her chin tipped up. "You know why. That company is more mine than it is his. Kyle wasn't going to take that away from me too. Besides, you've met Kyle." She grimaced. "He isn't really a nine-to-five kind of guy, so I didn't have to see him often. The year we were separated was the hardest because it was a secret. The year after I filed for divorce, it was easier because I didn't have to put on a show anymore. Pretend that breathing the same air as him wasn't repulsive."

Olivia wouldn't have to worry about that for long, Declan vowed to himself. "Why didn't you file for divorce right away?"

"Two years ago, when he… I left. He stayed in our house, and I rented a condo. Richard had just been diagnosed, and I didn't want to add to his stress, so we agreed to pretend we were still together." Declan stared at her in disbelief. "It wasn't like we were a couply couple before that. Everyone knew our marriage was basically over after the first year or so." Her eyes hardened. "They just didn't know why."

He did a quick calculation. "If you didn't love him, why did you stay?"

Olivia's back stiffened. "You don't understand."

"You're right. I don't." Declan shook his head. "God knows you've never been afraid to tell *me* how you feel."

Olivia stared at her bowl. "It's different with you."

Her words went a long way toward dampening his anger. "Yeah?"

She rolled her eyes. "You know it is. With Kyle, with my family, even my friends… They all assumed the reason the marriage failed was something I did, or wasn't doing. I'm a bit of a workaholic in case you haven't noticed," she said wryly. "My friends were work friends. I couldn't exactly confide in them what was happening at home. Kyle is very good at showing one face to the world, then twisting my words to make me look like I am a ball-busting shrew. Which coincidentally fit perfectly with how my family already thought of me."

Declan remembered how Olivia told him she'd never fit in with her family, but he hadn't realized the extent of how disconnected she felt. How isolated she was.

"When I tried to tell my parents, or even Jessica, what was happening... that I was unhappy..." Her voice trailed off. "I don't know if it's that they didn't believe it—Kyle does a fantastic job of the ingratiating-golden-boy routine—or if they didn't *want* to believe it. I was finally married, and my parents were thrilled. According to them, it's a woman's true purpose. And Jessica is Kyle's cousin. Plus, if I'd left, I would have lost everything I'd worked for."

"You didn't want to go somewhere else?"

"I thought about it a lot. Richard is very conservative, and Kyle had already spun the story that I was to blame for our problems. I couldn't be sure that one of them wouldn't say something to a potential employer, and I would be seen as damaged goods." Olivia frowned unhappily. "Can we please not talk about this anymore?"

Declan reached for her hand, turning it over, and traced over her palm with his thumb. "Of course."

"Thank you for bringing me soup."

"You told me chicken soup was your favorite."

Her brow furrowed and then cleared, her eyes stared into his. "You remembered that?"

Declan lifted her hand to place a kiss into the center of her palm. "I remember everything. I always have, Petal."

"Then why—"

Declan pressed another kiss to her hand, trying not to smile at how her eyes narrowed. That bastard may have hurt her, but he hadn't crushed her.

"I *will* tell you. I promise. But first, let me take care of you. I *need* to take care of you."

Olivia stared at him for a moment, and then with an almost imperceptible nod, she picked up her spoon with her free hand and began eating her soup, while he held her other. Declan's shoulders relaxed. The storm that had loomed all day finally broke, and rain lashed at the tall windows along the back of her house.

"I need to tell you something." Declan heard the thread of anxiety and fear under her words, and braced himself for whatever fresh horror she was about to share. "I think I might have killed Kyle."

Whatever it was Declan thought Olivia was going to say, that wasn't it. "You *think* you did?"

Olivia's face paled. "I stabbed him… He ran out… I thought the police would come."

That's my girl.

Keeping his expression reassuring, Declan squeezed her hand. "If Kyle went to a hospital, the police would be here by now."

Olivia looked thoughtful. "Then he's dead."

She didn't seem particularly bothered by the idea.

Declan shook his head slowly. "Not necessarily. He could have patched himself up, or gotten a friend to. You don't need to worry."

"I don't want to go to jail." Her haunted eyes met his, and he squeezed her hand again.

"You won't."

"You don't seem worried that I might have killed someone in my kitchen." Olivia's eyebrows pinched together.

Declan held her gaze, letting her see the truth. "Some people deserve to die."

For several long beats, they held each other's gaze, and he watched as she processed what he'd said. He could have wept with relief when she finally nodded.

"I agree."

Later, when Declan cleared the dishes and put them in the sink, he noticed the glint of something tucked in the corner of the backsplash above the counter. He picked up a bright blue porcelain handle, turning it over in his fingers. His eyes flicked to the empty hooks in front of him.

"Can I make you a cup of tea?"

When Olivia didn't answer, Declan took a deep breath, vowing to stay calm. The broken end of the shard stabbed his palm, but Declan welcomed the sharp pain.

That piece of shit broke her tea cups.

Declan forced a smile and lifted his chin at the storm outside. "Do you have whiskey? This feels more like a whiskey night."

The relief in her eyes that he wasn't going to press the issue had the vise back around his chest. Declan pocketed the shard of porcelain, noticing the smear of his blood on it, and turned to run his hand under the water. There would be a lot more when he was done.

"It isn't night," Olivia pointed out. "It's barely late afternoon."

Declan shrugged, and she quietly laughed, walking past him to open a cabinet. He closed his eyes as her delicate rose scent swirled around him.

He hadn't quite figured out how he was going to make it all work, but he would never leave her again. Declan planned on waking up with her smell on his skin and the taste of her on his tongue for the rest of eternity.

"Jameson?" He inhaled the woody aroma of the glass she handed him.

Olivia's eyes twinkled as she clinked her glass against his. "A cocky Irishman once told me it's the only whiskey a true Dubliner would drink."

"Sounds like a wise man."

"Hmm." Olivia took a small sip, staring at him over the rim. "Not so much. He's made a lot of really stupid choices."

Declan set his glass down and settled his hands lightly on her hips, not sure what other bruises she might be hiding.

"He *is* a wise man, because he knows he is going to do whatever it takes to make up for all the hurt he's caused." Declan leaned forward and kissed the uninjured corner of her mouth, encouraged when she didn't pull back.

"It may not be as easy as you think." She arched a challenging brow at him.

"I'm sure it won't, Petal, but it sure as hell will be worth it."

DECLAN BROODED IN THE DARKNESS, while Olivia snored quietly, cocooned in the thick blanket in front of the fire. He had suspected the truth weeks ago, at the meeting where he took over, but he had done nothing about it. He'd assumed that since they were divorced her immediate threat was gone… that Kyle's punishment could wait while he dealt with everything else.

Images of Olivia's bruised face and the fingerprints on her throat flashed over and over in his mind. The bridge of his nose stung, and he squeezed his eyes shut. He'd let her down.

Leaving one hand resting over her as she slept peacefully, her head on his thigh, Declan pressed the fingertips of his other to his brow. Hard. His breathing fractured as he imagined the scene the night before. Declan tipped his head back, pain ripping through his chest. He had been so worried about keeping her safe from his world he hadn't looked hard enough at hers.

Rage bubbled inside him and Declan tried to concentrate on

the silky feel of her hair as he softly stroked her head. A futile attempt to calm himself and find reassurance that she was safe. Here. With him.

The light from the fire was too low for him to make out her injuries, but Declan knew they were there. Branded into his brain forever.

I could have lost her.

His petty revenge on Kyle had made things worse for Olivia. He should have expected that Kyle would turn his wrath on her. Declan had failed her like everyone else in her life.

Never again.

"I'm sorry, Petal," he whispered, bending to kiss her hair, before carefully slipping out from under her head. Declan wasn't sure why Olivia had accepted him back into her life so easily, but he certainly wasn't going to argue.

Earlier, they'd taken their whiskeys to her sofa, and Declan laid a fire, covering her with the blanket as she snuggled against his side. He'd held her in silence, watching the fire and listening to the storm rage outside. With his arm around her shoulders, his body felt truly at peace for the first time in twelve years.

"I missed you." The words were barely audible over the storm and the crackling of the fire.

"I missed you too." Declan pressed his lips to her temple and inhaled. "I'm never letting you go. That 'maybe' we talked about is now 'absolutely.'"

Declan tensed, waiting for her response. He wanted to believe that if Olivia said she didn't feel the same way anymore, that she couldn't forgive him, he was noble enough to let her go. To let her find the life she deserved with a man who wouldn't always have a target of one type or another on his back.

But Declan wasn't. He was a selfish monster.

Olivia set her glass on the table and snuggled into the space between his shoulder and chest. "Hmm. Your 'absolutely' sounds a lot like 'about damn time' to me."

Declan huffed a laugh before pressing his cheek to her hair. He didn't move for over an hour, content to hold her in his arms while she slept.

Now, he impatiently paced her garage, waiting for the call to connect. As necessary as this phone call was, he was anxious to get back to Olivia. Declan snorted, imagining what his family's reaction to all this would be.

"What do you want?" Alex Kovalyov sounded irritated.

Despite his urgency, Declan couldn't help but needle the Russian. "Maybe I just wanted to talk."

"You're the least social person I know. What do you want?"

"I need Kyle Armstrong picked up. Unless he's already dead. In which case, I need the body to disappear."

"What exactly am I supposed to do with him?"

"Take him to one of your places."

"I don't have places," Alex said curtly.

"Suit yourself. Wherever it is your brother has people taken. And I need it done as soon as possible."

"What's in it for me?"

"I'll owe you," Declan said without hesitation.

"It's not as much fun when you give in easily," Kovalyov complained.

Over the last twelve years, he and the Russian had traded favors back and forth—a fucked-up friendship of sorts. Because of that, Declan let Kovalyov hear the seriousness in his voice. "It's important. Let me know when you have him secured. I'll come as soon as I can."

"You'll come? Personally?"

"Yes."

"How extraordinary." Alex hummed his amusement. "This sounds important. Might be worth two favors."

“Fine.”

There was a pause, and Declan could practically feel Alex’s surprise. “What did he do?”

“He put his hands on someone he never should have even looked at.”

Declan heard a low growl and knew Kovalyov understood. “He was married to Olivia Adler, correct? Didn’t you carry her out of an event last month?”

Declan’s jaw locked. “I didn’t realize you read the gossip blogs or that you were such a fan.”

“Someone’s testy tonight.”

“You’ll do it?”

“Call you when it’s done.”

CHAPTER THIRTY-SEVEN

Atlanta—Present Day

Light streamed through Olivia's window. Had she forgotten to draw the blinds last night, she wondered fuzzily.

She froze.

Had it been a dream? She closed her eyes again and gingerly slid her hand over the sheet until…

"Unless you're planning on doing something with that, teasing me this early in the morning is downright cruel, Petal."

Olivia exhaled a breath that she felt deep in her soul.

It was real. Declan was here.

Olivia removed her hand from his erection and rolled to face him, folding her arm under her head.

Dark stubble covered his jaw, and his violet eyes, hazy with sleep, smiled down at her. Olivia lifted a finger and tugged at his lower lip. "You still snore like a cow."

Declan's firm lips spread in a smile. "That wasn't me."

She gave him a mock glare. "I do *not* snore."

"You do, and it's not even adorable." He smirked. "You sound like one of the old men slumped in the corner at the pub. One of these days I'm going to record you, then you won't be able to deny it."

Declan punctuated his teasing with a gentle kiss. "But seeing as I've always been partial to pubs, I can deal." He pressed another firmer kiss to her lips, and she ignored the slight sting from her abused skin.

"You are a wretched liar." This time when she kissed him, tingles skated through her at the feel of his warm lips. Olivia shifted, suddenly needing to be closer. Her tongue traced the seam of his lips, urging him to deepen the kiss.

"We can't. You're hurt." He pulled back.

"I feel great." Or she would in a few seconds.

Declan groaned. "It's too soon," he said, even as his hands slid under her top to palm her breast.

Anger spiked in Olivia, and she pushed on his ribs hard enough that his hands stilled.

"You don't get to tell me when and how I deal with this, Declan. This is my body, and I can do whatever I want with it. And right now, it's interested in a mind-melting orgasm."

Declan's eyes heated, his finger brushing lightly over her lip. "You can't tell me your lip doesn't hurt when I kiss you."

Olivia lifted an eyebrow, lowering her hand to wrap around his hot length, and he sucked in a breath. She stroked her fingers from base to tip and back again. "Then I give you permission to skip that part."

Declan's hands began moving again, and Olivia gasped as his fingers toyed with her nipple. "If I can't kiss your beautiful mouth, I'll have to make sure it's the only part I miss," Declan breathed, and then proceeded to do just that. He kissed every inch of her body, lingering on each bruise where he found them.

Olivia writhed under him, her skin tight and hot. But still he teased, trailing his mouth and lips over her belly and lower to her hipbone, until he settled over her center, his lips and teeth driving her wild.

"Declan," she cried out, when his fingers slipped inside her to curl and press until her hips bucked beneath him. "I need you."

Declan's mouth sealed over hers, catching her cry in his mouth as he surged inside her. Olivia wrapped her legs around his back, clinging to him, as his powerful thrusts drove her deeper into the mattress.

"I love you," he whispered in her ear. "I've always loved you."

Pleasure crashed over her in waves as he continued moving inside her. Moments later, Declan cried out against her neck, his arms wrapped tightly around her body as if he couldn't get close enough.

Declan chuckled when he finally rolled off her, his breath coming in ragged pants. "The way you feel... that was... I don't know what that was." She curled into his side, burying her smile into his chest. "I'm not sure I've ever been more grateful for anything in my entire life than for the fact that you're on birth control," he huffed out in a breathless laugh.

Olivia's cheeks heated, and it felt like a boulder had taken up residence in her throat. "I'm not on birth control, Declan." Her lips pinched, trying to keep tears at bay, and she flopped on to her back staring up at the ceiling. Declan's body stilled to the point she wasn't sure he was still breathing. "I should have said something before—"

"At the restaurant, you said there was no risk."

Olivia dared a glance. Declan didn't look angry, only confused. "It's not really something I wanted to bring up in a restaurant bathroom." She grimaced. "You don't have to worry though. I'm not trying to trap you with a baby." Olivia bit her lip when her voice broke a little.

"I know you better than that, Petal."

Olivia really, *really* didn't want to have this conversation right now, to see the disappointment on his face, but she was an adult, and she owed him an explanation.

Olivia sucked in a breath through her nose. "Before things got bad, before I found out about the cheating—well, before I found out the cheating was an ongoing thing—I tried to get pregnant. Kyle's tests all came back fine. The problem is me." Her last words came out in a whisper.

Declan sat up suddenly, his fingers threaded into his hair. Olivia watched his chest rise and fall until the air was audible coming out of his nose in angry bursts. Olivia could feel the tears creeping up her throat. This was worse than she thought it would be.

"I'm sure you want children, and I do too… I just don't think it will be possible without intervention and even then..."

Declan suddenly turned, and scooping her up, he pulled her into his lap, enveloping her in a tight hug. "Fuck, Petal."

Olivia could feel him shaking and that set the tears free. "I'm sorry. I should have told you I wasn't on birth control. But what's the likelihood, that after actively trying, the few times we—"

Declan's voice was ragged when he said, "You didn't know?"

"I don't have a diagnosis or anything. I was in the process of setting up appointments for tests when I found out about Kyle's other girlfriends. There wasn't any point then."

Declan wiped the tears off her cheeks, his face raw with pain. "I assumed you knew."

The hairs on the back of her neck rose. "Knew what?"

Declan closed his eyes, and when they opened again, they glistened. "Kyle had a vasectomy. It's in his medical records."

Olivia felt like all the oxygen had been sucked from her body. She went cold and then flushed red hot. She tried to make sense of what Declan was telling her. "Kyle had… why would he do that?" She shook her head. "How do you know?"

"At the meeting… where I took control of Armstrong… From

your reactions to him, I suspected something was wrong. I had him investigated."

"You got his medical records?" Olivia screeched. This wasn't happening. Kyle couldn't have… He wouldn't. All the nasty things he had thrown at her, taunting her with what he claimed his doctor said. No one could be that evil.

But Kyle was.

She had been the one who pushed for a baby, but Kyle never said he *didn't* want one… Did he have the procedure so he could sleep with as many women as he wanted without worrying about getting someone pregnant?

"I think I might be sick," she whispered.

"I've got you." Declan pulled her close against his chest and stroked circles over her back. "I'm so sorry, baby. I thought you knew."

Olivia felt like she was drowning as sobs wracked her body. The sheer cruelty of Kyle's actions took her breath away.

Declan held her, murmuring against her hair. When her sobs finally subsided, he pressed a gentle kiss to her lips.

"I hope I killed him," Olivia snarled against Declan's chest.

"I hope you didn't." He held tight when she pulled away. "I was rather looking forward to it."

After a minute, Olivia asked the question that was hammering in her mind. "Would you mind? About possibly not being able to have babies?"

She felt a heavy sigh run through his body. "There is no reason to believe you can't get pregnant, Olivia, but I love *you*, not your reproductive system. If it happens for us easily, then I will be overjoyed, and if it doesn't…" He shrugged. "There are other options if we decide we want our family to be bigger than the two of us."

Our family.

"Are you sure?"

Declan pulled back and caught her chin in his hand, forcing her to look up at him. “I meant what I said before, Olivia. I never should have let you go twelve years ago, and I will not make that mistake again.”

The intensity in his eyes made her whole body warm. “Good. Because I’m not letting you go either.”

~

“What are you doing?” Declan frowned at her as she emerged from the closet wrapped in a towel.

Olivia paused as she reached for her sweat pants. “Getting dressed?”

“No.”

“No?” Olivia lifted her brows.

“You have the flu. You need bed rest.”

“You’re aware I don’t actually have the flu, and I’m not going to get much rest in that bed.”

Declan grinned at her.

“Besides,” Olivia said, reaching for an oversized cardigan. “I’m starving.”

She wrapped her hair into a messy knot at the back of her head and looked back at him. Declan was staring at her with an odd look on his face.

Heat rose on her cheeks, and she tugged at the hem of her cardigan. Over the last two years of living alone, Olivia didn’t bother with cute lingerie anymore.

Kyle’s insistence on her looking good, even relaxing at home, had spoiled it for her. It hadn’t occurred to her until this second what Declan would think of her outfit. He was used to seeing her dressed for work. Now as he stared at her, the sheet puddled at his hips and his impressive torso on display, she was embarrassed.

"You are fucking perfection." The reverence in his voice made her body unclench.

"You don't have to flatter me to get me back in bed. Once I've eaten, all bets are off."

Declan shook his head. "I'm not. This whole..." He waved his hand at her outfit. "What do you call this look? Homeless chic? It's perfect." He rose from the bed and walked naked to frame her face. "I love you, and I love that you aren't afraid to be yourself with me."

He lowered his head to kiss her neck, and she felt him harden against her as her stomach growled. Declan laughed. "Okay, you win. Food first."

Olivia made a quick omelet while Declan made coffee and toasted some of the bread from the night before. They moved around each other, assembling breakfast in the same easy way they had at the cottage. It was as though no time had passed, instead of the twelve years since they last cooked breakfast together.

Olivia was feeling emotionally wrung out over everything that had happened, but she still had questions. She was about to test Declan's theory that he loved that she was herself with him.

"Why didn't you tell me who you really were in Dublin? Did you not trust me?"

Declan ran a hand back through his hair. "That wasn't it. It's hard to explain. When we met, you assumed I was the bouncer, the same way I assumed your name was Rose."

Olivia's cheeks heated. "I thought about telling you, but when we said it was temporary, I decided it wouldn't hurt to be someone else that week."

Declan's eyes met hers. "It was the same for me. You know about my family now—how complicated everything is."

"When I saw your picture on the cover of *Trend* magazine, it was a bit of a shock." Olivia gave him a wry smile. "The handsome Irish bouncer I fell in love with looked like the king of the world, and the news that actually hurt the most… He was an American. That did a number on my fantasy," she joked.

Declan took her hand, stroking his thumb across the delicate skin over her knuckles. "I am Irish—half, anyway. I didn't live full time in the States until I was twelve. Before that, I only visited my father for the summers along with my brothers, and Cara when she was old enough.

"It was decided that to be properly raised as my father's heir apparent, he needed to have more direct control over me." Olivia turned her palm over and interlaced her fingers with his. "Frankly, I'm a little offended you didn't recognize me," he teased. "I'm kind of a big deal."

Olivia's lips twitched. "Sorry."

"I loved it. You didn't know who I was, and you didn't care when you thought I was a bouncer helping at the family bar."

"Well, to be fair, you came with a super-hot body, poetry, and an adorable cottage, so…"

Declan laughed and got up to retrieve the coffee carafe.

"Once I knew who you were… I cyber stalked you," Olivia admitted. "I wanted to see if any of it was true."

"It was all true, Petal. The important parts."

Olivia took a deep breath. She needed to ask the question, but wasn't sure she wanted the answer. "Did you ever look for me?"

Declan swallowed hard. "No, I didn't let myself. I knew if I found out where you were, I wouldn't be able to stay away. And I had to."

"Why?" Her voice was small.

Declan squeezed his eyes shut for a beat before opening them again. "Something happened after you left. I had every intention of tracking you down when I got back to New York… but after… It was impossible." Olivia's fingers twitched in his, but Declan tightened his hold.

"What happened?" Declan shook his head, his lips in a firm line. "It was that bad?" He didn't break eye contact. "I told you I might have killed someone, and you didn't bat one of your ridiculously long eyelashes. It can't be worse than that."

Declan's nostrils flared, and Olivia suddenly understood. She drew in a deep breath. "Will you tell me the circumstances someday?"

"I would rather not, but if you really want to know, I'll tell you. I don't want there to be secrets between us."

Olivia considered for a minute. It wasn't like her to be so accepting of something without an explanation, but something had shifted in her. Stabbing a man can do that. She thought of what Declan said. *Some people deserve to die.* "I think we've had enough confessions over the last twenty-four hours. It can wait."

Declan blinked at her easy acquiescence, but before he recovered, she said. "So, you didn't know until XEROS."

"My team worked up dossiers on all the key people at Armstrong."

Olivia shook her head with a frown. "Then why didn't you—"

"You were married." Declan's face was tortured. "I thought you were happy, and I didn't want to take that from you." Declan rubbed at his sternum.

"You stayed away because you thought I was in love with Kyle?"

"If I'd known... If I knew what he was doing to you," Declan's voice turned savage. "I would have come for you. You wouldn't have gone through all of this. If I'd only read that damned dossier on him... I'm so sorry, I wasn't here for you, Petal."

Tears slipped silently from the corners of her eyes, but her lips lifted in a sad smile. "Don't apologize. You couldn't have known. No one knew. I doubt it was in the dossier. Most of the time, it wasn't physical. It was what he said, how he made me feel…" Olivia patted her cheeks dry with the back of her hands. "I never cry like this."

"I know you must be angry with me—"

A quiet, humorless laugh left her, and Olivia cupped his jaw with her hand. "Declan, you aren't god. As much as you think you are omnipotent, you aren't. You can't know *everything*, protect *everyone* all the time…"

Olivia stroked her fingers along the powerful line of his jaw and then up to trace his eyebrows, smoothing the lines bunched between them. "You beautiful megalomaniac. I'm not crying because I'm upset with you. I'm mad at myself. The magazine with your real identity came out before Kyle proposed. I was angry and hurt. I thought you'd lied in order to use me. There were so many pictures of you online with the most gorgeous women. Jessica convinced me I was essentially another in a long line of women. She knew how I felt about you and how I had always hoped that we would get our chance.

"Jessica wanted me to marry Kyle, and she knew I was already seeing red flags in him. I think she saw your identity as her chance to push me into the marriage."

"I hate your friend," Declan growled.

"We aren't friends anymore. Jessica is pissed about the takeover. Declan, I knew where you were before you'd ever even heard of XEROS. I should have reached out, but I allowed my pride to rule my heart." Her lips twisted. "And god knows I paid for it. I doubted you. I doubted myself and my memories."

"I gave you good reason."

The corner of her lip lifted. "True."

Declan took her hand and held it on the table between their coffee mugs, fingers interlaced. "I never pretended with you. I may not have told you my real name, or who my family was and all that entailed, but I never lied to you. I was more myself that one week with you than I have been at any other time in my life.

You accepted me for who I was. No expectations or agenda. You wanted *me*. Other than my siblings, no one has ever cared about only me."

Olivia's eyes softened, and she scooted closer to him. "It was the same for me."

Their words hung in the air between them. If it were anyone else, Olivia would be pointing out that she shouldn't let Declan back in so easily. That she had just gone through a horrific ordeal and her emotions couldn't be trusted.

But the rightness of Declan's hand in hers reassured her that being with him was exactly how her life was meant to be.

CHAPTER THIRTY-EIGHT

ATLANTA—PRESENT DAY

Later that afternoon, warm and completely sated with a naked Olivia tucked against him, Declan dozed. He never took a day off, much less to spend the day in bed with a woman. Olivia's head rested on his shoulder, and her nails drew lazy patterns on his chest that only made him sleepier.

"Why didn't you tell me to call the police?"

"Hmm?"

"The police. You were so upset when you saw... even before I told you I stabbed him." Olivia hesitated. "Don't get me wrong, I appreciate you not pushing me. I guess I'm wondering why you never mentioned it. Is it because you know it would be bad for my career?"

The fuck?

Wide awake now, Declan captured her hand under his. "Why would you say that? What the fuck does any of this have to do with your career?" His blood boiled that Kyle had so eroded her confidence.

"It wasn't easy being so young in the position I was hired for. There was already gossip. I think I proved myself as time went on. But then I got the promotion after I married Kyle, and the gossip started all over again. If people knew how weak I was, that I let him treat me that way…" She gave a little shrug, her eyes sliding from his. "How could they possibly respect me at work? Trust in my leadership?"

Declan cupped her chin. "What he did to you was solely about him. About the fact that he is a craven, insecure piece of shit who never came close to deserving you." He stared into her eyes, willing her to hear him. "Kyle knew that. That's why he tried to bring you down. He knew you were a bright, fucking, shining star, and he was incompetent. Kyle is the weak one, not you. And I hate that you didn't have the support you needed."

Olivia's eyes fluttered at his fervent words, and to his surprise, even his fingers shook a little with the emotion consuming him when he touched her face. "I didn't mention calling the police because there is no need for them."

A tiny frown formed between her eyes, and Declan leaned forward to kiss her before pulling back to meet her gaze. He was taking a risk letting her see this part of him, but it was imperative she understand. "Before I knew you had stabbed him, I had no intention of letting Kyle off easy by being arrested. When I tell you he will *never* hurt you again, it's because I can promise you he won't be around to do so. I plan on making sure of it personally. It's already in motion."

"How?" There was no judgment in her voice only curiosity.

"I have a friend, Alex, with close connections to some not so nice people. This is the kind of thing they do. He's looking for Kyle."

Declan watched her closely, as she processed what he'd said, and waited with his breath locked in his chest for her reaction. Silently hoping she didn't ask for details. Olivia's sapphire eyes suddenly cleared, and he saw she understood what he meant.

Instead of recoiling in horror or objecting, she tucked her head under his chin and snuggled closer. "Good."

He let out a startled laugh against her hair.

"I didn't realize you had a blood thirsty side, Petal."

Olivia shrugged, nuzzling his neck. "Like you said, some people deserve it. Now shhh, I have the flu. I need a nap."

A soft smile on his face, Declan stroked the silky skin of her back until her breaths evened out before letting himself relax into sleep.

She really was perfect for him.

"You keep checking your phone." Olivia pointed out when Declan lifted it for the third time in five minutes. "Is there something going on at work? Armstrong, I mean."

Declan shook his head and turned his phone over, face down. "I'm expecting a call from Brady." *And Alex.* "He's going to install a better security system here."

"I have a security system."

"You need a better one." Olivia opened her mouth to argue. "I have enemies, Olivia." It wasn't a lie.

"Is that your way of telling me you're staying here?"

Declan met her eyes, waiting to see if she'd object. With anyone else, it would be insane to move so fast, but now that he had Olivia back, he wasn't going to waste any time.

Olivia rolled her eyes playfully when he didn't answer. "Well, okay, if it makes *you* feel safer at night."

CHAPTER THIRTY-NINE

ATLANTA—PRESENT DAY

Olivia's heart raced as she adjusted the bow at the collar of her blue blouse. Declan leaned over the desk, his arms braced as he looked over the papers she'd laid out. The outline of his muscles clearly bulged under his tailored gray dress shirt, and her body flushed with the memory of how she had woken up that morning, with Declan's hot breath against her thighs.

"This could work," Stuart said. His words were like a bucket of cold water. For a second, she'd forgotten he was there.

Olivia shook herself.

You are a professional.

Declan glanced up, and met her eyes with a smirk, before he turned to Stuart. They hadn't discussed how their relationship would work when it came to decisions about Armstrong, and she was nervous.

"This looks good, Olivia. Very good." Declan's voice was its normal cool, impassive tone, but the heat in his eyes sent a thrill down her spine. "What do you think it will take to close this?"

"Senator Menendez wants to be courted. A few dinners and a contribution to his reelection campaign should be enough. They are as eager for this as I am." She beamed. "A high-tech manufacturing site in their constituency is a win-win."

Declan's lips quirked. "Great. Let's meet again in three days for a status update."

Stuart nodded and gathered his things quickly, rising to his feet. "I'm going to that salad place down the street for lunch, Olivia. Do you want to join me?" His cheeks reddened a little. "Mr. Bloom, you are welcome of course, but…" His eyes returned to Olivia. "I know you're busy, so I thought we could make it a working lunch."

She opened her mouth to make an excuse, but Declan beat her to it. "Olivia and I already have a working lunch planned."

Declan's tone was smooth, but Stuart picked up on the dangerous undercurrent and practically scurried out the door, mumbling apologies and promises to catch up later.

Olivia arched a brow. "You didn't have to scare him."

"Trust me, if I'd wanted to scare him, it wouldn't have looked like that."

"I'm starving, so that better not have just been something you told Stuart to get me alone."

Declan leaned back in his chair and rested his steepled fingers against his lips. "I'm hungry too." Declan's eyes hooded, then he shouted, "Todd."

They heard scrambling in the outer office, and then a slightly out of breath Todd appeared in the doorway.

"I have a special request for lunch. Sakura Kaze," Declan said, naming a high-end sushi restaurant in Atlanta. He then rattled off a large order while Todd took notes.

"I'll order it now."

"I want you to personally pick it up."

Todd's forehead scrunched. "That will take me almost an hour."

"It's worth the wait." There was no room in Declan's tone for an argument.

"I'll leave now." Todd cast her a look and then shut the door behind him.

Declan came to his feet and walked to lock the door. "You can't eye fuck me in meetings, Olivia. It's very distracting."

"Was that what I was doing?" she purred.

Declan took her hand and pressed it to where his erection pushed hard against his suit pants. "Certainly, felt that way."

Olivia's fingers curled around him, shaping him through the fabric.

"Fuck." The sound hissed out of him as he arched into her touch. One large hand reached behind her head, pulling her in to crush her mouth under his.

Declan's tongue dipped into her mouth, exploring and claiming every inch. Olivia's hands were on his belt, yanking it loose, as his hands tangled in her hair. Slowly pulling his zipper down, she looked up at him through her lashes. "I don't remember these perks laid out in your offer."

She walked him backward until he leaned against his desk. Then keeping a deliberate eye contact, she licked her lips and slowly sank to her knees, taking his pants and boxer briefs with her.

Declan's fists bunched at his side as she slid one hand up over the defined muscle of his stomach, and teased her nails over him. "Olivia," he growled. His hips jerked, as her lips brushed over his hot skin.

His body trembled, and his stomach muscles contracted when Olivia trailed a line of soft kisses down his length. A low guttural sound ripped from him as her mouth closed over him drawing him deep. Declan's hands threaded into her hair as she used her lips and tongue to drive him closer to the edge.

"Fuck, Petal." His breath rushed out on a harsh exhale. "Stop.

Wait." Declan roughly grabbed her under her arms, hauling her up before spinning and catching her behind her thighs to lift her onto his desk.

She heard the popping of stitches as the narrow-cut of her skirt objected to the move. Pens and paper scattered when she leaned back, supporting herself on her elbows as he shoved her skirt higher.

"I've been thinking about doing this from the moment you sashayed into the office in that tight ass skirt."

Hooking his fingers in the elastic, he pulled her panties down her legs before pushing her knees wide. Olivia cried out when his mouth closed over her.

"Shhh, Petal. We don't want to be the office gossip do we?" He chuckled against her, the vibration sending sparks of pleasure cascading through her nerve endings.

Olivia covered her moan with her hand, biting her finger to keep from screaming as he brought her to the edge over and over again. When her body finally exploded, Olivia smothered her scream as Declan stroked her through the last of her convulsions.

Declan stood, and in an instant, he was inside her thrusting deep. "Mine." He growled into her ear. His hands tangled in her hair before his mouth claimed her again.

Olivia's heartbeat thundered as Declan again had her body coiled tight with need.

"Declan!" His lips covered hers, swallowing her cries.

His powerful arm came around her hips to pull her to the edge of the desk, pressing her chest against his, as his rhythm became frenzied. Olivia could feel his heart pounding through the layers between them, their pulses almost matching pace. *This man.* Declan buried his face in her neck and let out a roar, only somewhat muffled by her skin.

When Todd returned, they were working again, but by his red

cheeks, Olivia suspected he knew exactly what had occurred in his absence.

"We are totally getting written up by Human Resources." Olivia giggled when Todd shut the door behind him.

Declan grunted, and put a piece of sushi in her mouth. "I'll give him a raise."

THE NEXT FEW weeks were the happiest Olivia had ever known. They did their best to hide their relationship from everyone at Armstrong, but she knew from the looks she got that they hadn't been entirely successful. Olivia couldn't remember being this at peace in her life, and she knew it showed.

There was still no word on Kyle which was worrying, but Declan assured her that if Kyle had died of his wound they would have heard. Even if he'd wandered off and collapsed somewhere that night, his family would have reported him missing.

"You don't need to worry, Olivia. I won't let him get anywhere near you."

Olivia had spent so long taking care of herself, feeling like she was alone, being told that her problems were taken care of was a heady sensation. She wasn't an idiot. When Declan's friend Alex found Kyle, he wasn't going to hand him a cookie and give him a stern talking to. Maybe it made her a bad person that she didn't care what happened to Kyle—but the truth was, Olivia didn't. Each night, as Declan's strong arms held her close, her sense of safety grew.

Declan had rearranged his life to be with her every day, but after a few weeks, there were meetings he needed to attend in New York. When he kissed her goodbye that morning, an uneasy feeling settled like a rock in Olivia's stomach. Over the years, she had learned to listen to her instincts. It often meant the difference between a dinner plate thrown against the wall and a semi-pleasant dinner.

"Wait," Olivia said, as he pulled away.

"I have to go, baby."

"I know it's..." She didn't know how to put what she was feeling into words without sounding dramatic or clingy. There was no concrete reason for them. There'd been no sign of Kyle. And with the Fort Knox setup Declan had installed at her house, Olivia knew she was as safe as she could be.

Declan smoothed her hair back and sank to the side of the bed. "Are you worried?"

"It's..." Words failed her, and she swallowed before trying again. "It feels like if you leave, it could all disappear."

Every day they had breakfast together, before driving to work separately, and then frequently saw each other during the workday, ending with a dinner at home, curled up on the couch reading or watching a movie. It was deliciously normal.

In the low light of the early morning, she saw how her admission affected him. Declan cupped her cheeks and brushed a kiss across her lips. "I will always come back to you, Petal. Always."

"I don't want to wait another twelve years," Olivia whispered, her throat clogged with emotion. It wasn't a fair thing to say, but it was how she felt.

Declan inhaled a ragged breath and lowered his head until his lips hovered an inch over hers. "Nothing," he whispered against her mouth. Then he repeated the word in a fierce tone. "*Nothing* will ever keep me from coming back for you."

His lips descended, and Olivia whimpered, opening her mouth, encouraging him to deepen the kiss—to stay with her a little longer.

"I'll be back in four days."

"Promise."

God, when did I become so needy? This is embarrassing.

Except Declan didn't seem to mind. He seemed to crave hearing how much she wanted to be with him as much as she needed to tell him. "I promise."

The panicky feeling in her chest settled a little. Declan hesitated, then said, "You will be protected at all times. Brady and Vincent's man will be outside every night I'm gone."

His words momentarily distracted her from her nerves, and Olivia frowned. "Someone will be watching me?"

Declan nodded. "It's only when I can't be with you. If something else less immediate comes up, call one of my brothers." He made a face. "Or my brother-in-law. Tell them who you are to me, and they will help." He stroked her cheek with his knuckle.

"And who am I?"

Olivia meant it to sound teasing, but Declan's face was serious as he stared down at her. "You are the most precious thing in my life." Declan brushed her hair back. "I understand if you don't like the idea of being watched, but I can't function if I don't know you are safe." He leaned forward and pressed his forehead against hers. "Don't be upset." He pulled back, his eyes burning into hers. "Without you…"

Olivia reached up to grasp his wrist. "I'm not. I don't love the idea of needing someone outside, but that's not your fault. It's Kyle's." Her voice was firm. "I love you, Declan Bloom. And while you can be autocratic and overbearing sometimes…" Her lips twitched. "Maybe more than 'sometimes'… Thank you for taking care of me," Olivia finished quietly.

"I will *always* keep you safe."

But even with Declan's assurances in her ear, when Olivia heard the beeping, that signaled him resetting the house alarm, and the front door closing, she couldn't deny the boulder in her stomach was still there.

CHAPTER FORTY

New York—Present Day

Declan tapped his pen impatiently as he listened to other members of Bloom Capital present what they thought should be the next target for acquisition. There was no reason he needed to be here in person, he realized, and mentally made a note to tell Todd to schedule these meetings virtually in the future. The trip to New York wouldn't be a complete waste, however. Declan planned on collecting more of his belongings from his apartment in the city to take back with him to Atlanta.

His family might think he was stubborn, but once he made a decision, he rarely veered from it. Declan had made the most important one of his life—Olivia was his future.

Declan glanced at his watch. It was almost time for lunch. He'd bet his fortune Stuart was angling to get Olivia to go to lunch with him. A smile toyed around his lips. He would prefer her to tell the man to get lost, but Olivia was too nice. Too afraid of hurting his feelings.

Declan looked forward to the day he could claim her publicly. The day he could finally let the world know Olivia was his. His attention strayed to Alan Carrol seated at the table. He knew the man couldn't be happy about his change of plans. Alan had been eager for the connection to the Bloom family.

What was Carrol even doing at this meeting? He wasn't involved in these types of decisions. Surely, Alan wasn't so stupid as to think he could change Declan's mind.

After Olivia's attack, Brady confirmed Declan's suspicions. Before going to Olivia's house, Kyle had been drinking at the Magnolia Country Club with a large group of people, Fiona included. There had been a scene when management informed Kyle that he was no longer welcome on the property. Declan had no doubt who filled Kyle's head full of poison about Olivia that night.

Following a very tense phone conversation, where Declan outlined *exactly* what would happen if Fiona came anywhere near Olivia, Fiona had wisely kept her distance from him. He couldn't prove she pointed Kyle in Olivia's direction, but she wouldn't get a second chance from him.

Alan lingered as everyone filed out of the Manhattan board room. "It's been a while since you've graced New York with your presence."

"I didn't know you missed me," Declan drawled.

The man pursed his lips, craggy eyebrows dropping over eyes glinting with anger. "I don't give a shit where you've been. I am, however, concerned about the unhappy calls I've received from my daughter."

Declan felt his hackles rise. *Fiona* was unhappy? She'd wound up a psycho and set him loose on Olivia.

"Oh?"

The man glowered at him. "Yes, *oh*. She told me you've been embarrassing her."

Declan struggled to hold on to his temper as his anger built. "Did she?"

"Yes, you cold bastard. I never expected that you were going to be some sort of Romeo for her. This is a business agreement, but I'll be damned if you are going to make a fool of my daughter because you can't be discreet."

Declan set the pen he twirled in his fingers down and rose to his feet with a smile. The older man scowled as Declan took a few steps closer.

"My daughter is a woman of the world. She knows what to expect. But I've made inquiries. You are openly living with this woman."

"I'd be careful with the next words you choose, Alan."

"Fiona deserves more than you parading some sl—"

Declan pinned Alan against the wall, his forearm pressing hard against Alan's throat. The gurgle Alan emitted wasn't enough to satisfy him. He was vaguely aware of the wide-eyed onlookers on the other side of the glass wall, but he didn't care. Declan pressed harder, watching as Alan spluttered and his face turned purple.

"That *woman*," Declan said, his voice silky soft, "will be my *wife*. And unless you want me to cut your tongue out of your mouth, I would suggest you never mention her again."

Declan released him, and Alan clutched his throat, glaring furiously. "Your *wife*? What about Fiona? You promised."

"I promised nothing. We discussed it as a possibility," Declan said, straightening the cuffs of his jacket. "Apparently, during all your phone calls with your daughter, she failed to mention that I made my feelings about her, and our lack of a future, crystal clear weeks ago."

Alan's chest heaved. "You can't do that. You need me. I won't stand for—"

Declan took a step forward, closing the distance between them. "You won't stand for what? I don't need you to regain what is rightfully mine."

His smile was so cold, uncertainty flickered in Alan's expression. "My father's murder might have distracted me for a moment, but I think it's time you and the rest of the world remember exactly who it is you're dealing with."

Declan tugged on the man's tie. "And if your viper of a daughter comes near Olivia again, or does *anything* I feel could be traced back to her..." Declan let his mask slip, allowing the man to see his rage. "I will bury you, and that is *not* a figure of speech."

"You'll regret this, Bloom. You aren't half the man your father was."

Declan didn't even bother looking back when he said, "Thank god for that."

A FEW NIGHTS LATER, after his plane landed, Declan made a brief stop on his way to the house to pick up Olivia's surprise.

Declan: I'll be there in about an hour need to make a stop first.

Olivia: I can't wait. I made spaghetti Bolognese hope that's okay.

Declan smiled. A year ago, he would have eaten at whatever exclusive restaurant Todd had made a reservation. Tonight, he couldn't wait to sit at her small kitchen table and eat a pasta dinner.

Using his thumb print to unlock the door, Declan adjusted the red bow around the neck of the puppy tucked under his arm. Olivia stepped into view, her face full of welcome, until her gaze fell to the bundle in his arms. Her hands flew to her mouth with a gasp, and Declan's stomach shifted.

Fuck.

Was it too much? Was he rushing her?

"You got me a puppy." Olivia's voice quivered.

"You said you always wanted one. He's a German Shepherd,

but if you'd rather..." Declan was having a hard time reading the emotion on her face.

Is she happy? Freaked out?

"He's perfect," Olivia exclaimed, rushing forward to take the now squirming puppy out of his arms. She held him close, smothering his nose with kisses. "Aren't you, Oscar?"

Warmth spread through him even as he rolled his eyes at her name choice. "Oscar? Really?"

"Don't listen to the silly man, Oscar." Olivia carried the puppy into the kitchen, Declan forgotten. He grinned at her retreating back. The look of sheer joy on her face, and the fact he'd been the one to put it there, made his chest swell.

Declan was clearing the dishes when Olivia's phone lit up on the counter. The contact displayed made his blood run cold before swiftly heating to sizzle through his veins. He snatched up the phone, his grip so tight he was surprised the screen didn't crack.

"What is this?" Declan barked, lifting the phone. When Olivia flinched, her face leached of color, his heart dropped to his stomach. "Oh, fuck. Baby. I didn't mean... I'm sorry," he said, setting the phone down, running an agitated hand back through his hair. "I'm not mad... I..."

Olivia's face was blank, completely devoid of expression, which had a terrifying combination of fear and fury running through him. When Declan got his hands on Kyle Armstrong, he was going to enjoy every second he made the abusive asshole suffer.

Declan kept his voice soft, his hands relaxed at his sides. "Petal, I'm sorry, I shouldn't have yelled. I'm not angry."

Olivia's chin tilted up, and he was relieved to see even that small sign of challenge.

"Not at you." He amended. Declan moved slowly toward her, his hand outstretched, almost like he would with a frightened animal. "But even if I were. Even if I were furious with you, I would never hurt you." His fingertips brushed her shoulders, running lightly down to her elbows and back up again. "I promised you I would never let anyone hurt you again, and that includes me."

Olivia released a long, shuddery breath, and her stiff shoulders slumped forward. "I know. I'm sorry. I hate that I still react that way sometimes." Her eyes met his, and his chest cracked open at the fear and vulnerability he saw there. "I'm trying, I really am. I know you wouldn't hurt me like that… it's… a reflex."

"I know."

"It doesn't make any sense." Olivia scowled, frustration evident in every line of her body. "I've done everything the therapist told me to do. It shouldn't happen anymore."

Declan tugged her to him and laid a cheek against the top of her head. "I don't think this kind of thing is a linear equation. *I did A therefore B*. Even if it were, it was only a couple of weeks ago that Kyle attacked you. I think you have been amazingly brave after what happened."

Olivia huffed an angry breath, but nuzzled deeper into his chest. His arms tightened around her. Declan wished he had been there for her during the years she had shouldered this alone. All the years Olivia felt like she had to hide what was happening to her.

"You are an incredible woman, and you have nothing to be ashamed of."

"Why were you upset about the phone?" He heard her ask against his chest, and he let her go when she stepped back.

The reminder had his temper brewing again. "Why is he calling you?"

"Who?"

"Chris Keller."

Olivia shrugged. "He mentioned helping me find a job." Her

mouth firmed, and her gaze caught his, her confidence seeming to have rebounded now that she was talking about work. "But I don't need to find a job, right? Because you are going to be so blown away with my final proposal on manufacturing XEROS, that you will see selling off Armstrong would be a colossal mistake."

The words 'you can have the company' were on the tip of his tongue, but he held them back. She wouldn't appreciate that. Olivia had worked hard, and sacrificed so much, making the company her entire life—Declan could understand that drive.

It was important to Olivia to earn what she had—and while she may not fully understand that he would give her whatever she wanted to make her happy—being gifted Armstrong Electronics would do the opposite.

Working with Olivia, it had quickly become apparent that she had essentially been running the entire company for years. Considering how hamstrung she was by her former father-in-law's conservative business beliefs, and the dead weight of her asshole ex-husband, it was remarkable what she had created.

Would he give her the CEO position along with the keys to the company just to make her smile? Absolutely. But he didn't need to. Declan recognized that, given free rein over the next couple of years, Olivia could double Armstrong's profit. He looked forward to shoving that down Carrol's throat when he told the investors of his decision.

Olivia set her jaw, and Declan sighed, realizing he'd been silent too long. "Definitely a *colossal* mistake, so you can go ahead and block him."

Olivia narrowed her eyes. "I know the two of you don't get along, but Chris Keller is influential, with a lot of connections. He may have lost out on XEROS, but that doesn't mean Armstrong might not have a product that Bloom Communications would want in the future."

Declan ground his teeth. "If your concern is Bloom Communications, let me assure you, you can pitch me over breakfast anytime, because *I* will be the one making those decisions in the future."

"Declan—"

He waved a hand, cutting her off. "It's not a pride thing. The fact of the matter is, after the shareholder meeting in two weeks, Chris Keller won't be the CEO. I will."

Olivia paled. "How?"

Declan frowned, not understanding why she was upset. "I'm going to call a vote of no confidence based on the morality clause in his contract."

"Based on what? The two of you have history, but I've never heard of him doing anything that would come close to the level that would get him removed." Olivia's throat bobbed as she swallowed hard, and Declan's frown darkened. What was she worried about?

He watched as Olivia straightened her spine and squared her shoulders. "Is the morality clause an excuse to call a vote, because you know that with Alan Carrol's votes, you'll prevail?"

Declan blinked, confused for a beat, and then understanding crashed over him. "I'm not marrying Fiona."

Olivia's body relaxed slightly, and he reached forward and caught her hands in his. "I told Fiona there wouldn't be a partnership the day after your attack. It's *been* over." Declan stared at her. "Did you think I was lying these last weeks? Telling you I love you, promising to take care of you..." Anger colored his words.

"No." Olivia shook her head. "I'm selfish, I haven't even thought about Fiona or your whole situation with…" She waved a hand. "I've let myself enjoy what we have together. I forgot all that was still out there." Her brow furrowed. "You won't have the votes without him."

"I will. Chris has some nasty skeletons in his closet, and one of them is willing to talk to the board. Once she tells them her story, along with the assistance of some photos I found in my father's vault, the shareholders won't want to risk the chance of a public scandal." Declan smiled. "They know that even if this woman doesn't release her story about Chris to the press… I certainly will."

Olivia still looked skeptical. "Courtney will still vote to support him, and now Alan Carrol will too. How many votes do you need?"

Declan grimaced. "I need every other major shareholder."

Her eyes widened. "Unless you have a witness to him murdering someone, I don't see..." Declan stayed silent, holding her gaze. Olivia's mouth fell open. "You're not serious."

"Deadly."

"But who? How? Why isn't he in jail?"

"This is going to be a long story," Declan warned.

Olivia pulled out one of the kitchen chairs and sat, watching him expectantly.

"A little over three years ago, Chris killed an escort while driving drunk in my car. Another escort in the car was injured. It seems Chris was already involved with Courtney at that point, even though she was ostensibly living with my father. The two of them saw this as an opportunity to further their plans."

"What does that mean?"

"My father was notorious for his relationships. Except for the women he had children with, at almost exactly the year mark, no matter who it was, he always ended the relationship."

Olivia made a face.

"To be fair, he was upfront with the women he dated, and was extremely generous during that year… But there were plenty of women who thought they would be the one to change him."

"Courtney?"

Declan nodded. "My father and I were no longer close when he got involved with her. Too many years of battling over business." His lips quirked sadly. "In some ways, he and I were very similar. We both wanted to do things our way. It led us to... We were barely speaking by then.

"When my father abruptly announced he was marrying Courtney—right at that year mark—we, my family, were shocked. Cara even said she had seen signs he was close to ending the relationship."

"What did he say his reason was for the change?"

Declan's jaw hardened. "He didn't. He refused to discuss it with Cara. The twins weren't really talking to him either." Olivia lifted her eyebrows. "That's a story for another day. He and Courtney married quickly, and soon after, my father became ill. Before the next year was out, he was dead. I immediately suspected Courtney had killed him, but his doctor, Chris Keller's father, signed the death certificate as natural causes. When they read the will, we learned everyone had been disinherited. Courtney got everything."

Olivia's mouth hung open. "That's the plot of a TV movie. Wouldn't that be easy to challenge?"

Declan shook his head. "They were smart. The only witnesses to the will were people my siblings and I trusted. Luke and James were convinced it was our father's last 'fuck you' since we wouldn't let him control us anymore."

"Chris was a witness," Olivia murmured.

"And his father. They didn't inherit under the will, so on paper it looked legit."

"Wow." Olivia let out a slow exhale. "That was genius. You and Chris were friends, and he gained nothing by the will, so why would you suspect him?"

"Exactly."

Olivia frowned. "What does this have to do with the car accident?"

"My father would never have married Courtney of his own volition. After the accident they, Courtney and Chris, manipulated some photos, with the help of Courtney's son, to make it look like I was the one driving.

"Courtney blackmailed my father with the photos, and he married her to keep me out of jail… Though it is just as likely he did it to protect the Bloom name and his precious company," he said bitterly.

Declan explained to her how he'd eventually convinced his siblings of the murder, and how they discovered the truth about the blackmail and Courtney's secret escort service.

Olivia pulled out the bottle of whiskey she'd bought for him and poured two glasses while he revealed how Cami discovered that Courtney's son Trey was a murderer and tricked him into confessing on tape. Caught up in bragging about his mother, Trey had revealed the details of how Chris and Courtney forged David Bloom's will and poisoned him in order to inherit.

By the time he was done, Olivia was horrified.

"And your father… He…"

"Believed them." Declan's voice was grim, refusing to acknowledge the dull pain that spread through him every time he thought about his father's lack of faith in him.

"Not in the end, though," Olivia insisted. "As ill as you say he was, your father wouldn't have risked traveling to Ireland to get the photos if he didn't believe something was wrong with them."

Declan snorted. "You sound like Cara. She still wants to cling to her vision of him—that he wanted to put things right. It's more likely that he was interested in protecting his legacy and wanted to keep the photos from coming to light. Under the terms of the will, his widow Courtney would have been the next one to open that vault."

"You're wrong. Your father didn't write that will," Olivia reminded him. "Courtney did. You said Trey confessed. Your father would have assumed whoever inherited under the old will would receive the pictures."

A crack formed in the wall he'd constructed around his feelings about his father.

"You *know* the will was forged now," she continued. "Maybe he figured out what Courtney was doing in the end, and wanted to fix things with you before he died." Olivia's voice gentled. "He didn't know he had so little time left."

Declan's ribs squeezed over his pounding heart. He'd been so caught up trying to prove his father murder, and getting the company back, he hadn't really taken the time to process what everything they'd discovered meant.

Could Olivia be right? Would his father have reached out to him? Declan rubbed at his chest.

Things had been a disaster between them for years. Once David Bloom realized that installing his son as president didn't mean he would still be running the corporation de facto, the battles began. When he was named CEO it only got worse. His father had assumed that Declan would still follow his lead. When his father finally grasped that wouldn't be the case, it eventually led to a nuclear level fight and subsequent estrangement.

"I built this company. You have no idea the things I've done. You think because I handed the position to you, it makes you more qualified than me?" His father sneered across the wooden desk in his study at the Rhode Island estate.

Declan clenched his fists. "The acquisitions of the last few years are entirely due to me. We are now positioned to be the most influential media company in the world. I earned it."

"You don't know what it takes to run a company like this. Raised up in prep schools, playing at being a gangster every time your brother gets in trouble. Look at that mess I had to clean up with the Albanians. Do

you know what that could have cost us? Not only you. The company? Your brothers and sister?"

Red mist curled at the edge of Declan's vision. "You've made hundreds of millions as a result of that deal. You may have had to pay them at the time to 'help Seamus,' but don't fucking sit in front of me, like the two of us don't know exactly how that agreement gave you access to Eastern Europe."

His father's eyes turned to flint. "Your brother would be dead if not for me."

"And you've never let me forget it. My benevolent father," Declan mocked.

Something passed across the older man's face but was gone too quickly for Declan to identify. "You don't know what it means to sacrifice for this company—"

"Sacrifice," Declan shouted. "You gave them money. Money that made you more money. I sacrificed everything that night."

Declan hadn't waited for his father to respond, worried that if he stayed in the room a minute more, he might do something he couldn't come back from.

He didn't know that argument would be one of the last times he and his father would ever have a private conversation. A year later, his father had married Courtney and refused to meet with him alone. A year after that, he was dead.

Declan felt Olivia's arms wrap tight around his waist, and he ran a hand down her hair. "I'll never know what he was thinking at the end." He closed his eyes and rested his cheek on the top of her head. "It's almost worse to think that if we'd had a little more time…"

The phone in his pocket buzzed. He ignored it not wanting to let go of Olivia, but when the phone kept buzzing, he released her and frowned.

"It's my brother."

CHAPTER FORTY-ONE

Atlanta—Present Day

"Are you sure this is okay?"

"No, but we're doing it, anyway." Declan smiled, and squeezed her hand on the center console where their fingers were laced together.

Last night, when his brother called, Olivia could clearly hear the man shouting through the phone. Another voice soon joined in.

"Why is Chris Keller still in Atlanta?"

"Why didn't you tell us Courtney is in some sort of rehab? And don't even try to fucking pretend you didn't know."

Two similar voices fired rapid-fire questions.

Declan pinched the bridge of his nose. "I know the two of you share a brain, but could you try not to speak at the same time?"

"Twin jokes. Hilarious."

"This is serious. Luke and I had dinner at the Magnolia Club, and Chris Keller was sitting at the bar like he belongs there."

Olivia widened her eyes, and Declan sighed, realizing she could hear the conversation. He pressed the button for speakerphone so that she could hear more clearly. Warmth spread through her at the obvious sign of trust.

"We really need to talk about your taste in women. Your girlfriend was there with him, chatting away like they were best friends. Though Dahlia says you are actually in love with—"

"Shut up, Luke," Declan snapped.

Olivia grinned as she jerked a thumb at herself and said, "He's talking about me, right?"

Declan rolled his eyes at her, but the stunned silence over the line had Declan glancing at the phone and then back up to grin at Olivia. "Never made them speechless before," he mouthed at her, and she bit her lip to keep from laughing.

"Are you still there?" Declan asked.

"I don't think so. I think I must be dead. Are you—Ow! James! I'm driving, jackass."

"Shut up, you moron," James muttered. "You must be Olivia. Thank you for the muffins."

Declan raised his brows at her. "I may have run into your sister and your brothers' wives this morning."

"Just one wife," James piped up cheerfully. "Dahlia won't let Luke propose yet."

"Don't be such a dick. That was just mean." Luke huffed.

"Again?" Declan's question was for Olivia.

"They were at the cafe again this morning when I was getting the Friday..." She trailed off. "They planned it." Olivia shook her head. "I'm an idiot. I told them I usually go on Friday." Her nose scrunched. "Why did they want to talk to me?"

"Um, I'm trying to think of a way to phrase this that won't send you running screami—" Luke began.

"Because we've never seen Dec so obsess—" James interrupted his twin.

Declan pressed the button on the phone, cutting off their simultaneous voices.

The phone immediately buzzed again, but he powered it down.

"Obsessed, hmm?"

Declan covered her lips, and she forgot all about teasing him.

Now, on their way to have dinner with his family, her anxiety ratcheted up. Last time she got attached to a family, she'd been doubly hurt. Olivia already liked the women in his family that she'd met, but she would be lying if she said she wasn't nervous about meeting his mother.

"You'll love Anne, and she'll love you." Declan assured her.

"And your mom?"

Declan's tense jaw hadn't filled her with confidence. When he switched off the ignition in the underground parking garage of Luke's high rise, Declan didn't make a move to leave the car.

"My family..." He hesitated, and Olivia felt her throat tighten. "More than likely they'll..."

Declan's uncharacteristic discomfort had her own nerves stretched tight. He cleared his throat. "They have certain expectations of me... And you..."

Olivia swallowed, refusing to let her emotions color her words. "I'm not what they are expecting," she finished for him.

A muscle in his cheek ticked. "No. You're not."

She hid the hurt behind an impassive expression. It wasn't as if she wasn't used to being a disappointment to people's families. "They are expecting a Fiona?"

"My mother is," he answered through gritted teeth.

She inhaled slowly as a sharp ache grabbed her chest, her face hot. "I won't pretend to be someone I'm not," she managed quietly, when Declan turned to look at her. "I'm never doing that again. Not even for you." Olivia blamed the winter air, rapidly cooling the car without the engine running, for the ice seeping through her veins.

Declan's face was inscrutable for a minute, then his brows furrowed. "It's not you."

"I'm here. Let's make the best of it." Olivia reached for the door handle, but Declan's hand shot out to stop her. He cupped her jaw, forcing her to look at him.

"I'm a bastard, but I'm not the same kind of bastard as your ex-husband, or even your family are." His voice was hard. "You've met the women my brothers have chosen to be with. Dahlia is a movie star, and Cami is the voice of one of the most popular podcasts in the country. And Cara… I don't even know how to describe my sister anymore.

"They *all* hated the idea of Fiona. Someone who had no larger ambition in life than to wield social power over those she deemed lesser than." His fingers softened, and his thumb stroked over her cheek, warm against her skin. "They are going to be as impressed with you as I am." Declan's gaze burned into her. "I'm proud of you. Of what you've accomplished, of what you've overcome… while still being kind and…" His hand fell away.

"They won't expect someone as warm and loving as you to have chosen to be with me. My family loves me, but they don't know me. Not the way you do." Olivia stayed silent while he clearly struggled to find the words. "I love them and would do anything for them, but they wouldn't understand or approve of many of the things I've done—choices I've made."

Declan looked so sad, Olivia's heart ached for him. "I don't know your family well, but I think you're wrong. From what you've told me about what has happened over the last year, it sounds like they are more like you than you realize."

Declan's lips folded in, clearly not believing her. "We should go up."

Olivia heard the laughter through the door before Declan knocked. Dahlia swung the door open with a wide smile. "You're late. You'll have to play catch up," she said, ushering them into the main room where a large group clustered around a large kitchen island.

Olivia recognized most of the people present, but she could feel the intense scrutiny of the two older women and man sitting on the sofa.

Cami pressed a glass of wine into her hand. "I walked this gauntlet a couple months ago. It's easier with alcohol, I promise." She gave Olivia a wink as the others waved hello.

The eyes on her were speculative, but Olivia quickly realized what Declan had meant. The moment they'd crossed the threshold, Declan's entire demeanor changed. He was cold and remote, his face unsmiling. Olivia wondered if it was more that Declan held himself apart from his family, than that they couldn't accept him.

"I know most of you have met Olivia before." Declan's voice was stiff.

"We haven't officially met," the twin with his arm around Dahlia said with a mischievous smile, his eyes flicking to his older brother. "I've been *dying* to meet you. I'm Luke, the more attractive twin."

Dahlia rolled her eyes and elbowed him in the side. "Try to behave for at least a few minutes."

An identically handsome man, his gray eyes more cautious than his twin's, stepped forward, his hand extended. "I'm James, and you know my wife, Cami." His tone was so proud Olivia couldn't help but smile.

Cara stepped forward and wrapped her arms around Olivia, jostling her wine glass, and whispered in her ear so that no one else could hear. "I'm so glad you are here." Releasing her, Cara gave Declan a look as he suddenly loomed over Olivia. "Relax, Dec. No one is going to bite her."

Olivia heard Declan half growl and half sigh. "She's worse since she met you." He directed the comment to the man leaning against the wall in the corner, one ankle crossed over the other.

"She's perfect," Wes said.

"Aww." Cami and Dahlia sighed, while Luke and James groaned.

"I hate to keep bringing this up, but... There's an agreement about the two of you being so nauseating," Luke said.

"I definitely remember that, but Cara and Wes keep ignoring our rules. Ow!" James pretended to flinch when his wife punched him in the shoulder.

"Are you done yet?" Declan asked.

"Just getting started." Luke's eyes gleamed, his attention turning to Olivia. "For example, where did the two of you meet?"

Olivia froze. They hadn't discussed what they would say. "Declan bought the company I work for, and we've spent a lot of time together."

Declan stepped so close she could feel the heat of his body down the side of hers. To her surprise, he caught her free hand, and lifted it to kiss the back of her hand. She wasn't the only one shocked. The entire room had gone silent, everyone watching them with varying degrees of wide eyes and open mouths.

"We first met while we were both in Ireland twelve years ago."

The twins exchanged confused glances, but Olivia's attention was drawn to the woman with thick dark curls who had risen from the sofa.

"Were the constellations out of alignment twelve years ago or something?" Cami's brows rose high.

"What do you mean?" Cara cocked her head.

"It seems like a momentous year for this family."

If it was possible, Declan stilled even further, but Cami continued, oblivious to his tension.

"Twelve years ago, James was an idiot, letting me slip through his fingers, and joined the Navy." She smirked at her husband.

Dahlia turned a thoughtful look at Luke. "That's true. That would be about the time you said that Declan and—"

Luke silenced her with a hard kiss, a look exchanged between them before he asked, "What happened in Ireland?"

Olivia licked her lips, nerves swirling.

"None of your business." The woman standing by the sofa finally spoke, her Irish accent strong.

"Declan's never hesitated to interfere with our lives," Luke objected. "It's only fair."

"Luke," James warned.

Luke made a face. "Fine. It's nice to meet you, Olivia."

She managed a smile. "All of you as well."

"You never mentioned her before." Declan's mother's voice was unyielding, despite her shutting down a similar line of conversation by Luke. "Does her presence here mean you've changed your plans about marrying Fiona Carrol?"

"Yes."

Olivia's chest tightened. His mother did not look happy. "What is your plan to sway the other votes?"

Siobhan's eyes landed on Olivia, but she couldn't read the woman's expression. Declan tightened his hand on hers, but when she looked up, his face looked like it was carved from stone.

"If you don't marry his daughter, you won't have the votes you need."

Is that all that mattered to the woman? What about her son's happiness?

"Nothing personal against you." Her eyes bored into Olivia in an eerily similar way to her son. "I'm sure you are a lovely young woman, but for Declan to throw—"

Olivia could feel Declan's muscles bunch against her side. "Mam!" he snapped out, harsh enough to startle everyone. "Be very care—"

To everyone's surprise, Cara suddenly stepped forward, standing in front of Olivia, and cast a bright smile on the older woman. "Siobhan, have you ever seen Declan's tattoo?"

Siobhan's face gentled. "*A leanbh,* I appreciate—"

"It's the most gorgeous, white rose," Cara spoke quickly. "It's over his heart. He's had it for years."

"Cara." Declan's voice rumbled with warning, but his sister continued unfazed, her expression determined.

"I had forgotten all about it, because even though I only saw it one time—and Declan was drunk off his ass—he was practically incoherent, quoting poetry and raving about the lost wild white rose. Have you seen it?" Her gaze took in the rest of the family.

"I thought you said you got it after a pub crawl?" Luke said suspiciously.

"Of course, we've seen his tattoo, but you're babbling Car-bear," James interjected, angling his head to where Siobhan had her arms crossed over her chest. "If you've got a point, you might want to get to it."

Cara lifted her chin. "Do you remember a few weeks ago, I mentioned Olivia's perfume..."

Olivia's cheeks flamed, and Declan stepped slightly in front of her, as though protecting her from his family's examination. Because they were *all* staring at her now.

"*Wild White Rose*," Dahlia murmured, her wide eyes shooting to Declan. "Your tattoo is a white rose."

"There was no way it was a coincidence. The name of her perfume being the same phrase he said to me that night. You all saw him at the ball in New York. He was practically feral over her." Cara challenged her brothers before turning back to Siobhan. "I love you and know how protective you are, but you have to see... This whole time... It's always been her." Cara's voice cracked, and Wes strode forward to put his arm around her, pulling her close, glaring at the rest of the family, like they had been the ones to upset her.

Cara pushed away, her eyes glossy. "It took someone new to recognize the pain Declan's been living with." She gestured at Dahlia and Cami. "They saw right away what we've all missed. We've all been complacent because Dec is well..." She waved her hand at him. "Declan. The impenetrable, unfeeling fortress. But the second Olivia came back into his life..."

Siobhan stared at Cara for a moment, and then her eyes returned to Declan, before going past him to Olivia.

Siobhan's shoulders relaxed. "At least you got there in the end." She turned to the couple still seated and lifted her eyebrows.

"Don't gloat, Siobhan, it's unattractive," Anne said mildly.

"I'm not gloating, Anne," Siobhan said gleefully, in direct contradiction to her words, "I'm simply saying I told you so."

What is happening?

Declan's thoughts must have run along the same lines. "What the fuck are you talking about?" he snapped.

Siobhan picked up the glass of whiskey she'd set on the side table and took a sip before she spoke. "I'm your mother. Did you think you could gallivant around Dublin and stay in my mother's cottage with a woman you called your wife, and I *wouldn't* hear about it? Claire couldn't wait to ring me up after you left her pub that night."

A horrified giggle escaped Olivia at the stunned look on Declan's face.

"Your wife?" Luke stared.

Declan's jaw worked back and forth.

"Don't worry," Dahlia patted Luke's chest. "I'll get the story from Olivia and fill you in."

"You will *all* leave her alone." Declan gritted out.

"This is fascinating," Wes drawled from his position next to Cara.

Cara nodded. "It's kind of like when Q was outsmarted by that girl whose parents pretended to be human and got killed in a tornado… But they didn't have tornados on Earth anymore… And then Q got in trouble with the collective."

"I swear to god, if this is another Star Trek reference," James groaned.

Luke wrinkled his nose. "Why are the two of you such huge dorks?"

"Star Trek isn't dorky," Cara shot back. "It's full of philosophy and…"

Wes squeezed her tight and lifted her chin to kiss her. "It's okay, baby. They'll never get it."

Cara huffed something angrily under her breath that sounded like "jerks."

Declan's muscles slowly relaxed next to her.

"Is that it then?" Olivia whispered as his siblings began to good-naturedly squabble.

"Not quite. Thank you, honey," Anne said to her husband, as he helped her to her feet and handed her a cane. She walked forward slowly to stand in front of Declan and motioned for him to bend down. She kissed his cheek and stroked his arm with a gentle smile. "I'm so happy for you. You deserve this."

Declan's jaw relaxed, and for the first time since they had entered the luxury apartment, he looked like *her* Declan.

Anne continued. "I worried you'd never find peace."

"I don't have peace yet. But I will soon."

James sent an apologetic look to Olivia before saying. "If you aren't going to marry Fiona to get the votes, what *is* your plan?"

Declan squared his shoulders. "The escort who survived the car accident has agreed to talk to the board. She doesn't want to get involved in a criminal prosecution, but her story, plus the photos and confession Cami got... I'm going to call for a vote of no confidence. I have been working on the rest of the board. No one is interested in all of that being leaked to the press. It would seriously affect the share price if it gets out that Bloom Communications' CEO is a murderer twice over. I'll convince them to vote with me."

James nodded, but Luke frowned. "That doesn't explain why Chris is still in Atlanta. The deal for XEROS was completed weeks ago."

"He hasn't been here the whole time," Declan's voice was grim. "I was informed this morning that Chris and Courtney have gotten married. I'm not sure why he's here, instead of with her, or exactly what his plan is, but I suspect it has something to do with Olivia." His hand tightened almost painfully on hers.

The faces around them sobered. "You are friendly with Chris Keller?" Cami's tone was diplomatic.

"No." Olivia shook her head. "I had dinner with him after New York, but that's it."

"Why?" Luke's eyes were sharp.

A tiny warning growl emanated from the back of Declan's throat, but Luke glared right back at him.

"He claimed he wanted to help me find a job," Olivia explained.

This time, it was Wes who frowned. "Is that supposed to be a coincidence?"

"I knew nothing about what had happened with your father, and it was before..." she trailed off, not wanting to share that Declan had been pretending she meant nothing to him. "Originally, it was as an apology for what Courtney did... It seemed harmless."

Her face heated as she felt the full extent of Declan's attention.

"What do you mean, *what Courtney did?*"

The fury in his eyes made her stumble over her words.

"At the gala... when I thought I was drunk... Courtney admitted to Chris that she'd put her pills in my drink, and he said he felt responsible..."

Declan snarled a vicious curse. But it was the tsunami of energy rolling off him that had Olivia more concerned.

CHAPTER FORTY-TWO

Atlanta—Present Day

He was having a heart attack. It was the only explanation. Declan could feel his heart thundering painfully as it tried to break out of his ribcage, but he also felt ice cold. "Courtney did *what?*"

"That makes sense." Declan heard his sister-in-law faintly through the blood pumping furiously in his ears. "We said it at the time. It happened so fast. What did she give you? Did Chris say?"

Olivia's wide eyes were still looking up at him. He was probably crushing her fingers, but Olivia didn't complain. "Xanax. She thought I was flirting with Chris... and Declan."

Declan tried to rein in his anger, making a conscious effort to control his breathing. He wasn't successful.

"She could have killed you." Air sawed painfully in Declan's lungs. "As it was, Chris almost got you out of the building." His nostrils flared, and through his rage he heard Cami agree with him.

"That was really dangerous. Courtney didn't know if Olivia was on other medications or—"

"Not helping, sweetheart." Declan heard James say.

The memory of Olivia's clammy skin as she took shallow breaths that night, and how he'd ripped her dress in half trying to make her more comfortable flashed in front of him. He'd held her hair when she was sick twice and slumped to the floor, before he cleaned her up and put her in his T-shirt... He thought she was drunk... He should have gotten a doctor.

Declan let go of Olivia, and spun to give his family his back, his fists bunched at his side. He felt her hand on his back, rubbing firm circles.

"I'm okay."

His control was rapidly slipping away, and he needed to hold on. Declan didn't want to frighten her.

"Where is she now?" Luke's voice was hard.

"A spa in New York," James said. "It's too late to press charges."

His brother's calm words snapped the last tether holding him together, and Declan pivoted to face his family. "Press charges? I'm going to kill her with my bare hands," he snarled.

"Declan," he heard Olivia's voice trying to soothe him, and saw the looks on his family's faces.

He jabbed a finger at his brothers. "I told you the time was coming. The time is now. Courtney could have killed her." A shudder ran through his body. "Because of me."

"Declan," Cara began, but he held up his hand.

"No."

"Declan, if you kill her, our father's fortune will go to Chris. They're married."

"Without our father's remains, we need Courtney alive to get a confession," Luke said, but his eyes were sympathetic. "But after..."

"And since we can't find the ashes," James added.

They both watched Declan warily, and he knew by the looks on the others' faces he'd rattled them.

"Damn it!" he roared.

"I know where the ashes are, or… at least, where they were a few weeks ago."

All eyes turned to Olivia. "Chris told me at dinner. Looking back, I realize he was making the case about why I should feel bad for Courtney. Apparently, she had the ashes of her sons and David Bloom sent to one of those companies that make fake diamonds out of human remains. Chris says she doesn't take it off. She's wearing it around her neck."

Dahlia's face wrinkled. "That's bizarre."

"It's worse than bizarre," Wes said. "The ashes are compromised now. It will be almost impossible to prove the presence of thallium for one set of remains."

"They didn't use them all. Chris mentioned she left enough to have earrings made. The company should still have the individual ashes," Olivia added.

"If we could somehow get our hands on them," James said.

"I'll call Vincent and Brady" Luke said. "I'm sure they have someone who can get it done."

The words were slow to process in Declan's brain. He seemed to be stuck in a loop as his family made plans around him.

If she'd been under my protection all these years, none of this would have happened.

"Declan." He felt Olivia's cool hands on either side of his face, forcing his head down to hers. Declan's eyes focused on the clear, deep blue of her eyes and sucked in a breath, his body settling when she smiled at him. "Ashes first. Then deal with her."

Declan couldn't fathom what he had ever done for the universe to have brought Olivia into his life. But he knew he didn't deserve her.

Her hands fell away, and he dipped his chin in a tiny nod. Declan looked at his family, who were all staring at him like they'd never seen him before.

"Don't worry about Vincent. There's no time for all that. I'll buy the company."

They hadn't stayed much longer. Declan's nerves were so badly frayed from what Olivia revealed, he wanted to be alone with her. Sensing his discomfort, Olivia whispered, "Are you ready to go home?"

Home.

Declan wanted nothing more than to be wrapped around Olivia in front of the fire. Ignoring his family's objections that they hadn't eaten yet, Declan practically dragged Olivia to the elevator.

They were barely through the front door before Declan was kissing her, needing to feel her alive and warm in his arms. To reassure himself that she was safe and with him.

"Puppy," Olivia panted as his teeth scraped along her collarbone. Her hands pushed at him gently when he yanked at her buttons. "Seriously, Oscar needs to go out."

Declan lifted his chest off of Olivia, where she lay sprawled across the kitchen island, hearing for the first time the whimpers from the crate in the corner. He shoved a hand back through his hair and exhaled hard, but released the lever and the puppy bounded out. "I think I hate you," he told the dog.

Olivia stared at him from her semi-reclined position, face flushed with arousal and laughter. "Don't talk to my baby like that."

Declan pointed a finger at her as he strode toward the front door, grabbing Oscar's leash. "Naked."

"Hurry up," he muttered to the puppy as Oscar sniffed, circling the same spot of grass for the fiftieth time. The sound of a car approaching had Declan looking toward the road. However, because of Olivia's steep lot, Declan could only see headlight beams slowly sweep the cul-de-sac, illuminating his car parked halfway down the driveway.

The beams slowed for a moment, and the hair on the back of Declan's neck rose. His body tensed, but the car continued on, leaving the street in darkness again.

Closing the front door, Declan set the alarm, and as soon as he unclipped the leash, the puppy galloped off. Declan cast one more look at the door. With his car in the driveway and the alarm set, he didn't think Kyle would try anything, but it infuriated him that the man was still walking around.

All thoughts of Kyle vanished when Declan reached the kitchen and found Olivia exactly where he had left her, but this time she had laid out her bare skin for him like a feast.

"ARE YOU AWAKE?" Olivia whispered.

"No," he muttered. "You wore me out."

"Did you sleep with Courtney?"

Declan reared up on his elbow and looked down at her face, lit by the moonlight coming through her sheer drapes.

"Why would you even ask that?"

Olivia's face was serious. "I had put most of the night in New York out of my mind, but after tonight, I was thinking about the things Courtney said… and what you said tonight."

"What did I say?"

"That I could have died because of *you*."

Had he said that? "I was angry—"

"Don't lie to me," Olivia said quietly.

Declan traced the delicate lines of her face and then sighed, sinking back down next to her, and pulling her into his arms.

"I swear I never touched her. Though she tried… relentlessly.

Before she went after my father, Courtney came on to me, hard. Chris was there the night we met at a party. I have to believe that was where they first met as well—or at least they didn't seem to know each other."

He threw an arm over his eyes. "But looking back… I don't know that I can trust anything Chris ever said or did. He completely fooled me. I turned her down at the party, but over the next several months, she seemed to be everywhere I was, always making it abundantly clear she was available."

"How did she end up with your father?"

"I don't know. I think she had her eyes set on the Bloom fortune and thought she could manipulate me. She's a beautiful woman, but there was no chance I was going there."

"Because you're impervious to manipulation?" Olivia drawled.

"Yes."

She snorted a soft laugh. Declan tucked her hair behind her ear and stroked his fingers down her cheek and over her lips. "In order to be manipulated you have to have a heart."

A tiny frown formed in her eyes. "You have a heart, Declan."

He shook his head with a soft smile. "I'd already left it with you."

THE NEXT TWO weeks passed quickly. As much as Declan hated leaving Olivia, it was necessary to fly to each of the major shareholders' homes around the country to meet with them in person. He was on his way back to a private airport outside of Billings, Montana, when Brady's name appeared on his screen.

"What's wrong?"

"Your girl's got a visitor. Want us to intervene?"

"Who?"

"It's a woman. She sat in her car for awhile, so we ran an image search. It's her ex's cousin."

The friend. *Jessica*. Declan's jaw tightened. This woman, who should have looked out for Olivia, and had let her down. As much as he would like to get revenge, once he learned the woman had two small sons, he'd held off. That didn't mean Jessica got off completely free. One of Brady's cyber guys added some questionable items to her internet search history. For the rest of her life, Declan hoped Jessica wondered why TSA always selected her for additional screening. It was petty, but it made him smile.

"What do you want us to do? She's at the door."

"Olivia let her in?"

"Yeah."

Declan wanted to tell Brady to instruct his man to swoop in and remove the traitor, but he knew Olivia would kill him if he interfered.

"Tell them to keep their eyes peeled. I'm on my way home now."

"You're going back to New York?" When Declan didn't answer, Brady chuckled. "Just kidding. You Bloom men are so sensitive about your women."

Declan ended the call and immediately dialed another. "I need a favor."

"Anything," his sister's voice immediately responded.

"I need you to take dinner to Olivia's house."

"Um, okay?"

"Right now. Ask Cami and Dahlia to meet you there."

"I think Dahlia left for set this morning, but I'll call Cami."

Declan heard Cara whisper something to who he assumed was her husband.

"Wes wants to know if he should come with me." He could hear the eye roll in his sister's voice.

"No. But I need you to go, now."

"That's all I get?"

"Please, Car-bear."

He heard a beep. "I'm already in the car. Now hang up, so I can call Cami."

CHAPTER FORTY-THREE

ATLANTA—PRESENT DAY

"What are you doing here?"

Olivia stared at her former friend. Even before she moved out of state, Jessica had never shown up at her door unannounced. Normally, she let Olivia know weeks before she scheduled a trip to Atlanta. On the heels of Kyle's attack and how they had left things, Olivia's nerves were on high alert.

"Can we talk?" Jessica shifted her weight from one foot to the other.

Olivia opened the door wider, letting her former friend inside, and gave a wave to the man in the SUV at the top of her driveway.

"Who is that?" Jessica asked, angling her head toward the closed front door.

"Security." At first, she'd balked at the idea of having someone outside her house while Declan was gone, but Olivia had to admit after her first night alone, facing the large dark windows, she felt relieved knowing help was only a shout away.

Jessica let out a heavy sigh. "Is this the Kyle thing? He called me, told me what was going on here."

"Did he?" Olivia kept her voice neutral.

Kyle is alive!

"Don't you think this has gone too far, Livvy? I mean, I know the divorce was ugly, but your boyfriend somehow had him banned from all the good clubs. He really embarrassed Kyle in front of his friends, not to mention this guy has stolen Kyle's birthright from him.

"You're happy now, right? Your dream man came back. Why can't you leave Kyle alone?" Her eyes accused. "Kyle's afraid to show his face. Did you know that? Terrified your thug boyfriend will hurt him. He's not the white knight you made him out to be."

Declan was definitely not a white knight. More like a fire-breathing dragon. Her dragon.

"What are you smiling about, Livvy? This isn't funny."

"You're right, it's not." Olivia stared at her former friend. "When you spoke to Kyle, did he tell you he broke in and attacked me?"

That I stabbed him?

Jessica reared back. "He wouldn't do that."

"He would do that. He *did* do that. And it wasn't even the first time. I pretended to have the flu because he split my lip and left bruises all over me. I couldn't go into work."

"You're exaggerating." Jessica shook her head, denying Olivia's words.

"You never wanted to hear the truth. You were more than happy to explain away all of my unhappiness for years. I stayed longer than I should have because I was worried about losing you, losing a family I'd come to love, my own family's expectations… my job.

"Kyle wants to complain about his 'birthright' being taken. What did he ever do besides use company expense accounts to cheat on me?"

"Livvy." Jessica spread her hands wide. "Come on, this is me. I was there for the whole thing. It wasn't one sided, was it? You are as much to blame for your marriage falling apart as he is."

Olivia gaped at her. "I know you don't want to hear this, but your cousin is an abusive piece of shit."

"And you are a massive workaholic with my uncle wrapped around your finger," Jessica snapped back. "You were so worried about succeeding, you didn't care about Kyle's feelings. He knew work was more important to you than him."

"Is that a valid excuse for cheating?" Jessica blinked. "Within the first year? Hell, probably before."

"And you were faithful?" Jessica shot back.

"Yes."

Jessica scoffed. "Maybe you weren't sleeping with anyone else, but you never gave Kyle a chance. You refused to see what a great guy he is, because you convinced yourself prince charming was out there waiting. You were so wrapped up in the fairy tale of your 'Irish true love,'" Jessica mocked bitterly, "that you refused to see reality. It wasn't true, and now this guy has sucked you in again, like he did before. I get it. Declan Bloom is hot and rich, but he's *using* you, and you're too stupid to see the truth. The second he's done with you, Declan will drop you again, but this time I won't be there to pick up the pieces."

Jessica's voice had risen to a shout, and Olivia could only stare at her, stunned. How had Olivia never recognized her friend's resentment before?

"Thank goodness for that," a sunny voice said from the front door. Cami's smile was so sharp Olivia was surprised Jessica wasn't bleeding. "I knocked, but you didn't hear me."

Olivia's cheeks blazed, embarrassment sweeping up her spine, but Cami breezed past them, setting a bottle of wine and a bottle of sparkling grape juice on the kitchen counter. "I was on my way home from work when Cara called wanting a girl's night. It's a work night, so I brought alcoholic and nonalcoholic so all our options are covered. Sorry for the ambush, Olivia."

"I…um…"

Jessica glared at Olivia and then Cami.

Cami's eyes glinted as she tapped a finger against her lip, pretending to think. "*Irish true love,* huh?"

Olivia hadn't thought it possible for her cheeks to get any hotter, but she was wrong.

"We *are* talking about Declan, right? It makes me so happy to hear that's how you feel about my *brother-in-law*. After all, he has you permanently inked on his body." The smile she turned on Jessica was anything but friendly. "Isn't it the most romantic story you've ever heard? Almost like star-crossed lovers, but in this case, there is a happy ending. Like all good love stories, they had to tackle some monsters along the way."

Jessica's mouth opened like she wanted to argue, but Cami kept talking. "Cara is going to be here soon, and Dahlia will be here straight from her meeting. Luckily, she was still in town." Cami paused for dramatic effect and then turned to Jessica. "I'd invite you to stay, but this is kind of a *family* girl's night, and considering how you feel about Declan, you might want to go before his sister gets here. She's a tad protective."

"I'm so disappointed in you," Jessica hissed and then slammed the front door. Despite herself, Olivia winced. Jessica had known her long enough to know how those words would affect her.

"Oh my gosh." Cami grimaced. "I've never been so mean in my entire life, but that girl… I'm sorry if I overstepped."

The bridge of Olivia's nose tingled, and she bit her tongue.

Do not cry in front of this woman. Do not cry.

"Hey," Cami's voice was soft as she came forward hesitantly. "It's okay to cry."

Olivia sniffed. "Thank you for that."

Cami waved her hand. "Don't thank me. No offense, but your

friend is a bitch." She twisted off the top of the wine and smiled. "Don't judge me. Twist top is still good."

"She's not my friend. Not anymore."

"I think that's for the best," Cami said, opening the other bottle. "I didn't mean to eavesdrop, but I heard a bit of what you said… about your ex-husband."

Shame cascaded through Olivia.

"The Kyle in hiding thing… I assume that means Declan knows what he did to you?" Cami asked. Olivia managed a small nod. "In that case, he's smart to hide."

"Who's smart to hide?" Cara's voice sounded, as she paraded in holding three pizza boxes. "I took pity on the delivery guy in the driveway getting the third degree from your watch dog. I'm surprised Dec didn't insist it be Brady or Vincent personally."

"Personally what?" The door shut behind Dahlia.

For a minute, Olivia felt like she couldn't catch her breath. Her kitchen was full of three, vibrant women, and all appeared willing to accept her with open arms, whereas her oldest friend in the world thought the worst of her.

"Declan called you, didn't he?"

Cara shrugged. "He knew I would jump at the excuse to pump you for information." She turned her gaze to Cami. "I thought I might actually beat you here. I know your offices are around the corner but I hit every green light on Peachtree, and for once, the roads weren't jammed."

Olivia shook her head, biting her lip to keep it from trembling, overwhelmed by the emotion.

"Who's the angry chick in the car parked on the street? She was yelling into her phone when I pulled up," Dahlia asked.

Olivia took a deep breath. She felt like she owed them an explanation after they'd essentially dropped what they were doing to come to her rescue.

"Can I have a glass of wine first?" Olivia asked with a rueful smile.

An hour later, Olivia finally stopped talking and wiped a few lingering tears off her cheeks. She hadn't meant to tell the women the entire story of her marriage, but other than her therapist, she'd never told anyone. Once she started talking, the words poured out of her. Her shoulders dropped, feeling like forty pounds had fallen off.

These women made it easy. They listened quietly, only stopping her to ask a few questions, while wiping away their own stray tears.

Dahlia's face was tight. "I understand more than I'd like to. I was married to a weak asshole, too. When did it get physical?"

The immediate denials that usually sprang to mind evaporated in the face of Dahlia's sympathetic eyes. "After we were married for a year. It started small… pushes, pinches, gripping my arm too hard… I left the morning after it got really bad," Olivia admitted.

Dahlia made a soft sound. "Then you were smarter than me."

"I didn't know that," Cara said, resting her hand on Dahlia's knee where she sat next to her on the floor.

Dahlia rolled her shoulders. "It was a long time ago. My ex-husband is dead now, which is lucky for him, because when Luke found out about it, he was thinking of a more drawn-out way of ending the piece of shit than an overdose."

"I think that's the main reason Jessica came tonight. She doesn't even live in the state, so it had to be serious for her to come."

Cara's eyes were careful. "Because Declan is hunting for your ex?"

Olivia blanked her face, and Cara sighed. "I know Declan likes to think we don't know about things he's done or been a part of… And I'll admit I don't know it all, nor do I want to. He's my brother, and as much as he has tried to shield me, I overheard enough of my father's meetings during the summers I spent with him. Knew the fear people had of my name, of my father, and Declan. Hell, Declan even had my stalker locked away." She shrugged. "I'm glad he's on our side."

"James shot my psycho ex-friend who was obsessed with me," Cami piped up, but then her shoulders slumped. "Fine, it was self-defense, but I was feeling left out."

They looked at each other and laughed.

"What is wrong with us?" Cami asked.

"I don't know about you, but I was born into this family, so it's in my DNA. You ladies fell in love with the crazies."

"I think I shocked Declan when he told me what he was going to do, and I didn't get upset. Which I'm sure my therapist would have a lot to say about," Olivia said ruefully. "I don't know the details because his friend is handling it."

"Friend?" Cara laughed. "Declan doesn't have friends."

Olivia scrunched her nose. "It *sounded* like they were friends. He told me they do each other favors—it kind of sounded like a game. Declan was definitely smiling when he told me about it. He said Alex was secretly thrilled to do the last favor, so it shouldn't have counted on their tally. But also, that Alex was happy to help with the Kyle situation, because it put Alex ahead, and Alex loves when it's Declan's turn to owe the favor." She shrugged. "It was more than a little confusing."

"Alex?" Cami's voice was strangled. "Alex Kovalyov?"

Shit. Did I say too much?

"I don't know his last name. I might have misunderstood."

Cami shook her head. "I bet Declan was talking about the shooting at my studio. When Trey tried to kill me, Alex shot him. But Declan told me afterward that he thought Kovalyov did it because Madison was in there with me."

"Who's Madison?" Olivia was totally confused. "Wait, I thought *you* shot Trey Crawford."

Cami looked uncomfortable. "It's a complicated story. You should ask Declan about it. Madison is my best friend. Kovalyov has some weird obsession with her."

"That's terrifying," Dahlia said. "Don't get me wrong, he's got the whole fallen dark angel thing going for him, but he's scary as hell."

"I know. What makes it worse is, I think Madison has gotten herself involved with him." Cami shook herself. "That's a story for another night." Her lips quirked up. "However, if Alex Kovalyov is the one looking for him, Kyle should get a new identity. The Russian Bratva doesn't mess around."

Olivia's new puppy clambered into Cara's lap and happily plopped down. "Oscar," Olivia scolded. "You can push him off."

"No way," Cara said, scratching his ears. "I can't believe Declan got you a puppy. If I hadn't seen the two of you together with my own eyes, I'd swear we were talking about someone else."

"Why Oscar?" Dahlia asked.

Olivia blushed. "It's kind of an inside joke."

"Declan has inside jokes?" Cara looked skeptical, and even though Olivia knew his sister was teasing, she felt defensive.

Olivia got to her feet and pulled the worn paperback from the bookshelf and handed it to her.

"When I met Declan in Dublin, I asked him what the last book he'd read was. He gave me his copy to take with me."

Cami shoved her lower lip out with an, "Aww. You kept it."

Dahlia took the thin book from Cara, pursing her lips. "I'm impressed. Though I'm having a hard time picturing Declan reading this."

Cami stuck out her hand, and Dahlia handed her the book.

"You think that's surprising? I didn't even know he liked poetry until that night he was drunk and started quoting it at me," Cara said, as Cami flipped open a page and began reading silently.

"Really?" Dahlia's eyes were wide. "He quotes poetry?"

"It's actually really romantic." Olivia's mind wandered to the night before Declan left on his latest trip.

"If case you ever foolishly forget: I am never not thinking of you," he'd whispered against her heated flesh, as his lips trailed down her body.

"Oh my god!" Dahlia exclaimed. "You are bright red." She bounced on her crossed legs. "Does he quote it in bed?"

"I *told* you he was the romantic in the family," Cami crowed.

"I'm buying Luke a poetry book," Dahlia sighed.

"Ew! Stop. My ears are bleeding." Cara held her hands over her ears.

Sudden doubt flooded Olivia. It must have shown on her face because Cami gave her an understanding smile. "We won't say anything." She drew a circle in the air around the women. "We have to stick together, because these men are *a lot*."

"You can save the talk about my brothers' sex lives for when I'm not around." Cara pretended to gag, and they all laughed.

It was well after midnight when Olivia waved goodbye to the women as they drove off. She couldn't remember the last time she'd laughed so much.

Olivia hadn't realized how much she'd missed having female friends until tonight. She had always told herself that work was enough, but she now realized that she needed to make time for other things in her life.

Her body overflowing with emotion, she sent a text, knowing that Declan was probably still in the air.

Olivia: Thank you.

Declan: For what?

Olivia: For knowing tonight would be hard and sending back up.

She paused, chewing her lip.

Olivia: And for loving me.

Declan: You are my entire life. Landing soon. Love you.

Olivia shrugged into her coat and clipped Oscar's leash on, letting him drag her to the front door. She saw Rhodes's outline, on duty in his SUV, keeping watch in the freezing air.

Oscar sniffed all over the front yard, but apparently, the best spot eluded him. His brown nose suddenly lifted in the air, and then he was tugging her around the side of the house to the backyard. The lights from her family room cast out through the windows, illuminating a few feet beyond the deck above her.

Oscar let out a low puppy growl, and Olivia felt goosebumps rise that had nothing to do with the winter night. The fur on the back of Oscar's neck rose, and he let out a small bark before growling again.

Suddenly, there was a crashing sound from the thin stretch of trees separating the grass from the banks of the river. Olivia opened her mouth to scream, but closed it again when three deer darted across her yard, sending Oscar into a frenzy of barks. Yanking against his leash, he tried to give chase.

"Ms. Adler?" Rhodes called before the sandy-haired man came around the corner of the house at a full run, gun drawn.

"I'm fine," Olivia exclaimed, her hand pressed to her chest as if it would calm her heart rate. "Deer."

Rhodes scanned the trees with a frown. "I'll walk you to the door, clear the house, and do another perimeter check."

Olivia wanted to object that it was overkill, that the disturbance had been her overzealous puppy, but she kept her mouth closed, because honestly, she felt better with him making sure.

~

A WARM KISS against her ear woke her as Declan slipped into bed and tugged the blanket over their shoulders. He wrapped his heavy arm under her breasts and pulled her tight, pressing her back firmly against his hard chest. He nuzzled into her hair. "What happened to Oscar's crate?"

"He was lonely," she whispered back.

Declan grunted and sat up. He flipped a thick throw blanket until it draped over the dog sleeping on the chaise at the foot of her bed. Olivia relaxed into his warmth as Declan lay down again, her heart swelling.

This was the side of Declan very few got to see. The world saw the ruthless billionaire, and she got the handsome man who worried whether a sleeping puppy was warm enough.

CHAPTER FORTY-FOUR

Atlanta—Present Day

"As you can see, by manufacturing XEROS in house, we not only save a tremendous amount in expansion costs—based on the tech grant the state will award us—but also realize significant tax savings on next year's bottom line."

Declan kept his face neutral, aware that as many eyes were on him as on her. Cecile had informed him that he and Olivia hadn't been as discreet as they thought. Getting caught making out against the refrigerator in the second-floor kitchen was most likely what had given them away, he thought with a smirk.

He wasn't sorry. Declan wanted the entire world to know Olivia was his.

"In addition," Olivia continued her presentation. "As you are all aware, this technology is poised to change the way streaming services operate. While there are a handful of other products in development, XEROS is the only one market-ready. Which means, it is a prime target for intellectual property theft.

"By keeping our designs in-house, we can virtually guarantee the intellectual property stays safeguarded." Olivia beamed at the

Armstrong engineers and technicians she'd invited to the meeting. "I know I can trust every member of this company."

Declan steepled his fingers in front of his mouth to hide his smile. Olivia thought he didn't know about the next step in her restructuring plan—to offer stock options to all current employees. He *might* have glimpsed her notes while he was waiting for her to get ready for work the other morning.

"Look, your charts and things look pretty and all," Frank Townshend's voice dripped with condescension. Declan stifled the urge to strangle the man with his tie.

There was no reason for Townshend to have come, but as a significant shareholder in Bloom Capital, he had the right. Declan knew it wasn't a coincidence that Alan Carrol's good friend had flown to Atlanta specifically for this meeting. Though he would like to know how the two men even knew it was taking place. The other few board members left operating decisions to Declan's discretion. They were more than happy to simply collect their share of the profits he brought in.

When the man began making snide comments to Olivia, Declan immediately recognized what was happening.

"You are young for a CFO. Do you have these agreements in writing from each of the government agencies? In my experience, you can't make decisions based on someone's cocktail party promise." Townshend tapped his pen on the page in front of them that detailed the grant and tax cuts.

Declan stayed silent. Olivia had this. He watched with pride as she lifted one eyebrow at the older man, her expression calm.

"I do," she said simply.

Townshend gaped at her, and Declan couldn't help the smile that stretched across his face.

"Well, then," Declan said, sitting straighter in his seat. "If there are no other questions?"

He met Townshend's eyes. The man frowned, but clearly had

no further legitimate concerns. "Excellent." Declan brought his hands together. "I'll review it and let you know by the close of business today."

"This is extremely unusual." Townshend evidently felt like he needed to give it one more try. "We aren't in the business of holding onto companies. You are essentially putting us in the electronics business." He pivoted in his chair to face Declan, who noticed a thin sheen of sweat on the man's brow.

Briefly, Declan wondered what Carrol had on the man, because no one had ever questioned Declan's decisions before. Declan had been fully prepared to listen to the man's complaints before sending him on his way, but the idiot made the mistake of smirking at Olivia before turning his gaze back to Declan.

"I understand there are certain other *incentives* here—"

"Out," Declan barked. The Armstrong staff jumped, before scrambling to their feet. He didn't dare look at Olivia, because if she looked even the tiniest bit embarrassed, he was going to lose it.

"Declan, I don't mean any offense. I'm sure Ms. Adler is—"

"Declan," Olivia said.

"Out. Now." He didn't look at her, but there was no mistaking the command in his voice. Declan heard her sigh, and then the door clicked shut behind her.

"I don't know what's gotten into you lately," Townshend said, his voice trembling slightly. "Alan told me you called off your engagement. He's not an enemy you want, Declan."

"Am I?"

The man blinked at him.

"You said *he* wasn't an enemy someone would want." Declan's voice could have cut glass. "Are you implying I am? Because that is exactly what you are doing—making me your enemy."

"Declan, I've known you a long time. This woman seems to have—"

"This is the last warning you will ever receive from me." Declan stared into the man's eyes, satisfied when Townshend jerked back. "If I ever hear you refer to Ms. Adler in anything but the most glowing of terms, I will destroy you. You, your son and his ridiculous photography business, and whatever useless businesses your grandchildren grow up to create. Because god knows if they've inherited any of your intelligence, they will be disasters anyway."

"Declan," the man pleaded.

"We will repay you in full for the funds you have invested in Bloom Capital," Declan said, rising to his feet. He lazily buttoned his suit jacket and walked away.

"YOU CAN'T THREATEN everyone who challenges me," Olivia said, her lips pinched, when he entered her office, closing the door behind him.

"Yes, I can. Besides, that wasn't about you. That was Alan Carrol thinking he could flex some imaginary muscle." Declan shrugged. "A message needed to be sent."

"To Alan Carrol?"

"To everyone."

Olivia chewed her lip. "Can I ask you something?"

"Of course."

"Without you going all cold and angry?"

He gazed back at her for a long moment until she sighed. "Is Bloom Communications really what you want, or is it you can't stand to lose?"

Declan narrowed his eyes. "Is that what you think this is? You think I've done all this because I don't like to lose?"

Olivia came to her feet and walked to where he stood rigid in front of her desk. She ran her hands over his biceps, coming to rest on his forearms. "I know it's not *all* about that. But I'm worried regaining that company has become an obsession. Not the actual company, but the regaining control part of it. Of course, you want to avenge your father, regain his fortune for your family… but the actual running of the company? Is that what you want to do?"

Anger surged through him at her words.

"You said it yourself. No one ever gave you a real choice." Olivia's eyes pierced into him, like if she looked hard enough, she'd find the answer deep inside. "That job was forced on you, and yes, you were wildly successful, but you'd be successful at whatever you chose. Look at how fast you've built Bloom Capital."

His body vibrated with tension. He couldn't believe his ears. Bloom Communications was everything he had worked for. How could she ask him that?

"That's an interesting question coming from someone who is fighting tooth and nail to keep a company that doesn't even belong to her."

"You're angry. I understand. I'm only asking because… I don't know…" Olivia blew out a breath. "Have you ever asked yourself if you're happy? Truly happy?" She searched his eyes.

The muscles in his body relaxed slightly when she studied his face. "It's my family's legacy, Olivia. I can't turn my back on what we built." Olivia nodded, but he could see the shadow in her eyes, and he leaned down to press a soft kiss to her lips. "Trust me."

"Always."

His arms felt empty when she stepped away and put a few steps between them, her work mask securely in place. "Which way are you leaning on the proposal?"

Declan laughed, the rest of his tension dissolving. "And *I'm* obsessed?"

Her lips parted, but before she could speak, her office door swung open. Melissa burst in, her eyes wide. "Olivia, there is a crazy woman in the parking lot destroying your car."

"What?" Olivia gasped, but Declan was already striding from the room.

"I called the police," Melissa continued, hurrying along behind them.

Not waiting for the elevator, Declan took the stairs two at a time, ignoring Olivia's calls for him to wait. Bursting through the door in the lobby, he could hear screaming before he spotted Fiona, swinging what looked like a golf club, repeatedly into Olivia's BMW.

"Fucking whore!" Fiona screamed, as Declan shoved past the employees watching wide-eyed.

"Back inside," he ordered. A few people tucked their phones behind their backs, and Declan saw Stuart and Melissa tugging at people's sleeves to turn them back to the building. The group retreated into the lobby, where he was sure they would continue to watch the show through the windows.

"What the fuck are you doing?" Declan bellowed, striding towards Fiona.

"Declan, stay back!" Olivia yelled.

The windshield shattered under the next blow, and Fiona's chest heaved with the exertion, her eyes finding Olivia. "You ruined everything. He is mine!" she screeched.

"Put down the golf club, Fiona." Declan said, making sure he stayed out of her swing zone.

"No!" Fiona's eyes were wild, and he could see the wide pupils across the short distance. "She's a nobody. No one beats me!"

Her eyes lasered onto Olivia, and she took a few steps forward. "You think you're hot stuff now? Let's see how pretty you are when I'm done. My father always says you can't rely on anyone else to get the job done." She panted. "I gave that idiot

Kyle so much coke, all he had to do…" She sucked in a breath. "Never mind… I'll do it myself."

Faster than Declan thought she could move, Fiona swung the golf club over her head and charged at Olivia.

Declan stepped to intercept her, grunting as the shaft of the club came down hard on his shoulder. They grappled for a moment, then Declan yanked the club from her hand, and Fiona howled like a wild animal.

He wrapped his arms around her from behind, trapping her arms against her chest. Declan didn't know if it was adrenaline or something she'd taken, but it took more effort than he expected to restrain her. Fiona kicked back at him, thrashing to free herself.

"I'll kill her. You are mine. My father promised me I could have you."

"You sent Kyle?" Olivia looked appalled.

"All we had to do was give him a couple of bumps and gas him up about you and Declan's history… *Rose*," Fiona sneered.

Every muscle in Declan's body locked. "Who told you that name?"

Fiona threw her head back, but Declan dodged so that the back of her head glanced off his cheekbone rather than squarely on his nose.

"My father will break you, asshole. He won't let you get away with this," she hissed. "Chris has a plan. You'll both be sorry."

Fiona yelped when Declan's fingers bit into her arms. Declan's gaze lifted to Olivia. "Did you tell Chris?"

"What?" Olivia looked from Fiona trapped against him to her ruined car and back again.

"Did you tell Chris about us? Could Jessica or Kyle have told him?" Declan persisted. "Does he know your name is Rose?"

Olivia shook her head, then stopped, paling. "Chris asked

about the initials on my purse. I never told Jessica what the false name was that I gave you. Only that I gave you one."

Declan spun Fiona to face him, gripping her biceps to hold her still. "Was it Chris? Did he tell you Olivia is Rose?"

Fiona stayed silent, but the flash of hatred in her eyes gave him his answer.

"Declan, the police." He turned slightly as a police car came to a stop nearby. Declan abruptly opened his hands, so that Fiona stumbled back.

It didn't take long to give the police the story, particularly as Fiona's tantrum had drawn so many witnesses. After Olivia confirmed she wanted to press charges, Fiona shrieked as the officers placed her in handcuffs. "Do you know who I am? My father is going to have you all fired." Her voice was thankfully muffled when they shut the door of the cruiser.

Panic and dread swirled inside him.

Chris knew who Olivia was which meant Chris knew how to destroy him.

"Declan?" Olivia's voice came to him from a distance over the rushing in his ears. His heart seemed to beat in a two-part erratic rhythm: *He knows.*

Declan pulled out his phone. "Everything is fine. Let me call one of my brothers. They'll meet us at the police station. We need to give formal statements. Can you get our coats?"

"Declan, what are you going to do?" Olivia asked, moving to stand beside him.

"Keep you safe."

Olivia's gaze didn't waver as she continued to watch him for a moment, and then turned on her heel. Through the window, he saw her swarmed by the employees still lingering in the lobby.

Declan hadn't lied. He had every intention of calling his brothers, but first, he had other phone calls to make. It only took a minute to tell Brady the situation, and to instruct him that if

Declan wasn't physically with Olivia, he wanted at least one man guarding her at all times, not just at the house.

The next call was to Alan Carrol.

"You crossed a line," Declan said, as soon as the call connected.

"You're done, Bloom. I know you think you've got some trick up your sleeve for tomorrow, but I promise you it won't be enough—"

"Your daughter is in jail. If you hope to see her again, I suggest you listen very carefully to what I say next."

"What?" the man exploded.

"She destroyed Olivia Adler's car with a golf club, struck me, and then threatened Olivia with it," Declan said, ignoring the interruption. "Serious charges, which I fully plan on supporting Olivia in pursuing. But Fiona let an interesting little snippet loose. She admitted she gave drugs to Olivia's ex-husband, and then encouraged him to attack her. I'm guessing, with the right prosecutor, that might be seen as accessory to attempted murder."

He paused, happy when the line stayed silent. "I think we both know when it comes to twisting arms, I have a bit more experience. This is what will happen. Tomorrow, you will support my bid for CEO. In exchange, I will see that your daughter spends some time in a cushy drug rehab, and she gets the psychiatric care that she clearly fucking needs." Declan felt his temper slip and held tight to his control. "Your daughter will then take an extended trip abroad. When Fiona returns… You ensure she understands that I and anyone connected with me are off-limits. If I find out she has come within a city block of Olivia, I'll kill her."

"Don't you dare threaten my daughter," Carrol seethed.

"I'm not threatening either one of you. This is an accurate representation of what will happen."

"Fucking bastard."

"I'm losing patience, Alan, and your daughter is probably being booked as we speak. You'll want to get her out of general lockup as soon as possible. I don't think she'll fare well." The man spit out a vicious curse. "Do we have an understanding?"

"We have an understanding."

"Excellent."

"You arrogant piece of shit. You think this is over? Chris Keller is out for blood, and I will be cheering him on."

Declan had finished speaking with his brothers when Olivia emerged again, walking towards him with his overcoat thrown over her arm. She walked purposefully toward him, her heels clicking on the pavement, her head high. She flicked a glance at her ruined car.

"Taken care of?" Anger still simmered in her eyes.

"In process," he answered. He could see by her expression she wanted to ask more questions, but instead she shrugged.

"As long as it doesn't delay your decision." She sniffed. "I have a business to run."

Declan threw back his head and laughed before pulling her toward him and pressing a rough kiss to her temple.

"SHOULD I WISH YOU LUCK, or is that insulting?" Olivia asked sleepily from their rumpled bed, as Declan slipped into his suit jacket.

"Go back to sleep, Petal."

"I'm up now." Olivia pulled herself up higher on the pillows, the sheet covering her breasts slipping enough to give him the glimpse of one pink nipple. His feet brought him back to the side of the bed, his hand tracing over her soft skin.

"Me too." He chuckled, mentally calculating how long he

could delay his flight. His mouth sealed over hers and Olivia moaned, arching into his hand. His phone buzzed, and he bit back a growl. He nipped her bottom lip as he pulled back. "When this is over, we are going away. Just us, no phones, no computers, no family."

"Sounds like heaven."

Declan glanced at the phone screen and rumpled Oscar's ears. "That's Rhodes. He and another of Brady's men have arrived. There will be a car out front the entire time I'm gone, and they will drive you wherever you need to go until you pick out a new car."

When she didn't respond, Declan looked up from the puppy to see Olivia's lower lip trembling. Concern clutched in his chest. "What's wrong?"

"I don't know. I feel…"

Declan's heart twisted. "Are you worried about Kyle… or Chris? I promise they can't get near you."

Olivia shook her head, her eyes suddenly glistening. "I have this terrible feeling… You keep talking about keeping me safe, but what about you?"

Declan sat back, stunned. "Chris is too much of a coward to come at me like that."

"You aren't invincible," Olivia burst out. "You act like nothing can touch you and that it doesn't even matter if it does. I know you want to keep me safe. Why can't you understand that I'm worried about you, too?" Her breath hitched. "I just got you back, and I'm terrified you are going to be taken away from me."

"Hey," Declan cupped her face. "I'll be back in two days."

"Promise." Her hands clutched his wrists, gaze fierce. "Promise I won't lose you again. That you won't disappear. You'll stay with me."

Declan pressed his forehead against hers. "Always."

He hated walking away from her when she was upset, but by

the end of the day, it would almost all be over. After he regained control of the company, all that would be left was retribution.

In the early morning light, Declan climbed into his car and began backing up Olivia's steep driveway. Motion out of the corner of his eye had him glancing back through the windshield. "Damn it," he muttered, as Oscar galloped around the frost-covered yard, the front door cracked open behind him. "This is exactly why he belongs in a crate."

But Declan was more angry that the open door meant more than he hadn't pulled it shut. It meant that distracted by his thoughts, he'd forgotten to reset the alarm and that was unacceptable.

Putting his car in park, Declan swung the car door open and climbed out, whistling for the puppy. White vapor poured from the exhaust as he tried to grab Oscar's collar. But each time he got close, the dog raced the other way.

"Oscar." His voice was sharp, all too aware that the security detail was watching him chase a puppy around the front yard. "I'm going to murder this dog."

Declan walked to the front door, squatted down, and patted his leg. "Oscar," he called louder, over his car's idling engine. "Do you want a treat? Come on. It's fecking freezing out here, you eejit," he sing-songed.

The puppy's ears flopped as he cocked his head, considering his options. Declan rose and took a step into the house, holding the door open. "Come on. Treats!"

With what Declan swore was a doggy grin, Oscar raced toward him, ducking between his feet, before spinning around to face Declan, eyes bright and tail wagging.

"If you think I'm giving you a treat, no—"

The force of the explosion threw Declan forward onto the floor, shattered window glass raining down all around him.

CHAPTER FORTY-FIVE

ATLANTA—PRESENT DAY

Olivia pulled on the T-shirt Declan had discarded and snuggled back into the warm blankets. She heard Declan's sports car start, but the low throaty sound of the engine continued instead of pulling away.

What was he waiting for? The thought had barely registered when the house shook, and the world flashed bright around her, the glass of her bedroom windows shattered inward.

Adrenaline raced through her as Olivia bolted from the bed, a scream locked in her throat. Declan! She didn't register the sharp pain in her feet as she raced to what remained of her window casing. Through the thick acrid smoke, she heard shouting and could make out the charred outline of his car, flames licking high into the dawn light.

Olivia's legs collapsed beneath her, and she fell to the ground. "No!" White-hot agony lanced through her chest before the sound ripped from her throat again. "No! No!"

Her ears rung, and her head was spinning. She needed to move. Declan could still... Her feet and hands scrabbled beneath her as she raced for the stairs, oblivious to the bloody footprints she left in her wake. "Declan," she screamed. *He could still…* Her heart hoped, even as her brain tried to reason.

Sobs tore from her as she slipped, tumbling down the last two steps. Strong hands caught her shoulders, and then Declan's face was in front of her, streaked with blood. His mouth was moving, but her brain wouldn't engage.

Olivia launched herself at him, wrapping her legs around his waist, and clinging to his neck like a spider monkey.

He was alive. It was all that mattered.

Declan buried his face in her neck. "Are you all right?" His hands ran over her hair, pulling her head back so he could inspect her face.

"I thought..." Her voice broke.

Declan exhaled hard against her, his body shuddering. He held her against him, burying one hand in her hair and planting the other in the middle of her back.

"Clear." A voice shouted, and then Rhodes appeared, with his gun drawn low and blood running from a cut on his forehead. He charged past them, giving them a cursory look before proceeding farther into the house. Another man grabbed Declan's collar and spun him, with Olivia still attached, propelling them through what used to be her front door.

"Our vehicle is still operational." She heard a voice bark.

They were almost at the back door of the SUV when Olivia heard a whimper. Pulling her head back, her head swiveled until she saw Oscar limping across the front yard.

Following her eyes, Rhodes scooped her puppy up as Declan deposited her in the back of the car.

"He's all right, ma'am. Minor cut on his paw."

The doors slammed, and they raced away. Declan pulled her into his lap as she clutched Oscar to her chest. Olivia was conscious of Declan's arms tight around both her and the puppy, keeping them both secure, as the SUV rocketed away from her neighborhood.

Questions volleyed back and forth, but Olivia closed her eyes and rested her head against Declan's chest, finding comfort in his galloping heartbeat that matched the pace of hers.

"Do we need a hospital?" the man in the front asked.

"Petal?" His breath ruffled her hair. "Are you hurt?"

She shook her head, not sure she could manage the actual words. Declan's voice rumbled under her cheek. "Secure my family, and get us to the airport. Have the plane triple-checked."

They waited in the SUV, inside the airplane hangar, for what felt like forever. They were alone. The man in the driver's seat had glanced over his shoulder, and when he saw her shivering in just Declan's T-shirt, he had cranked the heat all the way up and immediately exited.

Olivia still shivered, but she wasn't sure it was from the cold.

"You're bleeding." Declan's voice sounded detached, and alarm shot through her.

"Don't do that." Olivia shifted in his lap, lifting her head. Oscar squirmed to get free, and she let him hop to the floor. She turned so that her knees were on either side of his hips, and she sat on his thighs, facing him.

Declan's face was like stone, except for the muscle ticking in his jaw. "Don't leave me." Olivia grabbed his jaw, forcing him to look at her.

His voice was as tight as the tendons in his neck. "I'm right here, Olivia."

"You know what I mean."

His nostrils flared, and he gave his head a slight shake. "You could have been killed."

"It was your car." She pointed out. Olivia glared at him. "Stop it." His eyes flicked down to meet hers. "You are pulling away. I can feel it." Emotion clouded his eyes, and she squeezed his jaw harder, her eyes refusing to let him look away. "You promised you wouldn't leave. I'm here and in this *with* you. So don't fucking leave me."

For a long silent moment, Olivia thought she hadn't gotten through, but then the corner of his mouth lifted.

"You are awfully bossy for someone who's sitting on my lap, bleeding all over my favorite suit."

Suppressing a relieved sigh, Olivia glanced down at the multitude of tiny cuts on her legs and feet. She sniffed. "I think that's the least of your sartorial problems." One hand toyed with the shredded fabric of his pant leg.

A knock on the window had her shifting to the side, off his lap. Declan cracked the door open and accepted a bundle from the man outside.

"We will have a convoy of armored vehicles on the ground ready to meet you," the man informed Declan.

Is this really my life? Olivia knew she should feel afraid. A car had literally blown up in her driveway, and there were conversations around her about how many men were necessary, and armored convoys...

She snorted, and then laughed harder when Declan looked at her like she'd lost her mind. "Did I break you?"

Another fit of giggles overtook her, but she shook her head, gasping for air. "No, I'm just thinking how absurd this whole thing is."

Declan watched her for a long moment, and then grabbed the back of her neck, pulling her in for a rough kiss. When he finally lifted, she was gasping for air, and his eyes burned. "I think, with you by my side, I could take over the fucking world."

Declan opened the bundle that had been handed to him and

revealed a pair of sweatpants and a hoodie. He pulled the hoodie over her head, and she lifted her hips to shimmy into the pants, wincing when the fabric rubbed against her cuts.

"What about you?" she asked, looking at his ruined suit.

"I have clothes on the plane."

Declan insisted on cleaning and bandaging the cuts on her feet, before Olivia finally insisted he let the medic, who had just arrived, treat the injuries to Declan's own legs.

At one point, someone handed Declan a phone, and he made call after call. Olivia only half listened, the image of his burning car in front of her. She could have lost him. Permanently. Her body shook, as the horror of how differently this morning could have ended played in front of her.

"I'm taking her to Connecticut. My estate there is secure." Declan told someone before ending the call.

"We're ready," Rhodes said, appearing at their window.

When they left the car, Olivia was surprised by how stiff and sore her muscles felt. Placing Oscar in her arms, Declan scooped her up and carried them both to the plane.

"I can walk," she muttered, looking at the thick socks he'd pulled over her bandaged feet.

"Let me," was all Declan said, and she sighed, relaxing against his chest.

He placed her in a buttery soft, leather seat and buckled her belt around her. Oscar squirmed, wanting to get down, and she set him gently on the carpeted floor. He shook his bandaged paw twice, before seeming to accept the annoying inconvenience, and sniffed around the cabin.

Olivia leaned her head against the back of the seat as the engines whined to life.

"I'd make a comment about him peeing in my jet, but since Oscar saved my life, I'll guess I'll give him a pass."

Once they were in the air, Declan disappeared to the back of the plane. When he returned, he wore black slacks and a soft gray sweater. He'd washed his face, and if not for the clotted cut above his eyebrow, Olivia could almost imagine nothing had happened.

"Still cold?" Declan asked, tucking one of the throw blankets around her legs before taking the seat next to her. Declan glanced at Oscar, curled up on a matching throw blanket on the seat across the aisle. They were alone in the cabin, a new security team waiting for them on the ground at their destination.

"Who was it?"

Declan didn't pretend to misunderstand. "I don't know." His lips flattened. "And that bothers me. It feels too sophisticated to be your ex-husband or Alan Carrol. He was angry yesterday, but he wouldn't have had time to arrange a bomb of that magnitude."

Bomb. The word ricocheted through her head.

Declan came within seconds of dying. If Oscar hadn't slipped out the door…

Unbuckling her seatbelt, she climbed over the armrest and straddled him.

"What are you doing?" Declan asked. His hands hovered over her back as she attacked his belt buckle.

"I need you." Her voice was hoarse as his zipper loosened, and she slipped her hand into the front of his pants and wrapped her hand around him. Declan's head tipped back with a groan as her fingers stroked over him.

Olivia could still smell the smoke in his hair, and it only made her more desperate. Her pulse raced, and she felt her eyes fill with tears. She needed to be as close to him as physically possible. Olivia's lips swooped down and covered his lips with almost bruising force.

She could feel Declan's hesitation, but her thumb brushed over the head of his erection, and like a switch had been flipped, he kissed her back with the same ferocity, his tongue sliding urgently over hers.

Declan's hand twisted in her hair, and Olivia lifted onto her knees, not breaking the kiss to pull her sweatpants down, making a frustrated sound when they caught at her knees.

Firm hands caught her hips and lifted so that she could push the fabric low enough to spread her thighs. She rocked forward, his erection caught between them, rubbing against her clit with delicious friction.

"I love you, Declan," she gasped into his mouth as she rocked over him. "I love you so much."

"Olivia." Then he was kissing her again, his lips moving over hers almost desperately.

Olivia writhed, her hands shoving underneath the cashmere sweater to splay against his chest. She could feel his heart pounding beneath her palm, and the need to have a physical connection with him was almost painful. She needed to feel him move inside her, an acknowledgement that they were all right—they were alive.

Olivia whimpered when Declan shoved the hoodie up, exposing her breasts, and latched on to one of her tight nipples, sucking hard.

"Yes! Declan. Please," she panted. "I need you. Now. Inside me."

Declan slid his free hand under her ass, squeezing and lifting as she positioned him at her entrance. His hips surged up into her and she gasped.

He let her set the pace, rising and plunging over him. Olivia felt his teeth on her breasts, and her legs shook. She was crying and trembling as Declan's thrusts became more erratic. "That's it, Petal… come for me."

She felt a thumb press hard against her clit, and she came apart. Declan growled, and his pace increased as she slumped against his chest. Then his face was in her neck, and they shook together.

His chest moved with ragged breaths against her, and Declan reached into the seat she'd vacated to retrieve the throw blanket. Draping it over both of them, he wrapped his arms around her, still intimately joined, and held her tight. Olivia felt tears streak down her cheeks, dampening his neck.

Declan stroked her hair until the tears stopped and she lay exhausted against him.

The plane landed at a private airport and taxied into a closed hangar, where Olivia was hustled into a dark-colored SUV. She dozed against Declan on the drive, only waking when the car made a hard turn and came to a stop in front of a large wrought-iron gate. The driver lowered his window, punched in a code, and the gates silently swung open.

Olivia wasn't sure if it was everything that had happened or simple exhaustion, but she barely took in the massive home in front of her before Declan swept her off her feet and climbed a grand staircase, depositing her in the middle of an enormous bed.

Declan looked grim. "I have to go if I'm going to make it in time."

"The shareholder meeting." Olivia nodded.

"I don't want to leave you."

Olivia smiled. "I'm safe here. You wouldn't have brought me here otherwise. Go get your company back."

Declan hesitated, emotions warring on his face. "There is a small army downstairs and on the grounds."

Olivia caught his hand and squeezed. "Go, I'm fine. *You* be safe."

Declan's jaw flexed, but then she watched as he assumed his public mask. A few minutes later, when he emerged from his giant closet, dressed in an impeccably tailored suit, Declan looked every inch the ruthless billionaire he was purported to be.

After he was gone, Olivia rolled to her side and tucked her

hands under her cheek, and exhaled a slow breath. Without her phone or a computer, she wasn't sure what to do with herself.

She must have slept because a knock at the door roused her out of a dreamless sleep. When she opened the door, a middle-aged woman stood smiling in the doorway, holding several large shopping bags and Oscar on a leash.

"Mr. Bloom thought you might want some variety."

CHAPTER FORTY-SIX

New York—Present Day

Cecile waited for him at the elevator. Her eyes scanned over his face, her lips narrowing as she took in the bruising and the cut over his eyebrow.

"He's here. And Daniella, your witness, is five minutes out. I'll wait for her downstairs," she said in an unperturbed voice.

Declan nodded. Ice flowed through his veins, keeping the fury that burned at bay. Someone had tried to kill him, and in the process, injured Olivia. Determination steeled his every move. When he found out who was responsible, they would beg for a mercy that wouldn't be coming.

He strode into the large board room and stopped at the foot of the table. Chris glared at him from his place at the opposite end.

Declan thought he would be consumed with anger in this moment—in this room—facing his former best friend. The man who had killed his father, and stolen from him... But all Declan was conscious of was the cold certainty that he was going to end the man across the table.

"You're late." Chris leaned back in the chair. "I hope nothing is wrong."

Declan's blood pulsed behind his eyes, but his voice was even when he replied. "Not at all. I heard felicitations are in order."

Something flickered across Chris's face.

That's right, fucker. You can't breathe without me knowing.

Several of the older board members looked between the two of them. Alan Carrol's skin was an unhealthy, patchy gray.

"Thank you," Chris responded with a self-deprecating smile. "We haven't announced it yet, but yes, Courtney and I were married a couple weekends ago."

Declan tilted his head. "Did the orderlies decorate?"

Chris's mouth tightened, and then he squared his shoulders and smiled broadly at the people around the table. "Perhaps we should get started,"

"We should," Declan drawled, his eyes never leaving Chris. "As a shareholder in this company, I'd like to call for a vote of no confidence for our current CEO. His term has been short, and I'm concerned that his extended tenure at this company could be detrimental to our reputation and stock price."

No one at the table moved. Everyone knew it was coming. "I have an individual here who will speak to the current CEO's connection to a fatal drunk driving accident." Chris narrowed his eyes, but Declan didn't blink. "I also have a report from a company I recently purchased, Everlasting Love. They will attest that Courtney Bloom gave them David Bloom's ashes. I also have here today a report from an independent lab that verifies the presence of thallium in those same ashes. These reports, in addition to a recording of Mr. Keller's late stepson Trey Crawford, implicating our current CEO in the murder of Mr. Bloom, are more than enough to violate the morality clauses in his contract."

"So, you paid someone to make up a story and falsify some documents," Chris scoffed, but his eyes had darkened. "So, what?

You look desperate, Declan." Chris's eyes darted to Carrol's, and when the older man stared at his hands on the table, Chris's jaw flexed. He'd get no support there.

"If you have proof, why haven't you gone to the police?" one of the board members asked.

"I haven't ruled it out," Declan said, not lifting his gaze from Chris. "However, I'm hoping to protect Bloom Communication's reputation."

"But if you think he murdered your father..." The woman persisted.

It was interesting that no one at the table had balked at the suggestion that it *was* possible.

"This is pure fantasy born of grief and guilt over his relationship with his father." Chris sounded confident, but his flushed face gave him away.

Declan's lips lifted in a cold smile, and Chris blanched. His old friend was no match for him. Not in terms of ruthlessness. If Chris wanted to secure the Bloom fortune, he should have killed Declan years ago.

"I'd like to hear what he has to say," someone else said. "Declan isn't a liar." Several people at the table nodded, and Chris's color flushed a deeper hue.

The door behind him swished open, and Declan turned with a gentle smile to greet the woman who entered, flanked by two Elite Security Specialists bodyguards. After the explosion this morning, Declan wasn't taking any chances.

"Ms. Doe," Declan ushered her forward, before meeting the gaze of everyone at the table with a hard stare of his own. "For now, she will remain anonymous. However, I'm sure if the story were to be leaked to the media, her name would be revealed." The implied threat was obvious.

The young woman stared at Chris, who seemed confused. He squinted. "Who is this?" His shoulders relaxed, but as the former escort spoke, the smile fell from his face.

"You may not remember me, but I remember you." Her voice only trembled a little as she gave a sanitized version of the event that had resulted in the death of her friend.

After finishing, Declan gave her a grateful smile, and Cecile escorted her from the room. Declan scanned the group around the table.

"I'm sure Chris isn't the first person to pay for sex, but the fact of the matter is he killed a woman in my car while drunk and then covered it up."

Cecile circled the table, dropping folders in front of each person, as Declan lifted his phone and hit play on the recording from the night Trey confessed to Cami.

When he clicked it off, Chris was pale.

"In front of you, you will find the photos used to frame me and blackmail my father. The reports included clearly provide evidence that someone manipulated the accident photos. There are transcripts of Trey's confession, implicating Chris Keller in my father's murder, and the lab reports on the thallium. These reports are all poised for release to the media." Declan cocked a brow. "Questions?"

The room was silent for a moment before a woman lifted a hand. "Motion to vote no-confidence on our current CEO, Chris Keller."

Less than five minutes later, it was over. The board removed Chris from his position, despite his futile attempts to sway the other shareholders. To Declan's surprise, upon realizing it was hopeless, Chris hadn't raged or cursed. Instead, he stood briefly, tugged at his cuffs to straighten them, and strode from the room.

But the look in Chris's eyes, when his gaze met Declan's on the way out the door, concerned him. Chris didn't look cowed or even angry. He looked smug.

~

"You have some nasty enemies." Alex Kovalyov's voice was unusually serious when Declan answered the call from the car on his way to the helipad.

Declan tugged at the knot of his tie. After being reinstated as CEO of Bloom Communications, he waited for the elation to come. The roar in his blood that always came with winning.

But it hadn't come.

All he could think about was getting back to Olivia.

"Who?"

"Agron Koci wants you dead." Declan felt his body still, dread filling his gut. He knew this day would come…

"Why now?"

"Someone tipped him off you were the one who killed his cousin. Not Seamus. I can assure you it wasn't us. Who else knows?"

Chris. No wonder he didn't look upset. Chris didn't think Declan would live long enough to fill the position.

Declan kept his breathing calm, but didn't answer Alex.

"Apparently, Agron's making a play for the big chair, and taking out a high-profile enemy will cement his position." Declan's jaw worked, but Alex continued, his voice lighter. "However, I'm calling with good news. It's being handled as we speak."

A coil of anger tightened in his belly.

"You've become remarkably unfun lately," Alex groused, when Declan stayed silent. "Fortunately for you, it turns out that my brother doesn't like Agron much. He's dipped his hand into too many cookie jars that weren't his, and on top of that, he tried to carry out a hit on you, in Atlanta, without Mikhail's permission. Everyone knows after the Lia Everton situation, my brother has a soft spot for all things Bloom."

"I never asked for Bratva help," Declan bit out. "I don't owe your brother anything."

"No, you don't. My brother did this as a favor to me."

"Why?"

"Would you believe I've become fond of your charming face?" Declan's nostrils flared. "Fine. Call it a wedding present."

"I haven't asked her yet."

"Not yours. Mine."

Declan was stunned into silence, but Alex continued. "I'm getting married soon, and I know your new sister-in-law doesn't approve. She or your brother will probably ask you to intervene —Don't."

The word was as hard as Declan had ever heard the Russian use. Alex's voice was deadly when he said, "Madison Amherst is going to be my wife, and nothing will stand in the way of that."

"Interesting." Declan's tone was bland, but he smiled, knowing the man couldn't see.

"It's not *interesting*. It's an exchange. A rose for an angel."

Declan understood. "Best wishes."

"Give Mikhail twenty-four hours."

Olivia greeted him at the door. "How did it go?"

"I told you there was nothing to worry about," Declan said, kissing her. "I promised an update to my family." Declan caught her hand in his, and Olivia hurried to keep pace as he strode rapidly through the house. He abruptly came to a halt looking down at her feet with concern.

She arched a brow. "Don't even think about picking me up. My feet are fine."

He debated for a second, but then resumed walking until he reached the door of his office.

"What about the car?" Olivia asked.

"Dealt with," Declan said over his shoulder, as he flipped on the lights.

He was opening his laptop when he realized she hadn't followed him into the room.

Olivia frowned at him from the doorway.

"If this is going to work, you have to let me know what is happening." Her chin jutted forward.

Declan couldn't help the smile that spread across his face. In the last twenty-four hours, she had presented a plan to save her company, dealt with an insane socialite, and rallied after a car bomb.

"Stop smiling at me and tell me what happened." But there was no heat in her words.

"With the evidence presented in front of him, Chris folded."

"Just like that?" Tiny lines bunched between her brows.

"There was nothing he could do. The assets are frozen, and with the evidence we've compiled, we will overturn the fraudulent will."

Olivia didn't match his smile.

"Then who tried to kill you this morning?" Her voice was quiet.

"Albanian Mob—relatives of the men I killed in a Dublin pub twelve years ago. I did my brother a favor, attending a meeting after I left you at the airport, and things got out of control. I told Chris about it once, and he must have tipped them off I was the one who killed Agron Koci's cousin, not my brother."

When she blanched, Declan wished he'd lied. "But it's okay."

"It's not *okay,* Declan." Olivia's voice pitched high as she practically stomped into the room. "They put a bomb in your car!"

Declan pulled her close, and ran his nose down the length of hers. "It's been taken care of, Petal."

"You've used that phrase a lot in the last twenty-four hours."

Olivia grumbled, but relaxed against his chest, her arms wrapping around his waist with an irritated sigh.

Declan smiled against her hair. "What can I say? I'm productive."

She muttered something against his dress shirt that sounded like, "You're something."

Declan smiled over her head and stroked his hand down her back. "It's still true."

"Can we go home?" Olivia asked, still not looking at him.

"To Atlanta?"

She nodded.

"Alex said to give it another day, but then of course, we will."

Olivia's arms lowered, and she brought her hands up between them to push back. "How is this going to work?"

His first inclination was to pull her back into his chest, but her expression was serious, and curls of apprehension crept up his spine. "How is *what* going to work?"

"Us." Her simple word sliced through him. "You are now the CEO of one of the largest media empires in the world. I run a company in Atlanta. We operate in two totally different worlds."

Declan's heart thudded. He hadn't allowed himself to think beyond the point where he regained Bloom Communications.

Her eyes were sad. "I want to be with you every day."

"You could move here," Declan said. "You could oversee Armstrong's operations remotely. There's no need for you to be there in person." But even as he said the words, he knew Olivia would never be happy in a role like that. Part of what made her successful was that she was hands on with her employees.

"We don't have to figure it out now." Olivia smiled, her eyes brightening. "We should celebrate. You are once again CEO of Bloom Communications."

Oddly, Declan didn't feel like celebrating, and Olivia picked up on his disquiet. "This battle with Chris… It's over, right?"

"For the most part. We still have to overturn the will, but we're in a much better position now. I've already sent the lab reports and the recording to the lawyers representing the various charities who filed a challenge. It will take time, but it *will* happen."

CHAPTER FORTY-SEVEN

Connecticut—Present Day

Declan paced over to the bar cart in the corner and poured them each a whiskey.

"Slainte." He tapped his glass to hers.

"I also have someone setting up guardianship for Courtney, to have the marriage set aside. Within the next few days, I'll have taken everything from him."

Olivia studied him. Despite his words, Declan wasn't as happy as she thought he'd be. Was it because of what happened this morning? "What will Chris do?"

"What can he do? Without the company, without my father's money, he's toothless. I win."

A wolfish smile crossed his face, but Olivia felt a weight settle over her chest. "You win," she repeated quietly.

Taking his drink to his desk, Declan sat in his giant leather chair and typed into his computer. Various tones sounded, signaling that each of his siblings had joined the virtual meeting.

Olivia understood Declan's confidence to some extent, but she didn't believe Chris would give up that easily. Not in a battle that had gone on this long. Declan filled his family in on what had happened at the shareholder meeting, but their focus was clearly on something else.

"And the bomb?" James's voice was hard.

"Unrelated."

"That's not good enough." James's jaw flexed on the screen. "Your car exploded, and Brady had people all over us at dawn. You owe us a little more than *unrelated*."

Declan glanced to where Olivia stood off camera. *Tell them* her eyes telegraphed. *They are your family.*

"Declan," Cara's voice pleaded.

"This is a secure transmission," Wes added.

Declan looked torn, and Olivia stepped closer. He looked up at her, and then tugged her down until she perched on his lap.

Small squares showing the various members of his family covered the computer screen. Siobhan looked livid.

"It was a problem from the past, but it's being handled."

"What does that mean?" Anne worried.

"Alex Kovalyov is settling it for me," he conceded. "I'll tell you more later." Olivia knew he would do everything he could to avoid it.

"You're coming Saturday, right?" Cami asked, leaning close to the camera.

"We'll do our best—"

"Declan," James snapped. "It's Cami's birthday. You need to be here."

"I said we'd do our best." Declan's voice was cool.

Olivia poked his side. "We'll be there. Send me the details."

"Thanks, Olivia," Cami smiled.

"I NEED TO GET BACK," Olivia insisted, as she dressed two days later in the clothes Declan had arranged for her.

She watched as Declan shoved a hand back through his hair. "I can't leave so soon after I've been reinstated."

Disappointment hit her hard. Olivia had known when Declan said they would go back to Atlanta right away that it wasn't likely. "I know. It's fine." She slipped her feet into a pair of heels she'd found inside the shopping bags. "I'll see you in a few days for Cami's birthday."

Declan looked at his watch. "If I move my meeting with the finance department, I can ride with you to the airport."

Olivia swallowed, anxiety thickening in her throat. They would make this work. They had to.

"It's fine. Oscar and I have your driver."

Declan's eyes clouded. "Alex has assured me that the Albanians are no longer interested in me, but your security will still be with you. I've made arrangements for us to stay at the St. Regis until the repairs on your house are finished. The contractor doesn't think it will take more than a week."

"I saw the email." Olivia said. "Structurally, the house is fine. It's only windows and doors."

Declan looked uncertain. "If it weren't—"

"I understand, Declan. You need to be here right now for the transition."

Olivia understood, but it didn't mean it hurt any less. Declan carried her bag and set it on the back seat of the black SUV that had stopped in the circular drive.

"I'll be back for the party. I swear."

Olivia forced a smile and pressed her lips to his. "You better, because I'm pretty sure they are announcing more than just Cami is a year older."

"What do you mean?" His brow furrowed.

She shook her head. "I mean, she didn't drink any wine at our girls' night, and the look on her face when she insisted you be there."

"She was being polite."

Olivia cupped his face. "No, Declan. Your family wants *you*. Not the CEO or the fixer. They want their *brother* there for all the important moments."

She resisted the urge to kiss away the tight lines between his eyes. "I'll see you soon."

Declan gave her a hand up into the SUV, but hesitated before shutting the door. "Olivia."

"I love you, Declan."

It wasn't until she was curled up under a blanket and staring at the clouds that it hit Olivia that this would be their life. Comparing schedules, finding windows where they could spend time together… a tear slipped down her cheek.

MEETINGS TOOK up most of her afternoon, but Olivia was finding it almost impossible to focus. Her thoughts were consumed with Declan and their future. He'd fought so hard to get Bloom Communications back, she couldn't ask him to give that up now. But she also didn't want to live a separate life from him. Only one real option remained. She would have to leave Armstrong Electronics.

Melissa popped her head in the door, interrupting her thoughts. "Stuart called. He needs you to meet him in the warehouse."

Olivia frowned. "Not in his lab?"

Melissa shrugged. "I couldn't hear him very well. You know how bad the coverage is out there. He said you needed to see something before your meeting with the senators."

That doesn't sound good.

Olivia closed down the file she was working on. Stuart wasn't a worrier, and if he said he needed her, something must be wrong.

Taking the elevator to the first floor, Olivia swiped her badge to access the hallway leading to the attached warehouse. The door slammed shut behind her just as a hand covered her mouth, followed by a sharp sting in her neck. Olivia immediately fought. A loud grunt sounded in her ear when her heel connected with a shin.

"You said it would knock her out." Through the fog quickly overtaking her brain, she recognized Kyle's voice.

Concentrate, Olivia. Stay awake.

But her limbs no longer responded, and Olivia felt her legs give out beneath her. Strong hands hooked under her arms, holding her up.

"Light it."

She knew that voice too.

Olivia tried to shake her head to clear it, but her head lolled back against a firm chest, and her heavy eyelids refused to lift. An acrid scent filled her nose. Smoke?

"Why?" Olivia wasn't sure if the words left her lips.

"Get her feet," Chris Keller demanded.

Olivia felt herself lifted in the air and then heard the creak of the outside door as she fought to stay conscious. She moaned when she dropped a short distance onto something hard. Her eyes fluttered open at the pain. "Why?" she repeated.

Chris loomed over her, eyes glittering. "I have nothing left to lose, but he does."

CHAPTER FORTY-EIGHT

New York—Present Day

Declan was ready to climb the walls as he listened to yet another presentation to bring him up to speed on Bloom Communications' current priorities. In this case, it was a financial snapshot of their European subsidiaries. He didn't remember the job being this boring.

He rolled his shoulders. This was what he wanted, Declan told himself. What he'd fought so hard to get back. This was the third meeting in a row that felt like a major waste of time. None of the decisions he made would have any immediate impact on the company.

The thing Declan enjoyed most about streamlining the companies his private equity firm bought was the challenge. Here, he felt like a cog in a giant system. All they expected from him was to make a check mark next to a decision that had been made months ago.

"The milestones for Q3 and Q4 are in the same range..." The man droned on, and Declan found his mind wandering.

I wonder what Olivia is doing?

Declan sighed. Having more fun than him, he would bet. His

phone buzzed on the glass conference table, and he turned it over to see the name illuminated. He sent Luke's call to voicemail.

When the phone immediately rang again, Declan lifted his hand to the man still presenting.

"Excuse me for a moment," Declan said, walking from the room. Normally, he would never walk out of a meeting unless something needed his immediate attention, but he was going stir crazy and grabbed at the excuse. "What do you need?" he asked his brother.

"Courtney's dead."

"What?" Declan halted in the middle of the hallway.

"Her housekeeper found her this morning. Looks like an overdose."

"I thought she was in rehab," Declan snarled. "Wasn't that the whole reason we couldn't get to her?"

"She checked herself out last night."

Frustrated rage coursed through him. He felt robbed, cheated of his revenge.

"Where's Chris?"

Declan heard a heavy sigh and murmuring. "Luke?" he snapped.

"Hang on." Luke's voice was just as sharp. "James is on the phone with Brady. I think something is happening."

Declan's breath came faster as he clutched the phone. "Problem?"

"Fuck!" Declan heard James shout in the background.

"What's happening?" Declan was already moving toward the elevators. His instincts telling him he needed to move.

"He had a fucking decoy." James took the phone from Luke. "And someone rammed the car following Chris Keller. Brady's guys were hurt, so we are just now getting the information. They've lost him and they aren't sure how long they were actually following the decoy."

Fear settled over Declan, so oppressive he couldn't breathe. "Olivia?"

The elevator door opened, and Declan thrust out a hand to hold the door open.

"Brady says she's still at work. Two guys are in a car out front."

"They were supposed to go in with her."

"Apparently she disagreed."

"I'm heading back now," Declan said, stepping into the elevator.

"We'll be—"

The call disconnected, and Declan looked down at the phone, resisting the urge to punch the elevator wall when he saw he had no coverage. The doors slid open in the parking garage, his phone already vibrating.

"There's a fire at the Armstrong building." Luke sounded breathless, like he was running. "They can't find Olivia."

In an instant, Declan's world crashed around him.

THE FLIGHT back to Atlanta felt like a lifetime, his phone attached to his ear the entire time. Declan dialed Olivia's phone over and over, his panic rising each time her voicemail immediately clicked on.

He struggled to hold on to his composure when Brady called to give him a status report. "A delivery van with the logo of an approved vendor entered the parking lot and pulled to the back of the building. It was out of sight for less than five minutes. Three minutes after the van left the facility, the fire alarms went off. My men went in immediately, but it was chaos as everyone evacuated. Her receptionist told them Olivia had gone to meet Stuart in the manufacturing area, but the man denied ever calling her. By that time, the warehouse was fully engaged, and they called in back up to search. Once the fire department arrived, they couldn't get back in the building."

"I don't fucking care what they did *after* they lost her," Declan roared. "She should never have been out of their sight."

Declan's chest heaved.

Where is she? Chris? Kyle? The Albanians?

"What do you want us to do, Dec?" James asked, his voice coming over the line.

Declan's free hand gripped at his hair. This was what he feared all along. She was in danger because of him. Olivia would pay the price for the life he'd led.

"Fuck," Luke hissed through the speakerphone. "I got a text from one of my sources. The police found Kyle Armstrong's body behind the wheel of a delivery van at Peachtree Executive Airport. Five flights have taken off since the fire was reported. All but one filed a flight plan."

"She's on that plane." The fissure in Declan's chest cracked open, the pain unbearable. He paced the aisle of the Bloom Communications jet, helpless rage coursing through him. Declan was stuck in the sky, and Olivia could be anywhere.

"I've got a guy at that airport," Brady said. "Let me see if I can get a copy of the security video before the cops get their warrant."

Alex called next to assure him that the Albanians weren't involved, and offered his brother's men to help with a rescue. Declan had no desire to owe the Bratva anything, but if it meant getting Olivia back, he wouldn't hesitate to sell his soul to the Russian mob. Vincent also confirmed that Alan Carrol was still in the city, and Fiona was on her way to a facility in Switzerland. With Kyle dead, the only person left was Chris.

Declan's chest ached. Chris knew Olivia was Rose—he knew what she meant to him and Declan only had himself to blame.

Intent on his revenge, he'd discounted what Chris would do when he was backed into a corner.

"Call me as soon as you have the footage." Declan dropped the phone into the seat next to him and buried his head in his hands. *Olivia.* It had been almost two hours since the fire. *Two hours.*

The phone vibrated in the seat, and with a weary sigh, he lifted it, expecting to see an email from Brady. Instead, his heart turned over when he realized it was a video call from Olivia's phone.

"Olivia!"

Chris Keller's smirking face filled the screen. "She's a little busy at the moment." Chris squinted at the phone. "Are you on the company jet? How convenient."

Declan locked his jaw, knowing he couldn't let his emotions get away from him. He needed to keep his head in order to save Olivia.

"What's your plan, Chris? If I were you, I'd be on my way somewhere without extradition, instead of playing games with me." Declan swallowed the questions he wanted to ask.

Where is Olivia? Is she hurt?

A gun appeared on the small screen as Chris scratched at his jaw with the barrel. Declan's blood ran cold.

"If it were anyone else, Dec, I might fall for the whole I don't care about anything vibe, but..." His smile turned cruel, and Chris extended the phone the length of his arm so that Declan could see Olivia tied to a chair behind him, completely limp.

Declan clamped his jaw against the bile rising in his throat.

She's not dead. He wouldn't call if she were dead. Would he?

"I see." Declan's voice was strained.

"Playing it cool." Chris chuckled, then stepped backward until he was standing next to Olivia. Declan's heart stopped as the gun lifted. With a wink at the phone, Chris stroked the gun over Olivia's hair before he used it to push her chin up.

Olivia's lashes fluttered, but she didn't make a sound. A tiny flicker of relief took root inside him.

She's alive.

"Not even going to ask if she's all right?" Chris dropped her head, and it rolled back at an awkward angle, making Declan's teeth clench. "Not even an 'if you touch her, I'll kill you?' I expected more from you, Declan," he mocked.

Declan felt sick. Fear and rage battled for supremacy inside of him.

"What do you want?"

"You groveling at my feet." Chris gave a dramatic sigh. "But also, money. Starting over is going to be expensive."

Declan's heart was pounding so hard he was sure Chris could hear. He wanted to negotiate. That was a good sign.

"Did you have an amount in mind?"

"Don't worry, I'll have it all set up by the time you get here," he said before ending the call.

Declan's hand trembled as he dialed his brothers. He didn't waste time on a greeting. "Chris has her at Dad's estate."

"We can be there in a little more than an hour," Luke said. "Olivia brought your jet back to Atlanta, right?"

Declan nodded, not trusting his voice, but then realized his brothers couldn't see him. "Yes."

"Wait for us, Declan." Brady's voice was serious. "You can't go in alone. We don't know what kind of manpower he has there. I have people nearby. I'll get them moving to meet you."

Declan stayed silent. He couldn't stop seeing the image of Olivia's limp body. It didn't matter how much money Declan gave Chris, his old friend was going to kill her, because Chris knew losing Olivia would destroy him.

"Dec," Luke's voice was quiet. "I know what you're thinking. If it were Dahlia... But if you rush in there, he'll be ready. The chances of either of you getting out alive are pretty slim."

"I'm not leaving her there."

"We are only asking for an hour," James said, and Declan heard an engine roar to life. "Wait for us."

Declan's breathing slowly evened out, acceptance bringing a sense of peace. "I'm going to get her."

"This isn't something for you to strategize your way out of, Declan. This is what Vincent and Brady and their people do. They are professionals," Luke persisted.

"*Fuck*!" James exploded. "It's a trap, Declan. He's going to kill you."

"I'm aware." Declan didn't care, if it meant there was a possibility she lived.

Ending the call, he walked to the cockpit to let them know the change in destination. Declan estimated his brothers and Brady would be in the air within the next thirty minutes, and then another hour to Rhode Island, and then twenty minutes to the estate. Realistically, they wouldn't be there for two hours. Declan could be there in a little more than one.

CHAPTER FORTY-NINE

Rhode Island—Present Day

"I have to pee," Olivia said. Her mouth was dry, and her stomach rolled, but she had remained still as long as possible, not wanting him to know she was awake.

With her eyes closed, Olivia listened carefully, trying to determine where she was, but the only sound was the tapping of a keyboard and a slight squeak, like someone shifted in a chair. It was the aftershave that gave him away. Olivia didn't know where she was, but she knew the man in the room with her was Chris Keller.

Where did Kyle go? Is he waiting nearby?

Finally, when Olivia couldn't ignore her bladder any longer, she spoke up.

"I really need the bathroom," she repeated, opening her eyes. He would have to untie her from the chair. That would give her a chance.

"Done playing dead?" Chris's friendly smile was entirely at odds with the situation.

"Yes."

"It really is a shame you met him first. I like you." His lips twisted bitterly. "Isn't that the story of our lives? Everything always cosmically lines up for Declan."

Olivia didn't answer, only stared at him, shifting uncomfortably to illustrate her point.

Chris watched her speculatively for a moment, spinning a lethal-looking letter opener between his fingers. He suddenly flipped it to grip the hilt, and then drove the tip of the blade into the wood desk next to a bronze bust. Olivia flinched as it quivered.

"Fine." Chris yanked the letter opener out of the desk with one hand and picked up the small bronze with the other. He snorted, staring at the statue, and then turned it to show her. "David Bloom. Next to Declan, he might have been the most arrogant man in the universe. Who has a statue made of themself?"

Olivia kept her mouth shut. Chris set the bust down with a thunk before approaching her with the letter opener in his hand. Olivia's eyes widened when Chris leaned over her, but he only slipped the point under the zip ties and flicked up, causing the plastic to fall away.

"I'm not going to hurt you." The smile he gave her was so chilling she felt it in her bones. "At least not until Dec gets here. I don't want him to miss the show."

Her heart sank.

Grabbing her around her bicep, Chris pulled Olivia to her feet, and her knees almost buckled. Her legs felt like jelly, and she stumbled as he marched across the room. "Pretty potent stuff." Chris observed. "I wasn't super clear on dosage, so I gave you all of it. Knocked you out for longer than I thought it would."

Chris walked her down a marble hallway and opened a door at the end, revealing a small bathroom. "Of course, you looked like you were dead, and your ex-husband freaked out that we wouldn't get the ransom. Like I was ever going to share with him.

Kyle was such a moron. I can't believe you married him." Chris shoved her into the room. "You have two minutes." His hand slapped against the door, preventing her from closing it. "Leave the door open."

"You want to watch me pee?" Olivia glared at him.

"Not particularly, but better that than you trying to barricade yourself in there. Clock's ticking." He made a shooing motion with his hand.

Nostrils flaring, Olivia took care of her needs as quickly as she could, lingering as she washed her hands. Her mind was blank of escape plans, but Olivia hadn't missed how Chris referred to Kyle in the past tense. Did that mean he was alone here?

"Declan will come for me."

"I'm counting on it." Chris leaned against the open-door frame, the gun resting by his leg, and he'd stuck the letter opener in his waistband.

If she could grab one of the weapons…

"I wouldn't," Chris said, seeming to read her mind. He casually stepped away from the door and beckoned her with the gun. "I don't want to hurt you before Declan gets here, but I will if I have to."

"Where are we?" The enormous house was silent, and through the distant windows she could only see green.

"The Bloom family estate."

"Rhode Island?" Olivia couldn't help the surprise in her voice. How long had she been unconscious?

Chris inclined his head and motioned for her to sit in the chair. To her relief, he didn't restrain her again. He didn't have to, she thought bitterly. He had a gun.

The computer monitor on the desk beeped. "Declan must have broken some sort of speed record." Chris sounded pleased and looked up to meet her eyes. "Lover boy is here." His eyes returned to the screen. "It looks like he's alone."

"Why do you hate him so much?"

Chris ignored her, flipped open a laptop, and typed for a minute or two. Olivia inched toward the edge of the seat, her feet flexing on the carpet. She couldn't sit there and let Declan walk into a trap. Her eyes measured the distance to the large plate-glass window that overlooked the side lawn of the mansion, and then at the paned glass doors that led back into the house.

The window was closer. If she feinted like she was going to the door, Olivia could throw herself through the window—they were on the ground floor, so she didn't need to worry about a fall. Olivia pushed the knowledge of what the sharp glass would do to her, out of her brain. Chris was going to kill her anyway, and she refused to be bait for Declan.

"You didn't answer my question." Chris's eyes darted to hers before returning to the computer. "What did Declan ever do to you?"

"That's an excellent question," Declan said from the doorway. "I've wracked my brain, and I can't come up with anything."

Chris's face contorted with satisfaction. With the gun pointed at Olivia, he stepped around the desk and pulled her from her seat, moving so that they stood with their backs to the window. Ten feet separated them from where Declan stood inside the doors.

What if I throw us both backward?

"Is it my natural superiority?" Declan cocked his head. "Or are you in love with me and can't handle it not being reciprocated?"

Chris's grip on her arm tightened. "You want to make jokes?" With his other hand, he shoved the barrel of the gun hard under her jaw, making her teeth snap together.

Declan's expression turned murderous, and he took a step closer.

"Now I have your attention," Chris sneered.

"You're insane, is that it? What a ridiculously clichéd motive." The planes of Declan's face grew harsh. "Because I can't imagine what you think your grievance with me is. You were my friend."

Chris's hand moved from Olivia's arm to wrap in her hair, yanking her neck farther back. "We weren't *friends*," he spat. "I was your lap dog. Even my father prioritized you and your father. *'Go to school with Declan, Christopher.' 'Stay close. Be his friend.' 'They have so much. There will be plenty left over for you.'* As if I couldn't accomplish something on my own. Apparently, I should be grateful for your scraps."

The gun lowered as he gestured at Declan. "You had everything. *Everything*. You didn't care, you never appreciated it. It was all handed to you... Everything you *ever* wanted."

"You sound like a spoiled child. *Daddy didn't love me*," Declan mocked. "I really had hoped it was going to be something more interesting."

Olivia stared at him in horror. Why was Declan provoking him? Chris was breathing hard, and the more Declan taunted, the looser Chris's grip on her became, and Olivia realized that was what Declan intended all along. He wanted Chris to focus on him.

Declan's eyes met hers and then flicked for a millisecond to the window behind her as Chris continued to rant. Olivia didn't dare show that she understood.

"You had everything, that is, until I took it from you. One piece at a time."

"Not very successfully," Declan drawled. "Considering I'm the CEO again, and you've been cut off from the money."

Chris gestured to the laptop.

"I have the transfer set up. You need to enter your password."

Declan stared at him, eyes burning. "As soon as I hit enter, you will kill us both."

Before Olivia realized what was happening, Chris hit her on the side of the head with the butt of the gun. She cried out, lurching sideways, as Declan lunged forward, but Chris raised the gun holding him off.

"Every minute you delay…"

Olivia could feel the warm trickle on her face, and she twisted to get away. This time the blow caught her jaw, stars exploding in her vision.

Declan's eyes were wild, but he was too far away to help. Jaw working, he stalked to the computer and punched in a series of digits and spun it so Chris could see. "It's done. This has nothing to do with her. This is between you and me. You want to kill me? Do it. You could be on a plane and gone before anyone else arrives."

"Not yet. I have to admit, I enjoy her company." Olivia fought the urge to gag when he suddenly turned and licked her face. "Maybe I'll take her with me instead."

Olivia opened her mouth to retort, but Declan gave her an almost imperceptible shake of his head.

"Maybe I'll let her live… If you ask me nicely. In fact…" Chris smirked. "That is exactly what I want you to do."

Chris's hand left her hair, landing hard on her shoulder as he pointed the gun at Declan. "But first."

The gun exploded.

For a second, Olivia couldn't hear anything, even though she knew she was screaming, as Declan reeled backward, blood blooming on his sleeve. His face contorted with pain, but he managed to stay on his feet.

"On your knees," Chris growled. "Beg for her life."

"Do you think I would hesitate?" Declan's voice was raspy, his eyes on her, *speaking to her*. He slowly lowered himself to the ground, one knee at a time. His arm hung useless, blood dripping from his fingertips at an alarming rate.

Sobs tore through her chest as Declan stared into her eyes. "I would offer my life for hers ten thousand times without a second thought. She *is* my life."

"Declan," Olivia's voice broke. Blood pooled next to him, soaking the carpet, and his tan face was paling rapidly.

"Don't cry, Petal. It's going to be all right." Declan's violet eyes clouded, but he gave her a sweet smile. "Don't be afraid. I love you."

Olivia saw his gaze go to the window behind her again and knew what he wanted her to do. Her heart tore in two. She couldn't save them both.

Chris's fingers flexed on her shoulder, no longer gripping her, his attention fully on Declan. "You know, I intended for your last moments to be listening to her die, but now I think you might suffer more, listening to her watch you die."

"No!" Olivia screamed as the gun flashed again. This time the blood bloomed over the crisp white of Declan's dress shirt, and he slumped to the ground.

Dragging her forward by the shoulder, Chris pushed at Declan's shoulder with the toe of his shoe, rolling him onto his back.

Declan grunted, his eyes cracked open.

"Oh good, still alive. Don't worry, Olivia, it shouldn't take long, and then it will be your turn."

Olivia didn't want to cry, didn't want to give Chris what he wanted, but the sobs that racked her body were impossible to hold in.

Declan was dying. Right in front of her.

His lips moved. "Love you."

Olivia heard the whisper and suddenly knew exactly what she needed to do.

"What?" Chris leaned closer to hear, and Olivia seized her chance.

Pivoting around the hand on her shoulder, she threw herself into Chris's arms and clutched at his shirt front, sobbing. Chris shoved at her shoulders, but his gun arm was useless with her pressed against him.

Using her sobs as cover, she swiftly pulled the letter opener from his waistband and immediately reversed it. There was a split second of shock and recognition in Chris's eyes before she plunged the letter opener deep into his stomach. He threw himself backward, staring in horror at the blade still protruding from him.

"You bitch!" The gun lifted, but his hesitation gave her time to grab the heavy bronze bust of David Bloom from the desk. Olivia slammed it down onto Chris's hand, forcing the gun down, and then swung upward with all of her strength connecting with a loud crack to his skull. Chris collapsed in a heap at her feet, but Olivia's only concern was Declan.

He was so still and pale, lying against the blue carpet. Pulling her blouse over her head, Olivia wadded it into a ball and leaned all of her weight on the wound on his chest. Tears slipped down her cheeks as the blood soaked through the silk.

"Don't leave me," she begged. "You promised. Stay with me."

Declan's lips moved, and though it was scarcely more than a puff of air, until the day she died, Olivia swore she heard him.

"Always."

CHAPTER FIFTY

Rhode Island—Present Day

A peaceful, rhythmic sound surrounded Declan. His body was comfortably warm and buoyant. It reminded him of a vacation he took in the Caribbean. He'd floated in the ocean, drifting lazily over the waves.

"*Whatever our souls are made of, his and mine are the same.*" The sound floated in the air around him, the words dragging at him, reminding him of something he needed to do. "Come back to me, Declan."

Declan wanted to relax into the soft feeling. It was so tempting… "Stay with me." The voice pulled at him.

"Stay with me," the voice whispered in his ear again.

"I think he's waking up," someone said.

Was that Cara? She sounded like she was crying.

"Car-bear," Declan licked his lips and tried again. Why couldn't he open his eyes? He tried to lift his hand only to have it drop as a sharp pain in his shoulder sent agony shooting through him.

"Easy," Luke said, his voice uncharacteristically concerned. "They backed off your pain meds. Take it slow."

Urgent need seized his chest. He needed to go. There was some place he needed to be…

Firm hands pushed him gently back, and his weakness only fueled his anger as Declan sank against the pillow.

"You're going to rip the lines out," James's voice was gruff.

Declan winced as the sharp pain returned, but his mind was a little clearer now, and he tried to grasp the thought floating on the edge of his consciousness.

He was on his knees, knew he was going to die, but he needed to…

"Olivia," Declan gasped. Panic crested like a wave in his chest, and he fought to sit up. "I have to get to…"

"She's here, and she's safe," Cara soothed. "Olivia is in the hallway talking to Siobhan and Anne. I'll get her."

Declan winced as he shifted. "I'm alive then?"

James glowered at him. "Not for lack of trying."

Declan grit his teeth against the pain. "Olivia is okay? You got there in time?" His eyes sought his brothers, needing to hear them say it again. Needed to hear that Olivia was safe and unharmed.

Luke nodded, a smile on his face. "She's fine. Brady's men got there before us. Lucky for you, one of them used to be a field medic." Luke's face twitched with emotion. "You almost died, Dec."

"Olivia." Declan's throat was raw. "Was she hurt? Did Chris—"

"She's a little banged up, but she's okay." James smiled.

"Chris?"

"Dead."

Declan hissed out a breath. "Good. I would have liked for him to suffer, but I'm glad they got him."

Luke and James exchanged a look.

"They?" Luke asked.

"Brady's men."

Luke coughed to cover up a chuckle. "Yeah. Chris was already dead when they got there."

Declan frowned.

"Olivia stabbed him and then cracked his skull open for good measure. They found her doing her best to save your insane ass," James informed him. "The two of you are perfect for each other."

Declan's eyes widened. "She was supposed to get out. The window was right there. Are you telling me she stayed?" The heart monitor began beeping rapidly.

The door opened, and Olivia, a bandage marring her beautiful face, strode in, glaring first at the machine and then at his brothers.

"He needs to stay calm."

James lifted his hands in surrender. "It wasn't us."

"You were supposed to jump out the window."

"I should have left you there to bleed to death with a psycho?" Olivia took his hand and squeezed, softening her tone.

"You killed him?" Declan asked, searching her eyes.

Olivia swallowed, but didn't look away. "I'm not sorry."

"You shouldn't be." James agreed grimly.

Luke clapped his twin on the shoulder. "Come on, we need to go help Car-bear run interference with the moms. Now that they know he's awake..."

Once the door shut quietly, Olivia studied him, her eyes filling with tears. "I thought I'd lost you."

He lifted his uninjured arm to brush weakly at the tears on her cheek. "I'm still here."

"You knew it was a trap." Olivia's eyes held his.

Declan nodded.

"Your brothers said you wouldn't wait for help." He stayed still under her perusal. "You almost died."

Declan interlaced her fingers. "But I didn't."

Exhausted, he closed his eyes, as Olivia brushed the hair against his forehead with her free hand. "Don't ever do anything like that again."

"I promised I would always come back for you," Declan whispered, before letting sleep pull him under again.

Declan spent over a week in the small private hospital before they transported him to his home in Connecticut for another week to recuperate. Olivia refused to leave his side.

"The repairs on my house are complete, but the Armstrong facility is going to take months." Olivia sighed. "The warehouse was a complete loss."

Declan walked slowly, his good arm slung over her shoulders as they maneuvered toward the atrium. He didn't need to lean his weight on her as much as he did, but Olivia had been so adorable fussing over him for the last week. Oscar barked happily, trotting alongside. Olivia glanced down at the puppy. "That dog has taken more private plane rides than I have."

"We couldn't leave him in Atlanta by himself," Declan said, smiling at the memory of how Olivia's face lit up when Todd arrived at the estate with Oscar.

"Are you sure you're okay, walking this far?" Olivia's face screwed up with concern. "We could just stay on the sofa."

"Olivia, if I had stayed on that sofa for another minute, I would have permanently fused to the cushions. The atrium is heated, so we'll be comfortable."

What Declan hadn't told her was there was a surprise waiting for her in the glassed room.

"I know you are going stir-crazy, but you'll be able to go back to work soon." Something in Olivia's voice had his feet stopping, and he straightened.

Looking down, he saw the vulnerability in her eyes, and brushed her hair back.

"What are you worried about, baby?"

She shrugged and tried to take his arm again, but he refused to budge. "Olivia?"

"This is going to sound so messed up," she muttered.

"Tell me," he demanded softly, cupping her chin.

"When I was with you on the floor in the study… and you were…" Olivia sucked in an uneven breath, and her eyes filled with tears. "I don't want to be away from you. Like, at all." She gave him a watery smile.

"I know you're stronger than you're letting on and that you are downplaying it because I needed to take care of you, but this time together is coming to an end."

Declan frowned. "Nothing is coming to an end."

"You know what I mean. When I'm back in Atlanta and you're gone."

"Where is it you think I'm going?"

Olivia met his gaze, her expression so unhappy his chest burned. "Bloom Communications is in New York. I know you need to be here. I know things will have to change."

It was true. Even during the two weeks he'd been recovering, he had been inundated by one issue after another. But Declan had also had a lot of time to think while he healed.

He nodded thoughtfully and took her hand, pulling her along with him. Declan abandoned his façade of using her as a crutch and stopped at the door of the atrium. "Things will have to change," he echoed her words, and then swung the door open.

Olivia gasped as she took in the space in front of her. The early evening light flooded the glass walls of the room, giving the entire room a golden glow. White roses cascaded from the ceiling in wide garlands, framing another floral canopy over a small table. Olivia stared at the candelabra on the table, the chilling bottle of champagne, and the pair of flutes next to it.

"Declan?"

He smiled at her, leading her further into the room, her eyes huge. Declan's heart pounded. He felt as if he'd waited a lifetime for this moment. Olivia's eyes shimmered in the candlelight as Declan took both her hands in his.

"We have always shared a love of poetry, and there have always been the same lines that came to me over and over since I met you. *Through the storm, we reach the shore. You give it all but I want more, And I'm waiting for you.*"

Olivia's brow furrowed. "I don't recognize it. Who wrote that? One of the Romantics?"

"Only the greatest Irish poet of all time," Declan deadpanned.

"Who?"

"Bono." When she still looked confused, he shook his head. "The singer? U2? It's from the song 'With or Without You.' Sorry, we didn't all go to Oxford." He joked, but then Declan sobered.

"I've known since the moment I saw you in that pub, we were meant to be together. There hasn't been a single second that has passed in the last twelve years that I didn't love you… That every ounce of my soul didn't miss you…"

Declan lifted a hand to wipe away the tears trickling down her cheeks. "You aren't supposed to cry yet, Petal. I'm trying to tell you how much I love you," he teased. And then, because he couldn't resist, he pressed a kiss against her lips.

"Olivia." Declan slowly sank to his knee and pulled a ring from his pocket, still holding her hand. He slid the ring onto her finger. "Petal, my rose, my heart, will you spend eternity with me?"

Olivia was already nodding through her tears, reaching to

help him stand. "Yes, but get off your knees before you pull your stitches."

Olivia stared at the ring. "I've dreamed of this moment for twelve years," she admitted.

Declan's thumb rubbed over the top of the ring. "It's my grandmother's Claddagh ring," he said quietly, before pulling out another velvet box from his pocket and opening it to reveal an oval-shaped sapphire surrounded by diamonds. He slid it on to sit snugly against the antique ring. "Something old and something new. And the blue reminded me of your eyes."

Olivia stared at the rings with a soft smile. "The grandmother that gave you the cottage?"

Declan nodded. "She and my grandfather loved each other fiercely. I wanted to ask you with their ring. I told you my grandmother moved to the cottage because she couldn't bear to stay in their Dublin house with all the memories." Declan took a deep breath. "I never understood until the day I left you at the airport. I wouldn't even be able to breathe in a space where I'd loved you, knowing I couldn't have you."

Olivia's brows drew together. "Are you saying you haven't been back to the cottage?"

Declan shook his head. "I knew it would be too painful. It was *our* place… It wouldn't feel the same… after."

"Declan," Olivia's voice broke.

"We were apart for so long, I don't want to wait another minute to start our lives together. You said things were going to change, and they will."

Olivia lifted her eyes from her rings to meet his. "I know. Nothing is as important as being with you. I am going to manage Armstrong until I can find my replacement. I want to stay here with you."

"Now you're just trying to steal my thunder." Declan

pretended to scowl at her. “We aren’t staying here. I’ll be able to fly in another week. It’s time to go home.”

“But your home is here. Your *job* is here.”

“This is just a house, Petal. I have a lot of houses. I don’t plan on getting rid of it. Atlanta will be ridiculously hot in the summer.” He grinned as cautious hope flit across her face. “My *home* is wherever you are.”

“How will that work?”

Declan framed her face with his hands and pulled her in for another kiss. “However we want it to.”

CHAPTER FIFTY-ONE

County Kerry, Ireland—6 months later

Her wedding day started with rain. She woke in Declan's arms to the sound of a steady patter on the roof of the cottage. Olivia smiled and pressed against Declan's chest. "We have to get up."

"I disagree," Declan grumbled, pulling her closer, sliding his hand down to cup her thigh and pull it over his hip. "We have time."

Her body stirred to life, but she pulled away and rolled out of bed, reaching for her robe, before padding barefoot to the door. "I'm going to put the kettle on. Your moms and sisters will be here soon to get ready, and you're supposed to meet your brothers."

"Come back to bed," Declan called after her, but she only laughed, setting the teapot on the Aga.

They had spent a lot of time at the cottage over the last six months, and she loved the simplicity of their life there. Sometimes, they only had enough time for a long weekend, but it was worth it to both of them. When they were in Ireland, they could be themselves, away from the responsibilities of their jobs.

Olivia, now the CEO of Armstrong Electronics, was excited

for production on XEROS to start next month in the rebuilt manufacturing building. Since Atlanta had become their primary residence, Declan had taken offices nearby so they could still see each other during the day if they wanted to.

It was still necessary for Declan to travel occasionally, but they arranged it so that Olivia could accompany him on those trips and work remotely. Fortunately, with Declan's new role, he was in Atlanta more often than he was away.

Olivia had been worried when Declan stepped down as CEO of Bloom Communications to a less supervisory role.

"I don't want you to do this for me?" Olivia chewed her lip. "You worked your whole life for this. It's what you've always wanted."

"I'm not doing it for you," Declan assured her. "The way I've structured the new position, I'll still have significant influence over major decisions, and I'm still one of the majority shareholders. It just won't be what I do every day."

"We can spend more time in New York," Olivia blurted out.

He smiled, pulling her into his arms. "That's not it, Olivia. I'm doing this for me." Declan kissed the tip of her nose. "It wasn't until you asked if I was happy that I even considered there was a different way. It's funny what almost dying can do for your perspective. I will always be extremely vested in what is happening at Bloom Communications, but I also realized I love what I do at Bloom Capital. Why can't I do both?"

"This is really what you want? Promise?"

"No question."

She was eating toast on Declan's lap when there was a brief knock at the door before it opened, and all five of the other Bloom females spilled into the room.

"Put the dresses over there," Siobhan ordered the three women trailing her, weighed down with a variety of dress bags and boxes. She had insisted that even if the ceremony was only family they should all still have their hair and makeup done.

"Anne, you and Cami sit there." She pointed at the sofa.

"Dahlia, you and Cara, make *him* leave. Declan can get her back in a couple of hours." She narrowed her eyes at her son.

"Please come in," Declan drawled from beneath her. Olivia giggled and moved to get to her feet, but Declan's arm locked around her hips. "Mam, you need to calm down. I don't want you to stress Olivia out."

Siobhan rolled her eyes. "I'm not stressing Olivia out." She eyed her soon-to-be daughter-in-law, and her expression softened. "I've never seen a happier bride."

"Hey! I was an extremely happy bride." Cara huffed from where she was pouring herself a cup of tea. "And Cami, you were freaking glowing when you married James."

"Leave me out of it," Cami arched a brow at Cara.

"Siobhan said 'she'd never *seen* a happier bride.' We didn't get to see you on your wedding day." Anne pointed out tartly.

"You walked right into that one," Cami laughed, both hands supporting her giant belly. "Ow! Dang it, now I have to pee. Can someone help me to my feet? I swear they both jumped on my bladder at the same time." Dahlia took her hands and helped hoist her to her feet, and Olivia pointed Cami in the right direction. They all watched her waddle away.

"It's been over a year," Cara groaned. "Are you ever going to stop giving me a hard time about eloping?"

"No." Siobhan and Anne said at the same time.

"You know what? I think you should take all the things you imagined my wedding would look like and put that energy into planning the next wedding." Cara grinned.

"Cheeky little madam," Siobhan groused. "Plan our dream wedding in two hours, pfft."

"Oh right," Cara's eyes gleamed, and she turned to stare at Dahlia, who was definitely giving the petite blonde a death glare. "I meant the *next*, next one. Have you and Luke picked a date yet?"

"I'm going to kill you," Dahlia mouthed.

"You're getting married?" Anne covered her mouth with her hands. "Why didn't you say something?"

Dahlia looked sheepish. "It just happened, and I didn't want to take away from Olivia and Declan's day."

"I knew," Declan said smugly.

"You didn't tell me." Olivia smacked his shoulder. "Okay, that's it. I have to get ready, and you have to go."

Declan set her on her feet and then stood, his violet eyes smiling into hers. "I'll see you," Declan's lips covered hers before he pulled back. "And you," he dipped his head to kiss the small swell of her bump. "Under the arch."

"And all of you make fun of me and Wes," Cara complained. "Go. The guys are waiting for you at the hotel. Let's hope the rain stops soon." She angled her head to look at the sky out the window.

Siobhan smiled. "Rain on your wedding day is good luck."

"We don't need luck," Declan said, kissing his mother and Anne on the cheek before heading for the door. "We have each other."

Olivia thought her heart would burst two hours later, when she and Declan legally confirmed what they'd already promised each other. The sun had come out, but rain drops still glistened on the castle ruins just as they had thirteen years ago.

"I really, really love you.

"I really, really love you too."

And Olivia was the only one who heard him quote Shelley against her lips before he kissed her.

"Soul meets Soul, on lover's lips."

EPILOGUE

County Kerry, Ireland—10 years later

"Your dog is snoring." Declan kissed her bare shoulder.

Olivia lifted her head to see Oscar asleep on his bed in front of the fire and pulled the blanket farther up to cover him. "He's tired from running through the snow all afternoon."

"What time do we have to be in Dublin tomorrow?"

"I told your mom after lunch."

"I vote we leave Oscar with her next time."

"I think the twelve grandkids she's had for the last week are enough," Olivia drawled.

"I'm only responsible for three of them."

"Well, there might be thirteen for next Christmas break."

Declan reared back, and Olivia laughed, rolling so that they lay chest to chest. "Bite your mental tongue. I'm talking about Cara and Wes."

"Did their adoption approval come through?"

"I don't think they know for certain, but Cara is optimistic. They've done the foster child to adoption route once already, and she said she recognizes the signs."

"That's great news." He pretended to shudder. "Five kids though? Our three are more than enough."

"That's only because our sons are just like you. I've never met a more stubborn group."

Declan's fingertips found her ribs, and she pressed her lips together, trying not to laugh. "I'm sure their mother's genetic makeup has *nothing* to do with it."

"Nothing what so ever." A laugh broke free, and Declan's tickling fingers grew more deliberate in their movement, and Olivia gasped when they found her peaked nipples. Declan trailed kisses across her cleavage.

Olivia's breath caught as heat flowed through her. "While you're in a good mood," she gasped. "I should probably mention something else."

"Mmhm," Declan sucked at the spot under her ear he knew made her wild.

"I told Dahlia and Cami we'd keep their kids for spring break. Since they are all in the same school."

Lips left her skin, and Declan looked up at her. "*All* of them? Luke's twins and all three of James's hellions?" He looked appalled.

"You'll never know they're there." Olivia laughed at his expression.

Declan shook his head. "It's the cross I bear for being everyone's favorite uncle."

"If that's what you need to tell yourself." Olivia's chest shook with laughter, and Declan's eyes dipped.

"If I only have one more kid-free night, I'm going to make it worth it." His lips closed over hers.

"You aren't really upset?" Olivia broke the kiss.

Declan brushed her hair behind her ears and smiled into her worried eyes. "No, not really. You, our boys, this family... It's the life I never knew I wanted."

"Happy?"

"More than anyone deserves," he said, stroking a thumb over her cheek, but then Declan smirked up at her. "However, there is a clock on when we have to go get our little demons. So, stop talking."

THE END

~

NEED MORE of the Dangerous Blooms Universe?

Look for Alex Kovalyov and Madison Amherst's story

Coming 2025

*****I hope you enjoyed reading this book as much as I enjoyed writing it. If you did, I would greatly appreciate a short review on Amazon or your favorite book website. Reviews and Star Ratings are crucial for any author, but especially for us Indies. Even just a line or two can make a huge difference!***

XOXO Kate

CONNECT WITH KATE

Don't want to miss another Kate Breitfeller release—sign up for the newsletter: https://katebreitfeller.com/contact/

Links to everything: https://linktr.ee/katebreitfellerauthor

ACKNOWLEDGMENTS

As always, there are so many people I need to thank!

First off, thank you to my mom for her constant help and support when I need to vent.

But most especially, thank you for being one of the best editors around, and for putting up with my insistence of "voice" over grammar. Your endless patience with my run-on sentences and sentence fragments are definitely appreciated.

Thank you as well to my Dad for being so supportive and encouraging throughout the author process. I particularly appreciate when I escape to your house to plot out a series or have a writing retreat and you bring me cocktails on demand. All authors should be so lucky!

Thank you to Michelle, for being such a great beta reader and for reminding me when I spiral that I always feel that way at different points in the process.

Thank you to my good friend Brandie, for not only speaking the same romance novel language, but for inadvertently giving me the inspiration for both series. Two different WhatsApp video clips of live music helped me shape this book and find the essence of these characters. You're encouraging words ten years ago put me on this path, and I will never be able to thank you enough. Love ya!

Thank you to the rest of my family for always recommending my books to your friends!

Thank you to Jo at Covers & Cupcakes for my absolutely stunning covers. I love them so much!

Thank you to my husband who was extremely understanding of the crazy hours I put in on this book and for always being willing to either pick up takeout or accept a frozen pizza for dinner when I'm working crazy hours. Also, thank you for helping keep me organized for all of my shows and for encouraging me to keep going when I'm feeling discouraged.

Thank you to the outstanding book community: Booktok, Bookstagram and Facebook—specifically, @BookwormBecca-Anne and @BookrecsbyKearstin.

Every time I put out a book, I make new friends and your support has made a huge difference! I truly appreciate it! However, I also blame you for the fact that my TBR is ridiculously long and growing every day with your outstanding content!

Thank you Becki Lee, Kerry Evelyn, Marian Griffin, Chrissy Chiccory, and Kimberley Keyes for the writing sprints, your experience, and endless encouragement when I'm ranting. And for being the best book convention friends anyone could wish for!

ABOUT THE AUTHOR

Kate's character driven romantic suspense and romantic mystery series serve as the perfect escape from reality! She frequently refers to her books as "hanging out with her imaginary friends" and enjoys putting them in a variety of precarious situations.

Kate currently lives with her husband, and her rescue dog/writing partner, Charlie, on Florida's Space Coast.

ALSO BY KATE BREITFELLER

The Caribbean Series

Becca Jumps Ship

Becca Dives In

Becca Swims On

Dangerous Blooms

See You Soon

See You There

See You Again

See You Maybe

Made in the USA
Columbia, SC
24 February 2025